A LIFE TO REMEMBER

A LIFE TO REMEMBER

A NOVEL

DENIS GRAY

A LIFE TO REMEMBER
A NOVEL

iUniverse books may be ordered through booksellers or by contacting:

iUniverse
1663 Liberty Drive
Bloomington, IN 47403
www.iuniverse.com
1-800-Authors (1-800-288-4677)

ISBN: 978-1-5320-7821-7 (sc)
ISBN: 978-1-5320-7873-6 (e)

Library of Congress Control Number: 2019910120

Print information available on the last page.

iUniverse rev. date: 07/22/2019

CHAPTER 1

Pop Warner football was a quick remedy for a bitter winter's day in Pittsfield, Massachusetts.

The Wild Stallions were playing the Golden Bears in a Pop Warner football game at Anchor Field Stadium. If there had been a fire sale in the stands, it would have been for these few precious items of winter clothing: gloves, scarves, thermal underwear, and beaver hats (the really furry, funky, warm kind).

Jimmy Boston was the quarterback of the Golden Bears, and Billy Mack was the running back. Today, Jimmy Boston and Billy Mack were in top form.

"Wow, what a throw Jimmy Boston just made!" Ron Hammaker's eyes practically popped out of his head.

"Yeah, what an arm!" Frank Bosco said, driving his point home like a hammer hitting a nail square on its head.

"Jimmy laid the ball right out there, Frank. All the kid had to do was run under it and catch it," Ron said.

"If only the guy had a little more *umph*. Just a little more octane in his tank."

"There definitely would've been six more points on the board for the Golden Bears and Jimmy Boston," Ron said, as if he could taste a touchdown. "But don't you worry—"

"What—me worry? Hey, I know what's up next," Frank said.

"There goes Billy Mack, Frank! Straight up the gut of the defense like a battering ram!" Ron said, with exclamation points dangling from his breath like icicles. "Billy Mack knocking the Wild Stallion kids down like bowling pins. Anything that gets in his freaking way, man, is a goner!"

Frank Bosco and Ron Hammaker were rival high school football coaches but only on game day. On any other normal day of the year in Pittsfield, Massachusetts, they were the best of friends. They had grown up together and played on the same Pittsfield High School football team that won the state championship two years in a row—and on Anchor Field, when they were Pop Warner kids.

"Can you imagine if a coach got Jimmy Boston and Billy Mack—the two of them—to play for them? They could count their lucky stars—and a state championship to boot. Man, would it be a dream day."

Frank Bosco, blowing on his hands more out of habit than need, nodded; he fully appreciated Ron's astute remark.

Ron Hammaker, who was the same height as Frank Bosco (five feet ten), looked into Frank's see-all eyes like the old flanker he was. And Frank Bosco looked into Ron's elude-all eyes, his old quarterback, both about to hook up on a long downfield connection that had six points and the end zone written all over it.

"Guess the all-out recruiting war is on between us. Huh, Frank?" Ron said, like a vulture circling the sky. "You," he said, thumping his chest, "and me?"

Frank Bosco stopped blowing on his hands. "That, my good and loyal friend, it most definitely is."

Ron stuck out the hand that had a state championship ring adorning it. "And so, Frank, may the better man win, my man."

"You bet, Ron!" Frank laughed, shaking Ron's hand in a firm grip. "And so let the games begin!"

Jimmy Boston was twelve years old. Jimmy Boston was white. Billy Mack was twelve years old. Billy Mack was black. At twelve years old, they were the best of friends—inseparable.

They were in Anchor Fields's locker room, changing out of their gold-and-black Golden Bear uniforms.

"Hey, hurry up, will you, Jimmy," Billy Mack said anxiously.

"How come, Billy?"

"Uh, why are you asking me that, Jimmy?"

One then looked at the other dumbfounded.

Billy had buttoned up his parka and had donned his woolen gloves. Jimmy was now at the stage of tying his shoelaces.

"Spend your weekly allowance yet, Billy?" Jimmy said, looking up at him.

"Uh-uh, not yet. Working on it though. You know …"

"So you feel in the mood to head over to Rockwell Mall and buy some records?"

"Yeah, Jimmy. Why—"

"Billy. Jimmy."

"Hello, Coach Bosco," Jimmy said.

Frank Bosco had made his way into Anchor Field Stadium's old fieldhouse. He stuck his hand (the one with the state championship ring on it) out to Billy, who was nearer to him.

"Hello, Coach Bosco," Billy said.

Jimmy was still tying his shoelaces, but when Coach Bosco got to him, they shook hands.

"Hey, I'm not disturbing you guys, am I?" Frank said, looking first at Jimmy and then at Billy.

"Uh, no, uh, Coach Bosco," Billy said quickly. "Jimmy's usually the slow one. Uh, when it comes to getting dressed—that is, sir. After a game," Billy said, for better clarification.

"Oh." Frank laughed. "I figured I'd give you guys at least enough time to get dressed before barging into the locker room. Uh, to talk to you."

There was a patient pause. "Because I can wait. We don't have to talk today. It can wait until another—"

"It's okay," Billy and Jimmy said in unison and then laughed at the coincidence.

"It's like how you two play," Frank Bosco said, "in perfect harmony."

"Thanks, Coach Bosco," they said—again laughing.

"Great feeling, isn't it, how you guys play the game of football out there on the field?"

"Yes it …" they began to say, but Jimmy was the one who completed the sentence, not Billy, "is, sir."

Frank Bosco still appeared to be athletic, a real stud. His weight was a few pounds above his playing weight, but he had no reason to squawk. His wavy black hair was neat and trim. He had dark Italian eyes that were true winners on anybody's scoreboard. His posture was straighter than a steel beam.

"I was going to talk to each of you, uh, individually—but uh …"

Billy and Jimmy looked at each other with knowledgeable smiles, as if to say, "There goes the trip to the Rockwell Mall."

"But since I have you, the two of you together. Do you, I mean, you don't have any plans for this afternoon, do you? Like say the Rock—"

"No, Coach Bosco," they replied ever so politely.

"Oh, because I know what young people do around here on Saturday afternoons after a football game—take off to the Rockwell Mall."

"No, uh, not us, Coach Bosco," Jimmy said, smiling. "Uh, B-Billy and I are, well, we're different, sir. Y-you know …"

Even Billy could hear Coach Bosco laughing at that huge whopper with cheese Jimmy had just served him with a wide grin.

Connie Mack's den was representative of Connie Mack's whimsical side, not his creative one. In other words, it was a man cave: rugged, unmanageable, and without grace or any embarrassment or excuses from him for its macho state of existence.

Billy had just gotten in the house and was at his father's den door.

"Hey, Billy. How'd it go today?"

"We won, Dad!" Billy said, entering the den.

"Congrats."

"Thanks."

"So … come on. Come on. Out with it."

"What?"

"The score, Billy. Why hold out on it?"

"The score, sir?" Billy smiled.

"Too ashamed to say it, huh? That you beat the pants off those kids. Beat the living tar out of them?"

Pause.

"Sixty, uh, sixty-three t-to three, Dad."

"How many touchdowns?"

"Four, sir."

"And Jimmy?"

"Five."

"With a field goal tossed in for good measure, huh?"

"Yes."

"What, you guys couldn't score from the—"

"Thirty-five-yard line, Dad." Pause. "Well, you see, Dad, Royce fumbled but recovered his own fumble on a third and inches. So it was fourth and a foot, and Coach Kelly—"

"Figured he'd let you test your leg to see if it still had life in it. If you could nail one from—"

"Forty-five yards out."

"Billy, was it dead-on? Am I right?"

"Yes, dead center. Split the goalpost. You're right, all right, Dad!

After the momentary elation, Connie saw signs of fatigue in Billy.

"Tired?"

"A ... a little."

"Sorry about this afternoon, but damn, uh, what the heck—what's the sense in me complaining? This project I'm involved in is challenging," Connie said excitedly.

Connie motioned to Billy to come over to his messy-looking desk. His fingers then did something quite tricky on the computer's keyboard. Something bounced up on the screen as if some splendid life had been born deep inside the computer's motherboard's chip.

"Hey, Dad, I like it. It looks cool. Not that I understand any of it, sir."

"Understand it? Well, neither do I, Billy, to be honest. But like you said, it does look kind of cool. Yeah—come to think of it."

Connie and Billy were looking at something on the computer that Isaac Asimov might have invented in a blissful state of overwhelming confusion.

"I'm going to have to do a cut-and-paste job on it. You know, the usual stuff. Process with these things."

"Dad, look, I have every confidence in you. I do," Billy said, laying his hand kindly on Connie's shoulder like a divine spirit.

"Why, thanks for the vote of confidence," Connie said mockingly.

Billy shifted his weight. "Dad, after the game, Jimmy and I had a visitor, sir."

"And who may that have been?" Connie asked.

"Coach Bosco. Frank Bosco, sir."

"Oh. Why doesn't it surprise me?"

Pause.

"And, Dad, guess who shows up right behind him?"

Connie had a strong suspicion who it was.

"Coach Ron Hammaker."

"You don't say. It means the recruiting war is on. Has just been officially declared. The run for the roses to hit the jackpot," Connie said, slapping his hands together with a thud.

"Two great friends. Two great football players. And now, two great football coaches. Archrivals. Each coaching different schools. Each trying to build football powerhouses. Those two were some special pair, so I hear, when they played for Pittsfield High, Billy."

"Yep, Dad. Sort of like Jimmy and me, sir."

Connie ran his hand though his dark brown hair. His skin was a glowing light brown. He wasn't handsome but was attractive. He was a combination of confidence and a powerful physical presence. His Afro was toned down to medium length.

"I didn't know much about Ron Hammaker until I got here. But Frank Bosco, Coach Bosco, well, Billy, he was well known, publicized nationally. Swore he could've turned pro. But the pro scouts claimed he was too damned short."

"How tall is—"

"They put him at around five ten."

Connie crossed his leg. "But you know how it is in sports, Billy: they're always making you a few inches taller or a few pounds heavier. Man, it's all about size in football. The bigger, taller, stronger—the better."

Connie sighed. "But I still say to this day: Bosco could've been a Fran Tarkenton type, you know. Or say Theisman, Joe Theisman. Bosco could sit in the pocket but could scramble with the best of them. Run like a deer. Had a big heart. And, hell, tough as nails."

"Dad, your kind of guy, huh?" Billy chuckled.

"You bet. Bosco is a winner." Pause. "So how did they pitch themselves?"

Billy, who was in sneakers, took a few quiet steps across the den's wooden floor. He looked at his father's picture on the wall. He was in a different type of sports uniform.

"About the same, Dad. Talked about their school's winning tradition. Made it sound exciting ... very."

Billy took his eyes off Connie's picture and looked back at him. "Dad, I like both of them. Both came across really well I'd say, sir."

Connie studied Billy. "And Jimmy, what about him, his impressions?"

"Identical. Same as mine, uh, I guess, Dad."

Connie chuckled. "You two act like an old married couple that's been married too long. You talk alike. Think alike. The two of you are beginning to even look alike."

"Dad ..." Billy frowned.

"Okay, I went a bit overboard with my analysis. Not look alike but damned near everything else, Billy!"

"Jimmy and I can't help it if we're lost twins, separated at birth."

Pause.

"It's just that color thing, Billy, that gets in the way of your hypothesis. A black baby, I'm sure, wasn't in anybody's house of cards!"

Connie stood. He walked over to an old, pathetic-looking leather couch against the side wall. He sat. It was a couch from his bachelor days when he couldn't afford much, but today, he wouldn't sell it for three times its weight in gold (even if there was no gold value for a couch like his).

Connie made himself comfortable by raising one leg up off the floor and stretching it out along the couch's full length. "Soon, the two of you are going to have to make a decision, Billy. High school's quickly approaching."

"Yes, I know, Dad," Billy said, wrinkling his forehead.

"And it's your call, Billy—not mine or your mother's. It's four years of your life. Four years being where you're happiest."

"Right, Dad."

Now Billy looked like a twelve-year-old, not someone who'd knocked the stuffing out of other twelve-year-olds today.

Connie Mack was back facing his dreaded computer. He was a concept/design engineer for Blast Aircraft Company in Pittsfield. He was a brilliant guy. He was from the South, educated at Brown University, summa cum laude, and a four-star athlete (lacrosse All-American).

Connie was looking at the design on the computer screen while painfully wincing. He had no idea, not the foggiest, of what he was going to do with the thing holding stage center on the screen; it stared back at him like a five-hundred-pound gorilla that'd just found an ideal spot in the zoo and wasn't about to budge. Connie stretched out his arms. His imagination, for now, was at empty. He'd been at this work since six something this morning, and now it was well after three o'clock.

"Talking about getting your pants beat off you. Hell, I'd say this project is doing just that. It's getting its licks in, all right. Dusting me off. Hell if it ain't!"

Connie looked over at his pathetic-looking couch like it was a consoling friend.

"Got room for someone who's taken too many lumps at his computer for one day? Who's battered and bruised and begging for relief? Whatever relief you can give me, I'll gladly take."

But the couch seemed to know Connie's fighting spirit. "Even though I'm down, you better not count me out. Not Connie Mack, my friend!" He sprawled out on the couch. "Ah … you're a lifesaver, all right," he said, patting the couch. "Better than a psychiatrist's couch."

The computer was still on, humming. He had not turned it off. He laid his head back on the couch. *Billy's bucking against the real world now, isn't he?* he thought. Billy's and Jimmy's names are in some other coach's computer—not just Bosco's and Hammaker's but a college coach's.

"Touchdowns. The more you score, the more they roar. The attention. The celebrity."

Connie twitched his shoulders (and he had shoulders you could set a mountain on). He was a six footer with muscles in his ankles. He kept in shape by a combination of routine exercise and a healthy diet, helping to keep the fat off and the muscle on.

"The system never, ever changes. The baton twirler never drops the baton. The beat goes on. And now it's Billy and Jimmy's turn to join the human parade."

They'd talked about it before, Connie and Billy. He had told him that one day these football coaches would come after him hot and heavy, would be knocking at his door. He and Susan, Billy's mother, didn't present the cynical side of the picture, the dark side of the recruiting game—what could be its terror. They only presented the reality of what could come: his and Jimmy's football prowess one day could be in great demand.

Connie put his hands behind his head, then dropped them down on the couch and planted his feet to the floor. They'd been slowly preparing Billy for the inevitable—college coaches beating down their door during the recruiting process. Recruiters trying to sweep Billy off his feet as if he were All-World, nothing short. Not someone whom he and Susan hoped was a teenager more concerned about teenage acne and dating girls than a college coach's pitch with wild, exaggerated promises.

"My son has character. Integrity. Plenty of it."

Connie glanced over at the computer, where his conceptualized design stared back at him like a five-hundred-pound gorilla who now owned that spot on the computer screen, its computer chip.

"He's not going to get bigheaded, think he's better than anyone. Even though …" Connie hesitated. "One day, my boy's going to be the top high school football player in the country. There's absolutely no doubt in my mind."

Ethan Lane was a grand neighborhood for raising a family. Its houses maintained a strength of character built with that specific mind-set. Ethan Lane was tree-lined. Squirrels inhabited the trees and made daily nuisances of themselves for the most part. But New Englanders accepted these cute little creatures as more of a necessity than a burden since they, of course, inhabited the land well before humans arrived—so the squirrels did have the upper hand in this most unnatural of arrangements.

Houses on Ethan Lane were built big with New England pride. The lawns were quite wide and healthy. Elm trees on hot summer days did an excellent job of blocking the sun, but in winter, their snow-coated limbs could pose a real danger to the neighborhood if they fell on telephone lines and created power outages for hours or days.

The Bostons lived at 18 Ethan Lane.

"Gosh, what a game, son!" Jim Boston had come out onto the porch, which was shaded by a huge elm at the left side of the house.

"Dad, where's your coat?" Jimmy warned his father.

Jim Boston had an Irish grin on his face, flush with four leaf clovers. He was slight of build. He was short, no more than five five, with a fine grade of dark brown hair that was neatly trimmed.

"Jimmy, I feel as warm as Irish stew, me lad. Do not worry about me." Pause. "Gosh, you played another great game today—you and Billy." Jim paused. "Uh, maybe I'd better get into the house before I catch my death of cold, uh, like you said, son."

Jimmy was surprised by his dad's sudden acquiescence—but for only a second, for he sensed just what was going on with him.

So Jimmy turned around, and there Sally Ann Schumacher was with a red bow tied to her soft, brown, lustrous hair. Sally Ann Schumacher stood out on her house's front porch, out in the cold air, and waved to Jimmy shyly. She smiled like an eight-year-old would to a twelve-year-old she had a huge crush on.

Jimmy waved back to Sally Ann, then hustled into the big house where it was warm and toasty (no drafts).

"Help you with your coat, Jimmy?" Jim asked, as if what happened with Sally Ann never had.

"Dad, uh—let's not get carried away, Dad, okay?"

"You hear that, Marion?"

"What?"

"Jimmy doesn't need me—his dear, old dad—to help him with his coat. Gosh, I figured he'd be arm dead." Jim laughed. He ran his fingers through Jimmy's close-cut blond hair. "I mean, you did throw a ton of passes today. And mostly completions."

"But there were a few drops too, Dad."

"Yeah. Too bad it has to go against the quarterback. Hurts your percentage rating."

"But Jimmy can live with it," Marion Landers Boston said, entering the wide vestibule, joining them. She was in a long, plain skirt hitting her at her ankles and a midsized, patterned apron.

Jimmy had hung his coat in the coat closet. "A quarterback has to live with it, Mom," Jimmy said, turning to her.

Marion kissed Jimmy's cheek. "Our stadium seat was as cold as your cheek, Jimmy."

"I told you you didn't have to come to the game today, Mom," Jimmy said. The three were heading into the kitchen, which meant they'd passed the living room and dining room first.

"Oh, but your father could?"

"No ... I ..."

"Well, I've—the cold doesn't scare Marion Boston off!"

Jim winked at Jimmy.

"I've known colder days. I was a high school cheerleader, let's not forget. We had to stand out in the cold and freeze in our cute little knee-high skirts as our big Saturday football heroes ran up and down the football field scoring touchdowns.

"Remember, Jim?"

"Oh, yes—the cheerleaders, not the touchdowns, Marion. Byron High wasn't that good. Touchdowns for us were scarce. It didn't have Ron Hammaker at its helm, not like now."

"Hot chocolate, Jimmy?"

"Great, Mom."

"In fact, I saw Coach Hammaker and—"

"Frank Bosco."

"Yes," Marion continued, "Frank Bosco at the game, Jim."

"Billy and I saw them too, Dad, Mom, after the game. It's why I'm a little late getting home."

"Oh, your father and I thought you and Billy had gone to the Rockwell Mall," Marion said from the kitchen stove, looking over at Jimmy and Jim at the kitchen table.

"Uh, well, Billy and I were going to hit the mall after the game. Billy wanted to go—"

"But Coach Bosco—"

"And then Coach Hammaker—"

"Showed up first."

Marion looked at Jim, and Jim at Marion.

"Talked to you and Billy, uh, separately, Jimmy?"

"No, Dad. They talked to us together. At the same time."

"Oh, I see," Jim said.

"Here's your hot chocolate, honey."

"Mmm …"

"Forgot your marsh—"

"Don't sweat it, Mom. I'll get one," Jimmy said, hopping out of the chair.

Jimmy came back with the marshmallow and put it dead in the middle of the hot chocolate.

"What would you do without that marshmallow in your hot chocolate, Jimmy?"

"Oh, I think I'd survive, Mom." Jimmy grinned.

"So what did they say?" Jim asked uneasily.

"Why, uh, nothing new, I guess, Dad. They want Billy and me to go to their school to play, right? It's about all, sir," Jimmy said, stating it simply.

"Not to just play, Jimmy," Jim said, with some degree of nervousness in his voice. "But for you and Billy to make their team a winner. A championship team."

Jimmy had finished drinking the hot chocolate. He said he was going upstairs to call Billy.

Marion and Jim were at the kitchen table, Jim on one side and Marion on the other, in this spacious kitchen with one wall patterned in wallpaper and the other painted pea green. Marion liked knickknacks, and in her kitchen, they thrived like a tiny colony: colorful, zestful, and quite unique.

Jim looked across the table at Marion. "Are you worried like me, Marion?"

Marion, who'd been reading the city newspaper, removed her reading glasses, and her sparkling brown eyes dimmed somewhat. "Jim, we've been through this before."

"I know we have hypothetically. But …"

"We can't protect Jimmy forever. He's an athlete."

Marion was taller than Jim even though both were sitting. Marion was tall and slender. Jim, of course, was short and trim figured. If Jimmy grew to be tall, it'd be because of Marion's side of the family, not Jim's. Marion and her five brothers (Casey clan) were all tall.

"A hell of an athlete, Marion. Not like me."

"Well, Jimmy Boston's father happens to be good at other things."

"Like, uh, what? Selling insurance policies?"

"And providing a good home for his family."

"Now don't you sound like a paid commercial for Jim Boston's Allied Insurance Company."

Marion's hair was blonde, thick, and styled in a neat ponytail with bangs. She reached across the kitchen table and took hold of Jim's hand. "But I know your fears, Jim. They're mine. I've counted them and numbered all of them in my head by now."

"It's just the pressure. It grows from year to year, you know. Pop Warner football, then high school, then college. Gosh, the pressure never seems to end for Jimmy, Marion."

"But you know our son's basic temperament."

Jim stuck out his hand. "Even-keeled, all the way."

"Sometimes I think these are just parental concerns anyway, not our children's."

"But what do they know, Marion—twelve-year-olds?"

"Why, you'd be surprised." Marion smiled.

"Look, are you just saying that?" Jim said, questioning Marion's sincerity. "I mean as a kind of convenient cliché?"

"No, of course not. I honestly feel sometimes our kids—you'd be surprised what they can handle. How resilient they are."

"I just don't want all of this stuff, this grown-up stuff, to wear him down. That's my greatest concern. Hell, Marion, it's what bugs the hell out of me." Pause. "Win, win, win—at all costs."

"But it's athletics, Jim. It's sports. Competition."

"The score's not always going to be sixty-three to three like today. A cakewalk. The good thing"—Jim paused, his squared-jaw face relaxing—"is at least Jimmy has Billy. He and Billy are going through this together. Jimmy has someone else to talk to besides us. A peer, not just grown-ups."

"Right."

"And Connie and Susan are there for Billy the same as we are for Jimmy. You need a strong support system, because things are going to get rough and tumble, very soon."

"Jim, the chronic, inveterate worrier."

"Marion." Jim winked. "Hell, when'd you learn those big words?"

"In Mr. Heaney's English class."

"Oh, you mean that one I used to sleep through?"

"Yes, that one, Jim!"

"Gosh, I didn't know after all these years I'd missed out on all of that gobbledygook."

Marion's solid, big-boned body shook with laughter.

Jimmy had called Billy. They'd been talking for a few minutes. They talked to each other so much on the phone that it was a miracle the telephone lines hadn't melted.

"So what do you think, Billy? Forget about the other high schools in Pittsfield or what?" Jimmy asked, curling himself up neatly on his narrow bed.

Billy was wiggling his toes (habit), then stopped. "I don't know, Jimmy."

"Heck, I could've said that much."

"I know." Billy laughed. "But it's true, Jimmy." Pause.

"What about your mom and dad, Billy?"

"They're—"

"About the same as mine," Jimmy said, cutting Billy off.

"It's up to us," they said together, laughing.

"Good old Mom and Dad, huh, Billy?"

"You can say that again!"

"But we have to decide, don't we? Together, that is. So what kind of vibes did you get today, Billy?"

"Vibes? Both of them are great. I like both of them. And my dad thought Coach Bosco could've been a pro, but they said he was too short. Could've been a Fran Tarkenton or something like that."

"Too bad," Jimmy said. "I hope I grow."

"Jimmy, hey, don't sweat it. You will."

"I don't know, Billy. My dad's short."

"But not your mother. Your mother and your five uncles."

"Yeah, I know. But you don't have to worry. Your dad and mom."

"I should be a six footer."

"At least."

"Now, what about—"

"Hey, Billy, you know who I'm looking at right now?"

"Jimmy, none other than—"

"Johnny U. Johnny Unitas," Jimmy said, hopped up.

Jimmy had Johnny Unitas's picture on his bedroom wall, above his bed's headboard.

"And …"

"You're looking at—"

"None other than—"

"Jim Brown," Jimmy said with real muscle in his voice.

Jim Brown's picture had a place above Billy's bed's headboard.

"Yeah, my man. Dad says, 'Where are the great fullbacks today? Where did they vanish to?'"

"Probably carrying Jim Brown's jock strap, Billy. I bet."

"Yeah. Ha. Probably."

"I'm glad your dad showed us film footage of Johnny Unitas."

"Liked Johnny U. right away, didn't you?"

"You can say that again, Billy. Johnny Unitas was cool. That's all I can say—cool, man. He took tiny, birdlike steps when he dropped back in the pocket to set up to throw."

"And then …"

"Zip. The ball was out of his hand and in the air in no time flat. Billy, I want to be able to do that one day. Set up in the pocket and throw like him."

"You will, Jimmy."

"We'll be pros on the same team. The New York Giants."

"Uh-uh. Not me, Jimmy. The Dallas Cowboys."

"Whatever, whatever," Jimmy said dismissively.

"Whatever the guy says," Billy said, mildly miffed.

Pause.

"We'll be the new Unitas and Brown, except we'll be on the same team."

"Yeah, man, the dynamic twosome."

Billy was back to looking at Jim Brown in his Cleveland Brown's uniform, helmet, and shoulder pads, lugging a pigskin through some hole he'd just punched open like a Mack truck.

Jimmy frowned. "But, Billy, we, uh, do have to get back to Coach Bosco and Hammaker soon."

"Uh, right. Coach Bosco and Hammaker." Pause. "Jimmy … what record were you going to buy at the mall today anyway? You never told me."

"Something I heard the other night on the radio. It's cool, real cool. Maybe tomorrow we can—"

"Head over to the Rockwell Mall?"

"You bet."

"And check out the girls?"

"Right, Billy."

"And … Jimmy …"

Susan Antoinette Mack was tall for a woman. She was statuesque when wearing heels—and seemed to whisk by. She wore a pixie hairstyle with layers, and she had high cheekbones and sultry eyes. She was brown skinned and smiled with such sincerity it was her strength. Right now, though, Susan Mack was not in heels but a blue nightgown, with curlers extending from her short hair, and still, she looked quite fabulous and fashionable.

"Good night, Billy," Susan said, tapping on Billy's door.

"Okay, Mom."

Susan turned off the second floor's hall lights.

The lights in her bedroom were low when she entered, but she could see Connie's outline fill out the bed.

Susan Mack made a face that spoiled her gorgeous face. "Connie, don't tell me I'm going to have to fight for space in bed again tonight."

Susan was on her side of the bed.

Connie's head popped up. He smiled from tooth to gum. "Want to draw a line down the middle? Straight as a ruler? I can get my—"

"Funny. Oh that's funny, all right," Susan said, sitting on the side of the bed, slipping off her red satin slippers.

"Wasn't meant to be," Connie said, smiling. "I could put a chalk line down the middle, you know. Like a highway." His face beamed.

Susan swung herself into bed.

"Hey, watch it. You're on my side of the bed!"

Susan turned off the nightstand's lamp. "Whose side?"

Connie shifted a little to the left, much in the direction of the floor.

"That's better." Susan smiled.

"Good night."

They kissed, his tongue slipping into her mouth.

"By the way, how's the project coming along?" Susan asked, seemingly unable to resist.

"Oh—you know, Susan. You know how it goes at first. Fits and starts. Something that looks representative of something, and then the question marks within question marks without any solvable answers—then *bam*. The whole damn thing comes together like some planned, pristine miracle not of my doing."

"Wow. You mean I asked for … for all of that?" Susan grimaced.

"Apparently so." Connie laughed. "You know better than to ask at this stage of the game. Not when my feet are ten feet off the ground. Dangling. Just dangling in space somewhere," Connie said like a lost soul.

"Indeed, after these many years of marriage, Connie," Susan said wearily.

Susan and Connie Mack had been married for fourteen years. Their fifteenth wedding anniversary was in two months, January 21. The two had met in college, Brown University. Connie was the one to say hi first and kept his eyes drilled into Susan Tatum until she "weakened," "succumbed" (it's how it was later characterized by Connie)—until she had to say hi back. After that, whatever happened between two "hi's" took off!

"I'll be at Billy's next game," Susan said. "Come hell or high water."

"Yeah, me too. My job's project or not."

"It was just the Wyatts. The whole thing was so pressing. I couldn't back out."

"Same here. There are but so many hours in the day. Its cliché, I know, but true. There are but so many hours in the day."

"Billy's good, isn't he?" Susan said, her face on the pillow, turned to Connie.

"Great, Sue. Billy's great."

"But do you think, I mean, he might just be physically mature, more so than the other boys his age. Maybe, Connie?"

"Not on your life. Billy's got all the attributes: natural strength and speed. And ... there's something about his sensibilities, Susan, his keen awareness of who he is that's uncanny. That's really moons removed from anyone else's I've seen."

Pause.

"He seems to know his place in the moment, doesn't he? It, I mean, that's not in any way sounding too esoteric," Susan said.

"It's a, it is a bit highbrow, but I know what you're getting at. Billy does have a presence."

"What, of course, is what I was trying to say. He commands the moment." Pause. "But some athletes, they can peak too early, can't they?"

Connie chuckled. "Don't ask me, Sue, because you know I was a late bloomer when it came to sports. Hit my stride late in the game. But to answer your question, yes, you bet. There are some very gifted young athletes who peaked too early. Stories piled up on stories. There's a gallery full of would-be All-Americans who took quick tumbles."

"A fall, you mean, Connie," Susan said with conviction.

"It happens—isn't rare or unusual. It's certainly not a phenomenon." He took her hand. "So ... you're going to worry yourself, right? Sick, right?"

"No ..."

But Connie could feel worry throbbing in Susan's hand.

"It won't happen to Billy; our son's destined."

"Football's taken over his life, his and Jimmy's, Connie. It's all the two live and breathe." Pause.

"Suppose it's like being a child prodigy. If it's okay to use that kind of mind-set. A violin or, say, a piano prodigy."

"Most of them are just flashes in the pan, aren't they? Burn out early, Connie. Seem to be programmed for failure."

"Maybe," Connie said edgily, "that's a bad, poor example then. But young, gifted musicians like that—it's a competitive field, Sue, like sports. The competition …"

"The earlier you start—what, the better?"

"Yes, no—well, I mean it doesn't hurt. Billy and Jimmy shouldn't be hurt by it, I don't think. It certainly doesn't hurt your chances for success any, I don't think."

"I haven't learned patience, Connie, have I? The value it has after all these years, have I?"

"Susan, Susan, look, you're all right. You've done well under the circumstances. You've kept your concerns at a minimum. Kept them out of the way of Billy's excitement. You haven't taken the glitter out of his eyes. You haven't spoiled any of the fun for him."

"No, I mustn't do that. No."

Quietly, Connie said, "And I guess it's all we can ask of ourselves as parents—that is to encourage, not discourage, when it comes to our kids."

CHAPTER 2

The rain fell lightly on Pittsfield.

For a good portion of the day, it'd been overcast. Frank Bosco was in his dark blue Ford, a car that had a ton of mileage tacked on its odometer. The car didn't look like much but hummed surprisingly well—not like it would die at the first stoplight it stopped at on a dark, desolate road.

Frank Bosco's dark Italian eyes were busy thinking. There had to be an electrical network between his eyes and his brain, transmitting a load of red-coded energy pulses. Billy Mack and Jimmy Boston were on his mind (not necessarily in that order). Who else? Frank had been under their spell for the past three days. He liked those kids. They were great. He'd spoken to each before but not at such length as the other day. They really were good, solid kids. He found it a joy being in their company. They were more than brilliantly gifted athletes, far and away.

He was after them, all right—in hot pursuit. Who wouldn't be? You'd have to be crazy not to if you were a football coach. They were a beauty to watch play, even though there were still sizeable areas of their game where each could improve. But then came intelligence, toughness, desire, and plain courage. And each had it in boatloads, Frank thought. Billy Mack and Jimmy Boston oozed with the stuff.

He knew it was going to be the better man who won out between him and Ron Hammaker for Jimmy and Billy's football talents. He knew that for him to be successful, he must always size up the competition, and this is what he saw in him versus Ron.

Ron was an aggressive type, as aggressive as he was. Ron was as sincere and well-meaning as he was. Both loved the game of football. Both loved kids. Both loved to teach the kids the game of football. They were in many ways equal—parts equal in sum. If he had an edge over Ron, he couldn't see one, and vice versa. Ron didn't have anything over him either—nothing that stuck out like a sore thumb. To get someone like a Billy Mack or a Jimmy Boston at their tender age was not only a dream come true but a natural blessing.

So far, this chase he was on, going full throttle after these two kids, had been, as a coach, rewarding and self-fulfilling. He thrived on competition, and here it was in full flower. Ron was going to make it a dog fight for its duration. He was dogged. It was the way he had been on the football field when they played together. He thought every ball thrown to him could go for a touchdown; even if it was a five-yard slant over the middle, Ron felt it could go for a touchdown.

And now as a coach, on game day, his team was beautifully prepared, and they were fierce competitors. But what really separated the team from the litter was its coach, a field coach who could spot another team's weaknesses and be able to surgically exploit them at will.

"Yeah, Ron," Frank said, wiping his brow testily, "may the better man win. And I hope like hell it's me!"

It was a cold rain. It was coming down even harder now. It fell on this street that could be called Main Street, America, but it was Alice Street in Pittsfield, Massachusetts, where a lot of Pittsfield's main businesses were grouped. Lights on this day in Pittsfield shone out of the street's stores, making it look more like Christmas had come, with its usual penchant for sparkle.

Frank Bosco's Ford was parked in a public facility with a two-hour parking maximum. Frank was out the car in a flash. He bunched his shoulders. He wasn't carrying an umbrella but threw a rain hat over his head. He didn't have far to walk. He just hoped like the devil the rain wouldn't get in his shoes and make them squish and squeak.

Frank walked against each building's wall, hoping the roof's wooden or metal overhang would provide good shelter. He held his breath. He was right where he wanted to be. His eyes tasted one last drop of rain, and then into the quaint office building he strode.

"Frank Bosco," the voice rang out. "Come in, Frank. By all means!"

Jim's voice had all the cheer and welcome and upside aggression of an insurance salesman who owned his own insurance company, Allied Insurance.

"'As ya policy run out on ya, Frank?' As it, lad?" Jim said, applying a thick Irish brogue.

"No, Jim. Not that I know of. At least Maria hasn't told me—not yet."

There were three insurance agents in the office, plus a secretary, Mary Roberts.

There was an old-fashioned, knee-high wooden swing gate dividing the room. It was how customers got to agents. Jim's desk was to the right of them. His hand was outstretched.

There was a coat and hat rack. Frank removed his raincoat and rain hat.

"Frank, how is Maria, by the way?"

"Maria's doing great. Fine, Jim," Frank replied, shaking Jim's hand. The handshake was firm and friendly (in a way, both salesmen).

"Uh … did I catch you at a bad time?"

"No. Gosh, not at all. Have a sit down."

Frank sat.

"I was going to call—"

"Only, you decided to take your chances. Live on the edge?"

"Some life, huh?"

"Frank, you can say that again."

Frank's hand went up to his eyebrow to defend his eye from the remnants of rainwater taking a downward turn.

"So your insurance policies are paid up to date, are they? Car, house, life—"

"Jim, it's Jimmy. It's Jimmy. It's why I'm here. You know it's not for insurance but your son, Jim."

"Thought so," Jim said, arching forward in his chair.

"I'm out here recruiting. Out here trying to get your son to come to Pittsfield to play for me."

"You and Ron Hammaker. Jimmy told Marion and me all about it. What happened after the game the other day."

"Of course he did. I expected Jimmy to," Frank said, settling into his chair.

"Frank, look, I knew it was coming—this recruiting business."

"Oh, this day had to come, Jim. Sure." Pause. "Jim, how does Mrs. Boston feel about it?"

"She's a trooper." Jim laughed. "That one is, all right. Better than me."

"Sounds just like Mrs. Boston."

"Unflappable. It's just like she is around the house—hears every darn thing in the house. A bug's back leg could twitch, and Marion's on it. She's attuned to things. I'm the one with the concerns, the worrywart in the family."

"Why, I know what you mean, Jim. Ron and I will be gentle but not when it comes to those college guys. They're a different breed altogether."

"You know, I've heard about calls coming all hours of the day and night. Big-time pressure, Frank."

"Afraid so, Jim. It's what Billy and his parents, the Macks, have in store for them too, down the road. It's their life, the coach's livelihood. It is no-holds-barred at the college level. They'll run roughshod over you and not give it a second thought."

"Well … Jimmy's going to decide this one on his own. You should know that up front," Jim said, a certain sternness tempering his voice. "It's Jimmy processing, this baby."

Frank had to laugh. "You know I dropped by to fatten you up, Jim. It was obvious, I guess."

"Don't I know it," Jim said, slapping his leg. "But Marion and I are making it Jimmy's call. Both schools are excellent academically. So there's no qualm, any reason for concern on that front."

"And we both have fantastic football programs, Ron and I."

"You bet."

"Well, Jim—I won't take up any more of your valuable time. I'm just glad Maria and my insurance policies are paid. Up to date. All of them."

"But, Frank, I'd check with Maria if I were you. I know how you football coaches are about anything outside the world of football."

"Like the absentminded professor. Ha. That's us."

Frank got up to leave. He and Jim shook hands.

"So I can't get Jimmy's old man to put in a good word in for me, huh, Jim? Not one good word for Coach Frank Bosco, huh?

Jim slapped Frank on the back.

Frank turned to leave the office by swinging open the knee-high gate. He walked over to the coat and hat rack, where rain bled off the raincoat's slick veneer finish and where his rain hat still stuck to the top of the rack like a battered sack.

Slowly, Frank put on his rain gear. He heard the rain beating against the building's window like it was waiting for him and only him with a devil's glee.

"So, Frank, how far behind you do you think Ron Hammaker is? What, a hair's breadth?"

"Probably as soon as the storm breaks, Ron'll pop up out of nowhere," Frank said, opening the door to face the rains with greater grit.

Frank was in another section of Pittsfield. Frank was in hot pursuit, running toward the person who was heading for his black Buick Regal. The rain had stopped.

"Mr. Mack!"

"Coach Bosco?" Connie said, looking over his left shoulder.

There was a little heavy breathing involved on Frank's part, as if he'd run a short wind sprint and his lungs burned.

Frank stuck out his hand, and Connie shifted his briefcase from right hand to left.

Frank still had his rain hat on, looking like a lost New England fisherman or Detective Columbo at a particular distance.

Now there was a sign of annoyance on Connie's attractive face, as if asking, *What's going on with this guy? Why's he resorting to this kind of juvenile gimmickry, trickery? Is this supposed to have some kind of espionage, undercover objective in it?*

Quickly, Frank ascertained Connie's irritation with him. "This is a bad time, Mr. Mack? Am I catching you at a bad time?" Frank asked, gripping Connie's hand, his dark Italian eyes losing an element of confidence. Frank felt foolish.

"Bad timing? For what, Coach Bosco? It's according to why you're here."

The rain had stopped, but the day was cold and raw.

"Uh—need, need I tell you, Mr. Mack? Someone—a … an ex-athlete like you?"

"Well, we're not going to discuss Billy, not out in this nasty cold."

Connie inserted the key in the car's lock. He unlocked the other door through the car's electronic system.

"Are you getting in, Coach Bosco?"

"Sure, sure, Mr. Mack."

Frank headed around to the other side of the car. Connie was already sitting in the driver's seat.

"Now, about Billy …" Connie said.

Frank opened the Buick's door in the Blast Aircraft Company's parking lot reserved for employees only and withdrew his rain hat from his head, holding on to it precariously.

This was a pretty woman, no doubt about it. She had eyes that shimmered in the moonlight, beautiful hair, and a saucy shape. She looked like Gina Lollobrigidia's twin sister. But her name was Maria Lo Bianco Bosco. And she was in her workroom putting stitch to seam and hemline—not studying tomorrow's movie script for a hot shoot.

Maria Lo Bianco Bosco was a clothes designer. Not a world-famous one but world-famous in the eyes, hearts, and minds of the local Pittsfield women of fine, exquisite, and expensive taste. Maria Bosco's clothes designs were in increasing demand by women of good breeding in Pittsfield. Maria had a rich client base that she pretty much had sewn up exclusively for herself.

Maria let the sewing machine idle for a second. She brushed at the beautiful black strands of hair that had fallen across her eyes, practically blinding her. She blew at the annoying strands of hair, sexily. She stood. In size, she was petite. She sat back down.

"I'm doing a lot for nothing—and why?"

Maria was as much involved with her husband's work as he was with hers. They were like that: each took mutual interest in the other's profession. Frank loved to brag about her, she was told. And he was her football hero before he became a football star. She couldn't remember when she wasn't in love with Frank. It seemed as if she was always in love with him. They had a big Italian-style wedding but—oddly at the time—no honeymoon.

Maria would hear him come into the house but would always pretend she hadn't. Her back was to the room's open door. The house's floors were thickly carpeted. Frank would sneak up behind her to surprise her. She would let him, not let on she'd heard him—and then jump out of her skin.

Maria started the sewing machine back up. The stage was set.

Frank mustn't be too far away, Maria thought. *A few footsteps maybe. Prepare yourself, Maria. Prepare yourself.*

"Frank!" Maria said, practically jumping out of her skin.

While Frank laughed. His hands had covered Maria's eyes. "Maria, when are you going to catch on?" Frank asked, kissing Maria on her left cheek, which blushed like a polished apple.

"You get me every time, Frank," Maria said, winking.

"Every time. I guess with your sewing machine on. Going at the rate—"

"I can't hear a thing."

"And your concentration when you're sewing."

"Something you would do—"

"When I was in the pocket. I know," Frank said wistfully.

She and Frank kissed.

"Now, what kind of kiss was that, Frank Bosco?"

"I-I made a fool of myself today," Frank said, releasing Maria. "A donkey's ass."

Maria's arm snaked back around Frank's waist. They moved over to the short couch and sat. Frank bunched his shoulders in and bent forward. He played with his hands.

"Like a beggar with a hat in his hand."

"How, Frank?"

His dark Italian eyes looked across the room. "Guess where I went today after school."

Maria paused for a second. "Where?"

"You know, nobody has to paint a picture for me. Of what a fool looks like, Maria. An asshole. Because it'd be hanging over our living room fireplace if they did."

"Frank ..."

Frank laughed sarcastically. "I went chasing off to Jim Boston's office today, that's where."

"So?"

Frank looked intensely at her. "And then I went chasing off to Connie Mack's place of business, Blast Aircraft. Met him in the parking lot."

"In … in the rain?"

"No. By then, the rain had stopped."

Maria relaxed.

"Maria, what was I trying to prove?" Frank decided to answer the rhetorical question. "I know what. It's how they do it at the college level, isn't it? The next level up."

"What do you mean?"

"The urgency. The thrill, Maria. The passion. All of it."

Frank's eyes darkened. "Waiting for the recruit's father in a parking lot—ambushing him. Letting him know you've got to have his kid. You must have his kid at all costs. See what I'm doing? See how desperate I am? See what your kid means to me—to my future? My football program? See how I'd—see how I don't have any pride in myself, scruples? How I'll make a fool of myself if I have to, as long as I get your son? As long as he plays for me. Me!"

Maria offered no comment.

"I don't do these kinds of things, Maria. Normally."

"I know."

"It's not me or my style. It's not how I think."

"But like you said last night in bed, Billy Mack and Jimmy Boston are special, Frank. Unusual talents."

"I-I've never coached the likes of that kind of talent before. Man—the potential those two kids have is amazing."

"Mr. Mack—"

"He made me feel foolish. Not that I blame the guy. No, I don't blame him. Shit no," Frank said, fidgeting. "If I'd reversed roles, I'd done the same. If it was my son."

"It was an ambush?" Maria half-laughed.

"What a jerk. Yeah, I felt like a beggar with his hat in his hand—a donkey's ass."

"Don't say that."

"It was out of character."

"Of course it was, sweetheart."

"Connie Mack's a no-nonsense guy—a straight shooter though, I mean—if there ever was one. Definitely an ex-jock." Frank laughed.

Maria laughed. "You make it sound like a club, Frank. A special one athletes join. For athletes only."

"Well, it is, Maria. Once we hang our jocks, we're as honest with each other as a day is long." Pause. "Connie Mack did say I was a great quarterback in my heyday though."

"See? He didn't think you're the world's biggest fool."

"Now, Maria, hold up. I didn't come home saying I was the world's biggest fool now."

"Okay, all right. So I got my signals crossed. Carried away. I'm not a quarterback, an ex-jock, you know."

"He said he thought I could've been another Fran Tarkenton or Joe Theisman—given the opportunity. Someone of that kind of genuine talent."

"Frank, you know I thought so too, sweetheart. Even though I didn't know about Joe Theisman or Fran Tarkenton at the time. I still don't know why you—"

"I didn't want to put you through that crap, Maria. The craziness. Cut by this team and that one. Tryouts. Training camps. The whole nine yards' worth. I wouldn't put you through any of that garbage. Not you."

Frank frowned. "City to city. Uncertainty after uncertainty to deal with."

"It, you think it would've been that bad, Frank?"

"When you're borderline like I was, Maria, marginal, the answer's yes. It's tough. Either somebody has to get injured, the guy in front of you—or you have to play like Godzilla. It's the treatment guys like me get on that level. Yeah, you have to play pretty much like Godzilla to win a prized quarterback job in the NFL."

"Godzilla?" Maria's beautiful black eyes flashed.

"Didn't you know he once played quarterback for the New York Giants?"

Maria pinched Frank where it hurt.

"Hey, *mama mia*—that was my shoulder!"

"Your throwing arm, right?"

Maria stood. She had work to do. She walked over to her sewing machine chair and sat. What Maria was working on was going to be a knockout.

Frank got up and walked over to her. "Jimmy and Billy aren't going to have a worry in the world when their time comes."

Maria looked up at Frank. "No?"

"A brain surgeon I don't have to be."

Maria laid some of the material into the teeth of the sewing machine.

"The penthouse suite is going to open up to them at every stage of their progression through it. They won't have to carry their suitcases from team to team or tryout to tryout like vagabonds."

Frank smiled. "There'll be a lot more people who make fools out of themselves, stand in line with their hat in hand, to have those two youngsters on their football roster one day soon."

"Not just you, huh?" Maria winked. "We'll know soon though, won't we, Frank?"

"In another month—January. It's when the kids like to get things set on the official record."

Pause.

"Thank God."

"Uh-huh. Thank God. And then this nightmare will end—once and for all."

Frank was making his way toward the door when he turned.

"Maria," Frank said, like a kid of nine or ten. "Do ... do I really scare you, uh, surprise you when—"

"Frank, you do! You really do!" Maria said with a suppressed smile on her face but extreme fright in her voice.

Like I must have done with Connie Mack, Frank thought, heading through the living room. *Really scared the hell out of the poor guy up in Blast Aircraft's parking lot today. But Billy Mack. Maybe it'll be worth it a month from now.*

CHAPTER 3

September 8, 1987

Frank Bosco looked like a ticking bomb. He couldn't wait to get the team together. The team was assembling in the Pittsfield High School locker room, where he would run through the traditional player introduction bit as head coach to kick off the new football season (getting everyone there to get to know everyone else).

The Pittsfield High School football team's nickname was the Purple Eagles. The team colors were purple and blue. They'd been purple and blue since 1942, when the team changed its colors. They'd always been called the Purple Eagles though.

Mike Overbranch, Frank's assistant coach, threw open the Pittsfield High School's gym door (it was a swing-in, swing-out door). He was leading the pack out the locker room into the gym. Lockers for the players had been assigned. Now it was just a matter of them finding them (which was always fun to watch—only, that would be later).

Mike Overbranch was short and stocky. He looked like a fireplug dogs gravitate to. He'd been a defensive halfback, then beefed up to a middle linebacker in his salad days. Now Mike looked like a definite middle linebacker whose helmet had plugged up too many holes.

"All right, fellas. Coach Bosco will be here any second now!" Pause.

"For the new guys, your first time here: how do you like our facility? I know you've looked around."

"Rah! Rah!"

"Good, good. Coach Bosco and the school are proud of what we've done here. Awful proud of being a big part of this community. Of helping make this community shine."

The locker room's door swung open.

"And here Coach Bosco is, men!" Mike said, extending his hand to Frank.

"Thanks, Mike," Frank said, taking Mike's hand and shaking it as if they'd just met at a beer and pretzel party. "Great job!"

Frank's eyes took in the whole scene like a wide-eyed camera. "What a group we have here. What a fine-looking group of young men you are in this gym."

Everyone in the locker room got goose bumps.

"Of course, many of you already know each other, but I'm still going to go through this, read your names off like it's an official roll call. Let you know who's who by way of formal introduction. And after that, you're on your own."

Frank made a mighty sigh. "Then we can drop all formalities and get onto bigger and better things." He laughed.

Frank looked at his troops with purple fire in their eyes. "So here goes. Here goes this year's football team's official roll call ... uh, roster that is," Frank said like he was about to topple over by this thrill of thrills.

"First, we have Tom Oswald to my left. And next to him, Danny Burke. And then ..."

Frank wound his way through most of the Purple Eagle's roster. There were maybe six or seven players left.

"And then there's Everett Cannon and Louis Paladino."

And then for some reason, Frank paused as if he couldn't quite believe what he was going to say next, as if someone (preferably Maria, only she was home dressmaking) should pinch his posterior (hard!) to make certain his body hadn't floated into a liquid jar of unreality.

"Uh—forgive me, gentlemen. Please forgive me," Frank said apologetically. "Uh, as I was saying, uh. And next to Louis we have ..." And again, Frank's voice faltered.

Frank looked worse for the wear now, as if he'd lost his recipe for sanity.

"Billy … Billy Mack. And next to Billy, we have, uh, we have Jimmy, Jimmy Boston."

Spike Armstrong, last year's Purple Eagle's quarterback, and Joe "Pitbull" McNally, last year's starting fullback, had shivers run up and down their spines like a long, cold, torturous ski trail in—of all places—Greenland, Alaska!

Frank was in his office, which was large enough to accommodate a chalkboard on wheels, various-sized football trophies on top a cabinet's broad top, and a wall of framed pictures capturing special moments of Frank's football career, past and present.

"Frank, you should see your face."

"Don't tell me, Mike. I look like a glowworm."

Frank had his feet propped on top of his desk.

"Did you see Spike Armstrong and Jimmy Boston air it out today, Mike?" Frank asked.

"It was something else," Mike said, practically flopping out of the chair.

"What do we have here, Mike? Some kind of gold mine?"

"I wouldn't sell them for the price of gold or anything else you can name. I've never enjoyed practice so much."

"Jimmy's arm—it's gotten stronger by the day."

"Clotheslines, Frank. Everything he threw today was on a clothesline."

"A frozen rope."

"And touch, he has it. Loads of it." Mike sighed. "It's, uh, just around the corner, isn't it, Frank?"

Frank knew what Mike had just said without him actually saying it.

"Don't I. I'm beginning to count the seconds, never mind the minutes."

"Right. You should know better than anyone."

Frank's feet dropped off the desk. "Want my job for a day? What do you say, Mike?"

"No, thank you. Not on your life, old buddy. You can call the shots on this one. I'll head for the nearest exit."

The phone rang.

"Oh … yes, hello, Coach O'Malley." He spoke a few more words into the phone. Then, his hand covering it, he said, "Mike, you know Coach O'Malley and I will be on the phone for a while, so if you want …"

Mike, with a few hand gestures, pardoned himself from the room.

Frank did have a long talk with his old coach. After hanging up, he was going to put his feet back up on his desk like he didn't have a care in the world, not a one, only he thought differently: he had all kinds of cares and worries. His brain had been a steam pipe of late (hot).

It was Jimmy Boston and Spike Armstrong who were at his brain's nerve center. It was all about those two guys. One a senior quarterback, and one a freshman quarterback. One who'd led the Purple Eagles to the state championship round only to be beaten by Ron Hammaker's team, Byron High School, by the score of 28–19. His worries and cares were about them.

The new football season was to begin soon, and he had to cement the quarterback position. Spike was the quarterback. It was his position, until someone else won it. And Jimmy Boston, the freshman phenom, wunderkind, my God, was knocking on the door—or better still—pounding the damned door, determined to knock it to hell and back.

Frank smiled. Practice was thrilling as hell. Competition between Spike and Jimmy had heated up to the point of boiling over. Frank saw Spike out on the practice field looking over his shoulder, literally, more than once. Jimmy Boston, even as a freshman, was out to win Spike's job—and he was making no bones about it to anyone witnessing this rare, special competition unfold.

Frank smiled more.

And Billy Mack was surely after "Pitbull" McNally's starting fullback slot. Pitbull was running scared like a wild mongoose was on his tail. Theirs was a competition to be heard and felt. Theirs was a competition of grunts and groans and an awesome destruction of the Purple Eagle's linebacker crew (youthful humanity). On the football field, Billy and Pitbull were running over and through people, punishing anyone who dared get in their way. Surely they were possessed by demons!

But Billy Mack, as far as Frank was concerned, was simply phenomenal. He was a young man who had talent pouring out of his ears. Every time he touched the ball, it was like silver dollars had rained out of the sky. Every time Billy touched the ball, there was the possibility of greatness, of seeing something never seen on the football field.

But the days were closing in on him, and Frank knew it. Did h e ever! It was a matter of six more days. In six days, he would have to announce the eleven starting positions for the team. But even with his nerves flaring tiny rockets, Frank was relishing this kind of pressure, this kind of challenge. He was being forced to put on his thinking cap, weigh each option open to him tactfully, argue each point like a trial lawyer until he turned blue in the face.

Frank was going to field a championship football team again this year. It would have all the makings of an outstanding football season for the Purple Eagles. He rammed his fist into his palm.

"My God, I've got work to do. Six days," Frank said, as if those six days were already up—had vanished like a rainbow after a rainy day.

Six days later, after school, Jimmy and Billy stood at their adjacent lockers. The lockers were in the corner of the locker room, off to the side like a special little island that had mutated in that spot just for them. They were the first two in the locker room, so Billy and Jimmy could talk freely.

"Like I told you, Billy," Jimmy whispered, "you're a lock."

"Jimmy, I wish you wouldn't say things like that." Billy shivered nervously, removing his T-shirt.

Jimmy was moving a little faster than Billy today: he was down to his pants—taking them off, his hands practically a blur.

"But it's true."

"Right … t-tell that to … to Coach Bosco," Billy stuttered. "Tell him you've already made the coaching decision for him—o-okay?"

Jimmy was down to his socks; Billy, his pants.

"I think Pitbull knows it too."

"Jimmy," Billy said, taking Jimmy's arm, "can we change the subject—please? Talk about something else."

"First freshman to ever start for the Purple Eagles." Jimmy cleared his throat. "Ladies and gentlemen. We present to you, standing in front of his funky locker (which he makes no excuses for) and directly from Mr. Joshua Jacob's Algebra I class—"

"Where he scored a perfect one hundred on Friday's algebra quiz."

"Where he scored a perfect one hundred on Friday's algebra quiz: Mr. Billy Mack. Acne bumps and all!"

Jimmy had coaxed a smile from Billy.

But then Billy challenged Jimmy. "How do you know I'd be the first freshman to ever start for the Purple Eagles, anyway, if Coach Bosco picks me over Pitbull as starting full—"

"Hey, Billy, don't bug yourself with the minor details, man. They're only—"

"Right, Jimmy." Pause. "But, Jimmy, suppose we don't start. I want to, but if we don't ..."

Jimmy's handsome face looked like a teenager's who'd all but forgotten yesterday's disappointment and was looking forward only to tomorrow's triumph. "We'll just work harder, Billy. How's that? A deal?"

"Stay focused."

"And work our tails off," Jimmy said, wrapping his arms around Billy's hefty shoulders.

"We're lucky just to have a coach like Coach Bosco, Jimmy."

"You can say that again."

"And whatever goes down, hey, Coach Bosco picked the right man," Billy said cheerfully.

"Agreed, Billy."

Billy rolled the second sock off his foot. "But you want it, don't you?"

Jimmy had put on his jock (the rest of him as naked as the moon).

"Yeah," Jimmy said calmly. "I want it, Billy."

CHAPTER 4

There was a breeze but not with a chill in it. Frank wore a baseball cap. It was covering his thick, wavy black hair. It was a cap with no insignia, only the color purple. He had a light jacket on, more for official reasons than for the weather. He did look official, no less than a head coach of a successful high school football team.

But even with this air of correctness as he stood on top the bleacher's first plank, his players surrounding him like he was about to give away free tickets to a U2 concert, his dark Italian eyes radiated warmth.

Coach Bosco had a clipboard in his hands with the names of the players he'd selected for the Eagles' starting lineup (barring injury or some other unforeseen circumstance) come game day. He stood as rigid as a flagpole anticipating wicked wind conditions.

Mike Overbranch was on the first plank off to the right of Frank, like he was a forgotten domestic house plant just moved back up from a dark, dank basement. Nothing would hold any surprise for Mike but the announcement of the quarterback slot. Mike knew the other twenty-one players who would be filling the roster.

Frank did a two-step shift to his left, like a cha-cha minus the third step.

Mike did the same dance step to keep the distance between them exact. And to no surprise, this mass of humanity in helmets and cleats and shoulder pads did the same dance routine: a two-step shift like a well-drilled chorus line.

Frank saw what he'd done, so he thought it only best he kill the suspense that gripped Mike and his team by starting at the top of the honor roll with the man who was to lead them to what was hoped and predicted to be the state championship—the land of milk and honey.

"This suspense is killing me too, men," Frank said, tugging the bill of his purple baseball cap, adjusting it so it could sit more comfortably and correctly on his head. Then as if the whole weight of the world was about to be lifted off his shoulders by the beauty of one glance at his official-looking clipboard, Frank said chirpily, "The starting QB for this year's varsity football team will be Spike Armstrong. Spike!"

"Dad!"

"You did it, son. The fullback position—it's yours. You're the Purple Eagles' new starting fullback, aren't you? Coach Bosco penciled you in!"

They hugged extra hard.

"Congratulations, Billy!" Connie said, lifting Billy off the Blast Aircraft's employee parking lot pavement like Billy was as light as a feather.

"Thanks, Dad!"

This, Billy meeting Connie at his job like this, in the employee parking area, made Connie feel especially good. He was grinning from ear to ear. It was a moment Connie would not soon forget. Not on his life!

"So, Billy," Connie said, about to open the Buick Regal's passenger side door for him, "how, I mean, how did it feel, son? The, uh, point of impact? When Coach Bosco hit you with the good news."

Billy licked his lips first, and his brown skin reddened before shooting his fist skyward. "Super, Dad! Great! It was the best! The greatest!"

Connie looked at his son, knowing the feeling—the feeling of an athlete receiving good news from his coach that he'd made the grade, was top at his position.

Connie just let Billy stand there savoring his triumph.

"Getting in?" He motioned to the car. "You don't want me to leave without you."

Billy hopped in the car, chuckling. He buckled himself in. Nothing was said between them as Connie looked both ways at the stop sign before driving the car down the short incline. Then he looked both ways at the bottom of the incline, and the turn signal light flashed left.

Connie was feeling the glide of the ride when he said, "So it will still be you and Jimmy in the starting backfield come opening day? As usual?"

Billy snapped out of his euphoria. "Dad, no, no. Jimmy … he's not the starting quarterback, Dad. Spike Armstrong is. Spike won the quarterback job."

Connie practically drove the Buick off the road.

"Spike … did you say Spike Armstrong?"

"Spike beat out Jimmy, Dad."

It didn't sound right to Connie. It didn't even have the right sound or bite to it. "You said Jimmy didn't, that Jimmy's not—"

"I didn't want to ruin it for you or—"

"For yourself. Getting the fullback position and not Jimmy—"

"Yes, probably, Dad. Probably. But it feels awful. It's never happened before."

"You and Jimmy not playing together. I know, son. I know."

"I could've cried, Dad, when Coach Bosco stood there and said it was Spike over Jimmy. I mean all the guys, after they looked at Jimmy, everybody's eyes turned to me. I felt sick. Sick to my stomach."

"You had to." Connie's foot eased off the car's accelerator. He had to let this piece of jarring information stew more.

"How'd Jimmy take it?"

"He's a winner, Dad. He took it better than the rest of us. Much better."

"I feel for him. He's like a son. Like family. I'm taking this hard, real hard, Billy. I didn't expect this. Not in my wildest dreams, son."

"Before Coach Bosco made the announcement, Jimmy and I agreed, in the locker room, if we didn't make the starting team, then we would work harder at it, Dad. It's how we saw it."

"Right, Billy. Yeah, exactly."

"Jimmy and I agreed on that much. I mean, Jimmy just came right out and said it like he'd not given it any thought. None—none at all."

Pause.

"Jimmy thinks, he thinks like an athlete," Connie said respectfully. "So do you."

"I ... I do?"

"Yes, you do, starting fullback for the Purple Eagles varsity football team."

"I can't believe it."

"Believe it, Billy. Believe it. And you deserve it, son. It's one hell of an accomplishment for you. One hell of an accomplishment."

Connie and Susan were sitting in the living room, surrounded by exquisite drapery anchoring the two front windows that looked directly out onto the spacious front lawn.

"Tomorrow's my big day," Connie said, glancing over at Susan, then returning to his newspaper.

Susan sat on the sofa reading a book. "I know."

"Sometimes, through it all," Connie said melodramatically, "I thought the day—tomorrow—would never come."

Susan giggled. "Me too."

"You mean to say I was that much of a pain in the—"

"Butt? Yes you were, all right. A big pain in the butt."

"Come on, Susan. The project was driving me crazy, but I didn't let it affect my family, did I?"

Susan smiled. "You're right; you didn't let it affect us." She paused. "Only at night."

"At—"

"We'll discuss it later. Okay? In bed, where it happened a few—"

"Jimmy. I can't get him out my mind," Connie said.

"I'm glad Jimmy took it well though," Susan said, with strain in her voice. "You know, these are the things that worry me."

"Me too."

"Do you think it's the first time something like this has happened to him? Him not making first team?"

"Of course, Sue. Of course. This had to be one hell of a jolt. And he was vying like Billy. He was competing. Jimmy's a fierce competitor. And when you compete as hard as Jimmy was with Spike Armstrong, yes, it's going to hurt. It's a blow, Sue. Huge."

"Billy's feelings in the car were—"

"Ambivalent at best. All his life, Jimmy's handed the football off to him. Every step of the way. Every game he's played. And now that's been taken from him."

"Will it change anything in Billy's performance on the football field do you think?"

"No ... if you should ask me. No, it shouldn't, Sue. No, it won't," Connie said more assertively. "Once Spike hands the ball to Billy and Billy gets belted around a few times, it'll become just another football game. Billy won't have the time to think, only react. Billy will have to focus in on the game.

"But ..." Connie paused. "There'll always be that sentimental aspect of it that'll be there no matter what. It's just something you can't rule out, push aside that easily."

Pause.

"How about some cake?"

"As long as you baked it."

"Connie," Susan said fussily, "you know I spent all day Sunday at the oven!"

Connie watched her as she left the living room for the kitchen and smiled with appreciation. *I have a great wife*, he thought. *A great wife. A great family. A great life.*

Ring.

Ring.

"I'll get it, Susan—since you're getting my cake!" Connie yelled.

Ring.

"Hello. Mack residence."

"Jim Boston, Connie. Is your insurance paid up?"

"Uh ... I think it—"

"Better check with Susan then," Jim said.

"So I see you know who handles the bills in this household."

"Connie, you betcha. In nine out of ten American households, statistics point out it's the wife."

"What would we do without them, huh, Jim?"

"Gosh, sink as fast as the *Titanic*!"

Pause.

"I called to congratulate Billy. But while I have you on the phone, Con—"

"How is Jimmy taking it? Coincidently, Susan and I were just discussing it. We were sort of worried."

"He was in a funk, Marion told me, when he got in. A mild one, but he seems to have snapped out of it. Not all the way but—"

"It certainly was a hard-fought contest, Billy told me. Jimmy really went at it."

"With all his heart and soul, Connie. He didn't give an inch to Spike."

"I know it's the way Billy operates too. They're two tough, outstanding young men."

"And they're ours, Connie. All ours!"

"Hell—you're right about that, Jim!"

"We could brag on our sons all day, and we wouldn't run out of words or gas."

"Jim, you mean superlatives, don't you?"

"Right, Connie. Superlatives. It's what I meant."

Pause.

"So Billy's …"

"Studying." Pause. "And Jimmy …"

"Studying."

"What else is new with those two, huh, Jim?"

Jim laughed. "Uh, then don't disturb him, Connie. Just let him know I called, will you? And say hello to Susan for me."

"And Marion for me."

"Oh, by the way, Connie, check on your insurance with Susan, will you? I believe everything's paid up to date, but since I'm not in the office and can't look into my computer, I can't be sure."

They bid each other good night.

"Susan, where's my cake?"

"Oh … coming, dear," Susan said mockingly. "You know when my husband speaks—"

"You run like hell!"

Susan had a slice of cake on the plate. "Not this wife. You must be talking about your other wife. Not this one."

Susan handed Connie the plate of cake. "I should dump it on you!"

"Yeah, you should."

Connie took a big bite out of the cake. "Jim Boston said hello."

"That's nice."

"He called to congratulate Billy."

"Jim's such a sweet man."

"By the way, Susan, is our insurance paid up to date?"

Susan laughed; she couldn't help herself. "Jim gets you every time with that line of his. Of course our insurance is paid up!"

Susan went back to reading her book. And Connie went back to reading his newspaper, with slight interruptions allowed for his fork attending to his chocolate cake.

But slowly, Connie's mind drifted from what he was reading and to Jim and Marion and Jimmy. To what the Boston family meant to the Mack family in Pittsfield. A white family. A black family. Families who by now were colorblind.

He'd had his reservations about them, about any white family. His job had brought them to Pittsfield—not any desire to live among white people, to cross the racial divide, as it were. It was his job, the opportunity to work for a top flight outfit. He was no pioneer. No trailblazer. No Jackie Robinson. It wasn't his aim to be the first black at something; he simply had an opportunity based on his abilities in his field and took full advantage of it.

Initially, he frowned on Billy and Jimmy's relationship. Not Susan but him. The relationship made him feel uneasy, uncomfortable. He thought it would be unequal in every way. It had to favor Jimmy Boston. Jimmy Boston was white. It would always favor Jimmy Boston. And then somewhere down the line, either through parental intervention or by societal rules, Jimmy Boston would dump Billy Mack like a bad headache. Dump Billy like they'd not spent one day of their lives together. How, back then, he'd wished Billy had a black friend—someone black he could build a friendship with, depend on, trust. But it wasn't to be, not in Pittsfield, Massachusetts.

But what a true blessing the Bostons turned out to be for them. He couldn't have chosen a better friend for Billy than Jimmy. The whole Boston family was a gem. Billy was on equal footing with Jimmy. Jimmy was by the Macks' residence as often as Billy was at the Bostons' residence.

Jimmy shared in as many of Billy's interests and activities as Billy did Jimmy's. They were wired together by a mutual love and respect.

Connie couldn't wrap his mind around anyone or anything destroying what they had. Odds makers would lose their shirts if they bet against them, that any lifelong friendship was out of the question in the world they lived in.

Susan looked up from her book and saw a saintly smile on Connie's face.

"What, may I ask, are you thinking, Connie? What's that enlightened mind of yours up to now?"

"Oh, how another piece of your wondrous chocolate cake would do me and my stomach, right now, just fine."

"It's that good?"

Connie winked. "You stood at the oven all Sunday and baked it with your two lovely, delicate brown hands, didn't you, Sue?"

Damn if life ain't great! Connie thought.

CHAPTER 5

The Purple Eagles were winning football games. It had been predicted they would win football games, and the team was living up to its preseason hype without there being a hitch in sight.

The team was 5–0 in its nine game schedule. All the games were romps, lopsided victories posted by the Eagles. It was plain to see only the state championship loomed as a test. And that wouldn't be until December, when the Eagles would take on the best the state could offer.

Joe "Pitbull" O'Malley was lugging the pigskin. He went through a nice hole, fought off some burly tacklers, and was, finally, stubbornly dragged down after he'd made excellent yardage.

Jimmy and the offensive line were in a huddle, with Jimmy barking out the team's next play. Jimmy eyed his tight end, Britt Knobby.

"They're not looking for a delay up the middle, Britt. Block down, delay, and then off you go. Okay?"

Britt Knobby, tall as a steamboat and wide as the Golden Gate Bridge, nodded his head (helmet) elatedly. "Got you, Jimmy."

Jimmy thought to himself, *Might as well try to get Britt into the end zone. He's been sloshing around in this mud for most of the game like the rest of the guys.*

Most of the Eagles' first team was out the game. The score was Pittsfield High 36, Banner High School 6, with three minutes ticking on the clock. The first teamers still in the game were there for conditioning only, like Britt Knobby.

Jimmy looked over Banner High's defensive alignment and smiled. *Perfect!* he thought.

"Hut … hut … hut …"

Jimmy received the ball from the center, faked a handoff to Pitbull McNally as Britt blocked down on Banner's right defensive end, delaying him on the line, then positioned himself in the middle of the field as everybody and his uncle rushed at Jimmy. Jimmy uncorked a feathery light pass over the middle of the field to Britt, who had only eleven yards to lumber over before hitting pay dirt and doing a wild chicken-wing dance that put even more mud in his cleats.

Frank's hand struck the clipboard. "Boy, that kid's great—isn't he, Mike? Great!"

"Cute as a pigeon, Frank!" Mike said.

The game was over. Frank was congratulating everyone, any hand he could shake. And when he shook his men's hands, he patted their backs like he had stones in his hands.

By now, Frank and Mike were in Frank's office. Today's game had been a homer, played on Pittsfield High's football field.

Frank went to his portable refrigerator and pulled out a beer for him and Mike.

"Thanks, Frank." Mike popped open the can.

"Well, here's to another victory, Frank."

"Number six, Mike."

Both drank from their beer cans. Mike started in again, but Frank didn't. He let his beer cool.

"I just can't get over Jimmy. He's … I mean, the kid is out of this world, isn't he? From another planet, Mike."

Mike was on his third swig of beer. "Scary, Frank. Very scary."

"Intelligent as hell. And his finger has its pulse on the game. Knows what to do and when."

"Reminds me of someone. Doesn't he, old buddy?"

"Uh, yeah, sort of." Frank beamed.

"How about Frank Bosco when he ruled the roost? The holy terror of Pittsfield."

"Uh, yeah, I was smart, I must admit. Cute. But Jimmy, wait until next year. You think we're tearing the league apart this year, hey, you ain't seen nothing yet!"

Frank picked up his beer.

"When was the last time Britt scored a touchdown, Frank? Or has he?"

"Probably somewhere in his sleep." Frank laughed. "Not for us."

"A turtle in a five-yard dash could outrun Britt, I bet."

"I'd bet five bucks on the turtle too."

Frank swallowed more beer.

"Strictly a blocker, Frank. And a devastating one but a blocker with nubs for fingers."

"But you see what Jimmy was doing, Mike?"

"Oh yeah, without a doubt. Gave Britt possibly the biggest thrill of his life." Mike cracked open a big grin. "Never scored a touchdown in my life, Frank. Did you know that statistic? Never crossed an end zone except in practice."

"Not on a fumble or anything?"

"Nope."

"Or an ... an interception even, Mike?"

"Nope," Mike said, shaking his head like he had sawdust in both ears.

"Too bad."

"You're telling me." Mike looked sad. "A freaking linebacker. A hole plugger, Frank. The guy in the middle. Drats!"

"You could smell out a quarterback though."

"Could I. Could I. There's something about a quarterback," Mike said, smacking his lips. "Makes you want to rip their freaking heads off!"

"I think it's the cologne we wear."

They laughed.

"We're going to need him, Mike."

"You think so, Frank?"

"Yes. He's the better quarterback now. Jimmy's better than Spike. Has been for a few games. Jimmy was probably better than Spike when I put Spike in the starting lineup. Handed the quarterback position back to him."

"Experience. You had to go with experience. Frank, I would've done the same."

"Uh-huh. I had to go with experience over talent."

"With the blowouts we've had, it's given Jimmy a chance to gain experience on this level. Even if conditions are much different when you're a bunch of touchdowns ahead," Mike said.

"But it's still how you handle yourself, Mike. The poise you exhibit. Your play-calling abilities. And Jimmy doesn't try to rush anything or impress anyone out there. He doesn't get fancy. He just plays his game— lets the game come to him."

"So if you had to do it over again …"

Pause.

"Oh, I'm not second-guessing myself. Don't think that. That's not me, Mike. Second-guessing gives football coaches ulcers, and I like my black hair this color," Frank joked. "Jimmy can't help it if he's one of a kind."

"Him and Billy."

"Yes," Frank said, like he was holding a bottle of champagne in his hand and not beer.

"Jim-Jimmy and Bill-Billy …" Frank said it like he did when he first heard Billy Mack and Jimmy Boston had decided to play ball for he Pittsfield High School: swoon-like.

Billy was lost inside himself. He'd had another great game this afternoon. He scored a slew of touchdowns. He carried guys forward on his shoulder pads toward the goal line. He barreled guys over like an avalanche at spin speed. Six games. Six wins. But it still felt empty for him.

Oh, he gave it his best, 100 percent of it. But it wasn't the same without Jimmy handing him the football. Not that he had anything against Spike Armstrong—oh, no. Spike had won the Purple Eagle QB position fair and square, so there was no argument with that. (Plus, Spike was a teammate.)

He tried not to think about it at first. But it was like a missing factor, a missing quantity in algebra. It was missing, plain and simple. He wasn't getting the ball from Jimmy's hands. The football was the same but felt different. The game somehow felt different—cut from a different fabric.

Billy sat down on the bed and then lay down on his back and looked at the ceiling, as if it could tell him things without struggling.

Coach Bosco had made sure he and Jimmy were separated during practice. It was Spike always working with the first-stringers and Jimmy with the second-stringers. Spike always handing the ball off to him, and Jimmy doing the same with Pitbull. It was quite plain to see what Coach Bosco was doing. He and Jimmy had to get used to it. Like it or not, they had to get used to the new arrangement. And he didn't like it—not one bit.

He'd been stone-faced, showing no outward emotion, but inside was where it hurt all the time. Incessantly. At practice. During the games. Just to see Jimmy standing on the sideline and not out on the field with him.

Billy looked over his shoulder and saw the picture he had of Jackie Robinson. His dad had given him that picture. It was in a gold frame. Jackie Robinson, his father said, was stealing second base, sliding into the second base bag under the second baseman's tag. His father had given him the picture when he'd been called "nigger" one time too many in Pittsfield. His father sat him down and handed Jackie Robinson's picture to him.

"Nigger—what does it mean, Dad?" It was his first response to the slur. It had been delivered by a kid from another team, but he could feel the same words in the other players; their eyes said a lot that day.

That night, his mother and father explained the word to him. He wanted to beat the kid up the next time they played. His father told him the word was built upon years and years of hate. Years and years of white people passing the word down to their children until they didn't even know, by then, why they used it—but it had gotten into their vocabulary anyway. They knew how to use it when it counted.

He remembered his father getting up from the kitchen table, excusing himself first, then saying he'd be back. He was holding a picture when he got back.

"Do you know who this is?"

"No."

"His name is Jackie Robinson. He was the first black man to play professional, modern-day baseball, in 1947. Mr. Robinson was a called a lot of names, much worse than nigger—not that it makes the word nigger any less offensive. Mr. Robinson endured a lot in order to play the game of baseball. Actually, for a black man to play the game of baseball in the big leagues."

Connie had then handed the picture to Billy.

"I know there are going to be times when you're going to want to strike back. Punch the stuffing out of one of those kids using the word. And that's all right. But there's going to be a time when you're going to prove them to be jerks and ignorant—because it's what they are, Billy: ignorant jerks. You're going to have to prove them all wrong by what you do. By your performance. And then nothing can get in your way—not even the worst of them. Those bums."

It'd made him read up on Jackie Robinson. Jackie Robinson became one of his heroes. He read the things Mr. Robinson was called, the taunts and slurs, not by jerks or bums but by racists (he was too young to understand the word then, so his father had used the words "jerks" and "bums" to describe them). He knew all about the word now. It was everywhere. In the news, everywhere. He'd read up on a lot of things: slavery, the South, lynchings—all of that bad stuff. It was horrifying. And now he was thinking of himself, which was far less than what other people had to go through—all people, not just black people.

It was just that Jimmy not handing the football off to him felt like it was lasting forever—like next year would never come, not at the rate it was moving.

Billy took his eyes off of Jackie Robinson, his hero. He just shut his eyes, thinking about how things used to be with him and Jimmy. What a perfect time it once was.

Jimmy had been lethargic. He'd dragged through the day and managed it poorly. Jim saw it. It was worse today than it'd ever been. Jim assessed what was going on in his son's life. None of this was easy for him, being second-string. It was as if a rug had been pulled from underneath Billy and Jimmy (something that simple but effective).

"Jimmy, it's me. May I come in?"

The room's lights stood low. "Come in. Sure, Dad."

Jim didn't want to talk about football with Jimmy.

"The office sold twelve new policies today."

"Oh ... it did?"

Jimmy was at his bedroom window, sitting in his chair, looking out onto the fenceless backyard that pointed to a rock formation and then trees, no houses bordering the back, nothing to interfere with the view or the feeling of the free run of nature at Jimmy's back door, thus his fingertips.

"I'd say it was a good day at the office." Jim stood to the right of Jimmy like a shadow. "Jimmy, remember Eli Baron's son?"

"Yes."

"Tom bagged him today. Jason said he finally got fed up with Franklin Fund Insurance. He said their response time is the worst. The absolute worst. Said he knew about ours."

"Dad," Jimmy said, turning to Jim in tears, "it ... it's killing Billy too."

"You don't have to tell me." Jim held Jimmy's head in his hands.

"I love football, Dad. And being second-string isn't the worst part. It isn't. I got beat out, that's all. Spike's a better player. I can live with that, sir. It's just Billy, not practicing with him. Not playing with him."

"Do you talk about it, son? Ever?"

"No, never. We can't. We avoid it at all costs. It's like we've adjusted to it but really haven't."

His son felt so little to him, even though he was growing rapidly. *But he's only a teenager, tender as a twig,* Jim thought.

"I don't know if we're pretending everything's all right, the same. But, but—"

"You haven't released your feelings yet then, have you, Jimmy?"

"No, Dad."

Jimmy stood, he was much taller than Jim now. Jim felt the physical difference between them.

"It's what I'm here for—if it's what you want."

"A cry, Dad. Is that what it takes?"

"Sometimes it's the tears that need to come out first. And then things begin to feel better. Even *get* better."

"Yes," Jimmy said.

"Billy ..."

"He's going through the same exact thing. I know he is, Dad. But we don't want to be crybabies. A bunch of crybabies." Jimmy put his forehead against the window. "But it's just not fun anymore without Billy." Jimmy wiped at his tears. "We've always had this thing, Dad, Billy and I—you know. This incredible connection. When I look in the huddle …"

Jimmy didn't have to continue.

"Jimmy, you're going to have to think about next year. How it's going to shape up for you two."

Jimmy drew his forehead away from the window and turned his head to Jim. "Everything seems to be moving at a fast gallop but that—next year."

Jim knew the only hope he could give Jimmy was what he'd said, not some sentimental nonsense with no heart or backbone.

Jimmy and Billy were on their way to today's game. They'd crossed Stover Street and were about to enter onto Lane Street. A stoplight stopped them, and just like that, Jimmy's brain lit up like a lightbulb, and his blue eyes were a new sheen.

"Steamroller Mack, Steamroller Mack, Billy. I'm going to start calling you Billy 'Steamroller' Mack! What do you say about that? Do you think it's original? After all, it's what you do—steamroller guys. Why didn't I think of it before?"

"I don't know either." Billy laughed. "But original, I … Nah, it can't be, Jim—"

"And you heard it from me first. It was born here on … on …"

"Lane Street. Come on, Jimmy. We take this street practically every day, and you can't remember its name?"

The stoplight had turned green, and they were on their merry way again.

"Hey, don't bother me with details. I'm so excited, man. Don't, don't bother me with the small stuff."

Jimmy slung his arms around Billy's shoulders. Billy was taller than Jimmy but not by much.

"Don't let on. Okay, Billy? Because when you score your first touchdown, it's when I'll do it. Spring it on everybody. Billy Steamroller Mack. Billy Steamroller Mack! Yeah, it's going to be great, Billy. Just great."

It was cold that day.

"It's going to be a tough game today though. Like Coach said yesterday, Standard High's been on an upswing lately. Since their first two losses, that team has been putting it all together—and fast."

Billy quivered in his sneakers. "Their defense is really laying the wood on guys," Billy said.

"They've got a big front line, and it's quick to the ball. Do a lot of gang tackling."

"A lot. It's our first real challenge this season, Jimmy. Real big test of the year."

"Yep. They're big and bad."

"Bring them on, man. I'm ready for that!"

"Because Billy Steamroller Mack just bowls them over. Steamrollers them like a steamroller."

Billy and Jimmy were in their Purple Eagle uniforms. They had about fifteen minutes before heading out onto the field. They were sitting on a bench, as quiet as two mummies sharing the same casket. Pregame jitters were at work. Even though Billy was starting and Jimmy wasn't, it hadn't changed for them: they were anxious for each other.

Jimmy broke the silence. "I forgot to ask you, Billy. How'd your father's project go with Blast?"

Billy lit up like a pile of fireworks. "Dad pulled it off. They loved it. He's been walking around the house with his chest poked out for the past four days. It won't go down. I don't think the thing's retractable."

"That's—"

"Hi, Coach."

"Hi, Billy. Jimmy."

"Hi, Coach."

Billy and Jimmy got off the bench. Frank hugged each individually.

"Today's the big one, men."

"Yes, Coach."

Frank looked relaxed, under control. "You know, it's good. It's good. We need a game like this. A tough game like this under our belts before we take on the state." He laughed. "This'll help us see how we stack up. It's the game we need. It couldn't've come at a better time on our schedule."

Billy and Jimmy nodded like they were coaches from some other time and place.

"Yes, Coach. Yes."

"It's cold out there today."

"Yes … yes, it is," Billy replied.

"Wore my long johns though. Or do—are they still called that—long johns?" Frank laughed, eyeing Billy.

"No, Coach. Now they're called, uh, thermal underwear, sir. At least at the Rockwell Mall."

Standard High was tough. It was testing Pittsfield High School's will all right. It was midway through the second quarter, and the game was scoreless. Jimmy, in fact, had not had an opportunity to yell out "Steamroller Mack" all day—since Billy hadn't crossed the Standard goal line yet.

Spike Armstrong had called the play in the huddle. It was second down and sixteen, an obvious pass play. Spike did some checking off at the line of scrimmage but then returned to the original pass play he'd called.

"Hut-one, hut-two, hut … hut … hut …"

And then he received the ball from the center, and it seemed like the whole mass of humanity (the Standard football team) came at Spike, knocking him off his feet and onto the ground, not caring how high the pile of humanity got, as long as Spike was somewhere beneath it, buried alive.

Standard players and Purple Eagles players finally extricated themselves from the pile, but Spike remained on the cold turf, hurt.

Frank and Mike and the Purple Eagles' trainer ran onto the field. It looked serious for Spike. The trainer, Steve Tann, signaled for the stretcher. Soon, it was on the field, with Spike on it.

Jimmy knew what would happen next.

Bobby Morris, a second-string split end, tapped Jimmy on his shoulder pads.

"Wanna toss a few, Jimmy, before you go in?"

Jimmy grabbed a football from the football rack.

Jimmy began warming up his arm while Spike was being carried off the football field on the stretcher.

"How do you feel?" Bobby Morris kept asking Jimmy after each toss and catch.

"Great, Bobby." Jimmy's arm felt limber, loose.

They put Spike down on the sideline, about twelve yards behind the line marker.

Jimmy didn't wait for Frank to come to him; he went to Frank.

"How do you feel, Jimmy?"

"Fine, Coach."

"Well …" Frank sighed. "This is your opportunity."

Jimmy's eyes were focused.

"Don't force anything. Let's just get out of the first half alive. Ride it out, Jimmy. The second half, it's when we'll go bananas." Frank chuckled.

Jimmy dashed out onto the playing field but still had the practice football in his hand.

Oops!

Jimmy turned to toss the ball back to Bobby, who caught it on the fly behind the Purple Eagle bench, then put it back in the ball rack.

The Eagles' huddle formed. The players in the huddle waited for Jimmy to get there.

Jimmy stepped into the huddle, and the first person he saw was Billy, and he knew everything, for the rest of the game, would go okay.

"I-I was supposed to say, 'Billy Steamroller Mack!' from the sidelines, Billy—"

"Not in the end zone with me."

"Man, Billy, it was so exciting, man."

"Your arms up in the air, yelling—"

"*Screaming*, you mean. 'Steamroller! Steamroller!' I couldn't stop!"

"No, you couldn't. And all I was doing was wishing you'd pick me up and brush me off and let me get the heck out of there!"

"How many of those Standard guys did you carry into the end zone anyway?"

"Felt like the whole defensive line. All of them."

Billy and Jimmy had reached Lane Street and were about to cross over to Stover Street.

It was still bitter cold.

In the third and fourth quarters, Pittsfield High steamrolled Standard High to the tune of 31–10. Jimmy tossed the ball for two touchdowns, and Billy ran the ball for two. Both had big games.

"Too bad about Spike, though."

"I heard it," Billy said, turning to Jimmy. "When it cracked."

"Out for the season. A broken ankle. What rotten luck. I've never won anything like this before, Billy, through injury—someone getting hurt. It just feels funny."

Billy stopped Jimmy, put his hand on his shoulder, and looked straight into his light blue eyes. "Look, Jimmy, no matter how it happened, you still have a job to do."

"Man, Billy, don't I know it."

"And let's face it. I mean … look at the score. How we romped over those guys once you took over QB duties."

"Who knows? Maybe we were—"

"Don't say lucky, man."

"But maybe we were, Billy."

Billy shook his head. "No way. Ain't buying it. You're good. Luck is for somebody else maybe but not you. Not Jimmy Boston, man. Not the one and only Jimmy Boston with the golden arm," Billy said.

The Purple Eagles won their final game of the season. They'd gone unbeaten during the regular season, posting a 9–0 record. The State Division 1 Championship fielded eight teams with a combined win/loss record of 60 and 12.

There were quite a few outstanding teams fielded among the eight, including Brand High School (the "Bee Stingers") who, too, boasted an unbeaten record of 9–0. Pittsfield and Brand were the odds-on picks to make it to the championship round. There'd been plenty written in the newspapers about them.

Frank was at the chalkboard diagramming a play. It was one of those Xs and Os kind of things with the Xs looking more like crosshatches and Os more like misshaped zeroes. The chalkboard was portable, on rollers with a wooden frame, easy to maneuver.

Frank loved diagramming plays, setting team strategy. The chalk would strike against the chalkboard's black slate like it was a new idea born by genius. And he would unbutton the top button of his shirt (whether he was wearing a dress shirt or sports shirt), showing the beads of sweat that had formed like a string of red pimples; they'd bubble up so quickly.

"Men, I know I've thrown a lot at you in one day, but we have two more days on this, so please don't, in anyway, panic on me."

There was a vein in Frank's neck that was so pronounced it looked like it was about to pop out and slither across the floor like a slimy snake.

"I don't want you guys going crazy four days before our first playoff game, but I'm positive you can handle all of this stuff. Am I right?"

"Right, Coach Bosco!"

"So let's see what we can do with this stuff in the next two days," Frank said, looking at the chalkboard. "Something that looks like Picasso's last testament to man."

The roomful of players looked at one another askance. *Who's Picasso?*

Marion had a special gift: she heard everything. Her ears were highly sensitive (scientifically) to sound. In that house, from attic to basement, Marion's ears heard things. She'd had this gift since she was a child.

She heard Jimmy. His sound was in the house between the floorboards, which indicated he was stirring. Jimmy's bedroom was far down the hall. It was separated by a guest room, bathroom, and den. But maybe it was the nervousness in him she actually heard. Nevertheless, he was awake.

Jim was sleeping soundly. She knew how to slip out of the bed by now, after all these years of marriage, without disturbing him.

Marion was out of bed, in her robe. The room's light was faint, just enough for her to see as she moved around. Before opening the door, she glanced back at Jim. The quilted comforter was keeping him toasty warm.

Marion proceeded down the hallway.

"Jimmy," Marion said at his door.

"I'm up, Mom."

Jimmy opened the bedroom door. "What, Mom—you heard my eyelids open?"

"Practically." Marion laughed. "Something like that."

Jimmy looked very much awake but not at all rested.

"May I come in?"

"Of course, Mom," Jimmy said, moving to the side of the door, as if he'd been blocking it before. "Should I turn on the light?"

"No, Jimmy. It's not necessary."

"Do … do you know the time, Mom?"

Jimmy had an alarm clock he'd set last night but seemed to have forgotten it was there.

"Yes, honey. It's 5:22 or something like that. I'm sure it only took me a few seconds to get here from my room."

Jimmy nodded and then walked back to his bed and sat on top of it. Marion joined him. Jimmy grabbed his pillow and hugged it to his chest.

"The game's at one today, Mom. I think I'm going to do well … I don't know. But I think I'm going to do well today."

The room's blinds hadn't been opened. Both were looking at them.

"You feel it all the time, don't you, honey? The pressure that comes along with each game."

Jimmy smiled. "Not all the time. It's not all the time. It's fun most of the time."

"But when it's not?"

"Uh, you mean like now?" Jimmy said innocently.

"Yes."

Jimmy shut his eyes, then opened them. "It's still not all that bad. I mean, I can handle it. It doesn't get me down or anything. It's just that I want to do well every time I'm out there on the field. Do my best."

Jimmy tried to explain himself better. "It's like—maybe it's like finals, Mom. School finals. There's the same kind of pressure to do well."

"But what you do, Jimmy, is before hundreds and—particularly today—thousands of people."

"Uh ... I hadn't thought of it quite that way," Jimmy said.

Marion was furious with herself. *What am I trying to do? Make Jimmy more nervous?*

"Jimmy, I'm not a man."

Jimmy felt like saying he hoped not—that he wouldn't be there if she was.

"I see that look on your face."

"Hey, Mom, it's—"

"I've never thrown a football in my life. Now, you can laugh if you want."

"No, I can keep a straight face, I think."

Marion laughed for him. "So when it comes to things like this ... well, honey, it doesn't always come out right. Your father knows about these things better than I. He can relate to them far better than I can."

"But you're here, Mom," Jimmy said, laying his head on Marion's shoulder. "You don't have to be a man for that."

Marion went back down the hallway. More of the morning's light filled the hallway. She was as quiet as before. Her steps were just as light. She quietly opened her bedroom door.

"Marion, coming to bed?"

"Yes."

Jim's hand patted the open spot. "There's room." Marion got back in bed, and he turned to her. "Been down to Jimmy's room?"

She nodded.

"Thought so."

Marion's head on her pillow, she turned to Jim.

"Had a good talk?" he said.

"Not so much a talk, Jim."

"But a mother's love. Am I right?"

"Yes. That."

"Yep. Today's a big day for him."

"I thought it might be too big, but it's not. But what do I know about these things anyway?"

"Marion, why, you'd be surprised. Damned well surprised."

"I was just worried, that's all." Marion pulled the comforter up closer to her chin.

"Not the unflappable Marion Boston?" Jim joked.

"You said you're driving the car up to Sage today. Right, Jim? Not the Macks, Susan and Connie?"

"Right, Marion. I told Connie I'd drive."

"Any reason why?" Marion asked.

"Told Connie I didn't know if his car insurance was paid up or not. How do you like that one?"

"Look, I'll pretend I didn't hear that."'

"With those ears of yours, how couldn't you? Gosh—now *that* would be a feat to behold."

Marion's ears had served her well that morning. *Without a doubt,* she thought.

CHAPTER 6

Under normal conditions, it was an hour's drive to Sage County, Massachusetts, where the state championship game was to be played in venerable Lyon's Stadium.

"We'll be in the thick of traffic soon," Jim said.

"Do you think we'll get in the parking lot, Jim?" Marion said from the back seat.

"Why do you think we left early, Marion? What—so we can freeze on those cold stadium seats?"

"I think the game's going four rounds," Connie said. "Four quarters. The full distance until someone delivers the knockout punch. Two undefeated teams. Two teams playing at their peak, both hungry. Two great coaches—"

"And our sons," Jim said proudly.

"And our sons, Jim," Connie concurred.

"I don't care if it snows," Susan said. "I'm going to cheer for Pittsfield High even if my teeth are chattering. Or are brittle as icicles."

"That's the spirit, Susan!" Jim said.

And then Connie began singing the Purple Eagles' fight song. Susan and Marion joined in. The four of them, nearing middle age but still young enough where it counted, felt like they were back in those halcyon days in high school when a drive in someone's car, or their car, on a Saturday afternoon was the best time a teenager could think of—short of the school hop.

The parking lot at Lyon's Stadium was jammed.

"Well, Jim …" Marion giggled. "There goes your leave-home-early-and-we-won't-have-to-worry-about-parking theory."

"Yeah, you can say that again," Jim said, squirming uncomfortably in his seat.

Marion looked at Susan next to her in the back seat and winked.

"Don't worry, Jim. Your intentions were good," Connie said.

"But gosh—this is going to be some tight squeeze, Connie!"

"Right. Everybody and their brother's here!"

Now the Macks and the Bostons were even more pumped up.

"My adrenaline is at the top of the charts. What about yours, Marion?" Susan asked.

"Mine too, Susan. Totally. Absolutely!"

"Hey, not bad, Jim," Connie remarked. Jim had parked the Oldsmobile cleanly between two cars.

"No, not bad at all, Jim. We're only about … maybe a mile and a half from the stadium," Susan quipped.

Actually, they were about a quarter mile from Lyon's Stadium.

"You'd think they'd treat the parents of Billy Steamroller Mack and Jimmy Boston better—wouldn't you, folks?" Jim griped.

"Well, next year—"

"Yeah, next year, Jim," Connie said.

"We'll stick it to them—"

"Or else get an earlier start, Connie," Marion said.

The four checked to make sure they had everything—that nothing was left in the Oldsmobile.

"We all set? Got everything?" Jim asked.

Off they went.

Once their tickets were half-torn, they got into the capacious stadium and located their seats. The seats were perfectly located, front row on the sidelines. They were pleased as pink with their good fortune.

"Great. Coach Bosco and his staff did a great job with our tickets," Connie said, flashing his.

Marion and Susan were busy chatting, and already stomping their boots as if their toes were bone cold.

Brand's and Pittsfield's marching bands jarred the stadium with big band sounds, competing as if the two football teams who were to take the field were an afterthought and they were the king of the hill, at least for now.

The cheerleaders were zesty and at their colorful best, pom-poms of every color in their hands, their lungs containing the capacity of two big cities at war. They were cheering so frightfully hard.

Marion and Susan were looking at them in their short knit skirts and white, cotton, ankle-length socks.

"Ha," Susan laughed. "Oh, to be young. And with such exuberance."

"Isn't that the truth, Susan? They don't feel a thing, do they? Nothing out in this element," Marion said.

"Remember when—"

"We could do that," Marion said.

"Like we were impervious to anything, Marion. At least to anything like cold."

Marion's eyes had begun tearing from the cold.

"Are you ladies having fun in the sun?" Connie joked.

"Just remembering back to a time, Connie."

"Hmm. When you and Marion could—"

"We girls would rather not talk about it. Right, Marion?"

"Right, Susan," Marion replied, taking up arms with Susan.

"Guess we better not touch that one, Connie."

Connie checked his watch. "Nine minutes. Nine minutes ..." he said to no one in particular.

Suddenly, Jim thought of Sally Ann Schumacher and the red bow in her hair out on her front porch this morning (without a coat on, of course), waving goodbye to Jimmy, wishing him luck, probably wishing she could be at Lyon's Stadium in Sage, Massachusetts, with them to cheer on Jimmy and Billy.

Marion's mind wandered back to 5:22 a.m. when she and Jimmy shared the morning in an unexpected but special way. She hadn't known

Jimmy would need her more than he needed Jim before a game—a game she still didn't fully understand from beginning to end, even now.

Susan knew there'd be many more years of this for Billy. She looked at Connie and Jim, who weren't at all bundled up like she and Marion were. Would the thrill in Billy be as big three years from now when he danced through the morning with her and Connie? Susan and Marion had talked about it on their way up to the game. Was this too much too soon for their sons? They, as mothers, thought about such matters.

Connie's eyes were targeting the stadium's black scoreboard, but he was thinking about one thing: how he and Billy, in their own ingenious fashion, had planned this day. Connie felt goose bumps on his skin as big as the cheerleader's pom-poms. Connie was ready for the game between Brand and Pittsfield.

And may the better team win, he thought.

It had been a thrilling, fast-paced championship game between the Purple Eagles and the Bee Stingers. As thrilling and fast paced as any championship game anyone could remember. Both teams were equal to the task. The stadium's temperature had dropped markedly. The score was Brand 24 and Pittsfield 21. There were 2:56 seconds remaining on the game clock, and Pittsfield was driving the ball downfield.

The drive had begun on the Eagles' five-yard line but now was on its thirty-two-yard line.

It was third down and three when Billy burst straight up the gut of the Bee Stingers' defense for ten yards before being solidly stopped.

Jim patted Connie's back.

Billy had run for two touchdowns. One was from eight yards out, the other a thirty-yard romp in which Billy Steamroller Mack steamrolled everyone on the field, almost to the inclusion of the stadium's goalpost.

The Purple Eagles were on their own forty-two-yard line.

"Billy's getting the call again, Connie."

"Everybody in Lyon's Stadium, including the Brand players, knows that, Jim." Connie laughed.

"Billy's on a roll."

Neither Connie nor Jim had blown on their hands since the game started, only during halftime—which didn't count.

Billy busted back up the middle for seven more hard-earned yards, shedding one tackler after another until finally corralled.

The line judge moved the chain markers from the forty-two-yard line to the forty-nine.

Jim and Connie looked at the one yard the Purple Eagles had to cross as if it were some magical territory where the field would slant downward in their favor.

"One yard, Connie. One more yard, and the ball's on their side of the field."

"Things are getting tighter, Jim."

Jim blew on his hands.

"How did it feel in situations like this for you, Connie?" one nonathlete asked the ex-athlete.

"Jim, it's the best part of the game," Connie said, his cheeks red. "When everything's on the line out there, up for grabs, it's when you have to be at your best."

Billy busted the ball up the middle like a wild bronco for another eight-yard gain.

"We're there, Connie. We just crossed the fifty-yard line. Billy just got us there!" Jim yelped like it was some kind of hallowed ground the Eagles had entered.

This time, the huddle was longer.

"It's a pass play, Jim. Jimmy's throwing it. It's a perfect time, situation for it."

A pass was thrown but dropped.

"Damn! Paulie should've caught it!"

Connie agreed with Jim; it came by way of a grunt.

Jim blew on his hands again. "But ... but the—"

"I agree, Jim. It's cold out here. Paulie's hands—"

"They must be numb. Stiff as a board by now." Jim laughed.

"I know mine are," Connie said.

Game time had wound down to two minutes.

The two-minute warning was issued to both teams.

Play was back in.

"It's going to be strictly a ground attack from here on in, looks like. We have two time-outs remaining. Jim, that's all the time in the world."

"Connie, Jimmy and Billy have dreamed of this moment."

"Me too, Jim. Me too."

Bam!

They could hear the sound reverberate in Lyon's Stadium, the collision of helmets so powerful. But Billy had picked up nine yards. He'd earned every precious inch of them.

Bam!

It happened again, with Billy busting it open for a twelve-yard gain this time, punishing the Brand players.

Pittsfield was on Brand's twenty-two-yard line.

One minute and twenty-one seconds remained on the clock.

The Eagles called a time-out.

"Good time-out, Coach Bosco. Excellent!"

"It's a real good time-out, Jim. The kids need a breather. A chance to catch their breath for a second or two—the way they've been putting out. And also before they make their final march to the goal. Assault."

Jim seemed worried, even if, before, he'd agreed with the time-out.

"It won't hurt their concentration or momentum, do you think, Connie?"

"No, it shouldn't, Jim. Those guys out there, they're too keyed up. Been that way all game. They know what's at stake." Connie laughed.

Bam!

It was another enormous explosion.

This time, fourteen yards was gained by Billy right up the gut of the Bee Stingers' defense.

The Eagles were eight yards away from pay dirt. Everything was on the line. There were thirty-seven seconds left on the game clock—time for at least two more plays.

"Here … here goes, Jim."

"Yeah, Connie, here goes."

"My juices are in overdrive!"

Everyone in Lyon's Stadium had their eyes trained on two players: Jimmy and Billy.

Jimmy looked over the defense. It was to be a short count, like they'd all been up till now.

"Hut, hut, hut …"

As the ball was being handed off to Billy, Jimmy felt very little of it, and while it juggled in his hand, he handed it to Billy, whose hands felt the same as Jimmy's, as if there was no feeling or sensation in them, and since the handoff was not clean or precise like the others, the ball dropped onto the stadium's frozen tundra, and Billy and every other player on the field seemed to go for it. Billy couldn't hold on to it, and again, it squirted out of his hands, and finally a Brand player, using his body smartly, smothered the football at the Brand seven-yard line. Other players from both teams piled on his back while he held on to the ball at the bottom of the pile, every muscle straining in him.

There was a pitiful hush combined with a giant roar from the Lyon Stadium's crowd.

Brand High School's offensive team lined up with its quarterback Dante Romano at their own seven-yard stripe and eight seconds remaining in the game.

"We … we lost didn't we, Connie?" Susan said.

Connie nodded to Susan.

Marion, Susan, Jim, and Connie stood there in the stadium's cold in stunned silence but soon realized what they had to do—and quickly.

The Macks and Bostons were standing in Lyon's Stadium's underground tunnel just outside Pittsfield's locker room area, waiting for their boys. Jim was holding on to Marion, and Connie onto Susan. The cold was still in them, but it was not as bad as before.

The door opened, and Billy stepped out first, followed by Jimmy. Their eyes were damp, for they'd cried a lot in the locker room.

Jimmy ran to his parents, and Billy to his.

Then the two families joined. There were exchanges of hugs. Not a word had passed between them, but there seemed to be no disappointment now in either Jimmy or Billy, no blame or any head hanging.

"We're heading off to the team bus," Jimmy said. "Billy and I will see you when we get back."

"Yes, we'll see you and Billy when you get back," Marion said.

"Our teammates are waiting for us," Billy said.

Maria Lo Bianco Bosco was holding on to her brother's framed picture in her petite hands. She had a sunny smile on her face. Who would've thought, she thought, her older brother would turn out to be the mayor of Pittsfield? Certainly not her; she'd be the last to.

When they grew up in Pittsfield (he was four years older than she was), all she could remember Vito doing was knocking her around. He showed no diplomacy or goodwill during those days, certainly not toward her—none of the qualities a politician needed to exhibit in the political milieu. No city hall stuff.

Maria put Vito Lo Bianco's picture back on the mantelpiece. *Vito's going to have to stay in office for a long time to feed his brood.* Maria was the aunt of five little Vito and Teresa Lo Biancos. They seemed to have one after the other, Maria thought. Vito, from neck to ankles, was a bull of a man.

She felt guilty, but it was best for her to leave Frank alone. The loss—he took it hard. It took the starch out of him. She had been at Lyon's Stadium. They hadn't talked, not really, since she drove him out of the Pittsfield parking lot when he got off the team bus and walked over to the Ford. She saw the lump in Frank's throat.

When he got home, he retired to the bedroom. She followed. Frank pulled down the shades. She started to say something to him but stopped. Frank took off his shoes and then got in bed and under the covers with his clothes on.

It was then that she knew her place, that she had no business being in the bedroom with him. Only, she felt guilty, no matter how little her presence meant to him. She couldn't equate a dropped hemline to a football loss. Even as an ex-cheerleader for Pittsfield High School, she could never feel a loss like the players.

Maria was in her workroom. She had worked doubly hard yesterday to compensate for today, taking the trip up to Sage in the car. She knew there'd be a huge bite taken out of her time today. If Pittsfield had won, she'd probably be sitting down, doing what she was doing; her Pittsfield clientele were demanding. They could care less that she was a football coach's wife, win or lose.

Maria liked the dress she was creating for Emma Stuart, one of Pittsfield's grand socialites. She'd been working on the dress for over a week. Today, she'd bead its skirt. The beading would only be about two inches from the skirt's bottom. This was going to be a dress that would win awards; someone in Pittsfield would think it came from an exclusive Parisian salon to Pittsfield by some fancy, elaborate, exotic travel route.

"But it's just little old me," Maria said, her face warm and beautiful. "By my simple, inelegant hands."

Maria was busy at work, but as she worked, she began to feel dreamy. She was careful about what she was doing but so skilled at her work she could do both well simultaneously.

She and Frank were in their early thirties. It was time for them to think of things other than themselves. Today reminded her of a lot of things; it bore fruit for a lot of things. She saw things at today's championship game that gave her pause. There was a beauty in life she was missing out on. She saw a spark of energy that could light the universe a million times over. It was quite remarkable. It jelled her thoughts and put them in a better perspective.

She heard Frank. As usual, he was trying to surprise her—coming out his room, closing the door with no force or anger, as if to leave no traces of himself.

How am I going to handle this? This defeat went to the bone. Today's loss won't be easily forgotten.

"I could sleep the night away."

Maria turned to Frank.

"But tell me, Maria, what good would it do? It was an awful loss. A horrible loss. It's losses like these that make the game feel bigger than life. And young men like Billy and Jimmy have to live with this for the rest of their lives." Pause.

"I feel like calling it quits. Just chuck the whole damned thing in the garbage. You know what I mean, Maria!"

But Maria had some news for him, something that she'd brought home from the game and trusted as if she'd found a gemstone.

"Only, did you see their families, Frank? The Macks and Bostons? Them, Frank, sweetheart."

Frank shook his head; he hadn't seen them.

"You know, it made me think."

Frank sat on the sofa. "About what?"

"Us, Frank. About something I haven't talked to you about in some time," Maria said, dropping everything in her hands to quickly join Frank on the sofa.

"I don't quite get it," Frank said, his dark eyes showing some signs of life.

"A family. We haven't talked about kids in a long time, Frank. Bambinos. We're Italian, Catholic, Frank. We believe in—"

"Maria, please. Now? Hey, not now. Not after a loss. Today, my team just lost a football game. Now's not a good time for that kind of talk. Not now ... okay? Capisce?"

"But they have their families, Frank. Their—"

Frank leaned back into the sofa, and his head thumped the back of it. "I was upstairs thinking about my kids. My football family. And now, now you're badgering me with this? This crap?" Frank said, glaring at her.

"So you don't think any of this has any merit?" Maria asked coolly.

"What do you want from me? I mean—what, Maria?"

"Nothing, nothing," Maria said emotionally.

"I'm as low as I can get. Like someone's kicked the shit out of me. Feel rotten as anyone can feel right now, and here you are talking about a family, kids. For god's sake, Maria? Bambinos, Catholic—for god's sake.

"What are you ... crazy or sump'in'?" Frank said, laughing.

"You ... you should've seen them, Frank, the Bostons and Macks," Maria said, with absolute awe.

"It really was that special, huh?"

Maria's face just glowed.

Frank kissed her. "Hey, I've got a great family already."

"Not like the one we can have, Frank."

Frank's arms wrapped around Maria's shoulder, and Maria was talking into his chest.

"How many? Uh, one?"

"One!" Maria replied, alarmed. "Why, I was just looking at Vito's picture on the mantelpiece before you came—"

"No, Maria, absolutely not!" Frank shuddered. "Not on your—"

"So what's wrong with five since, after all, I'm the one who has to carry them for nine months?"

"But I'm the one who has to feed and clothe them for the rest of their lives. On a high school coach's football salary, Maria?" (Of course, Frank had left out him being a math teacher on staff at Pittsfield.)

"I know, Frank. I was thinking of that too. But a mayor's salary isn't much better, is it?" Maria giggled.

"I don't know. You'll have to ask Vito."

Frank took Maria's open hand. "Do you want to get started?"

"Only one, Frank?"

"Well, at least for now," Frank said, sticking one finger in the air. "So bear with me, Maria. Okay?"

CHAPTER 7

It was September 1988, a new school year.

Jimmy had just left Mr. Sorenson's science class when their eyes met. It was like a blunt punch to the gut. Jimmy didn't know how to respond to his feelings—so what could he say to this blonde, blue-eyed beauty? First, he would have to get himself under better control for this to work. This was his first priority.

And then he passed by her, only to look back to see if she was looking back at him (no).

Who was she? Jimmy wondered. Who was that girl who was new to Pittsfield High? Someone he hadn't seen last year—the entire year. Where did she come from? She was no freshman (make no mistake about that!), not the way she walked. *How did she get here? Did she step off some planet rock?*

Jimmy stopped and put his head against the hallway's marble wall.

"What—you have a headache, Jimmy?" brainy Tom Fulton asked.

"No ... uh ... Tom. I'm okay, I guess."

"It is the first day of school, and already you've got a headache? Don't tell me you've got Mr. Sorenson for science."

"Tom," Jimmy said hesitantly, "do, is there such a thing ... oh, oh never mind."

"Jimmy, hey, man—what's come over you? What has summer vacation wrought?"

"Oh nothing—like I said before."

"Our star quarterback. God help the Purple Eagles this year. God help us!"

"Ha." Jimmy laughed nervously as Tom scurried off down the hall for what was probably his next class.

Man, Jimmy thought. *But who was she? Where did she come from anyway? This blonde, blue-eyed angel.*

Jimmy was feeling off balance, completely out of it. All he could do was arrange his books in his hands a bit better. Then he was off to his next class, Mrs. O'Sullivan's French class just down at the end of the hall.

It was later in the day.

Jimmy had had lunch. During lunch, had he looked for the girl—that blonde, blue-eyed beauty. You bet your life he had. Did he see her? No. Had he told Billy about her yet at the lunch table? No. He wanted Billy to see this girl for himself. (She had to be seen to be believed!)

Jimmy was entering Mrs. Elliot's English II class when their eyes met as if they were standing at opposite poles of the earth and had finally found each other in a softly padded meadow.

Jimmy began clearing his throat's phlegm.

Judy Collins didn't look away this time. She kept her eyes steady and directly on the target.

Jimmy had liked a bunch of girls before, so this was nothing new for him. So why was he behaving so awkwardly toward her? He was a graceful, cool QB—yet he was acting like he was tripping over his shoelaces (hardly Fred Astaire dancing with Ginger Rogers on an RKO movie set).

"Hel-hello …" Jimmy saw no one else in the crowd of students around him.

"Hello."

Jimmy stuck out his hand. "My name's Jimmy Boston."

"Judy Collins. My name's Judy Collins. Nice … nice to meet you."

After shaking hands, Jimmy said, "You're new, new to Pittsfield."

"I am. My family and I just moved here."

"You, you did?" Jimmy said dreamily. "Oh, you did," he said more manly. "Well, welcome to Pittsfield."

"Thank you, Jimmy."

Now that's the way my name should sound when someone speaks it!

Judy sat at her desk.

"Do … do you mind?" Jimmy asked, sitting to her right.

"No, not if the teacher doesn't," Judy replied.

She has a sense of humor. This blonde, blue-eyed beauty has a remarkable sense of humor, Jimmy thought.

"You didn't say what—where you moved from."

"Oh, no, I didn't. New Haven. I'm a New Haven, Connecticut, girl."

"Oh, uh, that's nice."

The front of Judy Collins's hair was set in short bangs, the back, a long, even ponytail.

"Have you ever been in New Haven—or Connecticut for that matter?"

"No to both. No, can't say I have," Jimmy said, still in that manly tone of voice.

"I like … I like," Judy said, taking big breaths, "Pittsfield better already."

Now was that a come-on or what? Or what, man!

———

Jimmy was carrying Judy's books, but he could carry them only so far, for he had football practice (Coach Bosco would kill him if he was late for football practice).

"Uh … I-I play football," Jimmy said modestly.

"Why I—"

"Quarterback."

"Why I—"

"We call ourselves—the team, that is—the Purple Eagles."

Jimmy realized he'd cut Judy off twice.

"Judy, uh, forgive me for—"

"I'm a cheerleader."

"It was what you were about to say?"

"Yes, before I was cut off. Not once—"

"But twice. Forgive me, forgive me. I'm usually not like this—not at all."

"I hope not."

"Tryouts are—"

"Tomorrow."

"Are you counting?"

"Uh …" Judy seemed confused.

"Twice." Jimmy laughed. "Now you've cut me off twice."

"Oh, so I did. You're right."

They were at a point where Jimmy knew he and Judy Collins would have to part company like a fork in the road. But instead of a fork in the road, it was a statue of someone famous in Pittsfield who died way back when it is was said Pittsfield was cornfields and flat plains, with even colder winters than modern times.

Jimmy had slowed down. "Foot-football practice, I'm afraid."

"So I'm going to have to carry my own books the rest of the way. Is that it, Jimmy?"

Judy was looking up into Jimmy's light blue eyes.

"I'll be at the cheerleading tryouts tomorrow."

"You will?" Judy asked, taking her books back.

"Uh-huh. Coach Bosco, uh—the football coach, that is—lets us watch them. The guys, that is. The cheerleading tryouts, they're a lot of fun to watch, all right."

"Wonder why? I imagine all the pretty girls who try out for it has nothing at all to do with it, does it?" Judy said while walking away.

"See you tomorrow in English class. And, uh, at the cheerleading tryouts."

Judy twirled once in her sneakers, then twice. "Thanks for carrying my books, Jimmy." Pause. "At least partway home."

There was the usual after-school brigade of students mingling in front of Pittsfield High School. The hustle and bustle was on. But really, it'd been just another day of high jinks from the boys and girls talking and laughing, trying their hardest not to let higher education interfere with any of their teenage shenanigans.

Jimmy was still in dreamland, so Billy was getting a heavy dose of it.

"Billy, wait until you see her. Just wait!"

"I know—it's what you keep telling me," Billy said, appearing disinterested now.

It was the next day. Shortly, cheerleading tryouts would begin.

"I-I don't know where she is." Pause. "I-I saw her in class, in Mrs. Elliot's English class today. So she should be here soon."

"Maybe she got a bye, since she's already a cheerleader," Billy said, his hand shading his eyes from the sun.

"Funny, man. Yeah, go ahead and rub it in. Have your fun at my expense."

"Jimmy, I mean, you are fickle when it comes to—"

"Look who's talking."

"Hey, you don't see me flipping over every girl who—"

"There she is, Billy. There she is!"

Billy's eyes sped over to her like a cheetah off its chain.

"There's Judy!"

"She is—"

"Beautiful, isn't she? A doll, Billy—a living doll!"

"Yeah, yeah," Billy said suavely.

Billy found Judy Collins more dimple cute than beautiful, glamorous. *To each his own*, he thought.

There was time before the cheerleading tryouts began.

"Come on, Billy." Jimmy stepped down the bleachers. "I want you to meet her."

"Sort of get my stamp of approval, huh?"

"Yeah. Sort of," Jimmy said, bouncing a playful punch off Billy's big shoulders.

"Ouch!"

"What—Billy Steamroller Mack's not impervious to pain after all?"

"Not without my shoulder pads!"

Judy was looking at Jimmy. He was tall; she wasn't. He was the football team's quarterback; she hoped to be one of its cheerleaders. She would cheer for him good or bad—even though today, when she asked about him, she was told he was a star quarterback on a championship football team.

Jimmy and Billy had gotten to where Judy was.

"Hi, Jimmy," Judy said, as if it were the first she'd seen him all day, notwithstanding Mrs. Elliot's English II class.

"Hi, Judy."

The sun hit both their eyes as Jimmy stood off to her side. Before Jimmy could say what he'd planned to say, Judy Collins stuck her hand out to Billy.

"You must be Billy Steamroller Mack. I've heard all about you. A lot."

Billy's skin reddened. "You, uh, have?"

"Judy, Judy Collins."

"It's a pleasure meeting you, Judy Collins."

"How did—"

"Word gets around, Billy," Judy said, turning her attention to take in her competition. "I hope they're not too good. Or should I say not better than me."

Billy and Jimmy laughed.

Already, Billy could see why Jimmy liked this Judy Collins girl, besides her being blonde and dimple cute.

"Ah, they're going to fall down in, in your wake, Judy." Jimmy didn't know quite what he'd said, but it sounded good. At least he thought so.

"Wish me luck," Judy said.

She went and joined the other hopefuls who were lining up in the middle of the football field. There were about thirty to thirty-five girls in the competition.

"By the way, what was it you just said, Jimmy? What kind of parting shot was that, man?"

"Billy, I don't know, but personally, I thought it was pretty cool. For sure, Steamroller!"

The competition for the cheerleading spots had been stiff all right. The cheerleading captain from last year, Dora Bloom, was calling out the girls' names who'd made the squad. In the bleachers, Jimmy was a nervous wreck, to put it mildly. His head was on Billy's shoulder. His eyes were closed. He didn't want to look. But his ears were opened wide.

"Don't worry, Jimmy. Your girl's going to make it," Billy said confidently. "She was the best out there."

"I can't look, Billy. Man, I … I can't look at this." Pause. "What … what's she doing?"

"Judy's, uh, she's cool."

"You know, you never know about these things, Billy. The judges. What they're thinking and all."

"Judy's a cinch, man."

"Billy, you like her, don't you?"

"Yeah … hey, she's cool."

Dora Bloom began naming Pittsfield High School's new cheerleading squad. She had a megaphone up to her mouth, as if she needed one.

"May Evans, Judy Collins, Florence Anderson, Barbara Taylor …"

"Did Dora say, say Judy, Judy Collins, Judy Collins yet, Billy?" Jimmy asked, his head coming off Billy's shoulder.

"That she did. Oh, about two, I'd say two names back," Billy said nonchalantly.

"She did? Did? Dora did!" Jimmy's eyes popped open.

"It's what it sounded like to me: Judy Collins—about two names back."

Jimmy saw Judy jumping up and down like a pogo stick, like she had control over the sun that had grown brighter in the sky for some audacious reason.

"Billy, you're welcomed to—"

"No, you guys go ahead. I have something to do."

Jimmy smirked. "Yeah, Billy, I bet."

"Hey, man, I've got a life. I don't need you hanging around me all the time, all day."

"Come on, Billy," Judy insisted.

"No, no, that's okay, Judy. Really—I've got something important to do. No kidding."

Billy took off and then waved back to Judy and Jimmy. "See you guys tomorrow!"

Judy and Jimmy didn't begin walking immediately.

"He's nice, really nice. I really like him."

"Billy's been my best friend since … wow, man. It's been a long time, hasn't it?" Jimmy said as if to himself.

"Has race ever come between you and Billy? Being that he's black?"

Jimmy didn't seem in the least surprised or offended by Judy's inquiry; in fact, he was glad she'd asked. It hadn't been asked with any seeming motive or prejudice intended.

"Probably at one time or another, we might've talked about it. But for the life of me, I can't remember. Honest, Judy. Or what we might've actually said. We probably acknowledged it and then moved on from there, I guess."

They passed by Jonathan Baron's house.

"What a house!" Judy said, flabbergasted.

"Uh, mansion you mean."

"There're a lot in Pittsfield."

"There're a lot of rich folk in Pittsfield. The Bostons, well, we're upper-middle class. Strictly upper-middle class," Jimmy said, his nose tilted upward, sniffing Pittsfield's fine air.

"My dad owns an insurance business. My mom's a housewife. I guess anyone who lives in Pittsfield either has to be upper-middle class or rich."

"I guess so. Pittsfield is such a beautiful town. Are Billy's parents—"

"Rich? No, upper-middle class. Same as mine. Billy's father's a concept engineer for Blast Aircraft. His dad is great. And he's one of the top engineers in his company. Maybe I should say the top. Yes, Mr. Mack is the top engineer at Blast.

"And his mom is a party planner—parties, special events, et cetera. Mrs. Mack, she's great too."

Judy and Jimmy passed another fantastic-looking mansion in Pittsfield.

"Judy, what's your father do?"

"My parents?" Judy said, subtly correcting Jimmy. "They're college professors."

"College—"

"Mom's an economics professor, and Dad's a physics professor."

"No wonder you're so smart in English II."

"Jimmy, I said physics and economics." Judy frowned. "Not English."

"So what's the difference in the long run?" Jimmy said with bravura. They were walking breezily.

"I never had any black friends in New Haven. Only because of the town's racial makeup, not for any other reason."

"Well, that's changed already." Pause. "Did you have a best friend in New Haven?"

"Mary Lou Thomas!"

"Mary Lou Thomas? Where'd she get a name like that? Mary Lou?"

"I don't know, but Mary Lou hates it. I called her last night. We talked."

"Miss her, huh?"

"I do. I really do. This is a new experience for me. Brand-new. I lived in New Haven all my life. There are certain things, people I miss. I have to admit. But Tyler College, my parents jumped at the offers there, so here we are."

Tyler College was in the neighboring town of Tyler City, a short distance outside of Pittsfield.

Jimmy smiled. "I'd never leave Pittsfield—not without Billy."

Judy's eyes looked up at Jimmy doubtingly.

"I mean it."

"Mary Lou's going to be my bridesmaid at my wedding. I've already decided. We've discussed it."

Jimmy had never thought about the subject of marriage—not until now, not until Judy mentioned it.

"And Billy's going to be my best man."

"He … it's something you've thought about too, Jimmy?"

"Why, uh, sure, sure. You bet. A lot. Sure," Jimmy said straight-faced. "Billy and I have discussed it more, at least on more than one occasion, I'd say."

Judy's house was attractive, plus comfortable looking and well built. It looked like a house that was built for two college professors with a smart daughter. The house's lights were on.

"I see Mom's home. She always beats Dad home from school. Unfailingly."

Judy and Jimmy stood in front of a low white gate.

"I love this house. I had heard the Berrys moved out but not that the Collins family moved in," Jimmy said as if he were handing Judy a smooth line.

"Want to come in and meet my mom?"

"Uh …"

"Too soon, huh?"

"Uh …"

"That says it all, Jimmy. That expression on your face." Judy laughed.

"Your mom, she'll be thrilled to hear you made the cheerleading squad."

"My mom and dad. Both had their fingers crossed. They were really up for it."

"By the way, Billy said you were the best cheerleader out there. Of the bunch. And I have to agree."

"I'll thank Billy the next time I see him. And I'll thank you now." Pause. "Thanks, Jimmy."

"Even if I shut my eyes when Dora began calling out the new squad?"

"Boy, was I nervous."

"But Billy said you looked cool. Billy, he could stand to look, not me."

"Really, Jimmy, it was all show on the outside, but inside …"

"Do I know that feeling."

"I heard what happened last year in the state championship game to the Purple Eagles."

Jimmy didn't wince. "You know what? That was last year. But it's not going to happen this year. Billy and I made that resolve. I mean, I'm not bragging or anything, so don't take this the wrong way, but Billy, the team, and I are going to work our tails off extra hard this year. We're going back to the state championship and will win it. The whole thing. That much I can guarantee."

A very attractive-looking woman peeked out the house's front window.

"Judy, your mom? Professor Collins?" Jimmy gulped.

"You sure you don't want to come in, Jimmy? Sure?"

"Sure, yeah, I'm sure. Yeah." Jimmy handed back Judy's books, hurriedly.

"Mom doesn't bite."

"No, but I have to brush up on my economics."

"What about physics?"

"See you in Mrs. Elliot's English II class tomorrow."

Pause.

"Oh, Judy, where do you eat lunch?"

"It'll be in the cafeteria tomorrow."

"Billy and I, we sit—oh, you'll see us. So we'll make room for you at the table. Don't worry."

"Thanks."

"See you."

"Okay."

"Thanks."

Judy entered the house.

Professor Amanda Collins was short and petite like Judy.

"Yes, Judy, yes!"

"It's a yes, Mom! I made the cheerleading squad!"

Professor Collins grabbed Judy around the waist, and they jumped up and down (Professor Collins had been a cheerleader herself in high school).

"Glad it's over with, huh, honey?"

"Mom, you can say that again. It was nerve-racking. The cheering and then the wait."

Amanda Collins's arm draped Judy's shoulders, and she drew her in again.

"I'm happy as pink for you. I know it was one of the things troubling you when we moved—your cheerleading."

"It was."

"And tell me, who was the tall, handsome young man you were with? A new admirer?"

"His name is Jimmy, Mom. Jimmy Boston," Judy said, taking a few light steps away from Amanda.

"Jimmy's in my English class and is the Purple Eagles' star quarterback."

"I just love the name, honey—Purple Eagles. Never in my lifetime, in all my years, have I seen a purple eagle."

Amanda sidled up to Judy, her long blonde hair flowing. "Did you invite Mr. Boston in?" She laughed.

"Yes."

"And?"

"He said he had to brush up on his economics."

"So you told him I'm an economics professor? And you mean to tell me I'm that intimidating?" She laughed. "So what's he going to do when he has to meet your father?"

"That's what I said, Mom," Judy said, heading for her room on the second floor.

"You did?"

"Yep."

"Judy, don't tell me I'm beginning to think like a fifteen-year-old sophomore in high school. How ... how intimidating."

CHAPTER 8

Alexis Price's transfer papers had gotten screwed up through no fault of her own. Between the school she'd transferred from and Pittsfield High School, everything had gone haywire. It was a bureaucratic nightmare. She was supposed to have registered for her classes three days ago, but it was today. If there was anyone who looked like a chicken with its head cut of, it was Alexis Jewel Price.

All eyes were on her. She was stunning. She wasn't tall but gave the impression of being so. Her hair was black, wavy, and long. It was well groomed and had a startling sheen. Her shape was no different from her face. Alexis Jewel Price was going to be the talk of Pittsfield High School (girls, boys, teachers)—and fast. It was just that she had a bit of catching up to do with her classes.

But Alexis was smart, a straight-A student. It was only today that she looked like a chicken with its head cut off—a beautiful chicken, granted, but a chicken anyway. But anyone in a bureaucratic mix-up like this one would be going crazy too (such things are awful to behold!).

The cheerleading squad practiced right after school like the football team. The football team, of course, practiced on the field, and the cheerleading squad in the gym. The gym rang out with shrill, high-spirited, tender, young voices every ten seconds or so.

For those who'd never seen Alexis Price, their jaws dropped.

"She's the new girl in town who they made an extra cheerleading spot for—isn't she, Judy?" May Evans said.

"Yes. Her papers got mixed up or something. So Dora held a special tryout for her."

"She must be good," May said.

"I know she's pretty," Judy said.

"Girls, girls," Dora Bloom said. "May I have your undivided attention, girls?"

Alexis Price stood shoulder to shoulder with Dora Bloom.

"I'd like to introduce the newest member of the Purple Eagles cheerleading squad: Alexis Price."

The girls applauded.

"If you want to say hello to Alexis, do it now before we get down to some real serious cheerleading." Dora smiled sadistically.

Judy introduced herself to Alexis.

"I'm Judy Collins. It's nice meeting you."

"Thank you."

"I'm new to the school and Pittsfield, like you."

"You are?"

"Yes. And of course, to be on the cheerleading squad, even though I was on one back in my old school, is exciting."

"I was too."

"Small world, isn't it?"

"Yes, yes, it is."

Some teenage giggles erupted in the gym.

"The football team usually gets thirsty around this time of day—if you know what I mean, Alexis."

"Oh yes, I know what you mean. I can see what you mean."

"But there're more of them than usual. Word must've gotten around, I'd say," Judy said, looking at Alexis.

Alexis didn't seem to catch on to Judy's casual remark. But all eyes from the Purple Eagle football team were pointed at Alexis Price, someone pretty beyond description.

The football team and the cheerleading team had been practicing for some time.

Billy came into the gym for water. His thirst was the real thing. He jogged into the gym, carrying his football helmet by its chin strap. Billy's eyes met Alexis Price's eyes, and hers his.

Billy ducked his head and gulped water down once it'd sprung from the spout.

Again carrying his football helmet by its chin strap, he began jogging out the gym. But in the hallway, he stopped and put his back up against the tiled wall.

"She is beautiful," Billy said, flushing this emotion out.

It was the first time in his life Billy felt black. Billy knew he was black. Billy loved being black. But this was the first time in his young life Billy felt black. It was the first time in his life he felt different, that being black, that this thing he felt deep inside him, that it wouldn't work.

Billy Steamroller Mack was black, and Alexis Price was white. It finally hit him—being black in a white town. It'd taken this long for that fact to hit him hard in the gut.

Eight days later, Billy was on the P-6 bus. He'd gone to the dentist. The Novocain had worn off. After he'd left the dentist's office, he'd run over to the Rockwell Mall (which was nearby) with his weekly allowance to see what he could find in the way of clothes, but he came up empty.

Billy took to his seat on the bus. The bus wasn't crowded, so there were empty seats. If he had a bag or a large package, he could have put it on the adjoining seat for the time being. Right now, Billy was laughing at himself. Jimmy was lucky; he'd really found someone. Judy was a definite find, and she hadn't crowded him and Billy out of their relationship. They still ate (the three) in the school cafeteria; then there was the telephone (Graham Bell's magnificent invention) available to them.

Jimmy was walking Judy to and from school every day. Their football practice was always longer than the cheerleading squad's, but Judy would wait for Jimmy no matter how long it took. It didn't seem to bother her. Sometimes he'd walk with them, and other times not; it all depended. He wasn't going to crowd them. He kind of read Jimmy's mood, something he was good at by now. He could tell when Jimmy was extra juiced, so he kind of slipped out of the locker room (even though Jimmy's locker was next to his) undetected. Jimmy was definitely on cloud nine, and so was Judy. He truly enjoyed them as a couple.

The football team was shaping up well, even if they'd lost a lot of defensive starters from last year's squad. But the offense was sailing along, and Coach Bosco, as usual, was working his tail off. They really had a great bunch of guys on the team, guys with a lot of guts and pride.

Billy looked out the window when the bus stopped. His heart jumped when he saw her. She was putting her fare in the bus's coin box. Now she was heading down the bus aisle. Even with the bus being practically empty, she still was heading toward him. He couldn't hide himself (not at six feet two and 212 pounds) or duck his head (that would be rude, wouldn't it?).

"Hi, Billy."

"Oh hi, Alexis."

"Do you … do you mind if—"

"No. No." Billy stood. "The seat's empty."

Alexis Price looked fantastic. She was dressed in blues.

She sat next to Billy.

Suddenly, Billy felt nervous and black, again.

"I'm still learning my way around Pittsfield."

"Oh …"

"Slowly but surely. At least where the Rockwell Mall is—even if I didn't go there today."

"Oh."

"I love Pittsfield." She looked over at Billy. "Billy, you always seem to be ducking me."

Billy looked at Alexis, as if now it was all right for him to. "I do?"

"Yes. It's the impression I've been getting."

"No, it's, no, it's not like that."

"Am I imagining things?"

Billy began digesting the question that had been so plainly put to him.

"I know you're black, Billy."

To say Billy was jarred would put it mildly.

"Billy, am I being too frank with you?" Alexis asked, twisting around to him.

"How's that?"

"I … I don't know."

"Maybe I do," Billy said, finally with some assertiveness.

"It's no secret, at least for me, when I look at you … I like you, Billy."

Billy couldn't believe his ears.

"You do? I mean, all the guys—all of them—are chasing after you in school. I …"

"I know." Pause. "Only, I like you. From the first day I saw you in the gym, when you came in to get water. Didn't you feel it too, Billy? I know I did. You had to feel it."

Billy was trying his best to avoid Alexis's eyes at all costs.

"Alexis, maybe you, we, uh, maybe it was an overreaction on our part. Both our parts."

"No, uh-uh. Not me, Billy," Alexis said directly. "I mean, speaking for myself, I wasn't overreacting. No, not at all. In the least."

Billy still couldn't absorb what was happening to him, what he was hearing. He was sitting on the bus next to the prettiest girl in Pittsfield High School, who was white and who was telling him she liked him like it was love at first sight.

Billy looked straight up the bus's aisle.

"You were ducking me, weren't you, Billy? Be honest."

Billy liked Alexis's persistence, her determination; it was how he was on the football field. She seemed to know what she wanted.

"You know, Alexis, I never felt black in Pittsfield until I saw you in the gym that day."

He had Alexis's total attention.

"I mean, I've been called names before, taunted. But that was a long time ago, way back when. Out on the football field but never in any other situation. But that day, the day I saw you, right away, off, I said it wouldn't work even though I saw the way you looked at me."

"Me … I didn't say that to myself."

"See, Alexis, it's different. I guess it's what makes us different, even if I was raised in a white community and fit in. But to be accepted in the sense of dating someone who's white, a white girl, being black and all—it really scared me. Put a big scare in me."

Alexis sighed. "Billy, I was just looking at you as a person," she said innocently.

Billy cleared his throat. "Uh, yes. I know you were, Alexis. As a person."

Billy was home. He vaulted up the stairs like an Olympian mountain climber. He went straight to his room and shut his door.

"Is Jimmy home, or is he with Judy? I didn't see them at the mall. But what's that mean?"

Billy picked up the phone. "Jimmy."

"Hey, Billy."

"I got you on the first try. Good, good, man."

"Yeah, so?" Jimmy said, like it wasn't the first time in their long relationship it'd happened.

"Uh, just glad I did. Just glad about that."

"Billy, are you—"

"You and Judy aren't out at the—"

"Our date's for tonight. I told you that. The movies. This afternoon's my—"

"Right. I almost forgot, sorry."

Jimmy laughed. "Sounds like you did. That you did forget—to me."

Jimmy waited for Billy to say something, then couldn't wait any longer.

"Okay, Billy, what's up? What's going on with you, man? What's Billy Steamroller Mack up to now?"

"Who, me?"

"Yes … you."

Billy was fumbling through his thoughts. "You know how I told you I had to go to the dentist today? Dr. Raymond?"

"Oh," Jimmy said, like he'd just unmasked a mystery, "that's why you're acting so giddy. Dr. Singer shot you up with Novocain, did he? And it's now just wearing off? You're just now returning to normal?"

"And then I went over to the mall."

"What did you buy? Your weekly allowance is shot, I know, Billy. There went your weekly allowance. Flew straight out the window, man. Know how you are—"

"I came out of the mall empty-handed, Jimmy. Got on the bus—"

"That I figured: our limo, Benz for now."

"And guess who got on the bus?"

"What? Who? Jim Brown?"

"No. Better. Far better than Jim Brown, uh, Jimmy. Alexis—Alexis Price, man. Alex Price!"

"Stop the music. You mean that supergorgeous, beautiful, drop-dead creature, Alexis Price?"

"Yes, that package of, of—"

"And what—you went ape? Bananas? Where'd she sit, Billy—Alexis Price on the bus?"

"Next to yours truly—that's where. Right next to yours truly on the bus."

"Next to you?"

"Is my mouth working right, or did I just say Alexis Price sat next to me? I did say that, didn't I?"

"Man, half the male population in Pittsfield would cut its right arm off to sit next to Alexis Price on a bus. And the other half its left arm."

"Everyone but you."

"Right. I've got Judy. Yeah, I've got my girl already."

Pause.

"Alexis Price is the prettiest girl in school," Billy said.

"Except for Judy. Of course, ruling Judy out."

"Uh, right, I stand corrected, Jimmy. Right—except for Judy," Billy said devotedly.

"And you sat next to Alexis Price. I mean, who was on the bus first anyway? You or her?"

"Me."

"And she just came over and asked to sit next you? Just sauntered over to you like that to sit next to—"

"That's about the size of it, Jimmy. Yeah, just like that, man. It's how it happened," Billy said with worldly self-assurance.

"Cool, Billy. Cool."

"Very."

Jimmy, in his mind, was picturing the whole scenario—how it must've happened.

"So what did you two lovebirds talk about?"

Billy hadn't told Jimmy his feelings toward Alexis Price. How could he when he'd been denying them to himself—until today?

"We talked about a lot of things." Pause. "Love," Billy said.

"Love!"

"Yeah, Jimmy, love. Or at least about feelings—our feelings."

Jimmy was less playful now. "Billy, hey, wait a minute. What have you been hiding from me, man? Your best friend! What's going on with you?"

"Jimmy, I didn't know myself at the time."

"Know what?"

"I mean, I knew ... but it wasn't something I wanted to, well, deal with then."

"Billy, you're beating around the bush. And beating around the bush is something Billy Steamroller Mack never does. Not you, man."

"At least not on the football field."

"You roll right over anything or—"

"Yeah but—"

"What? But what?"

"Alexis. When I saw Alexis Price, Jimmy, it's the first time I felt black. First time in my life I felt black, man."

"But, Billy, you don't have any problems with that around here. Pittsfield. You or your parents. You never try to be white. Your heroes are black: Jackie Robinson, Jim Brown, your father—"

"I know, Jimmy. But a white girl. I mean, I felt something serious. Something they say happens ..."

"Like how it did between Judy and me. I know. That kind of jolt. Kind of an electrical shock wave."

"Exactly, Jimmy."

"It felt great, didn't it, Billy?"

"Sure did. And I knew Alexis—"

"Felt the same as you. Toward you. When she first saw you. Laid eyes on you."

"Jimmy, man, how do you know these things?"

90

"Beats me. Beats the heck out of me." Jimmy grinned.

"Some kind of chemical reaction." Billy laughed.

"Like a nuclear plant."

"Yeah."

Pause.

"Now I see why you didn't tell me."

"You do?"

"So I forgive you this time, Steamroller."

"Man, I was worried."

"You better get out of here!"

Billy bounced off the bed. "But this race thing, Jimmy. This race thing."

"What about it?"

"Alexis has parents."

"Yeah."

Pause.

"Would they be cool about it? As cool as we are?"

"Hey—look, Billy. Go for it, man. Go for it. What do you have to lose?"

"I am. Alexis and I made a date for tomorrow night."

"Hey, that's my man. Roll them over and knock them dead. That's my man, Steamroller!" Pause. "Listen, I can call Judy. Change our date plans tonight for tomorrow night. We can double-date. Go to the movies together. How's that sound?" Jimmy asked excitedly.

"Uh-uh, not on your life. My first date with Alexis Price is going to be just her and me. We're flying solo. Alone."

"Okay, have it your way. Okay, okay," Jimmy said, surrendering valiantly.

"I'm still worried though."

"Don't be," Jimmy said soothingly.

"But put yourself in my shoes, would you?"

"I wish I could, Billy."

"Yeah, I know."

"If I dated a black girl—"

"It's a little bit different, the reverse situation, Jimmy, you dating a black girl."

"How come?"

"Jimmy, it's like you'd be doing a black girl a favor."

"But with you—"

"It's like she's doing me a favor."

"Man, Billy. What a bummer."

"I'm going to tell my mom and dad tonight."

"Yeah." Jimmy laughed. "You'd better, Steamroller, before it gets out of hand," Jimmy kidded.

"I—it's just that I'm already serious about her—and I, we haven't even been out on our first date. Man, I don't even know her that well yet."

"Sure. Guess that's the fear of dating—when you like somebody so much, and things go badly. Poof—right before your eyes. That's not cool."

"But you and Judy—"

"It's working out like a charm."

"Tell me about it, man."

"But …" Jimmy paused. "If this thing between you and Alexis does work out, then both of us will have cheerleaders as girlfriends, man. Just think of that, Steamroller."

"The star quarterback and the cheerleader, as you and Judy are known at school now."

"And the star fullback and the cheerleader, as you and Alexis will soon be known at school."

"Hey, we've got it made—"

"In the shade, Billy."

"Wish me luck, Jimmy."

"It's a cinch, Billy. A cinch."

Jimmy and Billy were off the phone. There was movement in the house. They had to have heard him when he came into the house. Probably thought Dr. Raymond had injected him with too much Novocain for him to talk, Billy guessed.

Dad's probably in his den, Billy thought. *And Mom, on a Saturday, could be anywhere.* So he'd look for her first (since it might take longer), bring her to his father, and then tell them both about Alexis Price. The white girl he liked. Liked? Really, really liked.

"I didn't plan for this. Just like Jimmy didn't plan for it to happen with Judy. It's all biological. Blame it on biology. It's what they teach you in school—isn't it?"

The den door was closed. It was late. No lights were on in the room. The door opened.

"Connie, you can't hide away in here all night. You have to come to bed some time," Susan said, half-joking, half-serious.

"Don't turn on the lights, Susan, if that's what you're about to do. I know what I look like."

Susan all but bit her tongue. "Okay, Connie, have it your way."

"You know, my father named me after his great-great-grandmother, Constance, a slave."

Susan managed to sit down on Connie's old, worn couch.

"I know you know that, Susan. What the hell. What the hell."

"Connie, what do you want from Billy? Tell me."

"A slave name. I carry a slave name. You call me Connie. Everyone does. Everybody calls me Connie. But not my father. Not him. Uh-uh. Dad always called me Constance—God bless him. He didn't let me forget who I was. How our family got to where it was. What it took."

Pause.

"She's white, Connie. The girl's white. We moved here. We moved to an all-white town. Pittsfield. Billy was raised here. Pittsfield. We don't live in Macon, Georgia, or Washington, DC, anymore."

Connie sucked his teeth. "Upward mobility. It's what they call it, isn't it? Of course. Of course, of course," Connie said sarcastically.

"No, Connie, they call it a job," Susan said soberly, pragmatically. "You came to a place where you could work. Remember how excited you were? You do remember, honey?"

"Sure," Connie said, as if he'd pushed it far into the past. "Who in their right mind wouldn't?"

"Hired by one of the top aeronautical companies in the country."

"Make it the world."

Susan laughed. "The world."

"Yes, sure, it was exciting," Connie said with much reserve.

"I haven't forgotten. Something I'll never forget."

"Been with them for fourteen years."

"Wow. How times flies."

"Billy was a year old, Sue. It's how I can remember, timewise, my tenure at Blast—by Billy."

"We needed Blast Aircraft then. It came at the right time—the job offer."

"Didn't it? Never mind its historical significance: the first black and all the other stuff that went along with it. Hell, I needed a job and quick. I had a family to support. To feed. Responsibility was knocking at the door."

"I was just about to head off to law school when—"

"You found out you were pregnant with Billy. And we pooh-poohed that idea. Had to."

"Motherhood first and foremost. Why'd I ditch my dream, Connie?"

"Life's funny, Susan. You get caught up in things. Circumstances change, and then five, ten, fifteen years slip by off the calendar without a person taking notice."

Susan rubbed her feet together after removing her slippers.

"Maybe it was a bad move. We gave up too much. Too much for Pittsfield."

"For a job, Connie? For something you went to school for and were trained to do and were superior at? Your gift?"

"Billy ..."

"He knows he's black."

"But he's not living it that way, Susan. Don't you get it? It's all I'm saying, Sue. Wrestling with."

"Don't' make your fears his, Connie. Don't do that to our son," Susan said, turning in the dark to Connie. "First it was Jimmy, Connie. That Billy's best friend had to be black."

"Not *had* to be, Susan," Connie said brusquely, "I wanted him to be. I wanted our son's best friend to be black. One of us."

"No, *had* to be, Connie. I didn't misspeak. Had to be. You were dogmatic. That unbending. That—"

"All right, all right, I was. But it's all about trust. Trusting someone through thick and thin. Trusting someone with your life, practically."

"And look what's happened, honey. Look at what Jimmy and Billy mean to each other, what their friendship means to them."

"It's on the football field too, Sue. It's what makes them so great. What they have on the football field, it's intangible. It's something you can't buy."

"And now this girl, Connie. Alexis Price. Why can't we think it will work out the same as it did for Jimmy and Billy?"

Connie rocked forward, then back. His eyes stung, and there was bitterness in his voice. "Why must we always have to prove ourselves to them?"

"Every immigrant group—"

"Hell, immigrant group. Are you kidding! I don't believe you were about to say that, something as idiotic. Unworthy for discussion. We were brought here as slaves. Slaves, Susan. Slaves. We came here in slave ships. In the galley of a ship. We didn't come in here through Ellis Island. Our ancestors didn't see the damned Statue of Liberty when they got here!

"Damn. There was no view of the freedom land, of the great melting pot from the bottom of a ship. No such comforts for the Africans. It wasn't a freaking luxury liner they were on. They weren't tourists."

"Okay, Connie. Maybe I was being naive, revising, making over history, but—"

"Billy's going to have to stand before this white girl's parents and be judged as a black boy by them."

"Aren't we going to do the same with her, Connie? With this girl? Uh, young lady?"

"Hell, Susan"—Connie grimaced—"do you think she's afraid of us? Terrified by us? Don't make me laugh. Maybe nervous. A little nervous like anyone. What's natural? But afraid? Terrified. Oh no, not that. She's been taught that she's superior. That she's above us. I'm not blaming the girl, Sue, so don't get me ... The blame doesn't fall on her shoulders. But it's how white society has conditioned her. She was born into it."

Susan's head dropped.

"Our son, he's feeling his blackness now. Make no mistake about it. You heard him when he told you about her."

"Yes, yes, I did," Susan had to admit.

"It was all there in his voice, Billy's mannerisms. He's had to come to grips with who he is. On the football field, he was given a chance. No one denied him. Billy's the best. But here, in this situation, this girl's parents, they could judge him, Susan." Pause. "It could happen just like that," Connie said, snapping his fingers.

"I'm not going to think your way, Connie. I just won't let myself!"

"Then you go right ahead. You do that. But prepare yourself for the fall," Connie said.

"I have more faith than you."

"Is that what you call it, Susan? Faith? He's black. Our son is black. When are you going to get that through your head? You can work with them, socialize with them, but date them? Their daughters?"

Susan got up from the couch.

"Don't run."

Susan didn't like Connie when he was like this, when he held regrets up to the mirror.

"I don't regret moving here, living here in this all-white community, as you put it. I don't have any such thoughts. I'm happy here. I have friends here. People treat me well. Decently. If I were in an all-black community, I'd hope the same."

Connie clapped derisively.

"Brava. Brava. Well spoken. Why, so articulate."

Susan took immediate offense. She walked over to the light switch.

"Big deal, Susan. Big damned deal."

"Sometimes I think you regret you're black."

That stung him. Susan saw as much. "I'm sorry I said that," Susan said, frustrated.

"Don't be."

"I'm sorry, Connie. Maybe I went too far."

"Maybe you did."

"But can't you see this argument is becoming about you and me? Our opposite views on the matter."

Connie looked at her, startled by what Susan said. "How in the—how can we possibly avoid that?"

Susan's shoulders slumped. "I don't know."

"We have different backgrounds. Upbringing."

"See, being black, we're not in any way homogenous."

"Only there are some basic truths, Susan. To deal with. It's all I'm saying."

"Yes, Billy, he is scared. I saw it," Susan admitted again.

"Things like this, I'm not going to back off. Don't expect that. I'm going to acknowledge them straight on. Dead-on, Sue."

"I like the truth too. I'm a friend of the truth."

Pause.

"Want me to turn the lights off? Because I'm going to bed. I'm tired."

"Don't worry, Sue. I'm right behind you."

Connie stood and looked down at his computer. "Good night, sweetheart."

"Nightly ritual now," Susan said, the air now cleared.

"It's fast becoming that. She knows a heck of a lot about me. About Connie Mack, no denying that."

"Like a wife?" Susan smiled.

"Like a wife," Connie replied, patting Susan's bottom. "Except I can't do that to her," Connie said, taking hold of her hand that she put there for him.

"Does it ever talk back?"

"No."

"Not like a wife then."

CHAPTER 9

Billy was in the Hill Borough section of Pittsfield. He was at the front door of another elegant house in Pittsfield that had all the trimmings of refinement and economic attainment.

He was casually dressed—blue slacks and a blue, striped dress shirt, minus a tie. He wore a tan coat (after all, it was fall). He glanced at his watch to make certain it was two o'clock. He had nothing planned for him and Alexis. They were just going to walk around the Hill Borough area. She was trying to further familiarize herself with her new surroundings. Billy had his weekly allowance tucked away in his back pocket just in case their plans changed.

For a second, Billy doubted himself. *I do look okay, don't I? I have to. Ring.*

Mrs. Price appeared at the front door, and Mr. Price stood right behind her. There was shock and surprise and dismay on both their faces when they saw him; it could not be described anymore politely.

Alexis stepped forward, coming into Billy's view in an attempt to ease some of the palatable tension.

"Billy. Hi. Come in. You're right on time."

Billy was much taller than everyone in the house, but no one had moved any from the front door.

"Hi, Alexis."

Alexis was in casual attire—fancy jeans and a top and a white jacket that zipped.

98

"Mom, Dad, this is Billy Mack." Pause. "Billy, my mom and dad. Mr. and Mrs. Price."

"Hello, Billy," Mrs. Price said, her face still fresh with surprise.

"Hello, Mrs. Price."

Then Mr. Price's hand greeted Billy.

"Mr. … Mr. Price."

Mrs. Price was an attractive woman, Billy thought, but Alexis got her good looks from Mr. Price, her father. He was a handsome man even with his hairline receding. He was Paul Newman handsome, the exception being he had black hair.

Billy stood tall, his powerful physique exuding strength and grace.

Quickly, Alexis got to him. "We won't be long, Mom, Dad. Billy and I are going to take a short walk around the neighborhood."

The Prices' home was on Trotman Lane.

Alexis's mother was the first to respond. "Yes, Alexis, a walk."

"Of course, Billy grew up around here. Right, Billy?"

"Yes."

"So he knows the area quite well," Alexis said.

"Uh, of course," Billy said, responding to Alexis's eyes.

Mr. Price walked away.

Billy suddenly felt slighted.

Alexis reopened the front door.

"See you later, Mom."

"Yes, Mrs. Price, see you later."

"Yes, Billy," Mrs. Maxine Price said warmly.

Billy and Alexis were out the door. Alexis looked up at Billy.

"You look great, Billy."

They were off the porch and walking the long stretch of ground.

"You didn't tell them, your mom and dad. Alexis, why not?"

"Tell them what, Billy?"

Billy was peeved. He stopped walking.

"That I'm black, that's what. Come on. If you're not going to play it straight with me, Alexis—level with me—then this isn't going to work for us."

"Billy, come on," Alexis said, tugging his arm and then dropping her hand from his arm once she got him to move.

They were walking away from the house. Billy had been silent for the past few minutes.

"Alexis, why didn't you tell your parents?" he finally asked again. "Why did you put them through that with me?" he said as if scolding her, as if he were her parent, not someone who'd become interested in her.

They kept walking in what was Alexis's new neighborhood, one Billy knew like the palm of his hand.

"You wanted it to be an ordinary date with an ordinary guy. Was that it?" Billy stopped walking again. "Well, it's not. I'm black. It's something you should've told your parents. Something we all have to deal with."

Alexis came out of her nonresponsive state. "When I saw you, Billy, I didn't think of color. It was so instant. I didn't think of color then. Not that."

"But later, Alexis … you had to."

"But I didn't want to." Alexis put her hands in her jacket and went mum again.

"You just can't pass us off. I mean—it just can't happen that way."

"I'm not trying to," Alexis said, her pretty eyes growing prettier. "My mind doesn't think like that. I wanted to hold on to that moment maybe. When I first saw you, Billy. When it didn't matter, your color."

Abruptly, all kinds of thoughts invaded Billy's head. Maybe they were taking this thing too seriously. Maybe it was infatuation, a sudden burst of something. Maybe it wasn't what they thought—what they were saying and hoping it was. Could it be all of the above?

"I love that house over there." Alexis's finger pointed to the house.

"Mr. and Mrs. Andrew's house. They're natives of Pittsfield. Robert and Ann—their children moved from here. Left, oh, I'd say for some time now."

"Oh—"

"How many boyfriends have there been, Alexis?" Billy said, looking down at her.

"A … a few. But nobody—not anyone serious."

"Infatuation?"

"Like any adolescent, I suppose, Billy."

"Right." Pause. "But the first time you see them, you like"—he laughed—"go get all googly-eyed, right? Don't you?"

"No, Billy. Not like that. Say like a mutual interest kind of thing. At least that's how it is for me."

"Oh, so you were always cool about it? Always?"

"Yes, I guess," Alexis said cautiously.

"You never went ape? Bananas?"

"No, not at all, Billy. Not me. I mean, I'm full of fun and all—but I've never gone ape, bananas over a boy. I don't react to boys like that."

Billy looked at Alexis's pretty dark eyes; they were astonishingly sincere.

"So you're saying—"

"It's the first time I've felt this way about anyone. Reacted this way toward a boy before."

Pause.

"Whose house is that, Billy? I like that one too."

"Sutter. Mr. Sutter's house. He's a big shot something or other in Pittsfield."

"Gee, is he?" Alexis said, teasing Billy. "That sounds awfully important to me."

Alexis and Billy kept walking the Hill Borough neighborhood, reaching farther and farther into it like a deep pocket.

By no stretch of the imagination was it a short walk.

"We're covering a lot of ground suddenly, Alexis. Not that I'm complaining. Do you hear me complaining any?"

"Billy, what about you and girls? Girlfriends?"

"None."

"None?" Alexis said, surprised.

"Not around here."

"Then?"

"Oh, if you want to count two years ago in Macon, Georgia. Have you heard of Macon, Georgia, before?"

"Georgia—of course, but no, not Macon."

"My dad's home. It's where the Macks hail from."

"What were you doing in—"

"Staying there for three weeks with my uncle Billy."

"It's who you're named after, Billy—your Uncle Billy?"

"My dad's brother, Billy Mack."

"And the girl?"

"Uh—uh girl, right. It was nothing really. Okay, I liked her," Billy confessed, smiling.

"What was her name?"

"Alexis, let's drop it, okay? I mean, it wasn't like it was a summer romance, nothing close or anything. I mean, we just went out a couple of times—"

"And you made googly-eyes at her, did you, Billy?" Alexis said, making her eyes do crazy things.

Billy laughed. "No. Uh-uh. It wasn't like that—at all," Billy said, as if defending his honor or trying to prove that he didn't chase after rainbows either when it came to such matters of the heart.

"Oh … come on, Billy. Don't be so serious. It's the past. It is the past, isn't it?"

The wind had picked up.

"I know, but I don't want you to get the wrong impression."

"Everything up until now is in the past, Billy."

Alexis was the one to stop walking, putting the wind to her back. "I like you, Billy. Really like you a lot."

It was as if Alexis was asking Billy to take her in his arms—to hold her. It was how it was said.

"I've never had this feeling before for a boy. It feels good, real good."

For a second, Billy's mind went blank, but then it wasn't, not blank at all. If he was going to say how he felt toward Alexis, he would have said the same thing she said to him.

She put out her hand. Billy took it. There was a mutual, innocent swoon between them, a shiver of delight happening simultaneously.

"Billy, are you ready to head back to my place?"

"Uh, yes, Alexis, I am."

It was forty-five minutes later. Billy and Alexis had talked a lot. He didn't go back inside the Price house. He and Alexis stood outside for quite some time, and then Billy saw Alexis to the door. They said goodnight and that he'd see her in school tomorrow.

Billy was a quarter of a mile from the Price residence when, lo and behold, there was Sylvan Price walking on the same side of the street.

"Mr.—Mr. Price," Billy said, stammering.

"Hello, Billy," Price said.

The day was darkening.

"Good night, Mr. Price," Billy said, passing him.

"Good night, Billy."

Billy had taken a few strides more when he heard "By the way, Billy, did you and Alexis have a pleasant walk around the neighborhood?"

Billy stopped dead in his tracks. He turned back to Price.

"Yes, we did, sir."

"I'm glad Alexis got out of the house."

Should I walk to him? Billy thought. It felt as if this could turn into a decent conversation.

"I thought Alexis, with her cheerleading and all—"

"Alexis is new to Pittsfield, of course, so she hasn't really gotten around in it that much."

"Oh."

"Me, I get around a lot." Pause. "Has Alexis told you the kind of work I do?"

Billy was standing directly in front of Price. "No, Alexis hasn't, Mr. Price."

"I'm a Realtor. Own a realty company."

"Oh, no wonder …" Billy failed to complete his thought.

"I know what was on the tip of your tongue."

Billy waited for an explanation for his own actions.

"No wonder Alexis likes houses so much."

"Yours is a beauty," Billy said.

Price laughed. "I got a terrific deal on it. Let me just say that. You knew the Gates, the former owners?"

"Yes." Billy smiled.

"I like to take walks, Billy. Basically, I'm a loner by nature, you might say. I've been this way since little—so I was told. But today I was scouting out houses too."

"Mixing business with pleasure, sir."

With Sylvan Price being so short, Billy somewhat stooped.

"Look, I didn't mean to be standoffish at the house—if it's how you perceived it. I am a quiet, reserved man for the most part but not standoffish."

"Mr. Price, I understand, sir."

"Oh, what the heck, Billy. I'm not prejudice. Let's get that out the way. Clear the deck. But it was a shock—you bet it was—to me and Mrs. Price."

"Alexis should have told you and Mrs. Price that I was black. I told her as much, sir, immediately upon leaving your house. I didn't like how it was handled any more than you or Mrs. Price."

Long pause.

"I know from my research—the demographics of Pittsfield—that there are really no black families in the area."

"Other than mine, sir."

"Not in Maxine's and my wildest dreams—"

"Did you expect to see a black face appear at your front door, Mr. Price?" Billy said candidly.

"Later, Maxine and I laughed over it. It was like the picture *Guess Who's Coming to Dinner.* Do you know the picture I'm referring to? Seen it, Billy?"

"Yes, sir, the one with Sidney Poitier and Audrey Hepburn and ... uh—"

"Spencer Tracy."

Both laughed.

"Except, Mr. Price, I wasn't coming for dinner, sir."

Sylvan took his hands out his pockets. "But you're welcome to, Billy, at any time."

"Thank you, Mr. Price. Thank you."

Sylvan's eyes took the measure of Billy. "The Prices aren't big people. I take it the Macks are."

"Yes, my dad was an athlete too."

"He's a ..."

"Concept design/engineer with Blast Aircrafts," Billy said with pride.

"Why, of course. I know of the company."

"My dad's one of the top, one of their top ..."

Sylvan smiled. "I know what you're trying to say without seeming to brag too much, Billy."

"Yes, uh, yes, Mr. Price."

"Sports. I'm not big on sports." He threw his arms out in front of him, demonstrably. "Look at me. I'm a runt."

Billy did have to agree.

"Maybe I'm built for midget car racing or something," Sylvan said self-deprecatingly. "So don't at all feel offended if I don't come to any of your football games. Billy, I'm just not a fan. Not sports minded."

Billy had the urge to say, "But what about Alexis's cheerleading, being on the cheerleading squad?" but, of course, he wouldn't.

"But Alexis told me you and Jimmy Boston are simply terrific. And top-notch students."

"Yes. Straight-As sir."

"Like my Alexis. Now it sounds like I'm bragging, huh? Good night, son," Sylvan said, shaking Billy's hand.

"Good night, sir. It was a pleasure meeting you."

As soon as Billy got into the house, he called Jimmy to let him know what happened between him and Alexis. Homework was secondary to Jimmy. So he made the call before Jimmy exploded from anticipation.

By now, Jimmy had all the facts, the good and bad of Billy's date with Alexis. They were about to sign off, something that was always inevitable but elastic, being teenagers and all.

"All I have to say, Billy, is Judy feels like the right girl for me too."

"She does?"

"This is happening to us both at the same time. Cupid's arrow straight through the heart. And you know what? It feels weird. Up to now, we really didn't think that much about girls."

"Hardly at all."

"Right, but it's all that's on our minds these days. Usually on a Sunday evening on the phone, in September, we'd be talking about football exclusively."

"Not girls, man."

"Nope, Steamroller. Not girls."

"So what are we going to do now, Jimmy?" Billy asked, innocently.

"Roll with the punches, I guess."

"Wow, Jimmy, what a brain!"

"Or did you want me to say something more …"

Billy was off the phone with Jimmy. He was over at his desk. He looked down at his books. His algebra book was down at the bottom of the pile. He was excellent at algebra, but Mr. Armory was making the course difficult for everyone. He was a difficult man, odd. Billy cleared the rest of the books away, reaching for the algebra book. He twisted the book in his big hand. He wanted to call Alexis.

His parents were out of the house. He knew they were anxious to know how things went for him today. He would tell them they went great, as he'd told Jimmy. He really did get to know a lot about Mr. Price. Mrs. Price, well, he didn't expect as much in that department. Mr. Price had worried him, not so much Mrs. Price. Mr. Price was the one who'd put a scare in him last night.

And now he felt like Billy Steamroller Mack—like he'd bowled a big problem out the way. And this one was off the football field, something that had seemed far more intimidating. Far more serious than name-calling, racial taunts. Something that could have stood in his way forever. Something that could have been a permanent obstacle—ruining his first chance at liking someone as much as he did Alexis Price, a white girl.

And he did like her a lot. And he liked her parents. And Alexis would like his parents once she and they met, once the Macks and the Prices got together for dinner. Jimmy told him over the phone that the Bostons and the Collins families were scheduled to do so this Sunday.

Billy looked at his algebra book and thought of Mr. Armory. *What rotten luck*, he thought, *to have such a grumpy teacher for algebra.*

Most days in Pittsfield, during the fall season, resembled today. There was an orangey glaze to the days, and leaves fell freely from the dated trees, then were raked into gentle piles that looked like small pup tents from above. The piles were arranged evenly in the front and backyards of homes.

It was a lovely time of the year in New England, cool and refreshing, the nights comfortable, not chilly. Summer had ended yet was remembered by those who had profited, as if it had belonged to them exclusively by some quirk of their good fortune.

If Jimmy had dreamt of a girl's family he wanted his parents to meet, it would have been Judy's, the Collins family. The dinner had been planned for well over a week and was finally occurring.

Jim parked the car in front of Judy's house. She told them they could pull up into the driveway, being that there was ample space, but Jim chose not to.

"Physics. Gosh, Marion. What the devil do I know about physics?"

Marion put her arm around Jim's waist. "So what the devil does Professor Collins know about insurance, Jim?"

"Not a whole lot, I bet," Jim said.

"Then you're even. I'm sure both subjects will be avoided at—"

"Mom, how can you say that when Dad has his insurance forms sticking out his back pocket."

Jim grinned guiltily.

"Uh, at this rate, we're going to be late," Jim said, standing outside the lovely house's gate.

Jimmy was wearing a tie he had blown the dust off before tying it and a bright white shirt.

"We aren't facing a firing squad, just the Collinses, Dad. Judy's parents, sir."

The dinner had gone particularly well for both families. Professor Amanda Collins liked Marion Boston as well as Professor Patrick Collins liked Jim Boston.

Patrick Collins was tall and lanky. His face looked like that of a college physics professor who had been locked away in a room for three days with a tough, gloomy physics problem.

"Uh, by the way, Pat—"

Oh no, he's not! Jimmy panicked. *Not that! Grab him, Mom! Stop Dad! Now, Mom! Now!*

"… is your in—"

"Pat, what a striking portrait," Marion said, pointing to the dining room's far wall.

"It's Pat's great-great-grandfather, Marion," Amanda Collins said.

Phew! Mom came through!

"He served and fought in the Civil War. Marched straight through Richmond with General Grant. Granddad Collins had a pistol by which to prove it too." Pat Collins laughed, scratching a dark beard bushy enough for General Grant's platoon to hide in.

Jimmy looked across the dining room table at Judy. She was sitting in the middle of Marion and Amanda. There was something about Judy today he couldn't quite put his finger on, though he wanted to.

"Who has the pistol now, Pat?"

"My dad," Pat Collins said.

"Has he fired it?"

"Jim!" Marion said, admonishing him.

"Well, has he, Pat?" Jim said, undeterred, paying no attention to Marion.

Pat laughed. "I'm afraid it's an old Civil War relic, Jim," Pat said, scratching his beard. "It has a lot of age. I don't think Dad wants to tempt the Fates. Not at his age. It might backfire on him."

"More coffee, Marion?"

"Just a drop more, Amanda. Thank you."

"Marion has to watch her figure, Amanda," Jim said.

"Jim!" Marion said, admonishing him a second time.

"Now, Pat, about your insurance …"

Pat sat up straight in his chair.

"Is it paid up?"

Dinner was at three. The Bostons had left the Collins's house at five thirty—Jim and Marion, not Jimmy. Pat and Amy Collins were in different sections of the house. Jimmy and Judy were in the den with the forty-two-inch TV—supposedly looking at it but instead looking at each other. Jimmy would leave at about seven, it had been mutually agreed. It was six forty. Both had done their homework yesterday, all of it, right down to the last punctuation on the page.

Jimmy had his arm around Judy's shoulders as they sat on the couch (nothing new).

"Now I know what I've been trying to put my finger on," Jimmy said, snapping his fingers with his free hand. "You've been blushing all day, Judy, haven't you?"

"I have. And you know why, Jimmy? This has been a perfect day."

"Really?"

"Really."

"Judy, the feeling's mutual."

"Dad and Mom are already signed up with their new insurance policies to start off the new month."

"Dad made your parents drop their old policies like hotcakes once he showed them his rates and the company's rating."

"Mr. Boston is some salesman, Jimmy." Judy swooned.

"Dad could find a snail under a rock and sell life insurance to him and his family. Yes, Dad's some pitchman, all right."

"And your mother sat calmly by …"

"Habit, I suppose. Actually, an old habit by now." Then Jimmy looked into Judy's eyes. "Judy, I don't like the look you're giving me."

"Maybe someday, Jimmy, we'll be …"

"Uh—that's a long ways off, Judy. Uh, marriage, if it's what you're thinking. I mean a long ways off."

"I suppose you're right. First things first."

"Like high school, college, a job, career, setting goals—little life-consuming matters such as that." Jimmy smiled.

"Yes," Judy said impatiently. "Small things like that."

Jimmy kissed Judy's lips (nothing new between them).

"Now, about next weekend."

"You'll be cheering."

"And you'll be throwing."

"And Alexis cheering."

"And Billy running."

"Next week will be exciting, Judy. The Purple Eagles' first game. Our opener."

"And I'll be there to see my star quarterback in person."

"It will be like a first for you, won't it?"

"Uh-huh. And we're going all the way this year, Jimmy. State championship."

"State championship, Judy!" Jimmy glanced at his watch. "Uh, time to go."

Judy's heart sank. "Yes, I know."

"Don't want to get up, huh?"

"Not at all, uh-uh. I could stay like this here forever with you."

"I bet."

Jimmy had gotten up. Reluctantly, Judy stood.

"I'm glad you came from Fairfield County, Connecticut, and wound up here, Judy."

"Pittsfield." Judy paused. "Never heard of it before—not until Mom and Dad mentioned it. Alexis said the same thing," Judy said as she and Jimmy began winding their way through the house to get to the front door.

"Poor Pittsfield. It gets no respect."

"Jimmy …"

"Yes?"

"When are we going to double-date?"

"You mean with Alexis and—"

Judy pinched Jimmy's arm. "Who else?"

"How about next weekend—after our first win, say? We'll celebrate at the mall. How's that?"

"At Patty's Pizza Parlor?"

"All the pizza we can eat."

Amanda Collins had heard Judy and Jimmy.

"Good night, Jimmy," the voice said, winding pleasantly down the staircase.

"Good night, Mrs. Collins."

"My mom really likes you," Judy said.

"Billy and I agreed, though, that it's better to win over the father first in these matters," Jimmy said as if it were a truism.

"Him too," Judy said.

"You're sure?"

"Sure. Dad doesn't look at you like a perplexing physics problem anymore. You're no longer under tacit scrutiny."

Judy opened the door.

"Don't step out onto the porch; it's cold out," Jimmy said. "Especially when I can do the honors right here."

"Mmm …"

They kissed.

Jimmy twisted Judy's blonde ponytail lightly (something he enjoyed). "Now for the long walk home."

"And back in the morning," Judy said wearily.

"To walk you to your new high school."

"It's beginning to feel like I've been there forever."

Jim Boston was half-naked or half-dressed—all according to what side of the View-Master you were on.

"Did the afternoon's dinner remind you of something, Marion?"

Marion was in her jammies.

"Our first dinner with our parents, I dare say, Jim."

"Without a doubt. Ha, ha."

"It was fun, Jim. As fun as today's was."

"We were Jimmy and Judy back then," Jim said fondly, drawing back the curtain.

"Yep. This … this," Jim began hesitantly, shaping every word seemingly perfectly, "I think is the real thing they have between them."

"You can see it a mile away, can't you?" Marion said, propping her pillow, then picking up a book off her nightstand.

"Thick as Irish ale, Marion. It was similar for us; you could see it a mile away like mud on your face."

Marion slipped on her glasses.

"It does something to your spirits when you see that."

"What—love, Jim?"

"Gosh … you bet, Marion. You bet. It makes the things you do, once the responsibility of being a husband and a father take over, seem … well, worth it."

"Like it wasn't in vain, huh? You didn't get stuck on a sinking ship, after all."

"Oh … so the world-renowned Casey sense of humor has kicked in?"

"Come on now, Jim. You started it. You're making marriage sound as if it's a death sentence."

"Look, I'm all for it—hell, even if it means I have to wash the dinner dishes at night."

"Oh, don't make me laugh, Jim!" Marion curled up with her book.

Jim climbed into the bed.

"Jimmy's life's really beginning to bloom. And I hear Billy's not doing too badly either in the love department. He's found a nice girl. Alexis Price is a beautiful young lady, all right."

"It's what they tell me," Jim said. "Then you've seen her."

"Yes." Then Marion looked over at Jim askance. "And who are *they*, might I ask, Jim Boston?"

"Look, I've got my network of spies planted in all the right places in Pittsfield. Just like I know Maxine and Sylvan Price are going to need new insurance policies, with them being new in Pittsfield."

"Hounding the poor Collinses at the dinner table like that this evening," Marion said in a huff.

"Hounding them? Why, Marion, they were at my mercy. Like I was at yours when we were out on our first date."

"You were, Jim?"

"Absolutely. Gosh, you were a beautiful woman then, Mar—"

"Was!"

"Uh … uh *are*. Are, Marion—"

"It's getting deeper and deeper, Jim."

"Gosh, are … are," Jim said, slipping his head under the bedcovers.

I'd toss the book at you, Jim Boston! Marion thought. *If it wasn't Edith Wharton's* Age of Innocence!

CHAPTER 10

The cheerleaders were with the cheerleaders, and the football players with the football players. In other words, Billy was with Jimmy, and Alexis was with Judy. It didn't have to be that way, but it was. Over the past few weeks, Alexis and Judy had formed a bond. Both being new to Pittsfield was the centerpiece for the relationship, and they plain enjoyed each other's company.

During cheerleading practice, whenever Dora Bloom, the cheerleading captain, gave them a break, you'd find them stuck together like dough. They were becoming fast friends, and everyone on the cheerleading squad took notice.

Alexis was at Judy's front door.

Ring.

"Hello, Professor Collins."

"Why, hello, Alexis. Come in, dear."

"We don't have time for that, Mom," Judy said, squeezing herself into the picture.

"We have to get to the game."

"Hi, Judy."

"Hi, Alexis."

Amanda looked at this current of energy buzzing before her.

"Good luck, girls."

"Thanks, Professor Collins."

"Thanks, Mom."

113

Amanda and Judy hugged and kissed, and then Judy was out the door as fast as you can say Jiminy Cricket.

By now, the two teenagers were bubbling with laughter.

"Did Billy call you, Alexis?"

"No." Alexis giggled. "I called him."

Now Judy giggled. "The same thing with me. I beat Jimmy to it too."

"If Billy and Jimmy could only see us," Alexis continued, "they'd think we're so mature."

Giggle. Giggle.

"Boy, if they don't have something to learn about us," Judy said.

"When we get together."

"They're probably the same as us when we're not around," Judy said.

The opening game of the season for the Purple Eagles was at twelve. It was ten fifteen. They'd get to the Pittsfield High in less than seven minutes.

"This is so thrilling, Alexis."

"It was thrilling before when I was a cheerleader at Mt. Kiso High, but our boyfriends … We're cheering not only for the team, Judy, but for our boyfriends. And we're to double-date after the game."

"It's going to be a full day, Alexis."

"At the football game, Judy, and then the Rockwell Mall."

"At Patty's Pizza Parlor," Judy said.

The weather was mean and lean, perfect for a football game.

"I wonder if Sally Ann Schumacher—"

"If she saw Jimmy off from her front porch today," Alexis said, cutting Judy off.

Jimmy had told Judy all about Sally Ann Schumacher with the red bow in her beautiful hair, and Judy had passed Sally Ann's fame onto Alexis.

"She's Jimmy's good luck charm. Plus, she has an awfully big crush on him." Judy giggled.

"Who can blame her, Judy?" Pause. "I'm going to be Billy's good luck charm," Alexis said coquettishly.

"All the way to the state championship!"

The Purple Eagles had landed. They romped over their first opponent. The score was 73–17. Jimmy threw five touchdowns, and Billy rumbled for three. Jimmy threw for 402 yards (19–23), and Billy rushed for 318 yards on seventeen carries.

Jimmy and Billy looked fearsome out on the field. Each had grown bigger and stronger over the course of the summer. Each was determined not to get involved in preseason hype that had put them on the preseason national high school All-American team. No way would they allow themselves to get big heads. To be All-Americans, they had to play like ones. They'd agreed it'd be their philosophy for the new football season.

"Man, Jimmy, did the cheerleaders cheer today!"

"Didn't they?" Jimmy punched Billy's shoulder.

"Ouch, Jimmy! I told you about that, man!"

"Yeah, yeah, Steamroller. Yeah!"

"Jimmy … I wonder if it had anything to do with—"

"Our girlfriends being on the squad. Or everything to do with our girlfriends being on the squad."

"They did do a great job. The cheerleading squad, uh, did sound better."

"Yeah, Steamroller. They were a sparkle of beauty."

"Oh no. Don't tell me you're a poet now."

"No, just in love!"

And then Jimmy looked around the locker room. He couldn't believe what he'd just said, especially in the Purple Eagles' locker room.

"Wish, uh, want to say that a little louder, Jimmy—so everyone in the locker room can hear it?"

"Shhh," Jimmy said anxiously, downgrading his voice. "Man, Billy, I almost blew it big-time."

"Especially around these guys. They aren't going to understand."

"But you do," Jimmy said edgily. "You do, Billy."

Billy couldn't believe he and Jimmy were talking like this—that a subject like this had come up between them. Last year was history. This was this year. Alexis and Judy had come to Pittsfield. Out of nowhere. Like a bolt of lightning. And now here he was sounding like a forlorn poet.

"It … it's overwhelming, Jimmy. Simply overwhelming, man."

"It is, Billy," Jimmy echoed.

Billy sat down on the wooden bench. Jimmy joined him.

"We really got ourselves snagged."

"Jimmy, hey, don't say it like that. Not like that, man."

"Well, we did. Billy, I don't know what hit me. Our lives have changed."

"And for the better. *Alexis*. Wow, Jimmy. I'm a lucky man."

"She was going ape when you scored. Bananas. And you scored a lot today—so she had a lot to go bananas, ape about," Jimmy said. "And Judy, what about her?"

"You bet," Billy said, putting Jimmy in a playful headlock, then letting go. "She was going ape. Bananas for you too whenever you threw a touchdown. And you know how many times that happened. Do I have to count them for you?"

Both stood. Jimmy was taller than Billy by a good one and a half inches. Billy had teased him that his five uncles (Caseys) must've kicked their genes in all at once.

"Again, guys, great game!" Frank Bosco yelled into the locker room.

"Thanks, Coach!" the Purple Eagles yelled back.

"Even though, Mike," Frank said to Mike Overbranch, who was at his side, pretending as if the words were not to sail off beyond Mike's ears, "we're going to have to tighten up our defense."

"We don't want to give up seventeen points, Frank."

"Not to a team like Dear Run High School, Mike."

"Great game, Billy, Jimmy!"

"Thanks, Andy."

"Thanks."

It's all they'd been hearing since they left the football field, and on the bus to the mall, and in Patty's Pizza Parlor. Judy and Alexis felt like sunken ships out at sea; they were barely visible after today's game.

The four were sitting in one of Patty's glow-red leather booths.

"Did I put my makeup on crooked this morning?" Judy seemed to be talking to anyone who had a sympathetic enough ear to listen.

Billy had his arm locked around Alexis, and Jimmy had his locked around Judy. They looked as comfortable as old couches.

"It's how I feel, Judy. We might as well be buried away in a tomb for all it's worth. For all the attention you and I are getting around here. Maybe it is the makeup, like you said," Alexis said.

Billy chuckled. "Cheerleaders don't score touchdowns. Right, Jimmy?"

"How chauvinistic, Billy!" Alexis yelped.

"Yep—that's Steamroller Mack for you, Alexis. Chauvinistic to the bone."

"Oh, so you don't think that way, not like Billy, huh, Jimmy? Not for any reason, huh?" Judy asked.

"Be careful, Jimmy," Alexis warned him with shining eyes. "Because you're about to lose your best friend, I think."

"You tell him, Alexis," Billy chimed in.

Then they laughed.

"How do you do it, Billy?" Alexis asked, touching Billy's bulging muscles. "Shed those tacklers like that? They don't stand a chance."

"If we knew, Alexis, I guarantee you we would bottle it, put it on the market, and sell it. Right, Billy?"

"And the way you throw the football, Jimmy. At my old school, the quarterbacks didn't throw the football like you. Not any way near," Judy said, amazed.

"I'm just glad we won," Jimmy said.

"And that Coach Bosco was pleased with the team's performance," Billy added.

"It means a lot to you, doesn't it, Billy?" Judy asked.

"Judy, man, a whole lot," Billy said, drawing Alexis closer to him. "We love Coach Bosco. Probably from day one. Right, Jimmy?"

The four had nibbled at their pizzas even if they'd ordered a whole pie. They looked at the box with the four slices still in it.

"Looks like doggie bags for us," Jimmy said.

"Wrap it and carry it in a bag? No way. What, insult Patty's Pizza Parlor? Uh-uh," Billy said, his hand reaching for the pizza box, only to be converged on by three more hands with the same idea in mind.

"Not on your life, Jimmy!"

117

The four were at the proverbial fork in the road.

Billy hugged Judy. Jimmy hugged Alexis.

"You cheered great today, Judy."

"Thanks, Billy."

"You did too, Alexis."

"Thanks, Jimmy."

"Call you later, Alexis," Judy said, waving back to her.

"Okay, Judy."

"Steamroller, hey," Jimmy said over his shoulder, "you can call me anytime."

Billy laughed.

He and Alexis were holding hands.

"Bet you I know where those two are headed off to," Billy said.

"Cunningham Park."

"That's a huge park, Billy."

"Why, the biggest in the state. They've found a spot, a private spot no one knows about but them."

"Billy, not even you?"

"Not even me, Al." (Sometimes Billy would address Alexis as "Al." She liked it. Nobody before Billy had called her that.)

"So they go—"

"And get lost somewhere in there."

"But it's kind of chilly today for them to be spending time in the park, don't you think, Billy?"

"Hey, not when you're in love, Alexis." Billy paused. He, again, couldn't believe what he'd said.

"You know what you just said, Billy," Alexis said, looking up at him.

"Yes—I know. It's been said a lot today."

"They are in love, aren't they?"

"You can't miss it, Alexis."

"It's in their eyes, their voices. I mean everything." Alexis squeezed Billy's hand tighter.

"Do … do you think …"

Pause.

"That we're in love, Al?"

"Yes, I—it's what I was about to ask."

"They say love, true lovers never have to talk about things like love. It's what they say, Alexis."

"They—"

"Uh, of course they do." Pause.

"Coming in when we get back to my place?"

Billy was glad they got off the subject. Things were beginning to get a bit over his head.

"No, I'd better hit the books. Mr. Armory's giving us one of his crazy algebra exams Monday."

"Oh right. You told me."

"And I'm going to ace it. He's not going to hurt my grade point. I'm resolved for that not to happen."

"You tell him, Steamroller!"

"No, no—not you too, Alexis!" Billy said, putting her in a bear hug. They neared Alexis's house.

"Billy, I'm already going to hate for this day to end."

"It's been great. We won. The Purple Eagles won."

"It's first game of the year! Woo-we! Wow-wee wow!" Alexis cheered.

"It's going to be a great football season for us. The Purple Eagles."

"And think—just think, Billy—you and Jimmy are just sophomores."

"Yeah, Al. And you can bet Coach Bosco hasn't forgotten that either."

Alexis wanted to hop up on Billy's shoulders and kiss him to death. It was how she felt right then.

"Here we are, Al."

"I guess so," Alexis said, downcast.

"Now you're going to take the bloom off the day by sulking? And look at you. Pouting too?"

"That disagreeable Mr. Armory. He and his algebra class. His crazy exams."

"I love you, Al."

"You do, Billy?"

"Yes, yes—I do."

Billy kissed Alexis in front of her house.

The first time Billy kissed her, it didn't feel like she was white. It just felt good.

"I love you too, Billy."

119

"Next year, I won't have Mr. Armory to contend with."

"Why, I hope not," Alexis said, pouting.

"He doesn't teach geometry."

"Good," Alexis said.

The football season had peaked. The Purple Eagles were in full flight. The Eagles were devouring their competition with Jimmy calling the team's signals. The team had been marked for greatness. It was offering every indication it was a great football team. It was out to live up to its top billing.

Billy Steamroller Mack, at this early stage of his football career, was showing every sign that he could be the next Jim Brown: big, fast, powerful, durable—stubborn as a mule; refusing to be taken down at the initial point of contact, scratching out the last inch, that last breath out his body on the play. One sportswriter thought Jimmy and Billy must have come from the other side of the moon, a different solar system; and they might well have, if someone asked their opposition.

Susan and Connie were driving back from Roma, a local restaurant. They'd been out dining, something they tried to do at least once a month. If they missed a month, they'd try to do it twice the following month to compensate. Susan was driving on this occasion; Connie enjoyed being chauffeured.

"I guess the families are going to have to sit down and meet. I guess we'll be invited to the Prices' house for dinner sooner or later, Susan. That's my educated guess," Connie said with consternation.

"Is … that what's been bothering you, been on your mind all evening, Connie?"

"Yeah, I suppose so." Pause. "Jim and Marion, they had to do the dinner routine with the Collinses."

"And?"

"And …" Connie's voice went dead.

"Why are you letting things like this bother you? I don't get it."

"They're an interracial couple."

"Alexis is a lovely girl, Connie. A lovely young lady."

"Yes." Connie squirmed. "But I don't think like you. Not on this I don't. See, I think about what's in front of them. Down the road."

"An interracial couple."

"Yeah."

"You'll never get used to them, will you?" Susan glared at him, her eyes no longer on the road.

"No."

"Why not?"

"Because I don't want to."

Susan was at a loss. She didn't know what to say. For a second, she thought she was in the car sitting next to a racist. Some kind of bigot that had just popped up in the seat next to her.

"Do you like white people?"

Now Connie glared at her. "I work with them, don't I? Live among them, don't I? I just came from one of their restaurants, didn't I? Spent my money to eat their food, didn't I?"

"What's wrong, Connie? What has gotten into you?"

Connie shuffled his feet. "I'm tired. You hear me, Susan? Every day, lily-white faces. Everything belonging to them. Nothing belonging to us. I'm just tired, Sue. Sick and tired of this shit."

"But that's just in Pittsfield, Connie. Here."

"This is where we live, Susan. This is our home. Shit. We live here."

Susan took a deep breath. "I didn't know you felt like this, Connie. This way ..."

"I'm from Georgia, Sue. You know that. I want to think all of this integration business works, but does it?" His voice was less strident.

"What a broad question. You want me to answer you—"

"Did we raise Billy to date a white girl?"

Susan, of course, heard the question by Connie but couldn't answer it. She wasn't having a problem with any of this, what was happening to her son. They'd been over, she and Connie, the ground that dating a white girl, Alexis Price in particular, was a de facto kind of situation. It's how it had to work out for her son, for Billy in Pittsfield. To think differently would have been foolish and irrational.

Now Connie was back with another question.

"Is that progress? Is it how you determine, measure a black man's progress in America? By him dating a white woman? Is that a résumé for how far a black man's come?"

Susan felt the rest of the trip home in the car was going to be gloomy and heavy for her.

They were home. The black Buick Regal rolled slowly up the driveway. They parked in the middle of it. Billy's bedroom light burned.

"He's probably talking to that girl."

Susan had had enough of Connie. "That's enough, Connie. Stop making Alexis Price the enemy!"

"I'm not picking a fight with the girl."

"You are. You are, and I don't like it. It's going to start showing, exposing itself in your relationship with Billy if you don't watch it. If you're not careful."

"Now what are you, a psychiatrist? What, climbing into people's heads now?"

Susan unstrapped her seat belt. "You don't think Billy's going to feel how you feel toward Alexis sooner or later? Billy's smart, perceptive—"

"Hell, I know that. I know my son. You don't have to tell me about him. Shit no."

"I thought I knew you."

"And what's that to mean?"

"I'm disappointed." Susan got out of the car.

Connie stayed in the car.

Susan drew her house keys, opened the front door, and walked into the house. She'd turned on the lights and was making her way up the staircase when Billy's door burst open.

"How'd it go, Mom?"

"Your father and I just went out to dinner at Roma's. Nothing more fancy or extravagant." She laughed.

Billy leaned against the door frame and folded his arms.

"I know, but you know how I get, even though it happens every month—you and Dad going out to dinner. It's like you're newlyweds or … or like you're going out on an actual date."

Susan smiled but knew it was forced.

"Where is Dad by the way?"

"Oh … he's still in the car. I guess. He …"

"He's got a brainstorm. Another one of his brainstorms. I know what that means when he gets one. Genius at work," Billy said, unfolding his arms and painting a picture with his hands.

"Yes, Billy. Genius at work."

There is a grown look to Billy tonight, Susan thought.

"Well, I'm turning in. Just got off the phone with Jimmy."

See, Connie! It wasn't Alexis!

"He's doing the same. We're still in training, Mom," Billy joked.

"Steamroller needs his nightly sleep, after all."

"Now you're beginning to sound like Jimmy, Mom. Good night."

Susan moved down the hallway. She flicked on the room lights. Connie was still in the car parked in the driveway. He would probably sit there until Billy's room light went out, she thought. They'd been married seventeen years, but how well do you know a person? Did he really dislike white people? When did it happen? Or was it there all along, only his humor and ambition were large enough, like some dark part, to hide it?

She'd never had to think the way she was thinking now, not since she and Connie had married. Connie was having regrets. Both were forty years of age, and Connie was having regrets about his life. The what-ifs could kill you.

Susan began removing her clothing. *But what if this relationship between Alexis and Billy should go all the way? Marriage. Children. Grandchildren. Connie. Connie.* What had Connie started?

She felt bewildered. She had a black girlfriend when she grew up in Washington, DC. She had black friends when she grew up in Washington, DC. There was a sea of black faces in Washington, DC—like they rose out of the Potomac. She didn't have trouble with her identity then or now. But what was happening to Connie? Why was this happening to him? When did this happen to him?

Susan walked over to the back window of the room and looked out. From there, she couldn't see the side of the house where the car was parked. There'd been no inkling whatsoever of this struggle Connie was involved in with himself. Living in a world he'd made accessible to himself. In a world that she felt was home, a world she felt secure and comfortable in and with.

But suddenly Connie felt trapped in it. It's the impression she was getting. And when you feel trapped by something, first you feel frustrated, overmatched, set upon—and then you feel there's no possible, plausible escape from it.

But to infect Billy and Alexis with it would be wrong, out of the question. They weren't responsible to Connie Mack, a black man who was suddenly having second thoughts about his life—where it'd taken him and what he'd done with it up till now.

Alexis and Billy were innocent actors in this. They could only move through their lives one step at a time like everybody else. What had gone wrong with Connie? What was Billy and Alexis's relationship spurring in him? He said Billy and Alexis were an interracial couple as though the relationship had been condemned from the start, already consigned to the most evil assignments of hate and intolerance and abuse.

Susan stepped away from the window.

It's how it came off. How it sounded to her. What could she do? What was her role in this now, or had Connie emptied it out of himself? Did it have to breathe, be heard to be mitigated?

"Oh, how I wish. How I wish it were so," Susan said, taking her night wear out of her bureau drawer. Then her heart raced. "But what if this is only the beginning—the beginning, only the beginning of something?"

Susan raced her night clothing over her body.

In a matter of seconds, she was in bed, under the covers. She was aware anyone's mind can paint the worst kind of scenarios, given the chance. But she had to have faith in Connie, that he would pull himself out of this struggle and do what was right for Billy, for his future. Susan shut her eyes, hoping that was true. Hoping Billy would always come first in her and Connie's minds. Not them. Not the adults. Not them with their pettiness, the things they no longer thought necessary for them to explain to others with any clarity or clearheadedness.

Connie was at the door. And then the door opened. Susan could feel his bearish presence without seeing him.

There was a silence sharp enough to cut them, drive deep down into their bare flesh.

"I'm going to get a jump on them. Beat them to the punch. It's what I'm going to do. I'm going to get a jump on the Prices. Shit, Susan." Pause. "I thought about it long and hard in the car," Connie said, his fingers quickly unbuttoning his shirt collar and then speeding through the rest of the shirt's buttons.

"They're not going to get the upper hand, not this time. Shit no. Shit no. We're inviting them to dinner. We're going to invite that girl and her family over. We're going to get the jump on them, all right. They're going to have to come to our house. Our home, Susan."

And then Connie laughed, stripping himself of his dress shirt.

"See how black folk live in Pittsfield. Shit, yeah. Shit yeah." Pause. "Probably never have been, stepped foot in a black person's house in their lives. See how black people live. Well, they're going to step into ours, Susan. If they want to or not. They probably only know blacks through Huxtable reruns. Ha, ha. Television. Ha, ha. Bill Cosby. Phylicia Rashaad. It's going to be fun, Susan. Just to see their eyes. Their faces, yeah. Ha, ha. Put them on the spot, under the gun for a change, Sue. See how they feel."

And from Susan's perspective, what Connie was doing seemed like the beginning of something that was making no sense at all.

It was days later.

"There're here, Susan. I'll get the door."

Susan stepped out of the kitchen in her flowery patterned apron. Billy came crashing down the stairs.

Connie flung the door open.

"Hello, Mr. Mack."

"Hello, Alexis."

"My parents, Mr. Mack," Alexis said, turning to her parents.

"Come in. Why, come in, folks. Nice to see you," Connie said.

Once in the house, the greetings continued.

"And this is my lovely wife, Susan."

Susan shook Maxine's hand, then Sylvan's.

Billy hugged Alexis as both parents looked on.

"Let me take you good folks' coats. And I see you're wearing a hat, Mrs. Price. A lovely hat at that, I might add. Very attractive."

"You can all me Maxine, uh—"

"Connie."

"Connie," Maxine said.

Connie removed Maxine's coat and hung it in the hall closet.

"And I'll take yours, uh—"

"Sylvan, Connie. Sylvan."

"Sylvan."

Connie stood behind Sylvan, looming over him as if deliberately.

Billy took Alexis's coat too.

Susan and Maxine were chatting.

Sylvan looked around the house with perked interest. "What a beautiful home you have," he said, his eyes turning slowly from mark to mark.

"It's how the Macks live, Sylvan. Live in Pittsfield, USA."

"You know I'm a Realtor," Sylvan said.

"The house isn't for sale. Right, Sue?" Connie laughed, looking at Susan.

"Not for the right price?"

"Price," Connie quipped.

"Sylvan Price. Why, he always gives you the right price!"

The Macks and Prices laughed before Susan ushered them into the dining room.

Alexis had lingered a bit before joining her parents in the car. She and Billy were on the front porch, looking at each other as if the other had rainbows in their eyes.

Alexis ran her hand vertically across the front of Billy's shirt not once but twice.

"You'd better get back in the house, Billy, before you catch a cold. Uh, pneumonia," Alexis said, unconvincingly.

"Not with you standing this close to me, I won't."

"They're waiting, my parents."

"I know."

"Good night, Billy."

"I don't want you to go, Al."

"I don't want to go." Pause. "Good night, Billy."

"Is that it?"

"No."

Billy and Alexis kissed.

"Is that better?" Alexis said.

"Oh, a whole lot better," Billy said.

"Good night, Billy."

"Good night."

Billy watched Alexis walk away, this beautiful creature. This angel.

Then she turned. "It was great. The dinner. I had a wonderful time. So did my parents."

"Me too. My parents too," Billy said as he watched Alexis get into her parents' two-toned station wagon.

Billy felt deflated but soon bounced back up on the balls of his feet and shot back into the house like the All-American fullback football experts said he was.

The first place he headed for was the kitchen, where he saw Connie and Susan doing heavy-duty labor (Susan washing the dishes, and Connie was drying them).

"I want to thank you two big-time," Billy said, rushing to them, then hugging them. "Big-time. It was great. Alexis said it was. So it was!"

"It was, Billy."

Connie said nothing; he just enjoyed the hug from Billy.

"It was a great idea," Billy said, releasing them. "You just don't know how much it meant to me, Mom and Dad. Have no idea."

"It was our pleasure, Billy," Susan said, wiping her hands on the dish towel Connie had handed her.

"They're such nice people, Maxine and Sylvan Price. And I got to know Alexis better—whenever she wasn't under your spell."

Connie subtly pushed himself into the background.

"I monopolized Alexis that much?"

"That much." Susan laughed, shaking her head repeatedly. "She's a beautiful young lady, honey."

"That she is, Mom."

"Well … I guess you're about to call Jimmy."

"How'd you guess?"

Susan smiled.

"Have to let Jimmy know my little family gathering with the Prices topped his with the Collinses."

"Billy, now how in the world is that determined?"

"Oh, there are ways, Mom." Pause. "By the way, Dad, is it okay if I go on the computer?"

"Billy, oh, sure, sure thing," Connie said from the kitchen table, where he was sitting.

"Talk to Jimmy for a hot minute, then get on the computer. It tends to relax, uh, calm me down."

"Get out of here, Billy. Teenagers!" Susan laughed.

Susan went back to washing the dishes. Soon, she looked back over her shoulder to Connie.

"Hey, where's my help? Did it go? What happened to my helper, my automatic, built-in dish dryer?"

Connie stood. He walked over to her. Susan handed the damp dish towel back to him.

"Oh, here you are." Susan raised her head to kiss Connie's cheek, but he withdrew it.

"Did I behave okay, Susan? Up to your expectations?"

Susan's body reflexed.

"Was I white enough tonight?"

"White enough?"

"You know what I mean, Sue. White enough. You know. Did I dot my i's and cross my t's and get everything in between just right?" Pause.

"You know, we should've served up that girl, those people, her family, some real down-home cooking, Sue. Yeah—that's what we should've done. Some collard greens. Ham hocks and collard greens," Connie said, his voice gaining momentum.

"They wouldn't've known what hit them. They could see how *real* black folk eat, Sue. We really do eat!"

When was the last time she'd eaten ham hocks? Collard greens, yes, but ham hocks? "Real black people." Was she a "real black person"? Because she didn't eat ham hocks. Collard greens but not ham hocks.

Connie was lying next to her in bed. He was asleep. He was relaxed; that was how she could tell he was asleep. He was a big man who was gentle while sleeping.

Why am I letting him get away with the things he's saying? So much? Susan questioned herself. *Why don't I challenge him? Is it the fear of argument? Every couple argues. Every married couple has its disagreements, its ups and downs. Rough spots. We're no different than any other married couple.*

Susan had moved her body with discomfit.

"Sue … Sue," Connie mumbled groggily and then turned over on his other side.

Susan looked at his outline in the dark. She had to think through all of this again. *How much does Connie need me? How much?*

This thing swept up on her from nowhere, unannounced, abruptly. It was vigorous. Powerful like Connie. Powerful like Billy when he ran the football.

Connie is a pretender, no better than them. Insincere. No better than them. Is this how the black man began paying the white man back, by being as deceitful, as insincere, and as dishonest? I have to think this thing through, don't I? I have to bring it into some kind of context. I want to help Connie. It's my duty to help him. White, black—what does it all mean?

Washington, DC, seemed so far away. It was a place where Susan saw black faces coming out their houses, walking the streets every day. In the summer, there was that something in the air, like an Irish neighborhood or an Italian one—the power of a culture coming out of their stoves. It was present for the day.

Pittsfield didn't have that. It had its beautiful homes arranged beautifully, in beautiful detail. There was a blankness to Pittsfield, a blandness, a homogeneity. Many of the neighborhoods looked alike and pervasively empty. There were Italians in Pittsfield and Jews, Irish, and Asians but mixed together as one, not an ethnic enclave of identification. What had they given up, sacrificed in Pittsfield for a Pittsfield?

Was this what was at the center of Connie's sudden rebellion? Was the price they had to pay for what they had too much? Had all those neighborhoods somehow gotten lost?

The Prices were so nice, Susan thought. Maxine and Sylvan Price. And Alexis, she was a knockout of a girl. When she and Judy Collins did their cheerleading for the Purple Eagles, she noticed; both stood out. They were the brightest, the peppiest—the loudest of the lot. Jimmy and Billy were lucky.

But Jimmy and Judy had smooth sailing ahead. It was only Billy and Alexis she worried about. But not from Maxine and Sylvan Price who, honestly, she thought would be the problem but seemed perfectly at ease with their daughter dating someone, a boy who was black. It was Connie, her husband, the person a month ago she'd never have suspected to be the problem, to cause any trouble, not in Pittsfield—not in the way she'd just described it.

Blast Aircraft Company took up three and a half acres and looked like it could take up another three and a half acres, without a sweat. Architecturally speaking, it was twentieth-century modern. Blast wanted the office building to look ultramodern, cutting edge, up-to-the-last-minute hip, like it could jet away before your very eyes at any time, any second—and so it did look that way in every physical and spiritual aspect.

There were benches for sitting practically everywhere. And trees aplenty. In the summer, it was great for the staff who hung out in this comfortable, ergonomically configured space. Most of the 448 employees thought it an ideal workplace, shimmering with exceptional enthusiasm and brilliant talent.

"Connie, have you heard about the new project they're scrubbing up for sail? Senior management?"

"No, I haven't," Connie said to Ben Cleghorne III, another concept/design engineer. He'd entered Connie's roomy cubicle.

"High-powered stuff they're discussing."

"Ron Jones must be in on the mix, then," Connie said, without losing concentration at the computer.

Ben Cleghorne III took a closer look at the image on Connie's computer. "Looks great, uh, whatever the hell it is."

"Yeah." Connie grimaced weakly. "As usual, Ben."

"You don't like the guy, do you?"

"Who?"

"Jones, Ron Jones."

"No."

"You don't have to be so damned loquacious." Ben's eyes left the computer screen. "Connie, have you seen the new dame down in graphics?"

Connie's head did the obligatory nod.

"What a pair she's got. Knockers on her. Soft as pillows, I bet," Ben said, pretending he was squeezing them and not the air.

"I recall you and Jones had a big stink. Were at loggerheads on the last big project you did."

"Yeah, Ron Jones doesn't like blacks."

"Oh, come on, Connie. You won in the end, didn't you? Your design."

"Right, in the end."

"Hey, what's with you today anyway?" Ben said, studying Connie through his horn-rimmed glasses. "Since when did you start talking like that? I thought it was the design Jones didn't like, not blacks."

Connie swiveled around in his chair to Ben. "Say what you want. I saw how the guy looked at me in those freaking meetings when things got tough, hot, heated. I know that look."

Connie stood. "It's in a person's voice, his eyes," Connie said.

"We're okay, aren't we, Connie? You and me, aren't we?"

"Yeah, Ben. Yeah, we're okay." Pause. "Fine."

Except there was a coldness in how Connie said it, sitting down in the chair, looking back at the computer.

Ben began walking out the cubicle, then stopped. "Connie, really, I am surprised by what you said before." Ben's hair was balding; it was patchy in spots.

Connie's fingers pressed down harder on the computer keys.

"After all these years."

Connie's face became more intense.

"I never had any inkling of you thinking that way."

"What are you trying to start, Ben?" Connie said, turning to this man who was a few inches taller than he was but no way close to his thickness. "I don't have any friends here. I work here. You can understand that. Get that through your brain, can't you?"

"But, Connie, I thought we—"

"Have you ever invited me to your house or out to your summer home, Ben?"

"Connie …"

"Hell no."

"But it's not fair. Tell me that's fair, Connie," Ben said, backing away from Connie, "when I haven't invited—I don't socialize with any of the guys on the job. White or otherwise. You know that. You know how private I am about my life."

"But would you, Ben? Would you?"

"Connie, I won't stand here and allow you to attack me or think I have to defend myself because of what you think. I won't. Not like this. Uh-uh, man, not for nothing I've—"

"Man, man! Black folk say man, don't they, Ben? So it's okay to say it with me. But if I were white. Stereotypical, huh? Stereotypical, isn't it, Ben?"

"What, huh—I … I … Why, why are you picking on me, Connie? Picking on … on everything I say. I haven't done anything to you. Nothing. Ron Jones, you said it was Ron Jones. But now it's me. I came in here, in your cubicle, Connie. Figured you'd want to know about the new project coming down the pike. That it would probably be your baby, that they would, the company would probably drop it in your lap. Tell you to run with it. The top guy, the top concept design/engineer in the com—"

"Why you, Ben? Why do you know about it, the project and not me? Why you and not me, man. Man. Man!"

Ben Cleghorne stepped farther back from Connie. His face was in ruins.

"I don't—"

"It's not your fight. Right, Ben? Right, man!"

"I don't know what—"

"Know what, man? What!"

Ben thrust his hands in his pockets. His head lowered, he looked dejected.

"It's nobody's fight, Ben. Nobody wants to take it on, man. It, it's nobody's fight …"

Ben thought maybe he was watching Connie Mack break down right before his eyes in the cubicle, in front of his computer—a nervous breakdown.

"No, no—Ben … it's nobody's fight …"

Connie was in his Buick. He slammed the car door. He was steamed. He was about to start the car, about to slam his foot down on the accelerator pedal, when his eyes just looked at the car keys in his hands and he laid his head back on the car seat's headrest. He was having some difficulty breathing and could feel his blood barreling through him. Especially his temples, as if his head had stored too much blood in it before and it had to find an outlet.

What kind of world have I created for Billy? Connie asked himself for the hundredth time. *What kind of world have Susan and I created for him? Where does Billy belong? Where's Billy's identity? His best friend is white. His girlfriend is white.*

Right then, behind the wheel of the car, Connie wanted to shut out the world. Tell it to go to hell.

Who are my friends? What friends do I have in Pittsfield? I've lived in Pittsfield for fifteen years. Who are my friends? Who can I call a friend—a true blue friend?

"Who the hell are they?"

Connie's chest caved in.

I have none. I have Susan and Billy, my family. I have my family in Pittsfield.

"John Smalls and Sidney Williams, they don't live in Macon anymore. They left Macon too. John's in Los Angeles, and Sid, I don't know for the life of me where Sid is. They were my friends, best friends, John and Sid. The guys I grew up with. Who … who …"

When was the last time I communicated with them? Connie thought. *John, I know where he is. Honestly, I don't know where Sidney is. I—isn't that nutty, crazy? I don't know for the life of me, for the life of me.*

What did he and Susan know of summerhouses, retreats, a pied-à-terre, places to get away to for relaxation, to kill the week's stress from the job on the weekend? The guys on the job talked this way all the time, of going off to their weekend retreats. It was their lifestyle, what they knew and had seen, what their parents did—how they'd lived.

What if Billy left Pittsfield? What if? And say he lived among black people, people of his own kind, Connie thought. *How would he fit in?* How would Billy fit in with his own kind, his own race, black brothers and sisters, when Billy, his son, was white? When Billy Mack, no matter his and Susan's good, honorable intentions, his skin coloring was white.

"Susan and I gave Billy all of the right things: Jackie Robinson, Jim Brown. But we made him white. Billy, he … he could only live among white people, not his own."

Just saying it scared Connie.

"People Billy thinks he knows. Who Billy thinks know him."

But Connie knew what would happen to Billy outside the walls of Pittsfield, in a world he and Susan had not created for him. A world he now was feeling was all wrong for Billy, for anyone who was black. A world without the Boston family, or the Price family, or Coach Bosco to protect him. Even he and Susan had been tricked into forgetting what the world was like, how close to the skin it can feel when a Ron Jones could remind him in one of his heated meetings who he was, as if he knew the secrets of his own self-deception too, in whittling him down to nothing, a putrid state of being.

A world that could turn on someone like him on a dime—without warning.

Connie pulled the car out of Blast's employee lot. Connie Mack was a troubled man.

Maria could have gone to school to tell Frank. She'd thought about it, for sure. But then she ditched the idea; it would be much more fun doing it the way she'd planned.

She was in her workroom. Frank would be entering the house at any minute. He'd sneak up behind her, per routine. She'd pretend she was so engrossed in her work that she didn't hear him, not a whisper of him, steal his way across the room's thick, carpeted floor.

Maria stared at the material. She had a deadline to meet. Mrs. Ruth Chesterfield of the Chesterfields of Pittsfield wanted her dress on her back as of yesterday. She was under the gun (silent as it was).

Maria laughed to herself. "Pu-lease!" she said with oomph.

But now here Frank was, on time. His timing could not have been better.

She had the sewing machine going full steam. *The stage was set. Frank mustn't be too far away,* Maria thought. *A few more footsteps more at most. Prepare yourself, Maria. Prepare yourself—okay!*

"Frank!" Maria jumped.

"One day you'll catch on!" Frank said, his hands covering her eyes. "One of—"

"Frank, I'm pregnant!"

Frank's hands flew out away from Maria's eyes like a flock of birds.

"You're mama mia! Forgive me, Maria, but mama mia!"

When she stood, Frank grabbed her.

"Careful. Careful! I've got to be extra careful with you now, Maria!"

"Frank, not yet. I'm not in a delicate way. Not the first month. It's only the first month."

Frank kissed her. He stood back from her. He patted her stomach.

Maria was amused. "Frank, you can't tell anything. That'll take more time too."

"Mama mia!"

Pause.

"Dr. Jacoby—"

"Told me this afternoon. I—"

"And so how did you react? I mean ..."

"Mama mia! Of course, I said it to myself, not Dr. Jacoby!"

He held her in his arms. "You're a sneak though. A real sneak. That much I know."

"For someone who sneaks up behind me practically every day, at least when I'm at the sewing machine, you have the nerve to call me a sneak?"

Frank pulled away from Maria a second time. "So what do we do now?"

"Wait. Nine months is nine months after all, Frank."

"Can't speed it up, huh? I mean our son …" Frank looked embarrassed. "Oh, that kind of slipped out."

"Yeah, I bet it did."

Frank stumbled over to the couch as if drunk.

"Not going upstairs, Mr. Bosco?" Maria asked, sitting down in the chair in front of the sewing machine like an expectant mother.

Frank was on the couch with his legs stretched all the way out, looking as proud as any man whose wife has just told him a baby was due in nine months.

"But aren't you going to go upstairs to run over your playbook, uh, while I do Mrs. Ruth Chesterfield's evening dress?"

"Nope." Frank folded his arms. "I'm going to sit right here and stare at my wife for the rest of the night. How's about that?"

"Well, if that's the way you want it, Frank," Maria said, gathering Mrs. Chesterfield's material.

"It's the way I want it."

"Mama mia!" Maria said.

CHAPTER 11

The Purple Eagles had won the state championship game under the outstanding leadership of Coach Frank Bosco. It certainly didn't hurt any that Billy Steamroller Mack ran for three touchdowns, and Jimmy Boston had thrown for four more during their title romp over Brand High (the state defending champs), 49–6. It was sweet revenge for the Purple Eagles, especially after losing a squeaker to them the previous year.

Now it was the beginning of a new football campaign for the Eagles. The new season was to begin in a few weeks. Needless to say, the Purple Eagles were predicted to soar high and mighty once again. Jimmy and Billy were first-team high school All-Americans last year and picked to repeat. They were thought to be the best football players in the nation. There could be no more important awards heaped on them, not until they reached the next level, college.

Cunningham Park was many acres of land, trees, and lovely wildflowers that made the lowland of Pittsburgh sing a song of nature not just through birds perched on thin and fat branches, chirping throatily as if they were a paid symphony, but through Cunningham Park devotees who spoke proudly of the park's charm and literal seductiveness.

It was a park replete with white pines and marvelous pathways that snaked though it from the south end to the north end. Official park statistics noted that the park had at least three and a half miles of visible and hidden trails. It also had loop trails, lakes, and ponds. It was a nineteenth-century park. It had age and history and reputation, something making memory-conscious Pittsfield residents' chests visibly stick out. Cunningham Park served the Pittsfield community well in that it was well funded by a Pittsfield historical foundation whose written mission was that of the park's lifetime protection, restoration, preservation, and dedication.

The sun was aglow. It was as if it had dropped down in the sky. It was a low sun, about as hot as if a person were standing under a giant microscope. But from where Jimmy and Judy sat in Cunningham Park, the shade was refreshing.

"This is going to be a late summer, looks like, Jimmy."

"It won't bother me, not at all," Jimmy said. Judy's head was back on his shoulder as he held her from behind. They were sitting on a blanket they'd spread on the ground.

Judy and Jimmy were in their secret location in Cunningham Park. It was a spot only they knew, not Billy or Alexis, not even their parents.

"If you play your first game in eighty-degree weather, it won't surprise me."

Jimmy kissed Judy's cheek. "All the guys are itching for the new season to begin. They can't wait to get in—"

"Especially Coach Bosco, I would suspect, Jimmy."

Jimmy shook his head painfully. "The baby, you mean, don't you?"

"Yes. Mrs. Bosco's miscarriage."

"Man …" Jimmy's hand slapped the ground hard. "It still hurts to think of it."

"I know," Judy said. "She, Mrs. Bosco, she's really a great person."

"She found a way to pick his spirits back up." Pause. "Man, Judy, you can really feel the love Coach has for her."

Judy nodded.

"They'll try again. Don't worry. Coach all but implied it without being too personal about it."

"Right. Maybe there'll be a day when our son might be coached by Coach Bosco's son. Who knows, Jim—"

"Wait, Judy. Who said I was going to come back home to Pittsfield when I graduate college?"

Judy twisted her head around to him again. "I just assumed one day you would, Jimmy. After college and all."

Pause.

"I don't know. There's a big world out there to conquer."

"Yes."

"We can be a part of it, you know."

"Yes, but I thought—"

"Billy and I have talked it over, Judy. Lately, we've been really getting into discussions about our future. We're definitely going to the same college. That hasn't changed since grade school."

"And what about Alexis and me?"

"You know you two are ... are definitely going to follow us. Tag along. Be our shadows."

"That sure, are you?"

"Yep."

"We certainly are, and no one's going to stop us. Not a soul!"

Pause.

"Jimmy, your dad—how does he feel about you leaving the nest?"

"Dad." Jimmy laughed. "He'll get over it."

"I guess so, knowing Mr. Boston. What a cheerful man."

"Oh," Jimmy said, snapping his fingers. "I forgot to tell you."

"What?"

"The date. Billy and I figured we'd take you and Alexis, our girls, out to a fancy restaurant, not the Rockwell Mall. Not on this date."

"Who's paying?"

"Why, Billy, of course. He' going to talk his dad into giving him extra on his weekly allowance. At least as of yesterday, even though you know Steamroller and his weekly allowance."

"So it's going to be a step up from the standard fare." Judy laughed.

"No fries and burgers for you and Alexis, Judy. Our girls," Jimmy said like he was his father selling life insurance to a prospective customer. "Billy and I have matured a lot. Have we!"

Billy didn't know how to put this personal problem of his to Alexis, but he had to speak to someone who wasn't as close to his parents as Jimmy. Someone who wouldn't be as emotionally invested in them as Jimmy and could look at them objectively, as if they weren't the most perfect people on earth, without warts.

They were on Alexis's back porch. Actually, it was a deck. It was a little past seven. It wasn't a school night; it was a Friday night. The Prices had gone out. Alexis and Billy were alone. Billy was holding her close to him—his arms wrapped snugly around her, his lips on her neck and then her ear.

"Billy, stop. You know how that tickles," Alexis screeched.

"I know!"

"So why do you do it?"

Billy kissed her ear again.

"Oh … Billy!"

"For that reaction from you."

"Billy, I love you so much."

"I love you too, Alexis."

With a night sky so clear, someone could write their name across it in bold, giant white letters. Billy and Alexis looked into it, imagining things not there.

Billy began holding Alexis more intensely, something he hadn't realized.

"Billy, what are you trying to do, squeeze me to death?"

"Sorry, Alexis, I'm sorry," Billy said, embarrassed. He realized how his feelings had suddenly manifested. "There's really something that's bothering me …"

"It's not us? It has nothing to do with our relationship, does it, Billy?" Alexis said, anxiously grabbing Billy's hand.

"Not us, Alexis, but my parents." Billy's face was pained. "They're arguing, Alexis. Arguing a lot lately."

Alexis didn't expect Billy to hand her this kind of information.

"Over what?"

"Little things, it seems. Maybe they're bigger issues. I don't know. I have no idea what's going on between them." Pause. "Dad, the company didn't assign him the prized project he was banking on."

"I, yes, I remember you telling me that, Billy," Alexis said, rubbing Billy's hand.

"With him being the top guy, he always got the company's top project. But not this time. It hurt him a lot."

Billy put his hand on top of Alexis's. "The arguments ... man, Alexis. They began after that. My parents never argued. I mean, they've disagreed on things, sure. Don't get me wrong. But—"

"These arguments, they sound serious."

Billy was pleased by Alexis's quick and dead-on analysis.

"Yes. I'm glad you can see that too."

Alexis sighed. "I'm sure my parents argue."

"All parents do; it's only human. They have to."

"Yes, Billy, but your parents' arguing is at a stage where you feel ..."

"Helpless. Completely. Totally."

Alexis could feel the muscles in Billy's body weaken.

"There's nothing you can do? Nothing you can say to them, maybe, to better things between them?"

Billy's eyes shut. "It's like I'm taking the attitude they have to work it out, Al." He opened his eyes. "Like they've always done before on their own."

"So you feel confident that they can?" Alexis's face, its delicate beauty, radiated optimism. "Really can?"

"You're, yes, absolutely."

"But it is hurting you."

"Uh-huh. So why pretend it's not? Seeing them argue."

"But maybe if you tell them, Billy ... how disgusted you are about it ..."

"I've thought about it. I have, Al. Doing just that. But I either keep my door shut, pretend I'm studying—you know, when it begins, it flares up—or I walk away. Remove myself from it."

Alexis's voice sunk in her throat. "What did Jimmy say? His advice to you?"

She caressed his forehead.

"I haven't spoken to Jimmy about it. You would have thought I would by now, but I haven't."

This made Alexis feel good, not that she was competing with Jimmy for Billy or anything like that.

"I just don't think Jimmy would understand the seriousness of it. Not this, at least."

"I think it would be like Jimmy probably feels in a way," Alexis said, her forehead wrinkling. "They're his parents too."

"Oh, you're so smart," Billy said brightly. "Right. Jimmy, it would be too much of a shock for him. And then he would try to play it down, low-key it, minimize it if he could. Jimmy's too close to the situation to be objective. That I figured out on my own."

"Do you think your parents will straighten this thing out eventually?"

"Man, if I only knew, Al. If only …"

"Let's say they will. Okay, Billy? They love each other. That's something you can rely on, right? Right? They love each other," Alexis said as if it was the answer, the key to everything.

"That much I'm certain of," Billy said.

"They have to realize it too, don't you think?"

"I just hope what I feel for you, what we have, Alexis, never goes away."

"Me too," Alexis said.

"No matter what happens between us, Al. No matter."

Susan was in the bathroom, afraid to go back into the bedroom. *What are we becoming? What are me and Connie becoming? What are we doing to ourselves?* These steady rounds of arguments. This steady diet, regimen. It was always him, Connie, starting it. She tried backing down, but he wouldn't let her; it only made him more aggressive, more challenging and attacking. He wouldn't settle for peace, for some quiet, easy exit from his rantings and ravings. He wanted to be confrontational, in your face; this was his modus operandi, what he was after, and she'd fallen into his trap. She'd become good bait for him.

It was taking its toll on her. The arguing, Connie's rage, it was wearing her down. Two nights ago, they'd argued. And even today, while it was calm, she could feel something brewing in him. It had reached the point with them when she could feel the tiny tremors in him about to go off.

Connie was ruling over her, and she didn't like it. The marriage was beginning to feel unequal, out of balance, out of control. There were no magic buttons to push in order to stop it. In this age of push buttons and electronic gadgets, there was no magic button to make this thing that was occurring stop for her and Connie.

The bedroom light was on when Susan got in there. It was low, dim, as usual. Susan blinked, then felt him brooding as if he were transmitting messages to her. Already she felt trapped and cornered, with nowhere to go. She turned into the room.

He would let her move in the room freely like this. This Connie would allow her. For her to remove her robe or the other courtesies necessary in preparation for bed. This was the freedom he controlled by just letting it happen, Susan thought.

Now I have to get in bed with him. Lie down next to him.

The light. I almost forgot the light.

The room's light went off. Slowly the room settled into a dark, cave-like place.

She was afraid to shut her eyes; her nerves were so taut. She was turned away from Connie. Her body wasn't curled but straight, her feet reaching as far down in the bed as they could. She could feel the bed warming, circulating heat, some degree of density. She held on tightly to her senses, her nerves.

"Even Ben Cleghorne doesn't know about this. Ben Cleghorne."

Susan wasn't prepared not to answer Connie.

"Yeah, even Cleghorne doesn't know what I know about this baby, Sue. What's coming down the pike soon. Very soon."

Pause.

"The great Ben Cleghorne. Eyes and ears to everything that goes on in Blast. Even that white boy doesn't know. I'll be able to tell him something. The nigger boy, Sue. Oh boy. Oh boy."

"I wish you wouldn't say that, Connie. That word. Not that." She'd spoken up. She had to. "Not in this house. Our house, Connie."

"Where then? This is my house, isn't it? Isn't it, Sue!" Connie propped up on his elbows. "This is my house, isn't it!" Pause.

"Nigger boy, see. Nigger boy. It's what I am at Blast Aircrafts—a nigger boy!"

"Why do you persist at, want to talk like that? What makes you desire to talk like that?"

"You wait and see. Just wait. It won't go to me again. The project, Sue. New ... they've got plans. Do they ever. Blast. They'll skip right over me. Ron Jones will—like the cow over the moon. He'll make damned sure of that. Shit."

"What's wrong between you and Ron Jones, Connie, that I don't know—"

"Wrong. The woman says wrong, as if I have something to do with this. As if I'm in some way implicated in this in a ... some direct, overt way."

Susan was facing him.

"What are you doing? Taking sides?"

"No, no—I'm not, Connie. Why must you take my words and twist them any way you want to? Can't you try to be reasonable? Try to—"

"My job, about my job, my abilities, my talents? No, I won't. Not me. And nobody should ask me. Whenever there's a top prize, I want it. Connie Mack. I want it for myself. I worked hard to get to where I am—"

"I, yes, I know you have, honey. I—"

"And I'm not going to let anyone take it from me. Run over me. Shit no. Yield to them. Shit no. Shit no. Not at any cost, Sue. Do you hear me!"

"There's never compromise in you, is there, Connie?"

"And now you're finding that out?" Connie said bitingly. "Just seeing it, are you? The hidden me? After all these years of marriage. You don't like it, do you, Sue?"

Susan knew she was in a no-win situation. There was no victory here, just further frustration and verbal sniping.

"Well, that's me, Sue, 100 percent. Take it or leave it."

"Oh ... Connie, why are we fighting like this? Don't you see? Two nights ago, and then two nights before that, and ..."

"They're going to regret it though. Are they ever," Connie said, seething. "The last project cost them a bundle, a mint, I'm told. Came in way over budget. Didn't know their ass from their elbow without their nigger boy there to pull the strings. Keep their house in order. Get them to the finish line."

"Don't use that word, Connie. I hate it!"

"What ... nigger boy? Nigger boy, Sue?" Pause. "Shit. Don't you know that's what you are to them, Susan? No matter that they hire you or how many of those fancy parties or weddings you arrange for the rich folk of Pittsfield."

"I don't like this, Connie. How you're beginning to think, talk, act. I just don't like it. Not at all."

"Why? Because I'm no longer a monkey at the carnival? A lackey?"

"This is getting out of hand. Billy—"

"Billy should know."

"No. You leave Billy alone. You leave Billy, my son, out of this. Don't you dare go near him with this kind of talk. How you're—"

"Oh, one day Billy will feel like me, if he lives around whites long enough." Pause. "As long as I have. Lives and works around them. He'll feel like I do, like the blood's being choked out of me. Every day, every freaking—"

"Connie!" Susan cried.

"I feel for you, Susan," Connie said coolly. "I really do. You've been tricked, hoodwinked. You've bought into their lies. It's a hoax, Sue. A giant hoax. One freaking hoax after the other after the other."

Billy heard his father's large voice behind his bedroom door, and his mother's sobs. He didn't know what his father had said to her, but he wished his father hadn't. How he wished that he hadn't.

Word had been received by the company: Ben Cleghorne III was to head the concept/design team on the new Blast project. It was stapled to the company's bulletin board (the announcement) that morning.

Ben Cleghorne had never headed a design team. He'd never even been asked to; this was to be brand-new territory. When he saw his name on the bulletin board, it scared the living shit out of him. Ben actually thought it was a mistake—a big one. He didn't even know he was being considered as a candidate for the job. But at ten o'clock that morning, he would hold his first meeting with Ron Jones and his team on the new project. Ben was terrified.

It was 9:22.

"Good morning, Connie." Ben stood just outside Connie's cubicle.

"Congratulations, Ben," Connie said, not detaching his eyes from his computer.

"You, uh, you saw then, Connie? The bulletin board?"

"I did. You know they said it'd be posted today. The new project team and who's heading it. Congratulations."

"Look, Connie, I'm really sorry."

Connie turned around. There was generosity in him. "And for what, Ben? You don't make the decisions around here. You don't give the go sign; senior management does. It's their call."

"I ... I don't know, Connie. This is such a huge project. So much is riding on it."

Connie swung back around to the computer. "Ah, you'll do fine, Ben. Just fine, man."

Pause.

"It should've been you, Connie. Your damned project. I realize that. By all rights, account. Everybody in the company does. With so much at stake. So much of the company's money riding on it. You're the top man—the top talent in the company."

"Ron Jones made his choice, and we all have to live with it. I'm not going to cry over spilled milk. I'm bigger than that."

Connie looked up from his desk at Ben and wondered if he believed him.

"Are you sure, Connie? I mean, you're just not saying that, are—"

Connie turned to him, more sharply this time. "Ben, look, I told you before, didn't I? And this just confirms it, man. My worst fears. This is the handwriting on the wall. The smoking gun, if you will. Yeah, I'm the company's top dog. Yeah, the best man to head the project.

"Hell, Ben, everybody and their mother in the company know that, as you said. Something this big, vital—this meaningful to the company and its bottom line—and I'm left out in the cold? Now it's clear, obvious to everyone. Need I say more? Plain as paint."

"I don't know, Connie."

"What's there not to know and see, man?"

"Maybe it's just a clash of personalities."

"Don't be naive. Don't go there. Insult your intelligence. Something as big as this, where the company stands to lose so much dollarwise, and you don't have the best guy leading the pack." Pause.

"Come on. Don't get your signals crossed. I know what's going on with Jones, and what hurts so damned much is he's gotten away with it. The bastard in plain sight. Daylight."

Ben checked his watch. "I'd better get back to …"

"Yeah," Connie said, cutting Ben off, "you have a lot of work in store for you. A heap."

"Yes … yes, I know, Connie."

"Good luck. And congratulations. You're a good guy, Ben. Just do your best. The best work Ben Cleghorne can do. It's all you can ask of yourself."

"Thanks, Connie."

It was quitting time at Blast.

Connie was still at his desk. His spirit was down. All day long, he had felt his nerves wearing on him. He could have kicked himself for feeling that way when all along he knew how it would turn out. He wasn't going to head the new project. His name was never tossed in the hat, the ring. Ron Jones had made certain of that.

But it still hurt (as he'd told Ben this morning). It still hurt when he stood there this morning looking at the bulletin board and saw what was stapled there. To know he'd been skipped over, someone as valuable to the company as him. Damn if he hadn't felt like he could kill someone.

Connie looked at his desk phone. Should he or shouldn't he?

He picked up the phone.

"Sue. Hi, yeah … yeah … uh, hi."

He listened.

"Fine. Fine. Listen, I'm working late tonight, okay? … Yeah, something came up. I have the materials here, so there's no reason for me lugging them home. Listen, you and Billy eat without me. And listen, don't fix anything for me. I'll eat out … Right. Right, uh, and tell Billy I'll see him in the morning … Yes, I'll probably be that late. It'll take up that much of my time … And tell him I know he's going to have a great game tomorrow.

But of course I'll see him in the morning. Of … of course … Thanks. Thanks, Sue."

Connie hung up the phone. He looked at his hand on the phone as his eyes welled with tears. Then he stood up and went over and got his outer jacket off the coat and hat stand.

Connie was at Mitch's Sports Bar. It was on the outskirts of Pittsfield, on Falcon Road. It was roughly two miles from Blast Aircraft. It was a respectable place but accessible basically by car. Connie had frequented Mitch's Sports Bar before. They knew him there, though not as a regular. Connie was on his third bottle of beer.

"How many touchdowns is Billy Steamroller Mack going to score tomorrow against Citizens High School, Connie?" Chris Martin, a big, overweight Irishman with a friendly bowl of a face, asked Connie.

"How about four, Chris. No … that's a low estimate, a conservative count. Steamroller's going to score six. Make it six touchdowns tomorrow against Citizen."

Chris was bartending. He poured what was left of the third bottle of beer into Connie's glass.

"Thanks, Chris."

"Six …" Chris said, letting it roll around on his tongue.

"A cinch."

"And Jimmy Boston?"

"Six more. My boy Jimmy guarantees it."

"And Coach Bosco …"

"Coach of the year, again."

Connie was a beer drinker during his Brown University days. He'd chug a few with the college boys back then at the local bar, but since his college days, he drank an occasional beer at home just for relaxation. This included an occasional glass of wine, but that was more Susan's drink of choice.

It was a little over an hour later.

"How about one … one more for … for the road, Chis-Christopher, my good man?" Connie said, bleary-eyed.

"Connie, my good man." Chris laughed. "You're tanked. Hell, tanked to the gills."

"Never felt bet-better, Chris."

"It'll be beer number nine, Connie," Chris cautioned him.

"Been counting, huh?"

"Got your bar tab right here."

"How about, about for Billy Steamroller Mack and ... and Jimmy Bos-Boston's six touchdowns tomorrow. Celebrating that, Chris. "And oh ..." Connie said, covering his mouth capriciously. "Coach, Coach Bosco, uh, coach of the year, Chris!"

Susan was worried. It was well past eleven. Connie never stayed out this late. She'd expected another phone call from him, at least that, but hadn't gotten one. She was in the living room. She'd relayed the message from Connie to Billy, Connie wishing him a great game tomorrow. Before Billy retired to bed, he was worried about Connie too, but she allayed his concerns by telling him his dad said he'd be quite late, so not to worry.

"But where is he?" Susan said, looking at the hour and out the living room's bay window.

Susan knew what Connie was going through, so this added freight to her worry. He hadn't brought up the new project he'd spoken so strongly about a few weeks ago, so she didn't know its status—heads or tails of it. But it was something in the back of her mind, there on a daily basis. Connie was seeking the truth of something, the proof of it. It was what he was after.

She walked over to the stereo set on the far wall. Music, she thought, music might ease her worry. She turned on the radio.

"Miss Patti Page is coming up next on the dial with a smile—WPMC 92.3 radio on your FM."

Susan smiled. She liked Patti Page.

Susan turned. The lights were on the front of the house.

"Connie!"

Commercial announcements played on the radio.

Susan steadied herself, offering not to exhibit worry. She didn't want to be above this, but she did not want to be swallowed up by it either. She loved Connie—every last inch of him—no matter what they were going through together. She loved her husband.

He was at the door, opening it.

Susan ran to him.

"Hey, what's this?" Connie said. Susan was in his arms.

Suddenly, Susan was alarmed. She smelled Connie's breath and saw the unevenness in his balance. Her head drew back judgmentally.

"You've been drinking, Connie."

"Yeah, had a few beers at Mitch's Sports Bar. That's all. Why, nothing more."

"But I thought—"

"I had to tell you something, Sue," Connie said coolly.

"Something?"

"Now suppose, suppose I told you I was going to Mitch's Sports Bar out on the outskirts of town, Falcon Road. What would you have said? Tell me."

"But you told me you were working late. At Blast, Connie."

Connie walked past her. "I didn't ... didn't I just tell you I-I had to tell you something? Unless I'm hearing things. A second ago." Pause. "No, I'm not hearing things."

"You lied. You deliberately lied to me!"

"That's, hey, that's Patti Page singing, isn't it? Can't stand her. What, what, you can't get a little Aretha Franklin, Gladys Knight and the Pips, a little soul in Pittsfield, Susan, on the airwaves up here? What, they only let us niggers in Pittsfield? You and me, Sue. Think we're the only ones good enough to live here!"

What's happened now, Connie!

They hadn't argued in over a week. For a week, there'd been peace between them.

"I'm going to turn this damned thing off, Susan. Miss ... Miss Patti Page, she ain't no Aretha, baby!"

Connie turned off the radio.

"A girl from Washington, DC. From the capital, listenin' to some honkey chick. Ain't got no soul in—"

150

"What are you doing now, Connie? Self-parodying, mimicking—"

"I ain't mimicking nobody, Susan. Shit. Fuck. Tired of talking like whitey, dressing like—"

"What happened, Connie, at Blast Aircraft—to you today?"

Connie stared at Susan, then looked away. He saw that bulletin board with Ben Cleghorne's name.

"Please, Connie. You've got to tell me."

"I don't care to discuss it," Connie said, turning his back to her. "Forget about it."

"What must I forget about, Connie?"

"I didn't want it anyway."

Susan heard her inner self scream.

"Oh, Connie, I'm so—"

"Don't give me that pity crap, you hear me! Don't fucking dare!"

He was looking at her recklessly. "Look, I'm glad in a way glad it happened," Connie said casually. "You know, Susan, it confirms everything. Every suspicion I ever had. I was right," Connie said, smashing his fist into his palm. "Racism is alive and well at Blast Aircraft. It took a little time to pull the sheets off it. Fifteen years to get to me. To find the nigger."

Susan looked down at her hands.

"But did it show up like a good old loyal friend. Big and bold. Yeah, a black man's best friend, Sue." Pause. "They dress you up in tux and tails so you can be the fool at your own party. (Do the James Brown, baby!) Yeah, it's what white folk do to you, all right. And what a beautiful little party it is, until they … they take it, one day take it. Grab it, Sue. All of it away from you."

Connie had put it in the past tense, as if he knew something she did not.

Billy and Jimmy were at their lockers. Billy had football cleats yet to remove, and it was the same for Jimmy. Both sat bent over, untying their shoe strings.

"Jimmy, my dad, he's drinking," Billy said firmly.

"Mr. Mack?"

"Yes."

"Billy," Jimmy said, grabbing Billy's shoulder, "you've got to be kidding me."

"No. It's real, Jimmy."

"I ... man, but why, Billy?"

"It's his job. I just know it," Billy said sympathetically.

"His job? Blast Aircraft? But he's their top engineer. He gets the top jobs, projects, always, right?"

"It's just worrying me, Jimmy. I haven't seen Dad in front of the computer lately, working out designs and problems. Or talking about a new project in, in months."

"Because maybe there aren't any. Maybe it's that simple."

Billy shook his head, countering Jimmy. "Uh-uh. No, I'm not buying into that. There's always something new and exciting going on at Blast. My dad loves his job. Loves working there too much."

"Yeah, you're right, Billy. Yeah." Pause. "Drinking ..." Jimmy said to no one.

Billy stood, ducking his head into his locker. "My parents, they're arguing. I mean a lot, Jimmy."

In Billy's ears, the locker sounded like an echo chamber, even if the football gear muffled most of the sound.

"No, they can't be, not Mr. and Mrs. Mack."

Billy pulled his head out of the locker along with the sweater. "Jimmy, it's been for some time now."

Jimmy was at a loss for words.

"I told Alexis but not you. You're too close to the situation, Jimmy." Billy stepped over to Jimmy and slung his arm around him. "You couldn't help. Not at the time."

Jimmy seemed to understand as his body slowly wound down.

"Sure, I think I understand."

"It's the only reason. You know that. My mom and dad, they're like your parents too. Your feelings toward them."

"Darn it, Billy. What's happening? I ..."

"It's like I want to get to the bottom of it so badly, Jimmy, so badly, but I'm too scared to. Maybe it'll be worse than what it seems. And then maybe not. I just have no idea, man."

Pause.

"Your dad, he would talk about it—discuss it with you, wouldn't he?"

"That, I mean, that I don't know. We're close … We, as you know, we talk just about practically anything and everything. But this, whatever this is, I don't know. Really, I have no idea."

Jimmy and Billy knew Judy and Alexis were outside the locker room waiting on them and that they were taking more time than usual.

"We'd better hurry and get dressed. Judy and Alexis must be wondering where, I mean, what we're doing," Billy said.

"Yes."

But Jimmy couldn't relax. He was anxious, as worried as Billy. The Macks, Susan and Connie Mack, they were his second family, as Billy had stated. They meant everything in the world to him. Whatever was happening to them affected him. It meant as much to him as it did to Billy. Now it was he who had to talk to someone about it other than Billy. Now it had become his responsibility to do just that, as some moral duty or obligation.

Jim was watching TV. Marion was reading a book. Both were in the same room, their comfortable den. The TV hadn't distracted Marion; it never did. She heard only the words in the book, not the ones on the TV.

"Marion, I guess you want to know what Jimmy and I talked about privately earlier."

Marion could only chuckle. "Why, I knew you'd get around to it sooner or later, Jim. Even if my patience was about to run out."

Jim crossed his legs. "It's not good news. You see, Jimmy had a talk with Billy after football practice, in the locker room."

Marion laid her book in the middle of her lap, and then her glasses.

"Billy … Connie's drinking, Marion. It's what Billy told him."

"Drinking? Connie?"

Jim folded his arms and then was agitated by the gesture, running his hands hard through his thick brown hair.

"Of course, this information's not new to me. I was aware of Connie's drinking. Just last week, Tim Granger told Brian, in the office, when

Tim dropped by to add to his policy, that Connie has become a regular at Mitch's Sports Bar.

"Tim Granger said Connie has been bragging about Billy and Jimmy, about their football heroics. According to Billy, it sounds serious. Gosh, it's scaring the living hell out of him."

"I can imagine. But Connie of all people, Jim," Marion said in a hushed tone.

"And it's not just the drinking. Connie and Susan, it seems, aren't getting along. Are arguing a lot."

Marion gripped the book in her lap. "What's brought this on, Jim? Tell me."

"It's job related, Marion. It's all job related. Has to be."

"How could it be, Jim, when—"

"When he's the top guy at Blast? I know. That would be anyone's counterargument: mine, yours, Jimmy's. Anyone's guess. But who knows about these things. Whoever does?"

"Jimmy, he's wondering about what he can do to help, Jim? Is that safe to say?"

"No not so much that. I think he just wanted to talk to someone. Uh, air it out. Out of his system. Out in the open. I think it was more that than for any other reason."

"This is so perplexing."

"Marion, right out of the blue."

"They're like us, Jim. A mirror image. A strong family."

"The same values as us." Jim wrestled with himself. "It has to be job related, Marion. What the hell else? Maybe Connie's under too much pressure at Blast. Too much pressure to produce. Too much stress. It's not good. Not for anyone."

"His job is demanding," Marion said.

"The nature of it. It's idea to idea. Who's got the best idea today, the best concept at the moment? Who's got the best design? It's just lucky Connie's a brilliant guy, Marion. Creatively brilliant."

"He's been able to hold on. Keep his status there at Blast," Marion said.

"They'll push you out," Jim said. "They will. In that kind of dog-eat-dog environment. They're always looking to find the next genius. Who's hot. The guy with the next big idea. The solutions for any problems."

"Do you think that's it, at the center of Connie's drinking? That?"

"Could very well be," Jim said cautiously.

Pause.

"But his drinking's got to stop." Even to Marion, her words sounded simpleminded, hollow. "That sounded foolish, I know, Jim. Not smart at all, or realistic."

"We love them, Marion. They're a great couple. It's what makes this so damn hard for us to absorb this."

Jim was going to turn off the TV but just sat there staring at it. "Marion, it'll just have to play itself out, the whole thing. They are strong people, you know."

"Yes, like us. Somehow we'd find a way to fix it. Iron it out, Jim. I know, between us."

CHAPTER 12

"Connie, now what are you doing here?" Chris Martin asked, his bowl of a face much surprised.

"Had a sick day coming, Chris—so took it. Decided to call in sick this morning."

"And join the afternoon crowd? Is that it? This bunch?"

"Right. So what are you serving?"

"I should be asking you. What do you drink in the afternoon? The usual?"

"Yeah, Chris. Get the bottle out and pour." Connie laughed. "Steady."

The afternoon trade was in Mitch's Sports Bar. It had a few personnel on hand who prepared deli sandwiches and fried hamburgers and did a good job of preparing chicken and ribs.

"So there you go, Connie."

"Ah," Connie said, swallowing his first drink of the day. "Just how I ordered it."

Chris laughed. "Connie, you're fast becoming my favorite customer. Or didn't you know?"

"Yeah, Chris. I … I know," Connie said, looking down into his drink.

"Coming, Ralphie. Excuse me, Connie, for a second."

Connie's hand went up like it was some kind of patented sign between him and Chris, and then he got back to his beer.

Connie didn't quite know how to feel today. He was away from his work. He never liked to be away from his work. He felt odd sitting there on the barstool in the afternoon, but there he was.

The new project was stumbling along. Ben Cleghorne was stumbling along. It was in the company's airwaves. He heard about it every day. It'd become common knowledge. People were convinced that Ron Jones had shot himself in the foot on this project in putting Cleghorne in charge of a project of this magnitude, something he couldn't handle. Company scuttlebutt had it that Connie Mack was the only design engineer who could do the job Cleghorne was trying to do but miserably failing at. Ben Cleghorne was stumbling along like a drunk on a dark highway.

Connie would just shrug his shoulders when told something he already knew.

"Ready for another hit, Connie?"

"Uh, sure, Chris. Thanks. Thanks a lot."

And now Connie was doing designs that were interesting but inferior, not like he knew Ben and his project team were up to. He'd gotten some info, bits and pieces of just what the project was about, and he had ideas, concepts that he was dying to show someone but couldn't. This wasn't his baby. He had been shut out in the cold on this one. And could well be the next one too. And the next one and the next one, and the other one after that one.

Maybe I can work with the guy, Connie thought. He thought back to when Susan said there was no compromise in him, and he'd flippantly remarked, "Why, I thought you knew that about me. Maybe I am too arrogant too. My ass is too much up on my shoulders."

Connie took another swallow of beer.

This can't be the end for me at Blast.

Connie called Chris over. "Just leave an extra bottle this time, Chris. Okay? I'll pour."

"Okay, Connie, you got it. Hell, I see you're, uh, deep in the thought. Worried about Billy's game, the Eagles against Rider High this weekend?"

"Yeah, Chris. That—that's it, all right."

"Guessed as much. Know you by now, Connie."

Hell, have I hit the wall—reached a dead end at Blast? Have I? The end of the projects. Hit the wall. The projects I used to dream of and got at Blast.

I fought for them. My time had come. I put my sweat in my work. I made sacrifices for them. I worked my ass off for them. My blood.

Connie had cycled through another beer and was starting a new one. Shakily, he poured the beer in his glass.

Home in front of the computer. Always working, working. Susan understood. Billy too. My family understands me. Understands that I have to be the best at what I do.

Maybe I can compromise. Maybe I can. Ron Jones. Maybe I can work with the guy. I'm a man. I've fought bigger battles than this. My grandmother, Connie, fought bigger battles as a slave. A product of slavery. I have her name, Constance. Connie for Constance. Connie smiled warmly. *A slave name. There were days for her when she didn't want to get up, when the sun in the sky was too hot for her to move and the cotton clung to her sweat like it would not let go. There were days for her that are not to be forgotten, which can make this easier for me, not as hard. Difficult.*

Connie dug into his pocket and pulled out his wallet and left the bar tab on the bar along with the customary tip for Chris Martin when he left Mitch's Sports Bar.

"Connie, where're you going? You haven't finished your drink." Pause. "Hey, Connie, that's not like you."

The car moved into the employee parking lot. Connie parked the car. The six-pack of beer was on the passenger seat. Connie had picked it up along the way. It was reopened. Not a can had been touched, drunk from. Connie reached for the tab.

Snap.

Fizz.

Connie needed something to calm him. He took his first drink out of the can. It did calm him, he thought. He felt much more relaxed, much more in charge of himself. The beer helped. They always helped.

But now Connie had guzzled down two beers and was on his third. And once he'd finished, he felt he was ready. The empty beer cans were back in the carton. The Buick, inside, looked neat. Connie looked again to make sure. Then he opened the car door and got out.

He had a light jacket on. It was October, but it was an Indian summer with a super sun in the sky. Now Connie's back was to the sun. Connie was approaching the huge, gleaming structure, a building he'd walked in and out of thousands of times.

"Hello, Mr. Mack," Robert Burns, the portly security guard, said jovially.

"Hello, Robert."

"Didn't see you this morning."

"Called in sick."

Burns looked at Connie. "Yes, Mr. Mack, your eyes do look kind of, well, a little red, sir. Fuzzy. Sure you're okay?"

Connie walked toward the elevator banks and their gleaming doors. Connie stepped on the waiting elevator; he was alone. The elevator doors shut. Connie punched the button for the desired floor, a floor that was not his floor in the building, where his company cubicle was.

Connie could taste the beer in his mouth; it was stale, leaving a bad taste in his mouth. By now, he was used to the taste, so it was something he could disregard, jettison by, not giving it attention. He felt completely, totally in control of himself, though. Then he thought of the beers in the car. *Maybe I should have drunk more beer*, he thought. *Just one more.*

The elevator was on the desired floor. It opened. Connie got off the elevator. The hallway was long with a glistening marble floor, beautiful to view along with the pictures on the wall, like a modern art museum reflecting trendy tastes.

Connie had reached the office, the outer part.

"Mr. Mack."

"Hi, Linda."

Linda Chanel was young, blonde, and attractive. Her brown eyes made the inquiry first to Connie.

"Oh, sorry, Linda. I'm here to see Mr. Jones."

"Oh …" Linda looked back over her shoulder, at the door. "They've been in there for quite some time, but you know how those situations are, Mr. Mack. They can drag on and on."

"Linda, I'll wait."

"Okay, Mr. Mack. Uh, suit yourself, sir."

"Thanks."

"Oh, should I let Mr. Jones know you're waiting, sir? It's the least I can do, Mr. Mack—while you wait."

"No ... that's all right, Linda. Don't trouble yourself any."

Connie took a seat among the chairs. Ron Jones's office was classy.

It was a half hour later. Linda had gotten fidgety, not Connie.

"Mr. Mack, are you sure you don't want me to inform Mr. Jones that you're waiting out here, sir? It might speed things up in there."

"No, that's quite all right, Linda. Let him do what he has to without any interference from me. Uh, on my part."

"You're so patient, Mr. Mack. If it was me—"

"Sometimes, Linda. But not always. Don't read me wrong."

Linda still smiled admiringly at Connie.

"I'm certainly no saint." Connie laughed.

The beers, they'd worn off, had dissipated in his system. Even the beer taste in his mouth was gone. Suddenly Connie felt different about himself, like he was the same levelheaded guy who reported to, except for today, Blast Aircraft every morning at eight o'clock sharp for the past fifteen years. He felt no different, just the same. As if he'd just begun his workday.

"Oh, listen, Mr. Mack—I hear the meeting breaking up. It's like ruffled feathers."

Connie didn't hear it but figured Linda could probably sense these kinds of thing by now. Ruffled feathers.

Ron Jones's door opened.

A few bodies filed out. They all knew Connie, of course, so they acknowledged him. He acknowledged them. There was a visible, palpable dejection in them.

Ben came out Ron Jones's office.

"Connie," he said with great surprise. "I ... I thought you called in sick this morning?"

Connie laughed. "Don't believe everything you hear, Ben."

"No, Connie, you called in sick. I know for a fact."

Ron Jones came to the door. He was tall, erect, and youngish looking for someone in his late forties.

"Connie," Jones said.

"Mr. Mack's here to see you, Mr. Jones. He's been waiting for well over—"

"That's okay, Linda," Connie said. "Hi, Ron. Do you have time?"

Lengthy pause.

"Sure, Connie. Come in."

Connie turned to Ben, who hadn't moved, who seemed interested in this, why Connie Mack wanted to see Ron Jones in his office after calling in sick that morning.

"See you tomorrow, Ben, bright and early."

"Oh, right, Connie. Right."

Ron Jones had stepped away from the door and was in his office.

"Connie, shut the door."

Connie had. He turned back into the room. The room was big and impressive. A long wooden boardroom table sat in the middle of the room. And then there was Ron Jones's desk with the handsome furniture attending it. There was an area off to the side with furniture a person could sink down into like a bear hibernating for the winter.

Ron Jones stood erectly at his desk. "This is a surprise visit from you, Connie."

"Yes, I know," Connie said, drawing closer to Jones's desk.

"Especially since you called in sick this morning, something Ben mentioned."

"This couldn't wait," Connie said calmly.

Jones didn't blink. "What?"

"This," Connie said vaguely.

"Oh, this," Jones said, as if he'd said nothing. "This meeting we're having."

"Yes."

Jones's taste in clothes was exceptional, as was how each article of clothing fit him.

"Why, I didn't know that."

Picking up a pen, Jones looked down at the appointment calendar on his desk. He pressed the pen's point to the paper. "I don't have a meeting at—"

"Three twenty-five."

"At 3:25 penciled in my appointment calendar for this afternoon with a Connie Mack who called in sick to Blast Aircrafts this morning for work. None that I can locate."

"Look, Ron, look," Connie said, with what seemed every muscle straining in him. "We can work this thing out."

"We? Thing? What thing, Connie? Work what out?"

"Can we at least sit?"

"No, Connie, I'd rather stand. So what is that we can work out, Connie?"

"Uh ... uh ..."

"Why, you're a smart, articulate guy."

"I'm not going to beat around the bush. Not with this. Uh-uh," Connie said, shaking his head.

"Don't."

"The project's failing. Falling apart."

Ron Jones offered no reply.

"Ben Cleghorne can't do the job." Pause. "And you know it."

"But you can. Is that it, Connie? You can?"

"You know—"

"You're the only one in the company who can?"

"Let's be reasonable," Connie said, taking a big, deep, healthy breath. "Okay?"

"I don't have to be, Connie. Whoever said that?"

Jones sat behind his big desk and looked up at Connie.

"Ron, look. I'm willing to compromise. I can, you know."

"And so what's this?" Jones smiled. "The new Connie Mack? The new and improved Connie Mack who's brought himself down a peg or two. You, Connie?"

"Let's face it, Ron. You're running behind schedule. It's—the project's in the red. It's costing you money. The bottom line. You know how the company feels about the bottom line, Ron."

"I've got their backing 100 percent. The company's vote of confidence. Their blessing. They're behind me 100 percent on this. There's no need for me—"

"Come on, Ron. Get off it. Who are you trying to hoodwink?"

Connie saw it when he came into the office—the stand with the design. Calmly, Connie walked over to it and turned it around to face Jones.

"This, Ron? This piece of crap here? I could do this crappy design in my sleep. There's no imagination here. No—"

"Not a Connie Mack design? Original?"

"No," Connie said, stepping away from the design.

"Well, I'm sorry to disappoint you, Connie, but as far as Blast Aircraft Company's concerned, we like it. And from what happened at the meeting this afternoon, I think we're going to go along with it. Give it the go sign. Thumbs-up. You know how we say around here, Connie. What we do at Blast when it's a go."

Was Jones bluffing? Connie thought. Was he putting him on, teasing him, and trying to make him look the fool? No way were Cleghorne and his team's designs up to the company's normal high standards. And the team had come out of Jones's office just now ...

"We never got along, did we, Ron?" Connie said, looking back over to Jones.

And then Connie saw what he thought was that unmistakable look in Ron Jones's eyes that always told him where he stood, right outside the margins, on the periphery—never quite there, never quite making the grade with him.

"That ... that look ..."

"What look?"

"Fuck, man. That look ..."

"I didn't want to say this before, Connie, but now you've forced me: you've been drinking. And I'm not the only one in here, the company, who has knowledge of your—"

"Yeah. I've been to Mitch's Sports Bar. Have a six-pack in my car. There're three cans left."

"It's what you did before you got up here?"

"Yeah, Ron, it's what I did."

"And so you're going to blame your troubles on me. You're going to heap them all on me. Take me to task."

"Damned right!"

"Well ..."

"That look. Fuck. Fuck, man. There you go again with that fucking look again!"

"What look? What look are you talking about?" Ron Jones trembled.

"If … if you came from the South and were black, you'd know the look. If you came from Georgia, Macon … from … and were black, you'd fucking know that look. What it is. Looks like."

"I'm not—"

"A racist, Ron?"

"No, no—"

"Nobody's a racist until their eyes tell you differently. The meetings. The meetings we used to have, when you'd look at me like you looked at me a second ago."

"I'm sorry, Connie. I didn't know I was looking at you that way. Like that."

"But you were, man. Shit, you were. Don't you see?"

"No, no, I don't. I don't. It, it's how I—"

"Uh-uh," Connie said, shaking his head, "no you don't, not with anyone else, just me. Nobody else at Blast. Just me. The black man. The fucking black guy. The—"

"No, no, no, no. That's not me or who I am!"

"There were times, times …" Connie's face had peaked into a madness, a violence; it was there in his hands too.

"Over a design, Connie? A damned company design!"

"But it's more than that. It's always more than that with, with a white man who feels a black man breathing down his neck. With fucking guys like you, it's always fucking more than that."

"Connie, you've got to believe me!"

"I don't have to believe anything. A black man doesn't have to fucking believe a thing a fucking white man says."

Pause.

"You're out of line here. You're way out of line here. Out of bounds. This isn't a company matter anymore. This … this is personal. You're making this personal between you and me. Cursing at me. Using profanity and—"

"Yes it is, very. Shit yeah. Personal, Ron."

Connie's fist pounded Jones's desk.

Ron Jones jumped.

"You want to hurt me. Do me bodily harm, injury!"

Jones reached for the phone on his desk, his finger punching a button on the panel as if for dear life.

"Linda, get security. Robert Burns and security! Connie Mack's in my office and wants to kill me!"

"Kill all of you! Fucking all of you, man!"

Within minutes, security was in Jones's office. They'd burst through the door.

Connie turned.

"Mr. Jones!" Burns yelled. "We got here as fast as we could!"

"Get him out of here! Get this man out of my office, Robert! Now! Right now!"

With trepidation, Robert Burns and his security team approached Connie.

"I won't bite, Robert. Don't worry."

"No ... no, I don't expect you to—"

"I'm the same person you saw in the lobby. You greeted at the desk."

"Yes, sir, Mr. Mack."

"Escort him out my office, Robert. You and your men. Now. Do what you're paid to do. Do your damned jobs. Get this man out of here!"

"Yes, sir, Mr. Jones."

"I'm coming willingly, Robert. Don't worry. There's no need."

"Uh, right, Mr. Mack."

Connie went with the security team, letting them escort him out of Ron Jones's office.

But then he turned and saw Jones standing back at his desk, and he saw that look again—knowing Jones couldn't fucking hide it, not if he tried.

Connie had asked Burns and security to escort him back to his cubicle. He felt confused, dazed. They said they would let Mr. Jones know of his whereabouts in the building, that he was in his cubicle.

Connie hadn't been in the cubicle long when his desk phone rang. First he was going to ignore it, pretend he still had the day off—since he'd called in sick to Blast in the morning. But he picked up the phone.

"Hello. Connie Mack."

He listened intently to the trembling, frightened voice and then responded.

"No, Linda. Absolutely not. You can tell them I said no."

Linda had stopped talking.

"Thank you, Linda."

Connie put down the phone. He looked to his left, resignedly.

"A hastily called meeting," Connie said. "Wait for security. No, Linda, not me. I'm not going to any fucking meeting. Not Connie Mack."

Connie recognized the meeting was to be about him. No one had to tell him that. Ron Jones had gotten the right people above him in the company to conference.

Connie walked over to his desk and sat. He could feel all the days inside this cubicle push down on him. Him sitting there looking at his computer screen, inventing, always imagining something new, different—a brand-new design concept. Taking it home and doing more, always doing more to make it better, improve upon it, his creative juices just taking over—overflowing.

How he loved this job, what he did. He lived with it twenty-four hours a day. He remembered his favorite college professor at Brown University, T. M. Finlay, say how lucky the students were to be in such a selected field of "intrigue and wonder." He'd never forgotten that: intrigue and wonder. And it's what it'd been for him in his career up to this point—intrigue and wonder.

Connie got back up and walked over to the window. He looked at Blast Aircraft's magnificent grounds set in an area of woods, hills, and practically isolation.

"Professor Finlay, were you right, sir. That day, sir."

Connie saw people coming and going.

Ring.

"Hello," Connie said. "Sure, sure, Linda. I understand. No. Don't feel sorry for something you took no part in. Thank you, Linda. A lot."

The weight in Connie shifted for a split second.

"Mr. Mack."

Connie turned. They were efficient. Like clockwork.

Connie acknowledged them.

"We're here. Mr. Jones asked us to make sure everything goes smoothly with you, sir."

"That I leave peacefully, Robert." Pause. "There'll be no trouble. Not from me." Connie took a look around his cubicle. "Since I didn't expect—"

"Here, Mr. Mack. Joey," Burns summoned Joey Allen. He stepped forward with large paper bags.

"You can put your personal items in these, Mr. Mack, sir." Burns took the two big brown bags from Joey.

Then Connie took them from Burns. "I don't know how many I'll need."

"Uh, I can get more. I can always get more if necessary, Mr. Mack. No problem at all with that."

"We'll just have to see, Robert?"

Connie looked over at his desk drawers; they had to be cleaned out.

It was a little later.

Connie was immobile.

"Uh, ready, Mr. Mack?"

"Uh, yes," Connie said, snapping out of it. "Sorry. I'm ready to leave."

Connie was carrying the three bags (one half-full).

Connie, Robert, and the rest of the security team walked down Blast's hallway. They passed Ben Cleghorne's cubicle. Ben got out of his chair.

"Connie …"

"I'll be seeing you, Ben."

"Yes. I'll be seeing you."

Connie saw Cleghorne's immediate relief.

Connie and security were down in the lobby and a little beyond the cordoned-off area.

"Are … are you all right, Mr. Mack?"

"Fine, Robert."

"Then good evening, sir."

And then Robert and his security team pivoted and walked away together as Connie held on to his three paper bags.

The Buick Regal's door opened. Connie could feel his nerves burning in him when he sat behind the car's steering wheel. He was going to look out into the parking lot but instead buried his head and began to cry, feeling an enormous amount of pain pounding in his chest.

Soon Connie was looking at the three beer cans in the carton on the seat.

"Damn if I don't need you now."

The beer can popped open.

Three won't do, Connie thought. *Not three of these.*

The three cans were empty, and the car was pulling out of Blast Aircraft Company's employee parking lot for what would be the last time, and Connie knew where he was going to go in his car to get more beer, something he had been doing every night lately.

Susan sat by the living room phone and then stood. Connie had told her he was taking the day off. She'd gotten out of the house early that morning. She and Billy ate dinner without Connie. It didn't surprise them—not anymore. But now she was sitting by the phone, driving herself crazy. It was as if one night a call would come. Was she imagining too much? Was what Connie was doing? Was it causing her to overimagine things?

He was drinking. He was in a car. Anything could happen. And it stemmed from what? She still couldn't feel its pulse, what was causing this for Connie, why their lives suddenly felt like they was crashing headlong in space.

"It's already crashed," Susan said, glancing down at the carpeted living room floor, the color burgundy, as if their lives were lying there shattered and scattered.

But now Susan felt exaggeration again, this orderly system she was caught up in of overimagining things.

It scared her though. These nights (so many piling one on top the other) of Connie driving home on the road, drunk. How had he done it? Did the whirr of the car's engine or someone's headlights help him? Did they brace him in some miraculous way that it made him physically and mentally able to manage it?

But there she'd been, Susan thought, looking over at the phone, thinking the worst. Always thinking the worst. Waiting for the phone to ring. Bad news. Awful news. It would be awful news on the other end of the phone. It would be about Connie. Bad news. Awful news.

Susan had fallen asleep but now stirred. The car, Susan heard it. She came tumbling out of sleep, fully awake. The car's headlights set on the house and then vanished.

Connie and I mustn't argue, Susan thought. Why she thought this, she didn't know. But it's what she thought—that she and Connie mustn't argue. She was just happy that he'd gotten home safely, unhurt.

She turned the hall light on for him.

"Connie ..."

Connie was standing in the vestibule with three large shopping bags.

"I was fired today," Connie said, responding to Susan's shocked expression.

"Blast Aircraft fired me. I stand before you without a job. I am unemployed."

Somebody had to catch Susan. Her body was so—

Only Connie walked past her with the shopping bags.

"I thought ..."

"Yeah, it happened this afternoon," Connie said, settling into the living room.

When she looked at him, he didn't appear drunk, she thought, but he was.

"But, Connie, you didn't go to work today. You said you were going to use a sick day. So how could this—how could you be fired? How could Blast actually fire you when ... when you weren't there, honey? Never there in the office today?"

"Simple, Sue," Connie said with no guile in his voice.

The bags were put down on the floor.

The bags! The bags!

"I went to Mitch's Sports Bar. And from there Blast. That's all. Like I said, simple."

Susan sat down and leaned back on the couch.

He moved from the center of the living room where one bag and the other two were on either side of his legs. "I had to, Sue. They needed me on that project. They needed me," Connie said in a hoarse, dry voice.

Now it was as if Connie were talking to a ghost, a phantom figure who he saw and thought was in the room.

"The project's falling apart. I wanted to save it. That's all." Pause. "Maybe I went too far. Yeah, kill someone. Kill someone?"

Susan shuddered.

"It's only a project, Ron. Kill … but I did say it. I'd kill all of you … I did say it."

Susan couldn't move.

"So they called security, but I told them to relax. No harm was to come to anyone. I'm not a violent man, not the blacks, the kind they see on TV. No. Shit no. I … *You don't have to cuff me*, I thought to myself."

Susan was crying.

"The office, I went back to my office. The meeting, you called it hastily, didn't you, Ron? Hell yes. Fuck, man. All the big shots were there: lawyers, Mr. Remington, you know—the top bananas." His body blustered. "No, I told Linda. Hell no, I ain't coming up to Ron Jones's fucking office. Hell no! But I didn't, wouldn't talk that way to Linda. She wasn't responsible.

"But I waited for the call to come, flooded with memories. Professor Finlay snuck into my memory. Showed up. They were deciding my fate. Those bastards. And then the phone rang again."

Susan jumped.

"Hello, Linda. Don't feel sorry. You had no part, hand in it. Thank you. Thank you, Linda. Security, good old security. They're like clockwork. Blast brags about them. But seeing it firsthand. Man …

"Man, did I pack my things fast. My stuff in the bags security, Robert gave me, and off we went. Shit. Passed … I passed by Ben Cleghorne's cubicle, and I did say something like 'I'll be seeing you, Ben.' Something like that.

"And we were in the lobby, bags in my hands, and Robert asked me if I was okay, all right. So I told him I was fine. Doing fine. Fine, just fine, you know … And then I walked out Blast Aircraft, just like, you know, like I always do. You know … nightly …"

Sue looked at him and saw a shadow of Connie, the man she loved.

Connie bent over and picked up the three shopping bags.

"Sue, I'm tired. I'll put the things in the den if … if you don't mind. I'm going upstairs. I'm dead tired right now."

She was still on the living room couch. It was very late. She should be upstairs with Connie, she'd thought again and again. If she was a good wife, she'd be upstairs with Connie, but she wasn't. This was when he most needed her. But she had not moved from the couch since she had gotten the news. The way she got the news—he hadn't deliberately done it that way.

The way he stood in the middle of the living room, his eyes, face; there was all this stuff just below it, at its edge, ready to catch fire, anger, stir itself into a violence, but it had not. Connie was too defeated, too battered, bruised, ripped apart, and humiliated.

Here was a man who was enormously gifted. Here was a man who had genius in him, and now his company just told him he was no longer good enough, valuable enough to work for them. They took their project from him, a project that should had been his at its inception. He reacted poorly. It was treated like a crime. Connie loved his work too much. It was all that could be blamed.

Why wasn't she upstairs telling him this? He wasn't to blame for what happened today. The company was to blame; it was dead wrong. They tried to force him to tolerate something that was intolerable, that was not in Connie's nature to accept; it was not in his best interest. They expected too much from him. Connie had to be the heart of that project, what he lived and breathed for. Blast Aircraft drove him to do what he'd done.

Why am I not upstairs telling him this? "You're not to blame, Connie. You're not to blame for today."

But I'm here on this couch. Not upstairs with you, Connie. Why?

Had his drinking driven this much of a wedge between them? So much so that she couldn't go upstairs to console him, bleed her heart out to him? Try to help rebuild him, even now while his own grief had just begun?

And now Billy.

"Who's going to tell Billy?"

She was going to sleep on the couch. It was what she was going to do. How different would tomorrow be? How different was it already? Susan could only imagine.

CHAPTER 13

Billy had just told Alexis about his father's situation. He didn't want to tell her before school, so he chose to tell her after school. His father told him he'd lost his job at Blast Aircraft. He had called him into his den. He didn't drag it out or beat around the bush. He told him everything would work itself out for the better. What he didn't tell him was why Blast had fired him. It was never brought up. This was the awkward part for him in dealing with the firing.

He was glad he had Alexis, someone with such a beautiful heart and spirit, plus brains.

They were nearing Alexis's house. They were holding hands. Their conversation had been choppy, but it was understandable, neither having experienced anything like this before.

"I'm glad I have you, Alexis."

"Thanks, Billy."

Billy stopped. "And I don't want you to hide this from your parents, okay?"

"But—"

"No, tell them. Go tell them. I don't want there to be secrets. It's bad enough I'm just telling you about it today, two days later. After the fact."

"But you had Jimmy." Alexis smiled.

"Jimmy, man. Alexis, was that hard to do." Pause. "So you'll tell your parents'?"

"Yes, I will."

"My dad's not afraid of anything, and neither am I. I guess I got that from him." Pause. "And there's another thing you should know, Alexis, but ... please don't tell your parents this. Not about what I'm to tell you."

"What, Billy?"

"My father, he'd been drinking a lot before he was fired."

"Billy, do you think—"

"It's all I can think, that it's related to Blast Aircraft firing him, since no one, not even my mother, will tell me why."

Alexis was visibly upset and held on to Billy in the middle of the sidewalk.

"But since neither will tell me ... It's like my parents are the adults in this situation, and I'm the child. It's never been this way between us. I mean, Alexis, like all of this is too big for me to handle, to understand. Or for them to discuss with me so ... so they won't—have mutually agreed not to."

"But don't they know what it's doing to you?"

"They have to."

"Mr. Mack was the top man, wasn't he? The best engineer at Blast Aircraft? And they fired him, Billy. Let him go."

Susan was in her Dodge SUV. She'd just left Mrs. Edith Ramsey's house. She was arranging a Christmas party for her in October (it was the way it worked in Pittsfield).

Her and Connie's finances were solvent, Susan thought. They had no worries. They had saved and saved. Connie's salary was six figures at Blast. They were not lavish and did not live extravagantly. She'd inherited money from her mother's sister (childless), her aunt Julia, who'd left her valuable property in DC (which Susan sold), and a good portion of her savings.

Connie felt uncomfortable about the idea of the inheritance money being intermingled with theirs, so she had a separate account with Connie as its beneficiary. It was money that had gone untouched over the years, and it was substantial.

Is he going to look for a new job? She and Connie hadn't discussed it. But how many aircraft jobs were in Pittsfield? It meant they'd have to move from Pittsfield once Connie got back on his feet. He'd have to hit the ground running once he recovered from the Blast firing. She was preparing herself for when she would have to leave a place she truly loved.

And Billy, he would have to be uprooted. And Jimmy. These were scary thoughts, but regardless, they had to be considered for everyone's personal sanity.

What had she and Connie discussed the past few days? *Nothing*, Susan thought. Absolutely nothing. Their lives had been drastically changed by this event (the firing), yet they hadn't discussed it. They were walking in and out of rooms closing doors. Connie was in the den, and she was finding other rooms in the house to occupy.

They were letting this thing go beyond them, transcend them—but all she thought of when out of the house were things like that, things not even silence could eliminate or knock down to its knees.

Susan was on Hart Street, her street. She was on the street she loved. The house was pretty much situated in the middle, equidistant from corner to corner. The Richards (Peter and Brenda) lived to the left of her, the Monroes (Phil and Sandra) to the right, and the Millers (Brian and Pat) lived across the street.

How would she feel when the moving van showed up and moved up to their front door?

Susan pulled the Dodge up to the two-car garage. Connie's Regal was parked outside. His car hadn't moved from that spot for four days, not since the firing. Susan pulled the Dodge alongside it.

Susan reached for her handbag, then put the car keys in it. She retrieved her house keys. *What is Connie doing?* She wondered. The car's heat was turned off, but Susan still felt traces of it.

The one good thing about the past few days was Connie was no longer drinking. For the past three days, Connie hadn't taken a drink (she could tell). He was such a proud man. Was it out of defiance he'd stopped drinking, the motivation behind this, and his pride? That he wouldn't let those people, Blast Aircraft, kill his spirit and get the better of him? Was his defiance now his weapon?

She was out of the Dodge.

"Connie, I'm home." She had no idea why she said it. Her voice seemed to reverberate back to her. She hung her coat in the hall closet. When she walked up the staircase, halfway up, she said it again. "Connie, I'm home."

The door was closed at the top of the stairs. She called up the staircase and opened the door.

"Connie, I'm home."

"Susan, listen, we have to talk." Connie was on his couch. He was brooding. It was immediately evident.

Connie's hands were placed on top of his kneecaps. He waited for her to sit on the couch beside him.

"I agree," Susan said in a voice less weighty than his.

"This is the fourth day of this. I feel locked up in this room."

Why shouldn't he? Susan thought.

He shrugged. "I'm not blaming anyone. It's been my choice to spend my days in here in front of my computer and reading. I've elected to do this. Make it my routine."

Susan saw the computer was on, with a design on it, and books were scattered off to the side of the computer, on the floor. It was as if Connie had decided to camp out exclusively in that area of the den.

"Who the hell am I kidding, Sue? I'm out a damned job. Blast Aircraft fired me."

Connie rubbed Susan's hand briefly. "First, it hurt like hell. Then it felt like a fresh breeze. And now it's back to that—hurting like hell."

"I love you, Connie."

"Come here."

Connie kissed her long and deep. Suddenly Susan's head rested on Connie's chest, feeling its relaxed breathing. It was therapy.

"So you've been thinking too?" Connie asked.

"I have."

"A—"

"About what lies ahead for us: you, Billy, and me. I can't help but think of it, Connie."

"Of course. Of course," Connie said.

"It's what you've been thinking about? You too?"

"Tell me, Sue. What else is there to think about, really?"

"We have to discuss it then, Connie. I—"

"Now's the time. As good as any." Pause. "There aren't any—you know there aren't any jobs in Pittsfield other than at Blast that call for my specialty."

"No." Pause. "It's why I was thinking," Susan said, lifting her head sluggishly off Connie's chest, "that the only thing you can do, Connie, is to look elsewhere, honey."

"Elsewhere!"

"I ... yes, elsewhere. Outside of Pittsfield. We'll have to move from—"

"Uh-uh. No way. You've got this all wrong. Twisted."

"Wrong, how can I possibly have it—"

"Wrong. Not on your life are we moving from here. Pittsfield. It's out of the question."

"But why, Connie?"

"Billy. Billy's football!"

Susan, in the SUV, had remembered Jimmy but not Billy's football. Somehow she'd forgotten all about Billy's football.

"We couldn't do that to Billy or Jimmy. It wouldn't be fair to them."

"But ... but what about you, Connie? You, I mean, you've got to think about yourself, Connie, your career."

Connie stood. He walked over to the computer and then back to the couch and sat. "I'll tough it out. Listen, Sue, I will tough this damned thing out if it kills me. I can make it. Don't worry about me making it."

But how? Susan was about to ask but didn't. *How in Pittsfield?*

"You, hey, maybe I'll teach. I thought about Professor T. M. Finlay. It must've been for a reason. And Jimmy's girlfriend, uh ..."

"Judy."

"Judy. Her parents are on Tyler College's faculty, aren't they? So who knows? Maybe they could tell me something. You know, if there's a teaching position open at the college in my field of expertise. You know that's a possibility. Might be a darn good one at that."

"Teach ..." Susan said, frowning. "Is that what you want, Connie? Someone as creative—"

"Why not? You know how I am with people. And besides, I'll be influencing someone's future, like Professor Finlay did mine. It'll be challengingly, Sue, sure, a real challenge to undertake."

Susan began to see the possibilities but still couldn't buy into them this hastily.

"Yeah, why not! Maybe it's what this is all about. What is really planned for me? Who knows? But it's worth a shot. I'm going to arrange to meet the …"

"Collinses, Connie. Uh, Amy and, I … I believe, Pat. Uh, yes, Pat Collins."

"What do I have to lose? Tough it out. Did I say tough it out?" Connie ran to the door and flung it open.

"Let the sun shine in, Sue. Shit. Shit. Let it. Baby!"

By now, Jim and Marion knew of Connie's firing. Jimmy had told them. Billy wanted him to. For the past few days, their lives had gone along as usual, but all they could think about was Connie, Susan, and Billy.

Jim had just come in from Allied Insurance. Marion greeted him.

"I just saw Sally Ann. She's growing nicely, isn't she, Marion? Turning into quite a lovely young lady. No more glasses."

"Contacts, Jim. Sally's switched over to contacts, for your information," Marion said, taking Jim's coat from him.

"Jimmy, I don't think he knows what he's going to be missing out on down the road," Jim joked.

"Don't worry. Sally Ann will get over Jimmy."

"By noon tomorrow." Jim grinned.

Pause.

"So how was your day?"

"Busy. When's my vacation due?"

Marion walked away from him. "I refuse to answer—not the way it was just said."

"It's that I sound that desperate, huh? That overworked? That out of it? Totally?"

"Jimmy and I have eaten," Marion said, switching the conversation. "I had a feeling over the phone you'd be late."

"You know by now, huh, Marion?" Jim said, exhausted. Then he winked.

"Yep, I—you know it was probably like that for Connie and Susan at one time," Marion said, entering the kitchen.

Jim marched right behind her. When he sat down at the kitchen table, his head sank down into his hands. "It's in between paperwork and my clients and all the other things. It's all I think about nowadays, Marion: Connie and Susan. Connie and Susan. Our dear, dear friends."

"Who—how can you not, Jim? How can anyone help but think of them?"

Jim felt guilty. "I had to check with, dammit, Marion, pardon me. But Connie's back to drinking. Back in Mitch's Sports Bar. It'd stopped for a while but has started back up. He's there nightly."

"Oh no!" It was the worst news Marion could possibly hear. "Why haven't we picked up the telephone and called them, Jim? Our friends. Why haven't we invited them over for dinner, done something?"

"I don't know if we're supposed to know, Marion. Gosh, I just don't know," Jim said. "I don't know if Connie and Susan know we know."

"They have to."

Jim's hand reached for the sugar bowl in the middle of the table and disdainfully backhanded it. "But it's not that simple, Marion. Like you can pat Connie on the back and say everything will be okay—all right."

"Am I saying that? Did I just say that? I know I just didn't say that."

"No, you didn't. I'm sorry. I didn't mean to be—"

"It's okay, Jim. It is," Marion said, regaining her composure. "But like I said, it's like it's happening to us directly, this thing between them."

"God only knows how I've wanted to pick up the phone."

"Me too, to call my dear, dear Susan. Say something soothing to her."

"But what would you say?"

"I don't know, but I think it would do us more good than probably them."

"We're thinking about them too much, aren't we? And we're guilty on top of it, and that's not good, not for anybody."

"They have to know we're always here for them."

"Always in their corner, Marion. They must know that."

Marion got up to check the food on the stove.

"Do you think we should then, uh, get in touch?"

Marion held her breath. "Let me think about it, Jim. Okay?"

CHAPTER 14

Over the past three months, Connie had been drinking more and more. The college idea didn't pan out. He went through the full process of Tyler College's hiring procedure, only to discover there was no opening in his field.

The Purple Eagles had won the state championship for a second straight year and had their sights set on winning it for a third. If accomplished, it would set a new state record for consecutive championship defenses, three.

Jimmy and Billy had further improved at their positions. But someone had remarked that Billy Steamroller Mack was running angry. He'd run hard, fiercely before, but during most of the season, he'd run angry. Like an angry young man.

"I'm going home sweet home, Chris," Connie remarked to Chris Martin.

"Why so early, Connie?" Chris frowned.

"Got to get up early this morning and stare at the walls. Yeah!"

Everyone knew Connie Mack was jobless. It'd become common knowledge.

"Don't tell me that's what you do now that you're on vacation, Connie. Stare at the walls?" Chris laughed.

"Hell. A thrill. Let me tell you, man. It's a thrill a minute."

Connie went into his pocket and pulled out money. "Still have enough money for the night's entertainment and a tip for my babysitter/psychologist/father confessor. Hey, did I leave anything out?"

"Yes ... friend," Chris said, cleaning the top of the bar with a damp cloth.

"Yeah, uh, yeah, friend," Connie said, embarrassed to say it.

"Good night, Connie."

"Yeah, Chris. The place is all yours," Connie said. "I'm leaving you in charge."

Connie was on the road. He hated himself. He really did. He hated himself from the inside out. He was a quitter. A fucking quitter. It's all he was. A quitter. A fucking quitter.

"Connie Mack. Named after my great-great-grandmother. A slave. Connie Mack. Connie Mack. Connie Mack."

The things his grandmother had to endure to survive ... and here he was in this modern setting and was crumbling, falling apart. Connie Mack.

He thought he had what it took. He proved it on the playing field: All-American lacrosse. An All-American. He fought off any challenge and adversity on the field—conquered it. He was this wonderful amalgam of hard work and courage and bravery. He was his team's leader. It came naturally to him, leading people. He did it at Brown University and at Blast Aircraft. *But now look at me,* Connie thought. *Look at Connie Mack.*

It frightened him now to think the thought.

He needed a drink. Yes, that was what he needed—a drink. A fucking drink. A fucking drink.

"The convenience store's open twenty-four hours."

Connie still had plenty of money on him. Tonight he didn't spend as much as usual in Mitch's. He quit drinking early. But what Chris said was haunting him.

"But bars, I never, never had a friend in ... in a bar. Not in a bar."

But every night, he was going into that place—that bar.

The convenience store was two miles up the road. "I'll pass it. I don't need a drink, another one. I'll pass it by. Right by. I've had enough for one night," Connie said, listening to himself with concrete confidence.

"I have to fight my way out of this situation. Out of this mess."
Chris had said it sincerely, "Friend." He'd meant it.
A haunting was back in Connie. All of it, every steel inch of it.
Connie Mack.

He never took beer into the house. Not once. Connie looked at the two remaining beer cans on the seat. He would not drink them. They'd stay on the car seat overnight. What he'd do with them tomorrow, well, he'd decide then.

At the front door, he fumbled for his key chain. The front porch lights burned.

"Oops." Connie fumbled the keys out of his hand and then laughed wildly.

"Mus-mustn't wake the family. Dis-disturb them. Sue and Billy— mustn't do that … now," Connie said, placing his finger up to his mouth, quieting himself.

"Yeah, yeah shhh … quiet, man. Mum's the word."

Connie was in the house. He did the normal things like hanging his coat and turning off the downstairs lights.

"Billy's in bed, so be quiet, Connie. Quiet does it. Not a peep out of you, not a one. Do you hear?"

Quietly Connie tread his way up the staircase. He saw, midway up, his den door was closed; only, there was a slip of light underneath the door.

Connie stumbled but got up on the landing and quickly opened the den door.

"What are you doing to my den!"

The den was a mess. Susan was cleaning it. She was doing it at eleven thirty-five at night.

"I'm—"

"Leave my stuff alone! Leave it alone!" Connie said, slamming the door behind him.

Susan was petrified.

"I-I just thought I'd—"

"This is my room. What are you trying to do? Take this away from me too!"

"Connie, no, Connie. Why no. Why would—"

Connie stood before her and snatched the book out of her hand, throwing it to the floor.

"I'll tell you when to clean in here. Connie Mack'll tell you when this den needs cleaning!" Connie said, spitting his words at her.

"This is crazy, Connie. Crazy," Susan said, tossing her arms in the air. "This entire thing has gotten crazy. Is crazy."

"Thing! Thing!"

"Yes. Us, Connie, us—"

"Oh," Connie said cunningly. "That's how you feel. Finally it's come out. Out your veins, huh, Sue? The truth. I finally got it out of you, huh? The good wife. The loyal wife. The faithful—"

"Don't you ridicule me. Don't you dare make fun of me!"

"Well, aren't you? Aren't you? Stoic. Understanding. Courageous. Brave. Yeah, Sue, brave throughout it all. Stiff upper lip. Yeah ..."

Softly she moved to the couch and sat there. "I just hoped you'd stop drinking. It's all I hoped for. With all my heart, I hoped you'd stop."

Pause.

"Oh," Connie said skeptically, gesturing with his hands. "Now it's my drinking that bothers you—not me being out of—"

"It's what's bothered me from the outset. Since this began."

"Well, I like to drink. Okay, Sue? I like to drink. It makes me feel good. Damn good!"

"And so ... you don't see what it's doing to us? Us, Con—"

"Us?"

"Yes, you and me. Never mind our son ... Billy."

Connie slapped his computer chair, toppling it. "You just talk about us, Susan. Us. You just talk about you and me and leave Billy out of this."

"We're not intimate anymore, Connie. You and I. You and I are not—"

"Who needs sex? Who the hell needs sex? I can live without it. Shit, woman. Who needs it?"

"I can't, Connie. I ... I can't," Susan said, looking over at Connie calmly. "I'm a woman who ..."

"If that's all that's bothering you then—if that's all you want, then …" Connie began to unbuckle his belt.

"What's come over you! You're disgusting!"

"Why, I thought it's what you wanted, Sue. A good roll in the hay. A good screw! Fuck. Fuck, girl!"

Susan was rushing out of the room when Connie grabbed her by her arm and then held her by her wrists.

"And you leave Billy out of this. You leave my son out of this!"

"Let go of my wrists. You're hurting me, Connie! You're—"

The den door burst open.

"Dad, what are you doing to mom, dad!"

Connie let go of Marion's wrists.

"Sorry, I'm, I'm sorry. Sue … Billy."

Billy held her trembling body.

"Are you all right, Mom? Dad didn't hurt you, did he?"

She was crying, nonresponsive.

Billy looked at Connie with rage and disgust.

"Dad, what's gotten into you?" Billy asked as he and Susan walked out of the den.

Connie remained where he was, silent, sober, sweating.

Two days later, Susan had to talk to someone. She had turned to Marion. Susan had suggested they do lunch, but Marion thought it better for Susan come to the house. She felt it'd be more relaxing in that setting. More conducive for talk.

They'd had lunch in the kitchen. The two were in the living room. They sat on the same couch but were separated by a comfortable distance.

"Susan, full?"

"Am I." Pause. "Is that a Marion Boston recipe for—"

"Not for sale," Marion said.

They kept talking, as they had in the kitchen, about things in general until Susan finally said, "Marion, I had to talk to you. It was vital."

Marion had prepared herself for this.

"My life now, right now, Marion, is in shambles. Total shambles." Pause. "I don't know Connie anymore. Who he is. He's not the same man—husband—I knew. He's changed."

"The job? It's the—"

"It started before that, before Blast Aircraft let him go. Well before. It started with Billy dating Alexis."

"Alexis? Billy dating Alexis, Susan?"

"Yes. But I won't go into that aspect of it with you. It's too private."

"No, don't, Susan. There is no need to. For you—"

"It's his drinking. It's what's destroying us."

Long pause.

"I know about it. Jim and I."

"Everyone does," Susan said despairingly. "I tried to understand. A brilliant man being let go. Why don't I just say it, Marion? *Fired.* Fired by a company when it most needed him, out of spite. Connie didn't head up the company's new project out of pure spite."

Marion thought to dig deeper. Her information about the firing at Blast Aircraft and Susan's seemed to differ.

"I don't want to go into it now—not that. I just want you to know what it's doing to us, our marriage."

"It's what's important to all of us—"

"How it's destroying it and Billy at the same time. At the same rate."

"Billy. My dear Billy."

"He doesn't understand. He's been kept completely in the dark. Our arguing. Constant arguments. What seems unending between Connie and me. And then silences, long stretches. Long, dreadful silences, they are. Have become for us."

"It must be—"

"They're awful, Marion. Why are we doing this to Billy? Connie and I?"

"Counseling," Marion said uneasily, not sure how it'd be received. "Maybe you and Connie should consider professional counseling. Seek it out as a way to fix this—"

"He'll have none of it. Won't consider it. I've suggested it to him. He won't do it, refuses to. He's too proud. Connie won't give up his piece of ground."

Piece of ground, piece of ground. To Marion, that sounded intriguing—such a man's perspective on things.

"What are you going to do, Susan? I mean, what's left for you to do?"

"Oh, how I wish I knew. But I'm getting desperate. I've never felt like this, how I feel now. So anxious. So ... so unhappy. My life's turned into this thing, Marion, this awful thing. Do you know what I mean? Elusive, unruly, while I'm waiting for it to end. Hoping that it will just end. That Connie will come to his senses. Return to the person he was."

"But not knowing when or ... or how it will end," Marion said.

"Yes."

"It has to be a terrible strain on you every day, Susan. Oh, Susan ..."

"It is. There's no pretending on my part."

Pause.

"I'm only so strong. Only so willing. We all crack, Marion. We all have a breaking point. I don't know where it's at or when I'll reach mine. It's what frightens me. Scares the daylights out of me. Each day.

"That's elusive too. That's vague too. That I don't know either—just what is my breaking point. No, Marion, I really, really don't."

It was hours later.

"Jim." Marion was in the back office of Jim's Allied Insurance Company.

"I'm glad you called, Marion. Sit down," Jim said, pulling up a chair for her. He pulled one up for himself.

"I had to call you."

"The lunch, then. It went—what, that poorly?"

"Yes."

"You mean you couldn't help her?"

"No, not at all, Jim. There are no words for what Susan's going through. She's never had this kind of trouble in her life, in her marriage. This is out of the blue, beyond her. She's desperate. Do you hear me, Jim? Susan's desperate." Pause.

"Jim, I'm afraid for her. She and Connie and Billy."

"Why I thought things would go well, I have no idea. When two people have to make it work, Marion. Two, not one."

Marion bit her top lip, then pressed them together. "I'm worried. Susan might be at her, could be at her breaking point. Vulnerable for it. We all have one, Jim. Susan reminded me."

Jim lurched forward. "Look, Marion, I know where Connie is. Where he hangs out. Now it's my turn with this." Pause. "You sat down with Susan; now it's my turn with Connie. It's been a long time since we've sat down and talked—really talked, me and Connie."

Mitch's Sports Bar was at its busiest on this Friday night. With Pittsfield being geographically close to Boston, there was a rooting interest in the Boston Bruins and Celtics. One TV screen had the Bruins game, the other the Celtics. There was noise galore, as reactions to anything up on the two wide TV screens brought on throaty exhortations, whether they be groans or cheers from these macho men.

Connie was in the bar, not turned to the TV screen but looking in the mirror fronting him and the liquor bottles at the base of a shelf, strung from middle to end. Being an ex-athlete and sports fan, ironically, Connie wasn't in the bar to watch sports. He was on his seventh beer, and there was to be more drinking before the night's end.

"Damn, they just don't have it anymore; Connie. Don't have what it takes. Bird, Parish, Johnson, and McHale, Connie. All gone. What's happened to the good old days?"

Connie wiped his hand across his mouth. "Chris, don't ask me. I hated those guys. Hated their freaking guts. And especially Auerbach during his reign. Him and that freaking cigar of his. When he lit, would light that cigar, I—"

"Good old Red," Chris said reminiscently. "Can't blame the guy for smoking cigars. Hold that against him."

Connie laughed. "I did admire the guy though. Was cocky as hell."

"You mean good, don't you, Connie? Good?"

"Okay … good. Good and cocky as hell then."

A cheer went up in the bar and then a groan. It was hard to tell who the cheer was for, or the groan—the Celtics or the Bruins.

"Connie."

Even in the bar's din of noise, Connie recognized his voice immediately

"Jim," Connie said, practically ashamed.

Jim had laid his hand on Connie's big shoulders. Jim's warm smile was on display.

"Jim, I—"

"Hi, Chris."

"Coming up, Jim."

"Thanks."

"Hi, Jim."

"Oh, hello, Bob."

"Here, take my seat."

"No, don't bother—"

"Go head, Jim. I was about to shoot a game of pool," Bob Delany said, getting up from his barstool.

"Thanks, Bob," Jim said, patting Bob on his back as he left for the rear pool tables.

"Don't mention it, Jim. And by the way, my insurance is paid up."

"Mine too," Chris said, setting Jim up.

"Oh, I know yours is, Chris. It was Bob's I wasn't sure of. Hey, Bob, check with Irene anyway, will you?"

It was good for a laugh for those patrons near Jim.

Jim's Heineken was in the glass. He took a slow sip from it.

Connie looked at Jim intensely. They were eyes Jim felt combing through him.

"Connie—"

"I know what you're about to say, Jim. What am I doing here in Mitch's Sports Bar?" Pause. "Well, I don't know, for the life of me."

Jim had never seen Connie's eyes red, but then, he thought, maybe when they sat together in the cold bleachers a while back and the wind whipped into his eyes until they teared—maybe then.

"This is a bad time you're going through, Connie. A rough patch in your life."

Connie's shoulders tensed. "You know what? I don't know this road. I really don't. Don't know anything about it, Jim. But here I am anyway."

"It's why I'm here," Jim said, ignoring his flattening beer. "Maybe a good talk will help."

Connie lifted his glass of beer and drank a lot out of it.

"It's what I wanted to do—"

"When you heard I was jobless, out a job, Jim? When Blast fired me. I know, Jim."

"Yes, Connie, but I never picked up the phone to call. I didn't have the guts. I—"

"What for, Jim? I'm a grown man." Connie half-smiled. "It hurt like hell, the firing. It still hurts," Connie said, his eyes burning. "Ah, what can you do," Connie said, picking up his glass of beer and finishing it off.

Jim expected to find this kind of man, then he didn't. It was the strangest, weirdest dichotomy, this set of feelings he had, as if fantasy (playing through his mind) couldn't quite match reality.

"Connie, Susan was by the house this afternoon."

"Susan, Jim?"

Jim was aware this news would be received with great surprise by Connie.

"Yes, Susan."

Surprise still showed on Connie's face.

"She called Marion. They had lunch at the house."

"Susan, she should talk to someone. I'm glad it was Marion. There's no one better." Pause. "But you sought me out, Jim. Why?"

"I would have kicked myself if I hadn't. Gosh, I really would've."

"It's that bad." Connie's eyes were openly tragic. "What Susan had to say to—it's that hard to tell me. Is it, Jim?"

Jim caught his breath. "She's desperate, Connie. Susan. Marion says she doesn't know what to do, where to turn."

"It's what she said. Susan said to her, Jim?"

"We're afraid for you two, Connie. That plain and simple. Really afraid."

"What can I tell you, Jim? How can I tell you how I feel?"

"Connie, it's why I'm here. I'm all ears." Pause.

"Remember when I first came into this bar, what happened?"

Pause.

"Do I. I remember some jerk—"

"Maybe it was more than one, Jim. Who's to say. I'll never know since I wasn't out here but in the men's room. We never talk about me being black, do we?"

"Should we?"

"But that night, I was black. Who had the can of paint? Where did it come from, Jim?"

Connie stood and looked at the face of the bar. "They painted it. Painted it with a cross and put the initials KKK on it for good measure. Touched it up just right, Jim."

"Connie, it was awful. I know."

"If you only knew, Jim. Knew the feeling." Pause. "And now I'm fighting my own hell. As, as a black man. I'm fighting my own private hell." Pause.

"How, Connie?"

"It started, began, all began with Jimmy and Billy."

"Jimmy and Billy?" Jim said mildly.

"But I didn't know it. I didn't know it then, Jim. You see, I wanted Billy to have a black friend as his best friend at the time. Not someone white. Who was white."

Connie looked at Jim, hoping he'd understand.

"Yes, but—"

"But that was a long time ago. Back. Ancient history. I got over that. Of course Billy couldn't have a better friend than Jimmy. Loyal, someone he can trust, who'll stick by him through thick and thin."

"Sure, Connie. I see your point."

"There could've come a time, Jim ..."

"When we—"

"Yes, the adults. The adults, parents—"

"Could have drawn the line. Yes, I understand fully."

"And then there's Alexis," Connie said, looking Jim square in the eye.

"A ... a white girl."

"Not black, Jim. Not a black girl. And I had to confront that issue again. Examine it again, Jim. I'd ... Susan and I had given Billy his all-white world to live in—"

"Which could reject him at any time. At a whim. Am I on target, Connie, with this? Pause. "Gosh, I never thought of it quite like that."

"As a black man, it's the only way we can look at it. Give it perspective, you see. Think. There's just not much we can take for granted. There's just not that much leeway, Jim, or margin for error. And look at me, Jim," Connie said, turning to take in the totality of Mitch's Sports Bar. "Here I am in a sea of white faces."

"And me, Connie. Here you are confiding in me."

Connie shrugged. "Who knows, Jim? Maybe it's good. Who knows?"

"Chris," Connie said, pointing to his glass.

"Connie, be right there."

Jim tugged Connie's arm. "But, Connie, it still doesn't change—"

"Susan's visit with Marion this afternoon any. I know that, Jim. Damn if I don't."

"We're worried sick."

"Jim, look … I, I'm spinning out of control. And I don't know how to get off this thing, this merry-go-round."

"You start with that," Jim said, pointing at the empty glass. "That, what's in front of you, Connie."

"Here I am, Connie," Chris said. The beer was poured into the glass. "Jim, see you don't need a refill," Chris said. "You've barely touched yours."

"I'll see my way through this. This mess of mine."

"It's your family that's at stake, Connie: Billy and Susan."

"Damn if I don't know that."

"It's all I can say, Connie."

Jim got off the barstool.

Connie took Jim and put him in a great big bear hug. "Thanks for coming. For taking the time. For the concern."

"You'd do the same for me, Connie—if it was me and Marion."

"Sure I would. You know that."

Jim turned and walked toward the bar's front door.

"You're a good, good friend, Jim," Connie said above the clatter of noise that filled the sport's bar.

Nothing was going to change for them. Susan saw no hope. Talking to Marion this afternoon had been good for the soul. She had to air out her feelings. She had to hear them in order for her to understand how far down they ran. She was running out of options. She didn't want to think like this, but it was how she'd been thinking. She had to protect herself. She had to start thinking selfishly before all of this began to consume her.

"Connie …"

He'd just come into the bedroom, into the house from his night out.

Belligerently, Connie laughed. "I closed down the bar for another night. Yep, Susan."

Susan was dressed for bed, in her pink nightgown.

"How do you like that, Sue? Closed down the bar. Me and the regulars."

Connie threw himself down on the bed. Again he laughed.

Susan simply looked at him.

Pause.

"Jim dropped by the bar."

Susan was surprised.

"I love him. Jim Boston. He's such a sweet guy, Sue. I respect the hell out of him. He is a good, good friend."

"Connie, he told you?" Susan asked, seeing the light from the bedroom lamp sitting on Connie's brown face.

"Sure. You know he did. Jim told me all about your little visit this afternoon at the house with Marion."

"Connie," Susan said, "I had to go. I had to talk to someone."

"And why not Marion, Sue? That's better than someone. Marion's the best. Grade A. It's what I told Jim. Exactly."

"And Jim, he came by the bar to—"

"Especially—I don't know if you were going to, if it was the word you were going to use—but to especially talk to me."

At that moment, Susan saw that the talk Jim had with Connie had done him no good. It made her feel more hopeless.

"Yes, good old Jim. Good buddy Jim. Coming to the aid—a white man, that is—coming to the aid of a black man. What gallantry. What sheer, magnificent gallantry."

"So that's what you think of Marion and Jim? That's what you think of them? Why, you're no better than the white phonies you say you're fighting against. Why, no better than them!"

"But they have the power, Susan," Connie said, rolling across the bed and then ending up on Susan's side. "Remember, Sue. They have the power. All the power."

"The power!"

"Nothing but, Sue. Nothing—"

"Yes, they do," Susan agreed. "But now I feel your power, Connie. Your power that's over me."

Now this thing had been twisted, and Susan understood how it'd been twisted in her favor, to favor her feelings, the pain—how she must protect herself before she became something to step on, settling for something so damaging and regrettable and pitiful.

"Connie." Susan was clearly spent. "I have to get myself out of this situation."

Connie laughed. "You're not sleeping on my old, worn couch in the den tonight, are you? Hell. Not that?"

"No, I—"

"Look, it's my den. So I'll go in there and give you some space. Give you a break tonight. I'll rest my tired head there until morning comes." Connie laughed sarcastically. "Then stare at the four walls. Will that do it for you?"

Susan stepped out of the light. "No, Connie. No. I'm not saying that, what you're thinking. What you're saying." Susan drew in her breath. "Connie, I'm leaving you. We have to separate for everyone's sanity—not just mine but yours and Billy's too. We can't keep going on like this. Continue to live like this."

"Separate? A separation!"

"It's what it's come to. Separation. Now I've said what I have to say," Susan said.

Billy was in a good mood simply because of Alexis. She was always in a good mood, so he never wanted to spoil it, no matter where he was emotionally these days. He'd always enter the house with a smile on his face or a whistle somewhere inside him, even if he didn't whistle it out loud.

Billy stuck the key in the door, then removed his backpack in the vestibule.

"Billy."

This caught him off guard. "Mom?"

When Billy got into the living room, Susan and Connie greeted him. "Hey, what's—"

Connie took the lead. "Sorry we have to do it like this, Billy, but your mother and I have to talk to you."

Then Susan took the lead. "Sit, honey. This is important."

The three sat, Susan in a chair, Connie on a couch, and Billy in a chair.

Billy seemed badly worried. He seemed to be reacting to the grimness his parents had imposed on him.

"Billy, honey," Susan began, "your father and I have come to a decision about our marriage. About our situation."

Billy's eyes were focused solely on Susan and then shifted over to Connie. *Situation,* he thought. *What situation?*

"Your father and I are arguing too much. Much more than what is healthy for our marriage, Billy. It's not good for you, us as a family, to continue like this. Along this path."

Billy's eyes set more sharply on Susan.

"I'm the one who suggested it, not your father. No. It was my idea." Susan steadied herself. "Your father and I have decided to separate for the sake of our marriage and our family. Right now, we're not a family. Your father and I are not getting along. We're just not. We need to be apart, so maybe we can come back together. Make things work again.

"Oh … I can't believe what, don't believe I just said that," Susan said, flustered.

Connie wasn't comforting her or helping her through this ordeal.

"I'm—this is hard, honey."

Billy's head swung over to Connie, and he saw a piece of stone, impenetrable.

"But it's the only way, Billy. It seems to be the only way for now. Do you understand, honey? The only way to save our marriage for now."

Susan was moving toward Billy, and Billy unexpectedly, stood.

"I'm going upstairs."

Susan stopped in her tracks.

"I have my homework to finish. And … and then I'll call Alexis like always. I always do, Mom, Dad. Excuse me."

Billy headed for the staircase, retrieved his backpack, and walked up. Soon he was in his room. He closed the door. He flipped on the light switch and put his backpack on the desk chair like always.

Billy looked at his desk where he studied. He pulled his trigonometry book out of the backpack. He could barely hold it in his hand; his hand felt so dead, numb. He looked over at his bed.

Billy felt a chill, then a dizziness. Right now, he couldn't think. He ran his hand through his Afro and then shut his eyes.

CHAPTER 15

It had been settled and worked out amiably between Connie and Susan: Susan would move out the house, and Billy and Connie would stay. Susan said since it was her idea to separate, she should be the one to leave the house, not Connie. And as for Billy, he loved them equally, they agreed, so why should it matter. Indeed, everything for the Macks had been worked out between them amiably.

It was ten days later.

Susan had done everything on her own. She was, after all, an organizer of things, a party planner for people in Pittsfield (and was handsomely paid for her services). Now she was organizing matters for herself, for her move.

The Dodge was approaching the house on Hart Street, and hitched to the back of it was a small U-Haul van. Susan felt a twinge in her stomach. She was approaching the home she was leaving. It was depressing. She felt like she could die right then.

She pulled the SUV into the driveway and parked in front of the two-car garage. She turned off the engine. She was afraid, scared to death, but in an odd kind of way excited by what she was about to take on, to see if she could pull it off—this old life she was stepping out of and the new one she was stepping into. Adrenaline suffused her.

"Mom." Billy had darted out the house.

Susan knew he'd come out to help her.

"Mom, it's nice."

Susan looked back at the U-Haul van. Her things had to be removed from the house, clothes and certain artifacts.

The job was practically done. Billy was out in the driveway with the van.

The den door was shut. Susan opened it. Connie was sitting in front of the computer.

"I came up to say goodbye, Connie."

"Thank you, Susan," Connie said, turning to Susan. *She is a beautiful woman,* he thought, *delicate, refined, sophisticated, and smart as hell!*

He stood. She walked over to him and hugged him.

"You'll be in touch, won't you, Sue?" Connie asked.

"Yes."

Susan left the room. Connie shut the door.

Susan descended the staircase, and her eyes scanned the house. "I love this house so much." She laughed. "Maybe too much."

Susan walked to the front door. She opened it and closed it.

"Mom, I want to go with you. You know I can catch the bus back. It'll be no big—"

"No, Billy. I can't let you. Not that. I must do this alone. It's important to me."

Billy was crestfallen.

She hugged him.

"I'll see you soon. Who knows when but soon," Susan said, as if confused.

"Right, Mom."

"Then you can see my new place—apartment. How it looks, honey."

"Of ... of course."

"There'll be room for you, Billy. I made sure of that when I rented it."

"Yes, I know. You told me already."

"Billy, I love you, darling."

For a second time, they hugged.

Billy opened the car door for her. Susan looked up at him and was going to say something but didn't. Billy sensed this. He backed away from the car as Susan began backing the car down the driveway, carefully. The car was at the tip of the driveway, and then it angled narrowly to its left. Billy stood there stiff, as stiff as he was yesterday in the living room when his mother told him of this day, what was happening now right before his eyes, that the move to Tyler would take place today at eleven o'clock.

"Billy, goodbye."

Billy was standing on the spot alone, without Connie. *We really aren't a family anymore*, Billy thought. *The Macks.*

Susan was on the road. She was on Harrington Highway heading for Tyler, for her new four-unit garden-style apartment building. She didn't want to think about what happened to her today, but she was. There was this creeping guilt in her that maybe she had given up on Connie and their marriage too quickly. That maybe she and Connie, after all, could have worked the whole thing out. But then she recalled the nights; they were abominable.

She had no idea what direction Connie's life would take careerwise. He was not budging from Pittsfield—that was guaranteed—because of Billy's football and, of course, Jimmy being a part of that equation.

The stunning moment now reappeared, the one she was dead certain she was trying to erase from her consciousness: her about to say something to Billy out the car's rolled-down window.

"What was I going to say to Billy? Take care of your father? Was that the heartless thing I was about to say to my sixteen-year-old son. Billy, take care of your father while I'm gone? Away?"

Susan felt disgusted with herself.

She'd even thought last night that maybe with Billy being there as Connie's responsibility might turn Connie around. (*What sick, demented little psychological game am I playing anyway?*). Susan was trying to put the burden on Billy. She was trying to unburden it onto him, for him to be the centerpiece of Connie's life, dependent on Connie, and in doing this, turn Connie's life back around to its former self. And that would be when she would go waltzing back into their lives, her family's life, through the front door with all the benefits and none of the pain, fully intact. What a stroke of genius. Pure genius!

"No, it's not what I'm thinking. It's not that!'"

Susan pulled the SUV off to the side of the highway. Cars and other vehicles zipped by.

"This isn't going to be easy. Why did I think it would? No, I never thought it would. But I couldn't continue to live like that. Not another day. I had to take action. Had to take back some control over my life, unless …"

Susan hadn't turned the car's ignition off. The car idled. Susan just wanted to take one more breath, an easy one in her chest.

"I love them. They know that. No … there's nothing for me to answer to …"

She looked out the rearview mirror and then ahead through the car's front windshield. Then the car was back on Harrington Highway, pointing ahead for Tyler.

Connie had not moved out of the den. He sat in front of the computer. His mind had a range of creative thoughts in it, flowing at will. Blast's project had failed with Ben Cleghorne at its helm. The company had to call in a new concept/design engineer from California to head the Blast team. He was to arrive Monday morning (today, Saturday).

Susan's gone. Billy's here, Connie thought. *I still have Billy, don't I? Not all is lost. I haven't destroyed everything in my life. I still have my son.*

He got up. *Things will be different for us without Susan, for Billy and me. Much, much. Billy and I will have to set up some kind of viable system, some kind of operation—reliable, effective, efficient. Yes, it's me and Billy now. We'll have to fit ourselves into a pattern, into a way of conducting our lives from day to day like a well-oiled team, machine. We must be alert, sharp, disciplined—on top of things right from the beginning of the day to its end.*

This is the challenge. This is what's ahead for me, for us, Billy and me. Why couldn't I see this before?

Everything's in my court. The ball's in my court. I have to run this household, make sure it runs reliably, efficiently, smartly—on time. Now it's up to me.

Connie was at the den door. He opened it and walked down the hallway.

"Billy," Connie's voice rang out. "Billy!" Connie continued walking. Connie opened Billy's door.

"Billy, what do you want for dinner? I'll have it ready for you in … oh, an hour. Yes, no more than an hour. It's four forty-five. Give me no more than an hour. I'll have your dinner ready by—let's synchronize our watches, okay? What do you say?"

Billy was sitting on the bed. His body was positioned toward the window.

"That's okay, Dad. I'm not hungry right now. Okay?"

Susan pushed back the window's curtain. She looked out on this new street of hers, Langhorne Street. It was a beautiful street to look at, a well-kept street, not unlike Hart Street. While it didn't feel like home, she knew in time it would. But for now, it wasn't.

She had to look out the window. She was almost compelled to. Billy was coming to visit. They'd spoken over the phone Wednesday, and he'd said he'd like to go to Tyler. This was sooner than she'd anticipated. A week after leaving home, Billy said he wanted to visit her. She'd felt good with this development, since she had thought she wouldn't see him for another week, three at most.

She'd volunteered to go back to Pittsfield by car to pick him up, but Billy said he'd travel to Tyler by bus. He said all she had to do was tell him the connecting route. The trip was no more than thirty-five, forty minutes total.

In a way, she was relieved Billy chose to travel to Tyler on his own, since she didn't know how she would have reacted seeing the old house again, being outside of it in a parked car. It was bad enough last Saturday pulling up in front of the house with a U-Haul van. That was agony beyond comprehension. But to sit outside a house you love in a car, and everything you love's inside, well …

Billy said he would be at the apartment by one o'clock. It was 12:25. He sounded good over the phone. Now the cat and mouse game, the cheating. How much should she inquire of Connie through Billy? How much of a go-between should her son become for her? A conduit? But to use him this way, to exploit Billy—it upset her. Even if she asked how he was, how Connie was doing, its motive would go further than what it seemed. Billy would be serving her deception.

Susan's fingers released the curtain. Her life was now filled with doubts and struggles, and she was now fearful of them turning into regrets. She felt bitter about the whole thing. Sometimes it was self-pity. The nights had not been of any real comfort to her. She wasn't turning over new gems of wisdom. She had left her husband and son as if she'd abandoned them; what was happening to them had been too tough for her skin. It's what she'd done, and it had such a selfish feel to it, a grisly tale, similar to a crime.

She felt safe where she was, yet she wanted to fight to save her marriage. She loved Connie. Being away from him for a week had brought this feeling into clearer focus. It was never at issue, her loving Connie. It was never a question of that. But he'd gotten lost. He was rummaging through the past, something you can't go back to fix or rectify. Pittsfield was an all-white town when she and Connie arrived there, and it would remain that way if they were to leave. Pittsfield was Pittsfield, no matter anyone's regrets.

Susan glanced at her watch. Billy would be at her new apartment building soon. She couldn't wait to see him, to be with him, to hold him. It's all she longed for was to hold her tall, handsome son.

This time when Susan pulled back the window's curtain, she saw Billy and—treat of treats—Alexis too!

Susan, who was in flats, dashed out the apartment and onto the front lawn to greet them.

"Billy!"

"Mom!"

Her arms were outstretched, and Billy ran to her like Billy Steamroller Mack ran on the football field: full steam ahead.

Susan was lifted off the ground.

Alexis stood and watched with a pretty smile on her gorgeous face.

"Alexis, honey," Susan said as Billy put her back down on the ground. "What a treat—the two of you."

"Alexis wouldn't let me come alone. I guess she thought I might get lost."

"Oh, Billy," Alexis said.

"She knows how I am with directions."

Susan hugged Alexis.

"He's such a phony, isn't he, Alexis? A big phony at that."

"You can say that again, Mrs. Mack. I second it." Alexis smiled.

"Always trying to pretend how unsmart he is, when we know—"

"Billy's a brain."

Billy wrapped his arms around Susan and Alexis, standing over them.

"Now, Mom, may Alexis and I see this new apartment of yours? Your new digs?"

"Why, of course."

Susan got to the front door of the apartment and opened it for him.

"Wow, Mom. It's great!"

"Great, Mrs. Mack! Great!"

The apartment came furnished, but Susan, in a week's time, had added her own Susan Mack wrinkle to the place with great panache.

Susan had fixed lunch for Billy and Alexis. Alexis and Billy had eaten like ten hungry refugees. As active as both were, Susan knew they'd burn the calories off in no time flat. *Oh to be young*, she'd thought at the time, *and not have to worry about a waistline.*

Alexis had been quite up front with Susan and Billy. She told them she wanted them to have an opportunity to speak privately.

Susan, after recovering from Alexis's intelligence and acute sensitivity, thanked her.

Alexis had stepped into the living room. The TV was on. Susan and Billy remained in the kitchen. Billy was holding Susan's hand. They sat at the table, not one saying a word to the other. Billy's hand just lay inside Susan's, soothingly.

"Mom, I was going to call you to let you know Alexis was coming."

"I'm glad you didn't."

"Yes, I thought better of it. I know how much you like surprises."

"You mean *love*, Billy. Love, don't you?"

"Uh, love. Yeah—we can x out *like*." Pause.

"Mom, Dad …"

"Yes?"

"He's trying his best. The best he can, I guess."

A scare bit Susan. *What does that mean?*

"His best, honey?"

"This is all new to us, Mom." Billy frowned. "You not being in the house is brand-new territory. We're trying to do things the same, as if you were still there with us, but it's different. Things have changed."

The crime she had committed. This awful, grisly crime she had committed.

"You hate me, don't you, Billy? Don't you!"

Susan's hand fell out of Billy's, and she rushed to her feet. Then she turned back to look at Billy.

Why am I doing this to Billy? Why am I doing this to my teenage son?

"No, Mom. Hate you? How can I hate you? I kind of knew what Dad was putting you through. I mean, I did know. The arguing and all. The night I had to break you up. The two of you up. I, it's just that I don't know how it started or why. I have no clue, Mom."

Susan sat back down. Her hand slipped back into Billy's. "That, how it began, I can't tell you, Billy. I can't—"

"Then who will?"

"I can't. I don't know, Billy."

"It's like I feel I'm somehow responsible for all of this between you and dad, and I don't know how or why."

Pause.

"It … is it a secret? Is it?"

Susan was seeing firsthand what she and Connie had done to Billy, to their son. They had given him a perverted view of life that was growing more and more dangerous and persistent each day. But Susan knew she couldn't explain to Billy something she didn't believe—that she and Connie had gotten their community, Pittsfield, all wrong; that Billy had gotten his best friend, Jimmy Boston, all wrong; that Billy had gotten his girlfriend, Alexis Price, all wrong. Connie believed those things, not her. It was the cause of her troubles, and, of course, there was more.

"Is it a secret, Mom?"

"Billy." Susan was rubbing Billy's hand skittishly. "I can't think. I can't. I'm alone in this apartment, and it's all I have time to do, think. Yet I can't. All I do is worry but not think." Pause.

"When you think, you ... you want to come up with solutions, alternatives. It's why you think, honey. And I have none. No solution to this situation. All I do is worry about you and your father. It's all I've done for the past six days." Pause.

"Are you coming back to us, Mom?"

Susan had expected this. She tenderly brushed the tears from Billy's eyes with her hand.

"And thanks for coming, Alexis. You're welcome anytime you want to venture into Tyler." Susan laughed.

Billy and Alexis were walking down the walkway.

"And make sure you call me the minute you get back, Billy, to the house. Let me know you and Alexis got back safely."

"I'll make sure that he does, Mrs. Mack," Alexis said cheerily. "As soon as we get to my house, I'll march him over to the phone, Mrs. Mack."

"Thanks, Alexis."

Susan stood on the apartment's outer brick stoop, and then, soon, Alexis and Billy were gone. Susan stood there. The day was gentle enough for her to do just that—stand there. It was May, and summer was on the horizon.

"How long can I hold up?"

By asking this question, Susan knew she had to make her life the most important thing there was to her. That there was nothing more important to her than her. That she must involve herself and go after life with no signs of slowing down or letting up.

She only hoped this was possible, that she could redirect herself, her thoughts. It would have to be done by herself—within the sphere of some brand-new experience she must envision for herself. It'd always been family: Connie and Billy. For Connie to work out his problems, he had to have space. She had wanted to call him the past six days, badly so. But she resisted any such temptation. It was how she would have to train her mind to think—deliberate avoidance. Now was the appropriate time.

Susan held on to her arms. She'd had enough of the outdoors, she thought.

"In time, Billy will have to be sacrificed too," she said, shutting the front door behind her.

She fully understood what she'd just said. For the rebuilding of Susan Mack, Billy would have to be sacrificed in some tawdry, guilt-free way—in order for her to get on with it, for her to be able to put one foot in front of the other.

"He'll have to be sacrificed," Susan said forcibly.

Susan walked in the direction of the apartment's bedroom. "But today I'll wait for his call. To make sure he and Alexis got home safely." Pause.

"It's what matters most for me now."

CHAPTER 16

It was two months later.

It took a month before Connie went back to drinking. He was back in Mitch's Sports Bar, back to being a regular customer, to drinking beers and getting drunk. He was heading out the door, fumbling with his car keys.

"Night, Connie!" Chris shouted out. "See you tomorrow night!"

"You … you bet you will, Chris. On the dot. Just … just keep my barstool warm for me overnight."

Connie gained better control over the car keys. He looked down at them with strain, then grasped them.

The night was humid. It was mid-July, and the temperature had stalled. Mitch's was air-conditioned. Instantly, Connie felt the difference. But by now, he was accustomed to the abrupt change in climate when coming out of Mitch's bar at this time.

Shortly, Connie was in the Buick. He stopped for a second, for he could hear himself breathing hard.

"What's wrong with me?" He cried. "Susan! Susan!"

And like that, in a spurt, he felt like a beaten, downtrodden man. "Su-Susan."

He'd spoken to her twice over the phone, twice since she'd left him. And each time, it had something to do with finances. Nothing more than finances—not about them.

"Finances! Fucking finances!"

What is she doing with her life? Connie thought. *Two weeks ago, she sounded calm, so stable—nearly bloodless. And how did I sound? And how did I sound with no beer in me? Like the old Connie, the one who provided for his family and had that certain genius in him?*

Connie was on the road. The car wouldn't weave; he wouldn't let it. Every night, this was his challenge: to get home from Mitch's Sports Bar safely in his car and to make sure the car didn't weave in the road. This was his ultimate satisfaction from day to day. And the car wasn't weaving in the road. Not tonight, it wasn't, or any night, no matter how drunk he got. No matter how bad his head got.

The headlights were shining on the two-car garage. Connie could still hear himself breathing—a steady flow of unfiltered air.

"Home," Connie said, slapping the steering wheel.

"M-made it. Made it!"

Nothing had changed about the house since Susan left. Everything was as she'd left it, inside the house and out.

Shortly, Connie was up the staircase and on the landing. Then he was in his bedroom. He turned the bedroom light on.

"You drove Mom away! You drove her away!"

"Billy—"

"You drove Mom away with your drinking. You're drunk, Dad. Drunk!"

Connie couldn't get hold of himself. His head spun.

"You, you just let her go!"

Connie still couldn't find words in him big enough or powerful enough to appease Billy.

"You," Billy said, getting off the bed, "didn't fight for Mom, Dad. You just let her go, let her, her—"

Connie grabbed Billy and hugged him.

"You don't understand, Billy. You don't understand, son. You're too young to—"

Billy bolted from Connie. He ran out of the room.

Connie's body released its breath.

And now he was the one sitting on the edge of the bed, not in the dark, as Billy had, but with the ceiling light shining down on his mass. The beers in him had evaporated. This was serious stuff. This was the first time Billy had come to terms with his true emotions around him. The separation between him and Susan was real now. Two months and a week made it real now.

The days were dragging on them, painfully wearing them down. *How long had Billy been sitting in the darkened room waiting for me?* Connie asked himself.

He got up. He had to talk to Billy. He owed him that much of himself.

"Billy." Connie was in Billy's room.

"Billy …"

"I heard you, Dad," Billy whispered.

"I just want you to know that it wasn't your mother's fault, the separation. It is nothing your mother did to cause it. I was the problem. All of it stemmed from me. From me all along, son."

"But why? Why when you knew it could lead to this?"

Billy hadn't turned on his bedroom light, and neither had Connie. They weren't looking at each other, just hearing each other's emotions.

"I never thought at the time it could lead to this. Believe me, Billy. Please believe me. That much about this whole nasty thing."

"And why am I too young to understand what's happened between you and Mom, Dad? It sounds like a cop-out, a convenient cop-out."

"It's not, Billy. I can assure you—"

"I don't know what, who to believe anymore."

"Look, Billy. I know we've thrown your life into a tailspin. That—"

"Tailspin? Is that what it is, Dad? A … a tailspin? Man, Dad, man. It feels much worse than that. Much, much—"

"I know. I—"

"And I'm tired, Dad, of you saying that. I'm sick and tired of hearing you say that you know."

The lights shot on.

"You made those guys my heroes," Billy said, pointing at the two framed men. "Jackie Robinson and Jim Brown, Dad."

Connie looked at them as well.

"But it was you I looked up to more than anyone."

"Me?"

"I thought you could beat up the world, Dad. Thought you could beat anything in the world."

"No, I can't, Billy. I can't. I'm only human, son. Human, nothing more."

"But why? Why think that way when your heroes are … are my heroes?"

"They're heroes on the playing field. Only on the playing field. But real life's not—it's not always about sports."

Pause.

"But couldn't you have fought for Mom? Put up a fight?"

"Billy, not at the time, son."

"So you just gave up? Is that it? Chucked it?"

Connie's skin felt prickly.

"Not give up, Billy. But things must change in me before I can ask your mother to come back, to try over again. To make a go of our marriage again. To put our family back together, Billy."

"And can you, Dad, change? Whatever this thing is that's changed you, that you're holding … keeping from me?"

"Damn, Billy. I've let it fester in me for so long that now it's overpowered me. It's bigger than me."

"Overpowered you?"

"Some things I can't beat, Billy, like I said. Some things take time. Can't be fixed overnight."

The light in the room went out.

"I understand, Dad."

Silence.

"Good night, Billy."

"Good night, Dad."

Billy was running between his house in Pittsfield and Susan's apartment in Tyler. But lately, Susan didn't seem to have time for Billy. She was about to embark upon something she'd always wanted, her long-lost dream to become a trial lawyer. It was the dream she'd deferred when she'd carried Billy. She was to enroll in Tyler College in the fall as a prelaw student. All of her energies and attention were being turned to this end, and it was particularly felt by Billy. He could feel himself becoming less and less important to her, a shadowy light that moved in and out of her life, unnoticed and disregarded.

Billy was at the Bostons'. It was late afternoon. Jimmy and Billy were on the porch.

"Hi, Sally Ann," Billy said, waving at Sally Ann Schumacher.

"Hi, Billy." And then Sally Ann looked over at Jimmy. "Hi, Jimmy."

"Hi, Sally Ann."

"She's some stunner now, huh, Jimmy?" Billy said, watching Sally Ann enter the house.

"And she still has a big crush on you know who."

"Hey, that's passé, Jimmy. She's no longer a little girl with a red bow in her hair."

"She's a teenager."

"Yeah."

"A teenager subject to the vicissitudes of life," Jimmy said glumly.

"In other words, Jimmy, it was good while it lasted, my man."

Jimmy laughed. "Yeah. We all have to grow up sometime."

"I bet she has a crush on at least twenty other guys in the neighborhood by now."

Pause.

"Hey, Steamroller, feel like going upstairs into the chamber of racket? There's something I want your ears to hear. For your ears and your ears only."

"By special invitation, huh?" Billy laughed.

They zipped up the staircase.

"Billy, you're going to love it, man!"

"Just hope I still have all my hearing by age forty." Pause. "In my advanced years."

Billy and Jimmy had played more than one audio tape in Jimmy's "chamber of racket," as he called it. In fact, they'd played quite a few tapes by now. Now they were talking about girls—specifically, Alexis and Judy.

"Steamroller, so when are we going out on another double date, the four of us?"

"Why ask me? I'm not the one in charge. Alexis is."

"Oh, so she wears the pants in the family?"

"Hey, Jimmy, don't try to play cool with me, man. You know Judy's the boss in your family too. Queen supreme. Queen of the jungle. You ain't fooling nobody, man."

"Billy, ever since girls started wearing pants, my dad said."

"Mr. Boston's right."

"Wouldn't have it any other way though."

"Me either," Billy said.

"We can sit here and pretend all we want that we're henpecked, but we love it. Just love it."

"You don't have to say any more to convince me, man. Jimmy, we are two lucky hombres."

Billy picked up one of Jimmy's audio tapes, browsed it, and then put it back down.

"Only, how long will it last—this happiness—Jimmy?"

Jimmy knew just what Billy was alluding to.

"Billy, Alexis loves you. You love her. Every relationship's going to have problems. Ups and downs. You just have to work them out. Through them. That's all."

"Yeah, I guess so." Pause.

Jimmy was totally surprised by this negative piece of information Billy had handed him.

"Problems? What kind of problems could you and Alexis be having? It's the first I've heard."

Billy took a big breath. "Sexual."

"Wow, Billy. Judy and me too!"

"When or, better still, if we should have sex. Should or shouldn't we."

"You know, Judy and I are struggling with that same thing."

"It's tough, Jimmy. Really rough. My hormones are doing a number on me."

"Yeah, something fierce."

"Alexis's too."

"Ditto. Ditto for Judy," Jimmy said.

Billy and Jimmy spread both their long bodies across Jimmy's bed, with their legs dangling off it like fishermen sitting on a wharf.

"I can't believe we're talking like this, Jimmy—you and me."

"Believe it, Steamroller. Believe it."

"I mean, certain things maybe we should keep between, you know …"

"Billy, we're the best of friends, buddies. Look, Judy and Alexis wouldn't mind. They've probably shared the same kind of stuff between them by now."

"You think they've talked about sex? Really, Jimmy?"

"Come on, Billy, Steamroller."

"Yeah, yeah." Billy laughed, trying to undo his innocence. "Yeah, of course they have. For a fact."

"So have you and Alexis come up with anything? Because Judy and I sure haven't. Even though our hormones are raging."

"No, we're trying to do the right thing by everybody. But …"

"Tell me about it!"

"We'd disappoint a lot of people if, for instance, Alexis got pregnant. Her parents. Would the Prices be disappointed in me."

Pause.

"Judy and I, we were thinking about, uh, using a condom."

"Hey, Jimmy, there's no guarantee with those things either, man. You know that, don't you? Condoms can leak."

"Like a water balloon."

"With you in it!"

"Right!"

Jimmy glanced at the shine of a smile on Billy's cheeks. It was nice to see Billy smile for a change, Jimmy thought. He'd been under a great deal of pressure as of late.

"Teenage problems, huh, Jimmy? The stuff life's made out of, so adults tell us," Billy said, rubbing his chin.

"This sex thing is killing me though, Billy."

"Killing us both. I'm not even thinking about this upcoming football season. Not right now."

"Steamroller, uh, now … now let's not get ridiculous here. Absurd. Carried away. Okay?"

"Not until Coach Bosco gives us his forty lashes with his whip, I'm not."

"He said he's going to be extra tough on us this year." Jimmy winced. "No superstar stuff. No prima donnas on the team."

"Not on a Coach Bosco team. The Purple Eagles. No one's getting special treatment."

"Maybe Coach will hand out a new playbook this year, Billy."

"I can learn it faster than the quarterback. Outsmart you, Jimmy. Prove once and for all that fullbacks aren't dumb—can only punch holes in walls and make license plates with our heads for a living."

"Why, no contest, Steamroller. No contest at all. I look forward to the challenge!"

Jimmy was doing what Billy had asked him to. He was down in the kitchen with Marion. He took her by the waist and walked her over to the kitchen table. They sat.

"Billy has a favor to ask of us, Mom. He'd like to stay for dinner tonight, if you don't mind."

"Mind? Of course he may," was Marion's automatic response, but then she thought deeper about Billy's request.

"Thanks. But one other thing, Mom. Billy would like for you to call the house. Mr. Mack."

"He does? Why, yes, I can do that. Call Connie to—"

"Tell him Billy's staying for dinner."

Jimmy's eyes were telling her she had to do it right then.

"I'll call him now. Uh, this very instant," Marion said, getting up from the table.

Marion knew the Macks' telephone number by heart.

"Uh, hello. Good evening, Connie. Yes, this is Marion. Marion Boston."

Jimmy was back upstairs with Billy. "It's a go, done deal. Mom took care of it."

"I just don't want to go home tonight, that's all. Face him tonight. Face the guy, Jimmy."

They were heading down the staircase.

"Jimmy, your fa—"

Jim Boston came barreling through the front door.

"Hey, Billy! Jimmy!"

"Hello, Mr. Boston!"

"Hi, Dad!"

"Your father will be home early tonight," Marion yelled from the kitchen, "was what I was about to say before he showed up!"

"What? Dinner's on, Marion?" Jim asked from the hallway.

"Well, you said you'd be home at—"

"Six thirty, and it is six thirty."

Jimmy and Billy were down the staircase, and Jim went up to them, putting himself in the middle. He grabbed Jimmy and Billy around their waists, and the three marched gallantly in the direction of the kitchen, where the food was.

Marion had told Jim when he called that Billy was staying for dinner.

"Here we are, Marion." Jim beamed. "The Three Musketeers."

"Don't date yourself, Jim," Marion said while applying the finishing touches on the kitchen table's setting.

"Marion, these kids know about the Three Musketeers. Right guys? You know a—"

"Sure, Dad," Jimmy said, embarrassed.

"Sure, Mr. Boston," Billy said with muscle in his voice. "We know, uh, Jimmy and I know all about those three guys, all right, sir. They're not dated."

"See, Marion? No fear. The Green Hornet's here!"

"Jim, now that's enough!"

"Billy, you know where to sit."

"Yes, Mr. Boston—wherever you and Jimmy and Mrs. Boston aren't."

They laughed.

The food was on the table. Jim blessed it.

"Dig in, guys!"

"This looks like a training table, Mom. Huh, Steamroller?"

"The ones you see for college football players—all you can eat for free."

Plates of food were being passed around the table with great aplomb.

Billy looked at the Bostons. It felt so much like family, he thought. Something he missed.

They'd been at the table for a while.

"Billy, more corn?"

"Yes, thank you, Mrs. Boston."

Marion passed the platter of corn on the cob to Billy.

"Hey, Mom, what about me?"

"Billy's first in order. He's our guest tonight, Jimmy."

"Guest? Billy's no guest in the Boston house. You know Billy's family, Mom."

"Regardless, Jimmy," Marion said, passing the platter to Billy, "you'll have to wait." She laughed.

Maria had awakened. She glanced at the alarm clock on her lamp table. She knew the time Frank had rolled out of bed—5:42 a.m. It was 6:02 a.m.

"He's probably in …"

She got out of bed—destination bathroom. The first time she yawned, she didn't cover her mouth; the second time, she did.

"Frank, I knew where you'd be. Excited, huh?"

"A new season, Maria. And with it new thrills!"

"Frank, it's only the beginning of August. So why are—"

"But it'll be September soon. Oh, you know how I get once—ah …"

Frank was halfway out of the tub. Maria handed him a towel (it had blue and red polka dots).

"I should by now, shouldn't I?" Maria was in a magenta negligee.

"A football coach's wife shouldn't have an excuse for not knowing," Frank said. He was toweling his privates.

Maria stood in front of the wall mirror brushing her teeth.

"It's going to be a long day, Maria."

"Complaining already?"

"No. It's just this preseason hype stuff."

"Jimmy Boston and Billy Mack and the Purple Eagles going for their second consecutive state championship," Maria said.

"It's all those reporters. They'll be yakking about it all season."

"So ..."

"You know what could happen. So there'll be caution at every turn, right? I don't want the team to get ahead of itself. Bigheaded. Their heads outgrow their helmets. Sometimes, you're the cause of your own downfall."

"But there will be a second championship, won't there, Frank?" Maria asked, looking into the mirror vainly.

"Oh yeah, no doubt, Maria. Two in a row." Pause. "It'd look good on my résumé. It's like a pearl, a gem, about as gorgeous as you."

Maria turned to Frank, seemingly deflecting the flirtatious compliment.

"Frank, do you feel Billy and Jimmy are under a lot of pressure?"

He paused. He was putting on his underwear. He nodded.

"Could you be a little clearer?" Maria laughed nervously. "I'm not the press, you know."

"Well," Frank said, laughing, "yes in the sense that it's always hard to top yourself. That's the hard part. You know if Michael Jordan can come back and average thirty points a game again or better next season, say, for example." Pause.

"But no in the sense that Billy and Jimmy seem to be prepared for the pressures of performing. Like it's what they'd mentally, spiritually— whatever—prepared themselves for since they were born. Came out the cradle. They're so gifted.

"Hey, that's a real mouthful, huh, Maria? A real plate of pasta. But to see it every day up close and personal, why, it is exciting. I love those kids. Love them to death."

Maria smiled saucily. "Oh, you love all your players, Frank, not just them."

"I do. But especially Jimmy and Billy."

"I don't want to be around you when our little bambino comes. When he pops out of the oven."

Frank held Maria from behind.

"It's going to happen again, isn't it, Maria?"

"Well, we've certainly been trying hard enough. Doesn't seem like I get a day off of late. Sex, sex, sex."

"Sex." Frank grinned. "I've turned into the Italian stallion of Pittsfield. It's how I'm feeling these days. No kidding, Maria."

Frank pressed his hand onto Maria's pleasing, round rump.

"Not now, Frank," Maria said breathlessly.

"Yeah, come to think of it, I do have to talk to the press," Frank said, straightening out his particulars.

"And I have to finish Mrs. Meredith Winslow's new evening dress that seems to never want to get done this morning. Why, at least, not in this lifetime."

"Did, uh, you do that on purpose, the breath thing you just did when I was holding you?"

"Oh, just another talent of mine I didn't know I had until now." Pause. "Next you'll be singing arias like Renata Tebaldi."

"Who? What? Me sing like Renata Tebaldi, Frank!"

"Hell. Who knows, Maria, what you're liable to do," Frank said, exiting the bathroom.

Maria wheeled around to take a more serious look at herself in the mirror.

"La la la la la la la. Lu lu lu lu. Li li li li li li li li."

Frank felt like saying, "Oh no, Maria, I was kidding! Just kidding!" But instead, he applauded. "Brava, Maria!"

After all, he thought, she had to put up with far worse from him, what with her being a football coach's wife for how many years now?

Alexis was at Judy's house. They were in the huge backyard, sitting on elegant lawn furniture, batting at bugs.

"Ugh, got one, Alexis!" Judy shrieked.

"Good! That's one less bug in the insect kingdom we'll have to worry about."

Judy was scratching her arm. "It must've been a mosquito, darn it."

"I hate them. Especially when they buzz in your ears."

"Buzz … buzz," Judy said, imitating a mosquito.

"Judy, I could go for another glass of lemonade, if you don't mind."

"Good, huh, Alexis? Jimmy loves my lemonade too."

Judy poured the lemonade into the glass from the plain white pitcher.

"Love. We use that word a lot—don't we, Judy? It's really slipped quite conveniently into our vocabularies."

"We do. I guess so."

"Billy and I use it all the time," Alexis said. "Among ourselves, that is." She tightened the red band to her cute ponytail.

"Jimmy and I do too," Judy said, as if she and Jimmy were not to be outdone by Billy and Alexis.

"I guess we're at the age when we mean it. When we *can* mean it," Alexis said, taking a sip from the glass.

"Yes. I know I do, Alexis—mean it."

"Even if we don't have much experience at this," Alexis said more seriously.

"Sometimes, you know, I think you have to throw caution to the wind when it comes to our feelings, Alexis."

"You mean matters of the heart," Alexis said exaggeratedly.

"Alexis, ha! Don't make me laugh."

"Judy, honestly, though, we are in love, aren't we?"

"Very. Morning, noon, and night. There's nothing else to call it at this stage."

Judy poured lemonade into her glass. "Have you and Billy—have you two discussed sex yet?"

"Yes. What about you and Jimmy?"

"Yes."

"And I, we (I guess everything's we now)," Alexis said, shaking her head, "we want to …"

"But …"

"We want to be responsible."

"You know, Alexis, it's how Billy and I feel about having sex at this stage of our relationship."

"But it's bugging us, Judy."

"Oh no!" Judy shrieked. "I can't believe you said that. Not with these bugs buzzing around us!"

"I can't either. But it is an issue. A big one."

"It has to be. It's going to be an open topic though."

"I know. It's not going away. Not until it's resolved in some kind of adult way."

Judy smiled. "We're all sixteen. We're growing up. All of us, and fast."

"But with Billy, Judy, there's more on his mind than …" Alexis looked down at her half-empty glass of lemonade as if she were finished with it.

"Billy's parents and all. Mr. and Mrs. Mack," Judy said timidly.

"When's it going to end for him? I keeping asking myself. It's something I ask myself over and over, Judy. When will it end?" Worry lines were on Alexis's face.

"He's hurting so much inside. It's so painful, Judy. He, he tries to be …"

"Normal?"

"He's holding it in. So much of it. It's not good. Far too much as of late." Alexis sighed.

"Alexis, have you told him that?"

"No, I haven't."

Judy saw no reason why she should follow up on that question with another. How sure of herself could Alexis be about this thing they were just learning about?

"He just wants it to end in the worst kind of way. He wants his mom and dad back together. It's all Billy's asking for." Pause. "Is that too much to ask?"

"I'd never think of it happening to my mom and dad," Judy said.

"Mine either," Alexis said.

"But it does to other families like ours, all the time it seems."

"Uh-huh. You don't always know what goes on behind closed doors. Your parents' secrets. Even though Billy's parents, Billy said, had been arguing a lot. Openly."

Judy looked at her glass of lemonade, and it no longer looked appealing to her.

"Alexis, may I ask you a question? When did you stop seeing Billy as black?"

"The moment I saw him."

"Camelot," Judy said.

Pause.

""You know what? Let's think up some new cheers for this year. A little more razzamatazz," Judy said, springing from her chair.

"Why, that's not a bad idea."

"We need some new ones, and since—"

"You're team captain this year, Judy …"

"Why in the world not!"

"And ..."

Judy kind of mulled over the situation. Then she seemed to rise to the occasion.

"How about this one, Alexis!" Judy said, rising from the ground, emitting a shriek that could have quite possibly scared the entire bug population of the entire Western Hemisphere out of hiding in one fell swoop.

CHAPTER 17

Being high school All-Americans and again preseason All-Americans brought with it a lot of media attention, meaning interviews. Grinding interviews. Tiresome interviews.

"Man, Jimmy, I don't know about you, but I'm beat."

Jimmy and Billy were on the P-6 cross-town bus heading home.

"You? Today was no piece of cake. Uh-uh."

"Coach says if you can get along well with the press, then that's most of the hassle stripped from the equation right there."

"I know," Jimmy said, leaning back on the hard gray plastic seat, totally exhausted. "College level. Pro level."

"They'll be there, Jimmy. Heck, man, every step of the way. They have to get their copy, Coach says."

Jimmy stared at Billy. "Hey, Steamroller, what's Coach becoming? Some kind of guru to you, man?"

"Jealous, huh? Just because I listen to Coach Bosco, huh? Just because he's my main man, huh?"

"Hey, I listen to him too."

"But sometimes I think you're ... you're too much on cloud nine to listen to anyone but—"

"Judy."

"So you're seeing her later?" Billy slapped his forehead. "Why did I even bother to ask? What a dumb question. I'm usually smarter."

"Usually."

"Where?"

"In Cunningham Park."

"In a spot nobody knows but you and Judy." Billy rubbed his knuckles until they reddened. "Jimmy, suppose something happens out there? I mean, I don't want to bring bad—"

"Nothing will, Billy. It's cool."

"Cool? I don't know where my best friend in life and his girlfriend hang out in Cunningham Park, and he's telling me it's cool. An offhanded cool at that."

"It is, Billy."

"Jimmy ..." Billy looked at Jimmy intently, practically to the point of pleading with him. "You know, I sometimes worry about you and Judy out there. All joking aside, man. I do. Seriously."

"Don't, Billy. I mean, it's all right. Nothing's going to happen to Judy and me."

"I just thought I'd let you know."

"I'm glad you did. But there'll come a time—don't worry—when you'll know. It won't remain a deep, dark secret forever," Jimmy said reassuringly.

"Okay. Okay."

Long pause.

"So what about you and Alexis? What are you two up to later?"

"Home for me. Alexis and her parents are going out together. So I guess it's home for me."

They remembered there was a time when Billy wouldn't say it like he did.

Judy had gotten to Cunningham Park. She was sitting on a huge rock. The mountain range in the distance was at least eight hundred yards away, and there, a footpath could be found to begin the climbing of it, a majestic-looking mountain. The cluster of trees didn't hide its visibility from where Judy sat. But it was the scent of the flowers, the fine blend of them, that Judy was enjoying, having shut her eyes to better enjoy their friendly fragrances.

"Judy, hey, you got here first!"

Judy hopped off the rock and back on her feet in a jiffy.

They kissed.

"You're not supposed to get here first."

They kissed longer than before.

"But I did."

They held hands while walking loosely over to the same rock Judy had sat on (favorite).

"How'd it go with the press?"

"Boring."

"You said it would."

"And it was—very. This All-American stuff is great, but the crap you have to put up with Pepsodent smiles and—"

"Billy too?"

"Billy too. It was like we were poster children for a toothpaste commercial or—"

"A dental ad?"

"Ha. This stuff, Judy, man, is not what it's cracked up to be. It's for the birds."

Jimmy looked around at the clear blue sky.

"Judy!" Jimmy said excitedly.

"What!"

"One day, we should get hold of a can of spray paint and paint our names on this rock!"

"But that'd be graffiti, Jimmy," Judy said self-righteously.

"Hey, who'd know?"

"Right." Judy paused. "No one comes out here but us."

"So you're game, Jud? You're with me on this?"

"Am I. I'm all the way in!" Pause. "When?"

"No rush." Jimmy laughed. "But soon, okay?"

"That's a promise?"

"Come on, you know better. Of course it is. My word's gold."

Jimmy kissed Judy's forehead and rubbed her nose with his. "Now, how do the new cheers—how are they working out, by the way?"

"You want to see one?" Judy said, bouncing off the rock.

"Uh … wait a minute. Why don't you surprise me on game day! That'll be better, I think."

Judy rejoined Jimmy on the rock.

"Billy, Jimmy, how was he today?"

Jimmy hesitated. "Okay, I guess."

Judy sighed. "When do promises end, Jimmy?"

"What—that's a loaded question coming out of—"

"Will … will you always love me, Jimmy?"

"Yes, I will. Always."

"I mean, there's no reason to be afraid of anything?"

"Not with us, Judy. That, you'll never have to worry about. Not us."

Pause.

"Billy … I mean, he didn't want to go home after school. It was like similar to the other night at the house, you know, when Billy stayed for dinner. Go home—to what? For what?"

Jimmy was on his feet.

"There was a time … Man, was there ever. It seems like it was just the other day. Billy's world was perfect then like, like ours, Jud. Yours and mine."

"I know."

"I love them too. Mr. and Mrs. Mack. I miss that situation. I miss that situation over at Billy's." Jimmy's voice became more upset, disturbed. "And now Mrs. Mack, she's becoming a problem."

It seemed Judy didn't want to ask the obvious but instead let Jimmy clear his head and mind. There was pain pushing through his face. It seemed as if Jimmy needed more of Cunningham Park's air to calm him, to cap his anger.

"She's not there for him. All of a sudden, you see … Lately, Judy, she's been too busy to see him. I guess she's been …

"Billy wanted to go over to Tyler and see her last weekend, but she said, Mrs. Mack, told Billy she was too busy. Can you imagine Mrs. Mack saying that! Not her, Judy. Not her. Mrs. Mack. Even she's changed. The separation has changed her. Even her!"

Jimmy had said it with such anger it made Judy realize just how badly the truth could hurt.

"Alexis is worried, Jimmy," Judy said softly.

"She should be. All of us should be worried. Billy's tired of going from house to house."

"He told you that?"

"The same night we ate at the house. He's tired, Judy. Plain sick and tired of going from house to house like this. Billy hates it, man."

"I know I would."

"And now Mrs. Mack doesn't even have time for him."

"It seems that way. When Billy needs her the most."

Judy drew Jimmy to her. She'd stood.

"What can we do to help him?"

"There's nothing. I can't see any—there's nothing right now I can think of."

"Don't say that. It's like you're willing to give up, and you're not a quitter. Not one to give up."

"You're, no I'm not, Judy. I, no, I'm not giving up. But there's the football season, you know, maybe we can count on. Maybe that's the distraction he needs. It might do it for Billy. It should, Judy. I think it should."

"Last year, when Billy's parents were having problems, Alexis and I, we thought he was running angry."

"Yeah, I know. You told me."

"Yes, I did. That's not good, is it? Running angry on the football field."

"Look, Judy, I don't know," Jimmy answered, annoyed.

"Sorry."

"Football has to bail him out. You know, out of this problem. Billy has to find some distraction, something to put his mind at peace." Pause. "I know when I'm on the field, I don't worry about anything. I'm at peace with myself. It takes my mind off everything—exams, you know, stuff like that."

And then Jimmy suddenly realized what he'd said. "I realize exams aren't as big as the things Billy's going through. No comparison. But—" Jimmy kicked the grass. "I don't know what it is I'm trying to say. I just want it to work all the way around for Billy. For everyone, Judy."

Football season was supposed to be on his mind, but it wasn't. The Purple Eagles going for a second straight state championship was supposed to be on his mind, but it wasn't. Billy's mind was crammed with so many other things.

The world he'd known and felt secure in had fallen apart and was in a state of shambles, disrepair—and he still had no idea why. Every day, he was living with that thought. Every day, he was being forced into it. The thrill of a new football season with Coach Bosco and Jimmy and the Purple Eagles was not that now. Even Alexis was no substitute for what was at the center of the storm in his life: his mom and dad. It was all that mattered to him. The thought of separation, of it being a permanent fact in his life, of it staying that way, had fully worked its way into him. There were no more layers he could build. He had tried that, ever so feebly, and it hadn't worked for him; it'd made things worse. Today, his mom and dad were separated. Tomorrow, they could be divorced.

Billy had left Alexis's house early. He wanted to catch his dad before he went out for the night. He wanted to catch him before he was drunk, even if he knew he'd had a few beers in the house by now. He wasn't drunk, just working slowly toward it.

He had to know things, that's all. His dad had to know things. Nothing had been defined. Nothing was clear. It was his dad, not his mom, who had brought this whole thing about. It was he who had brought this chaos into his life, this disruption, disorder. It was his dad, not his mom. He was the one to blame. The fault lay with him. It was his dad who clearly ruled this problem from its beginning.

Where is he? Up in the den with his computer, drawing on some past events, stuck in the past, dwelling—not letting it go? Stuck there? Billy thought. *Blast Aircraft was a long time ago. Blast and him seems ages ago,* Billy thought.

Billy looked up the staircase. He was carrying a backpack that had in it new football plays Coach Bosco had diagrammed for this year's Purple Eagles offense. The backpack was strapped to his back. He wanted to face his father. He needed answers.

"Dad." Billy's taps on the door had grown louder. "It's me, Dad."

The door opened slowly. Connie stood behind it.

Billy entered the room.

Today, to Billy, his father looked like a beaten man.

Connie closed the door.

"Why do you keep the door shut, Dad?"

"Because I want to," Connie replied tautly.

Connie had reached his computer. He sat in the chair, unshaven, unkempt.

Billy looked at the computer screen.

"Dad, designs. Crazy designs, Dad. Dad, they fired you. Blast Aircraft fired you."

"What? What did you just say to me?"

"They fired you. Blast Aircraft fired you!" Billy said.

"Yes, they did, didn't they, Billy," Connie said rationally.

"I…I…" Billy did feel lost, unable to swim, in no way up for this. "Dad, I…I just thought. I…I…"

Connie just watched Billy stumble, struggle, and grope incomprehensibly.

"Forget it then. Just forget it then." Billy was in tears.

Connie's focus was back on the computer, to the screen.

Billy stood there watching him, this man he had always held above the stars. His only real hero.

Billy hadn't moved for some time, standing in the den as if poured in cement.

And Connie's eyes were looking into the computer as if the world in there had shut the world around him out. What he saw on the screen was valueless but still, for him, real.

Billy saw no hope. He began to retreat, move himself away from what he was witnessing, frightening him more by its possibilities.

Billy had reached the door and was about to close it when—

"They fired a nigger. Blast fired a nigger. It's what it did!"

Billy was stunned. He'd never heard that word used in the Mack household.

Billy turned and saw his Dad's facial expression. The facial expression jammed into his face hadn't changed, neither matching nor equaling the anger he'd heard in his voice.

"Shocked, huh, Billy? Are you?"

Billy was speechless as his hand let go of the doorknob.

"You're shocked, all right," Connie said, as if he were trying to shock Billy more.

"I was at first," Connie said, his eyes staring unchanged into the computer, "but not for long. Uh-uh. I had figured it out, all out before, but had forgotten my lessons. The ones I'd learn from home," Connie said deviously.

"The lessons of the past. Of the South. What the white man taught me down there in Savannah, Georgia. My lessons, Billy, the only rules of the game."

Connie's body came out of its slovenly slouch. "You can never be equal to him, only think that you can, or are. Oh … oh what perfect delusions, Billy. Oh, what perfect mental delusions you can perpetuate on yourself. Afflict yourself with. Deceive yourself into enduringly imagining. One year after the next and next and next."

Connie's body was alive. "Go to the right schools. Read from their books. Their literature. Share their thoughts. Talk like them. Yeah, even that. Move into their communities, neighborhoods. Their beautiful, marvelous, immaculate neighborhoods. The only thing I didn't do was take their women. It's the only thing I did right, Billy. That."

Billy felt an awful burn inside him.

"Yes, it's the only credit they'll hand me. It's the only concession they'd make to me, Billy, Connie Mack, is I didn't marry a white woman. Connie Mack didn't chase after white women."

"Dad—"

"Why couldn't your mother see it? The big picture? Why couldn't Susan see it my way? Like me?"

"Mom?"

"I told her. I told her we did it all wrong, Billy. I told your mother that. Why couldn't she see it my way? Why, Billy?"

"See what? Wrong?"

Connie came to his feet. He grabbed Billy by the waist. He led him over to his old, damaged couch. They sat. Connie was frantic, his mind tormented.

"We raised you here. Here. Here in Pittsfield. It was wrong. We did it all wrong. Your mother and I. But she couldn't see it. You're surrounded by whites here in Pittsfield. Your best—"

"But I'm black, Dad. Black."

"No. No. You can't be, Billy. Not that." Pause. "You wouldn't know how to survive where I came from, or your mother. They'd reject you, wouldn't know how to accept you, deal with you, Billy. This world is different. This world swallows you up and then wants you to, tries to make you forget who you are until it reminds you again. It always reminds you. Someone's always there to remind you. Slap you in the face. Ron Jones. It was Ron Jones at Blast Aircraft for me.

"Someone, someone always appoints himself, Billy. Always." And then Connie saw his own madness. That he was being perceived this way by his own son, by Billy, someone he now felt he had to protect no matter what.

Connie's speech slowed. He leaned back on the couch. "For God's sake, Billy. Your best friend is white. Your girlfriend is white."

"What—"

"Understand that, Billy. Susan didn't. Your mother didn't. They've got you, Billy. They've … they've got you."

To Billy, Connie sounded paranoid. Nothing less than paranoid.

"Jimmy, Jimmy—"

"I love him too, Billy. No less, Jimmy. No less than you."

"Mr. and Mrs. Boston—"

"Good people. Solid people. Good friends. Jim and Marion. They're good friends, the Bostons are."

"But—"

"But I'm not blaming them. The Bostons. I'm not putting the blame on them. Onus, onus of blame on them. I'm just blaming myself, son. I should have known better. Been smarter. Your mother and I should have done better for you!" Pause.

"It's our fault, your mother's and mine. No one—"

"I don't want to hear any more, Dad. Stop it! Now! Right now!"

Billy had to collect himself. It was worse than he'd thought. What had happened between his father and his mother was much, much worse than what he'd imagined.

"So you never accepted Alexis? Only Mom. Alexis was the wrong color. Alexis was wrong for me? Is that it, Dad? What you're saying, Dad?"

"Yes, Billy. Regrettably. But you see, it wasn't your fault. Any of it. You can't blame—"

Billy bolted out the room.

Soon Connie heard something crash and then crack. He ran into the hallway and into Billy's bedroom. The backpack was on the floor. One of Billy's football trophies was by it, broken, split in two.

"No wonder Mom left! No wonder she doesn't want to come back!"

Connie was looking down at the broken trophy, not Billy.

"Alexis, Mom—you're against everyone, Dad!"

"It's the world," Connie said, as if screaming to it. "The way of the world, not me. How the world runs. The world, Billy, the world," Connie said, slowing his speech.

"No, it's you, Dad. You!" Pause. "Mom doesn't see it your way."

"She wasn't fired by whitey. I was!"

"No, no it goes deeper. Jimmy and I started before Blast fired you. Alexis and I started before they fired you, Dad," Billy said, pointing at Connie. "No, Dad, it's you. It's you who can't change. It's you who—"

"What the hell do you understand? Tell me? A teenager!"

Billy sat down on the bed and bent over as if his stomach had cramped.

"Why didn't I see it, Dad? Why didn't I see you didn't like Alexis? Alexis just brought it out of you, didn't she? Brought the South out of you. Your hate!"

Connie ran out of the room. He slammed his door.

Billy chased after him.

"Don't open the door! Don't!"

"What are you afraid of!"

"Don't come in here!"

"I love Alexis. I'll always love her, Dad! Always! Always!"

Connie's hands covered his ears.

"I don't love a black girl, Dad. I love a white girl!"

The door was flung open. "And you're doomed, Billy. You and Alexis Price are doomed!"

It was over. Now Billy knew the argument between his mother and father. It was about the life they'd given him. The life in Pittsfield. The only life he knew.

Jimmy, their relationship was natural to him. They were born to be football players, were paired; it was natural. From the start, they hit it off. From day one, there was never any question of color, of black or white. It happened from day one.

Alexis, yes, his first eye contact with her, yes, there was fear. First seeing her, then knowing that she was the one. That of course she'd first have to like him and then look beyond the fact he was black, that somewhere down the road her parents would have to approve of him.

It wasn't natural between him and Alexis. It felt unnatural, as if he were trying to cheat at something he ultimately would get caught at somewhere down the road in the future.

"And I did get caught. My dad caught me. Didn't you, Dad?"

It pleased Connie that everything was finally out in the open for him and Billy, no matter how much it hurt Billy or how cruel it'd been. It would hurt Billy more if a white man had done to him what he'd done. *In time, I'll soothe his pain,* Connie thought. *I'll help Billy. But now he has to feel the lash of prejudice, of racism, himself. Billy has to know what it feels like, not taunts, not like it was when he was a boy and was taunted on the football field over his black skin. But now. He must know now how it feels to be black in a white man's world. The lesson he was never taught. The lesson he must learn. Only he can learn.*

This indeed pleased him. Susan had forgotten her roots, what they'd come from, but not him. He was glad Susan wasn't there when he and Billy mixed it up. Billy would have been bewildered. But this evening, he'd put something before Billy that he would have to work his way through, study hard. It was going to be painful, sure, but it's what marks progress—pain. *It makes a man out of you. It's what has to happen to reach that place and for it to shape you.*

Connie Mack, his great-great-grandmother, helped pass on that asset, that attitude down as legacy for the Mack family. Connie was proud of his grandmother Connie and to carry her name. Susan named Billy after her brother Billy (he went along with it). But he still wished he'd name Billy Connie as he'd planned, that he had fought her on that front. But at the time, he saw no reason to. Knowing what he knew now, being reminded of it, he would have fought Susan tooth and nail on that particular principle.

Connie checked the time. He was in his bedroom. He was dressed and shaven.

"Hell, I mustn't keep the guys waiting. Chris and the crew."

He thought of Susan but not for long. It was more like a flash.

"She has her life, and now I have mine," he said. "She was wrong about this. One day she'll see. In hindsight if nothing else. It was all for Billy's good. My son. My son, Billy."

Billy heard Connie's door open and close.

"He's going off to Mitch's Sports Bar. Dad doesn't give a damn about me."

The front door of the house opened and closed.

Billy's backpack, with Coach Bosco's newly diagrammed plays for the Purple Eagles offense in it, was still on the bedroom floor next to Billy's broken trophy from a long-ago football victory he and Jimmy had starred in in Pittsfield.

CHAPTER 18

Pittsfield High School's new football season was underway. Mike Overbranch commanded stage center until, of course, Coach Bosco made his grand entrance into the Pittsfield High School gym (what he always did at this baptismal event).

Billy remembered back to when he was a freshman and was introduced to his future teammates. How nervous he and Jimmy were. It produced a nervousness that was hard to explain to anyone who had not experienced it.

Overbranch had timed things out to perfection, for when his voice had peaked was when Coach Bosco entered the gym, striding through it like a winner of last year's state title championship.

Billy turned to Jimmy and hugged him. Then both applauded along with the other freshmen and upper classmen, rambunctiously.

Jimmy and Billy stood in front of their lockers, the first time since last season.

"Spring cleaning, huh, Billy?" Jimmy asked as Billy opened his locker.

"Hey, don't tell me you smell it too?"

"What, possibly a tuna fish sandwich you left from last year, Steamroller? Got sandwiched in there, man?" Jimmy sniffed offensively.

"Get out of here. It doesn't smell that bad!"

But it didn't stop Jimmy from pinching his nose.

"By the way, Jimmy, that name, Steamroller, it still hasn't caught on. You know that, right?"

"Yeah, thought it might by now. Heck, Steamroller, nobody has any imagination around here—in Pittsfield."

"Because maybe, just maybe, it's too lame. Corny!"

"But you do steamroll over people, Billy. Maybe on the next level, college, it'll catch on."

"Yeah, maybe so."

"Without a ... I won't be needing this!" Jimmy said, pulling out an overwashed jock.

The liner of Jimmy's locker had Judy's picture. Billy's locker had a picture of Alexis.

"College—how many letters have you been averaging a day?"

"Jimmy, egad, I didn't know there're that many colleges in the world!"

"Coach said it would be like this," Jimmy said, discarding a pair of frayed socks. "The recruiting wars."

"My, uh, my dad too. That we'd be besieged by colleges all over the map."

After hearing a tiny tremor in Billy's voice, Jimmy tried to protect himself from what he knew Billy was feeling but couldn't. "Your father should know the recruiting process all right."

"Even though, athletically, Dad said he was a late bloomer, but academically—"

"He was smart, man. Top student."

"Yes, Jimmy. I—"

"Hey, Steamroller, hurry up. Our girls are waiting!"

"Right!"

"Billy, look. Are we screwed up or what? Football heroes, huh? Being recruited by the top football schools in the country, huh? That's a load, man. We're both henpecked, Steamroller. This is torture—pure, freaking torture."

Alexis and Billy were holding hands. Judy, Jimmy, Alexis, and Billy had already reached the fork in the road, the great divide.

"Billy, does it ever … I mean, get boring to you? Being so good?"

The wind seemed to be teasing Alexis's beautiful black hair, tousling it with glee.

"Never. I've never been bored playing football, or that I'm that good."

"Oh … come on, Billy," Alexis said, nudging him. "Be honest. You know you can be with me. And drop your modesty. Any signs of it."

"Al, I am. I just play hard and hope for good results. Play hard on every down."

"Billy, what a terrific attitude you have!"

It was Billy's turn to laugh. "Do you ever get bored?"

"Me? From what?" Alexis asked innocently.

"Being so beautiful."

"Billy …"

"See? The same thing. It's the same, exact thing, Al!"

"It is? Oh, of course it is!" A gorgeous smile splashed her face.

Billy looked at her and knew that she was the girl for him. She would always be the girl for him. Black, white—it didn't matter. None of it mattered.

They were about to cross Horizon Avenue when Billy, still holding Alexis's hand, stopped.

"You're the girl for me, Alexis. Always. You'll always be the girl for me."

Alexis looked up at Billy cryptically. "Why are you telling me this?"

"I don't know why. I just want you to feel what my heart feels. So I guess that's it. Wraps it up."

They began walking again.

"Billy … is it college that brought this on?" Alexis said, brushing a thin strand of hair from her dark, sensuous eyes.

"Sure."

Alexis smiled.

"We, you and I are still going to the same college, aren't we? As planned?"

"Of course. Just how we planned it out."

"Whatever college Jimmy and I choose will be conducive to your—"

"And Judy's—"

"Yes, major."

"Don't we sound efficient." Alexis smirked.

235

"Like we have the world by its tail. But it's going to be great. It really is, Al."

"Just think, Billy, the four of us taking the campus—"

"Whatever campus it is."

"By storm!"

"You, me, and Judy, and Jimmy!"

Billy pressed his lips onto Alexis's.

"I love you, Alexis."

Alexis shut her eyes. "Me too, Billy. I love you too."

Billy was home. Connie wasn't.

Food had been cooked and left out on the kitchen counter, covered for reheating or for the microwave.

"Thanks, Dad. Thanks a lot."

His sadness hit him. Billy felt his mother's absence and his father's pretending that he still lived in the house, was still his parent, someone who cared for him. This was when it all hit home for him.

Billy moved the food from the kitchen counter to the kitchen table. He wanted to eat the food on the plate (covered), but a knot was in the pit of his stomach, a knot tying it together. But it was a word. A word couldn't explain how it really felt. From day to day, relief came only temporarily, in between other events that didn't matter as much, that mattered very little lately.

He looked at the food with disdain.

"I hate this, Dad!" he screamed.

Football, knocking people over, down—steamrolling them. What did it mean? Would they be at the championship game this year? Would they be in the stands? *Will they? Or one over here and the other over there, separated, apart—no longer together. Not like before. Not like Mr. and Mrs. Boston, Jimmy's parents, sitting in the bleachers together.*

The thought of the upcoming football season had begun to wear on him. It had begun to play tricks with his mind. He was looking forward to the new season, but then he wasn't. He loved football. He loved being out on the football field with Jimmy and the guys, the Purple Eagles,

Coach Bosco. It's what he loved with all his heart and soul. But his mom and dad ...

The knot in his stomach tightened. The food that he could see through the clear plastic looked nasty, as if it would make his stomach regurgitate. Billy shoved the food away so hard it landed on the floor.

Billy hated his life, how he was living. He hated this thing that now was his, that had happened a day at a time (inch by inch), which he could neither stop nor control, find any solution for. It was eating him alive—continually feeding on him with no end in sight.

Alexis was so beautiful today, Billy thought.

"You were so beautiful today, Alexis. Beautiful, Al. Really, really beautiful."

He felt grown-up when he told her how his heart felt. When it happened, he felt like a man.

"It happened like magic does, unplanned. Man, it ... it was unplanned, unrehearsed. I couldn't believe it, my ears, myself. How I said it, man. Said it. How much I meant it. My heart spoke to me, Alexis. Spoke to me today," Billy said, as if Alexis were standing before him, in front of him.

Ring.

Should I? Mom. Maybe it's Mom.

Ring.

"Yes, hello."

"Steamroller!"

"Jimmy ..."

"Who else calls you Steamroller?"

"Like I said earlier, Jimmy, you're the only one who has a corner on that market."

"Better be. Hey, I'm not disturbing suppertime, am I, Steamroller?"

Billy looked down at the big mess on the floor. "Uh, no, I've already eaten."

"So you can grow up big and strong. Remember our parents handing us that line when we were little? At our awkward age."

"Sure, Jimmy. Absolutely."

"And we did, Billy. Man, did we ever. We did grow up to be big and strong."

The silence between them seemed longer than it should be, and by now, Billy knew Jimmy well enough to know why.

"Billy, you looked … well, a bit down today. A little out of it."

"I did? I didn't know that."

"Like you had a lot of stuff … things on your mind today."

"Oh, college probably, you—"

"I should have known. What else." Jimmy laughed.

"It's dogging us, Jimmy. You know that."

"Us meaning you, me, Judy, and Alexis."

"We really have to start narrowing our choices down for their sake, since it'll be here before we know it. We'll be shipping off to college. And you never know from day to day what's going to happen. Never, man. From day to day."

Was there something veiled, a message in what Billy just said? Jimmy thought. *It was said neither cynically nor bitterly by Billy, but were his parents hidden in there somewhere?*

"Honestly, Billy, Judy and I were talking about it the other day, to be up and up with you."

"So have Alexis and I. Uh, today in fact. It's practically around the corner when you're a junior. Senior. Then graduation from Pittsfield High. Then college."

"So right. Maybe we better get a move on. Shake a leg, Steamroller. Set things in motion. So, uh, what do you say we sit down tomorrow on this. Is that too soon or—"

"Here or your place?"

"It doesn't matter. We'll begin sorting through our letters, let's say, and then start going after it hot and heavy. Of course, there are some obvious exceptions, like Moon County State. Ever hear of such a college? Moon County State? We can put those kind in a shredder right away, if you haven't already." Pause.

"It's going to be great when we bring Judy and Alexis in on it, Billy. Really great, man."

"Won't it, Jimmy."

"A big-time college football program and a great academic program as well. Are we in heaven or what, Steamroller? Tell me we ain't!" Pause.

"But I'll miss Coach Bosco, Jimmy, and all the guys. Man, will I."

"Me too, but let's not get too sentimental. After all, it's not like we're leaving tomorrow. Shipping off for college, you know." Jimmy grinned.

"No, not at all," Billy said softly.

"So why don't we make it official? We'll meet here tomorrow."

Pause.

"Jimmy, any new tapes? Anything new in the den of racket?"

"How'd you know that was going to be next on the agenda? Habit, huh?"

"Right, guess so." Billy looked down at the mess still on the floor, his stomach churning. "Tomorrow, when I'm there, I guess you'll be playing them, huh?"

"You know it!"

"Jimmy, you're the best friend anyone could have. Anyone, man."

"Why, thank you, Billy, so much. That's a major compliment. You are too, Steamroller. You are too, my man."

"And Mr. and Mrs. Boston …"

"My parents are the greatest."

"Especially Mr. Boston—whenever someone's insurance policy is paid up."

"Especially then, Billy."

"Okay then. I'll see you tomorrow. Be by tomorrow at, but wait—"

"Yeah, we didn't. Two. Make it two, Steamroller." Jimmy sighed. "Yeah, I guess I better hit the books. Get busy."

"There is a lot to do. A lot."

It was a strange sentence, especially coming from Billy, Jimmy thought.

"Just keep loving Judy, Jimmy. Just keep loving her with all your heart and soul. Okay?"

That too, Jimmy thought, was strange.

Pause.

"Nighty night," Jimmy said, hoping to loosen things up.

"Yes, good night, Jimmy. Good night."

Billy hung up the phone.

Jimmy, before hanging up, looked at the phone in a new, odd way.

The knot in Billy's stomach cramped him in pain. And his head felt in a bad swim. He was bending over, and then he went down onto one knee.

Billy didn't know what was happening to him as he struggled hard to get back up on his feet. When he did, it was a slow, gradual, tortuous struggle to get over to the kitchen table.

Billy was in a chair and reared back his head, but the pain would not leave him. His mind, Billy thought. If he could use his mind to numb it, become oblivious to it, similar to how he ran the football and his mind had this certain concentration in it, this elite focus in it that made the rest of him impervious to pain when it smashed into people or was smashed into by people. It was his mind that saved him, that absorbed the blows, the hurts—the punishment before the helmet, the football pads. It was his mind.

Billy sat at the table calming himself. And very shortly, the awful pain subsided enough so that Billy could declare being free of it.

Was he going to clean up the mess on the kitchen floor? He wasn't sure. Maybe his dad should see it when he came in from Mitch's bar tonight, Billy thought.

His mom—suddenly Billy thought of her. He ran over to the kitchen phone to pick it up and dial.

She's not home! Billy panicked. *Mom's not home.* The automatic answering machine had clicked on.

"My obvious problem is that I am not home to receive your call. If your message can't keep, please speak at the beep."

"Hel-hello, Mom. It's me. Billy, Mom. I-I love you, Mom. I-I just called to say that, that I love you. Just to say that, Mom. I love you. That's all."

He hung up the phone. Billy felt more confused and depressed, and his head was swimming again, but no knots in his stomach, no pain that knifed him.

"Dad … Dad …" Billy said, with some disorientation.

How right was he about all of this? Jimmy, his best friend, and Alexis, his girlfriend. How right was he about them? Him growing up in a white world, but he was black. He knew that now. What chance did he have? His father was smart.

"Dad said very little. Dad said I have no chance at all. But I love Jimmy. I love Alexis. They love me, don't they? Don't they for always? Always? Forever?"

College was in the future. All of them were to attend the same college. What did his being black have to do with that? Who would take that away from him? Who?

"Where are you, Dad? Why won't you answer my question? Where are you to answer my question, Dad!"

His dad was smart, brilliant. How could he be wrong about anything?

"You always figure things out so well, Dad. On your computer. On— so well, Dad. You do, Dad."

What would happen to him and Jimmy in life? What would happen to them when, like his dad said, someone "reminded" him that he was black?

Billy's head was pounding.

"And I want to marry Alexis. I want to marry you, and … and I want, I want us to have children, Alexis. Children. You and me. Not black or white children. Children. Our children, Alexis. Ours, yours and mine."

But they couldn't. They couldn't. *Someone would say we couldn't. Who? Who is that person!* Billy thought.

"Coach Bosco. Why am I bringing your name up? Why!"

Practice, full-out practice in two days. He and Jimmy were preseason All-Americans again. The best high school players at their positions in America. The Purple Eagles were all set to fly high again, go for the second consecutive state championship.

"I love you, Coach Bosco. But I can't do it. I just can't."

Now was the time, Billy thought. His mother wasn't home. His father wasn't home. *Now is the time*, Billy thought. The future had been snatched from him, cancelled out. It's what his father told him. Billy Steamroller Mack's future had already been decided. He and Alexis and Jimmy—it'd already been decided. His mother wasn't coming back. She was too busy with her life to be home, to be around when he most needed her. She was involved in a new life, with new things. His mom and dad would never get back together, reconcile, not in a million years. Divorce would be next on the horizon; it was the only thing left for his parents.

All the letters from all the colleges were in his room, stacked neatly, him having to give them some attention.

"Dad, you saw through this world, didn't you? Right through it. Didn't you? Thanks, Dad. Thanks."

Billy stood. He looked down at the mess on the floor. *Clean it up?* he thought. *It doesn't matter now. Why should it?*

"I never had a chance. They never gave me a chance. And … and they'll just take it away from me in the future. Everything. Everything I love. Thank you, Dad. Thank you."

Billy was going to write something out. That much he was going to do. Write something out no matter what, no matter what came out or how it came out. They'd be his feelings. His true feelings.

Billy was at the foot of the staircase, looking up.

"I love my life, though. I love it. Dad, I love it."

Susan's hip shut the car door (wisely done). As streamline as her hips were, they'd come in handy, Susan thought. She smiled. She was in great physical shape. Her hands were full, but in order to open the apartment door, well, everything would have to be put down for her to free her hands. Susan put her school books and lone grocery bag down on the apartment's front stoop.

Once she opened the apartment door, she regathered her possessions. Into the house Susan breezed like a sunny debutante. The sun was setting, so there was a charming glow flowing through the apartment's middle window. Susan noticed it. *I love this apartment,* she thought.

The books and grocery bag had become heavy, so Susan sped into the kitchen and put them on the kitchen table.

"There."

She was hungry. In fact, starved. She'd been in Tyler College's law library for some time this afternoon. She was finding school fun. Returning to it at her age, taking up prelaw, was fun.

"I'm going to be sitting pretty on the Supreme Court with Mrs. O'Connor and Mrs. Ginsburg. Ladies, make room for one more: Susan Mack!"

But then Susan held on to one of the prodigious books. "Who knows," she said, studying it, "anything's possible. Anything, if you set your mind on it. So I'm not ruling it out totally."

Connie hadn't damaged her, she thought. The way he thought, he was thinking—it hadn't damaged her.

Susan gathered the remainder of the law books and carried them into the living room, where there was a desk for her studying (she burned the midnight oil).

After doing this, Susan rubbed her hands together fiendishly. "Now it's time to eat. I'm hungry!"

She was back in the kitchen.

"But first, messages. Let me see if anything's come in."

Susan stepped over to the wall phone.

"He-hello, Mom. It's me. Billy, Mom. I-I love you, Mom. I-I just called to say that, that I love you. Just to say that, Mom. I love you. That's all."

Susan shut her eyes to slow down the day and herself. She hung up the phone.

"Billy, I've been an awful mother of late. No one has to tell me."

This brand-new life of hers had put her where she was. Now that it'd built up steam, it hadn't had a chance to glance back.

"Should I call him?"

Why was she asking herself this question when it was her son she referenced?

Susan touched the phone with a lightness, as if it were important she touch something, even if it was hard plastic.

"I'll call tomorrow. His football season begins in two days. I haven't forgotten."

In fact, she'd marked it on the wall calendar.

"The Purple Eagles will be in full swing in two days. Jimmy and Billy will be back on the practice field in full gear, ready for battle." Susan laughed. "Preparing themselves for another tough year at the helm under Coach Bosco. Another winning year. Exceptional. Exceptional.

"Tomorrow, I'll tease you about it, Billy."

Her high level of energy had snapped back, for now she had dinner to prepare, and those law books awaited her on the front room's desk.

"I love you too, Billy. But tonight your mother's got her work cut out for her. I'll be consuming one law book after the other," Susan said, not at all perturbed by the challenging prospect confronting her.

Connie had just pulled the car out of Mitch's Sports Bar's parking area. *The drinking is killing me,* he thought. *Just how much lower can I sink?*

It was beginning to sound like self-pity. He hated self-pity. It rubbed him wrong.

When Connie drove at night from the bar to home, he drove caringly, not angrily. Always caringly, looking at the car as an outside observer. The car was always driven on balance, correctly. It was some kind of miracle Connie was able to pull off—to drive the car correctly, on balance. Even he was aware of this odd talent.

It was just that his life wasn't being lived correctly, he'd think. That was out of balance. But when he began to think about it, his life, then he was back to self-pity, and he wouldn't do that, take a part in that; it was rejected at all costs.

But he was no longer a father. When he said it, it hurt like hell, but it was accurate.

He was driving the car, his hands gentle on the steering wheel, guiding the car ever so finely (like a spool of thread through the eye of a needle) along the wide, two-lane road. He could feel the beer in him but the balance in him too. When was all this going to end for him? When was he going to find himself again?

To continue to live as I am living, Billy's going to sink too.

"How has he held up this long?"

He knew Billy was but a shadow of himself. Without Susan, without something solid, his family, Billy was but a shadow of himself. It had been all wrong, Billy staying with him all of these months. He couldn't take care of himself, so how could he take care of Billy?

Billy should be with Susan, Connie thought. *Billy and Alexis get along well, but it is only the beginning for them. They don't know how much further in their relationship they must go. It's why I feared the relationship then and now. It's the only reason why: pressure on a black man is enough in society without adding a white woman to the mix. It's like suicide.*

"I know Billy hates me now. But maybe one day that'll change. One day, maybe he'll see I'm right. He'll see it my way. That I was right about him and Alexis Price."

He wasn't going to have another beer when he got back to the house. There were two beers in the refrigerator, but he wouldn't touch them when he got in. He was going to head straight to bed. His drinking would have to end, but when? He didn't know; he had no idea.

As usual, entering the house, he was extremely quiet so as not to wake Billy. He'd become good at that, weaving himself through the house solidly but quietly. Connie couldn't wait until his head hit the pillow. And this made him think more of his life, trying to put it back in perspective.

The car was parked, and Connie was in the house. The moment he stepped into the house, there was something eerie about it. Connie dismissed it as being his overactive nerves.

But then he had an impulse for another beer and stood in a darkened vestibule, torn, undecided.

"Uh-uh, not tonight. I don't need another beer. Hardly. What I need is to lay my head down on my pillow. It's the only thing I really need."

He was on the second-floor landing.

The feeling returned.

"But everything's normal," Connie said. "Normal in the house."

Into the dark, Connie looked. His den door was shut. The guest room door was shut. Billy's bedroom door was shut. The bathroom door was shut. Connie's bedroom door was shut.

Things in the house are normal, Connie thought. *Normal.*

When Connie passed Billy's bedroom door, he felt an enormous pain, something not even beer could block. It'd happened to him before. This wasn't the first, and he knew it wouldn't be the last; it was something that he would have to live with for now.

He opened the bedroom door. There was a sadness in him, not self-pity. *It must never be self-pity, only sadness. It must never reach the place of self-pity.*

He began undressing at the bedroom door, not bothering to enter the room. His clothes would remain where he left them, and then he would hang them in the morning. This was his routine. This was how he did things. He wouldn't bother to turn on the bedroom lights to do things properly, the correct way.

Connie could feel himself in the dark—big, large. He was worried about becoming a bitter man, but Susan, anyone who knew the mental condition he was in, would say he already was.

Connie pulled back the bedspread. "Ah ..."

He felt relief in his body as it fit into the bed. He felt as if he had crash-landed and now everything was okay, right. Connie's head was on his pillow, and soon he curled up on the side of the bed, as if two bodies were in the bed, not one.

Susan ... Connie thought of Susan. He used her name. It was in his mind more during the day than he would like. But here she was now, in his mind, showing up and lingering.

If only she could see things my way, he thought. Then he and Susan and Billy would be a family again.

But Billy had his football family. He would have his football family for another year, and that would make things all right. Jimmy and Coach Bosco would make things all right for Billy. Billy will be all right as long as he had his football back.

Connie felt the same he'd felt in front of Billy's door but refused to give in to it.

The house felt eerie, something new to him.

Connie awakened. When he awakened in the morning, he knew the time. He didn't need an alarm clock; hours and minutes were in him. This made it easy for him to wake in the morning.

With impatience, he rubbed his eyes. The room was dark. This was when he most missed Susan. Connie propped himself up, and before he could feel the morning's atmosphere, the eeriness of last night draped him.

"I don't understand this. Don't have a clue. This feeling. What's going on in this damn house of mine?"

Billy was up. He'd been up for at least twenty minutes. It's how it was. It's how the morning routine worked. Billy was up before him now, but only by fifteen minutes. When he worked for Blast Aircraft before, it was different. All different. He was up before Billy and Susan then. He was the first one up and readying himself for a new day, getting his day underway. The first to push back the sheets.

But now it was Billy setting the tone of the day. It was Billy who was getting ready in the Mack household for school, for a new day, for Alexis and Jimmy and Coach Bosco and all that went with it. Billy had so much to look forward to, Connie thought. High school, college, when every day had some spunk in it, bite, something glorious and astounding.

It wasn't like him. Why was he thinking like this? Maybe it was Susan; maybe it was not. But this eerie feeling, for some reason, he couldn't shake. It was crowding in on him, his senses beginning to make him feel more discomfort.

Billy was in the kitchen eating breakfast, Connie thought. He'd join him. He wouldn't avoid him this morning. He would join him at the kitchen table this morning and talk about something, anything.

Football. Maybe football. Maybe they could talk about football, Jim Brown, or Jackie Robinson. Maybe that was where they could find common ground.

Eagerly, Connie got out of bed. He went to the closet to get his robe, and while putting it on, he looked down on the floor, at the door, and saw what was left there from last night.

"Who's going to hang it up but me? There's no one else here to do it but me. Shit."

Connie walked over to the clothes lying on the floor and scooped them up one by one: shoes, socks, pants, shirt, outer jacket. He felt like a tramp, something awful, but he always did whenever he did what he'd done last night so irresponsibly.

Connie hung up or put away everything but his outer jacket. That jacket belonged downstairs, so he draped it over his arm. He opened the room door.

What was eerie about his room felt even eerier when he stepped out into the hallway. What he felt trapped in, draped by, had a worse feeling in the hallway. *What the hell is wrong?* Connie thought.

He passed by one closed door and then the other while carrying his jacket over his arm. Then he stopped at Billy's door and heard nothing—not as if he expected to hear something.

They would talk about football. He'd pinch it out of Billy. Things weren't that bad between them, him and Billy. Things weren't that bad that they couldn't talk about Jim Brown or Jackie Robinson—find some common ground, something that cemented their relationship. Billy still loved him. They'd hit a rough spot, a rough patch in the road—that's all. These things were temporary, nothing more.

Connie was at the top of the stairs. He was listening for Billy, for him down in the kitchen, but he did not hear him; everything was weird. Ever since he got in the house last night, everything had been weird, not approximating the normal. But why didn't he hear Billy this morning? Even when avoiding him, he'd still hear him in some manner or form.

How will I begin conversation with him? I'll simply say, 'Good morning, Billy.' It's what I'll say. How I'll say it to start conversation. Billy doesn't hate me that much. He'll say, 'Good morning, Dad.' I can trust him to say that much to me. He's never been mean. He's a kind young man—and loving.

Connie's knees felt brittle as he looked down the short flight of stairs. He could feel himself falling down them. *Isn't that freaking awful?* he thought. *What's come over me? I'm beginning to feel crazy. He's my son, for God's sake. Billy will talk to me. Maybe he feels what's in this house too. This weirdness. This sadness that's in here with us that, right now, is inexplicable.*

Connie was walking down the staircase. His knees no longer felt brittle. And his thoughts felt free. Maybe it was there, just on that floor, the memory of Susan. Sleeping in the same bed every night. Sleeping without Susan every night alone and then waking, nothing feeling the same, not having any confidence about anything.

Connie was in the hall closet hanging his jacket. His eyes stared into the closet, finding a darkness in there, a loneliness that felt only too real. Connie shuddered. And then he turned, thinking he heard Billy in the kitchen. It had to be Billy moving a plate around, making noise—some familiar sound.

"Billy. Good … good morning."

Connie tucked the robe more into his middle.

"Is that you, Billy?" Connie said, as if he saw the shadow of Billy on the kitchen floor, and then it quickly fled.

"Good morning. Is that you, Billy?" Connie was in the kitchen now but saw no one.

"Oh … I …" Connie looked up at the kitchen clock.

"Oh … I thought you were getting ready for school, Billy," Connie said, but not understanding why.

But then Connie looked with alarm at the mess on the kitchen floor. "Billy!"

It'd been there overnight.

"Why'd you do this? Something like this!"

And now Connie felt what he and Susan were doing to their son. He saw the anger of it; it was there, visible on the kitchen floor, the cracked plate and the rotting food. It was in the house, this weirdness, this strangeness and sadness. Billy was sick with it. He was being consumed by it. Running the football for the Purple Eagles and Coach Bosco wasn't what his son wanted. He wanted him and Susan.

Billy wasn't going to school today. He was in his room angry, angry at him and Susan. What had they done to him? To this beautiful young man? They'd kissed the ground he'd walked on. What had he and Susan done to Billy?

Connie ran out of the kitchen. He looked up the staircase. Billy was in his room, behind the door, angry at the world. Angry at everything.

"Billy!"

Connie was running up the stairs.

Tap.

"I'm sorry, Billy!"

Connie tried to open the door, but it was locked.

"Your mother and I, we're … we're sorry. Come out. Open the door. Unlock it, Billy. Parents make mistakes. Can make them too. We all make mistakes, Billy. Forgive me, son. Please, Billy. I love you!"

Connie's fists banged against the door, battering it. He was in a blind rage.

His shoulder was to the door, banging it. He had a fear in him, something horrible.

"I can knock it down, Billy. You know that. Off its hinges. With ease, Billy. You've got to open the door!"

Pause.

"Dammit, son. Then I'm going to knock it down. You're giving me no other choice, Billy!"

Connie's shoulder rammed into the door for what would be the last time. He stumbled forward, having tripped over the door and bumped the ladder. He looked up.

Billy's body hung by a leather strap from the vaulted ceiling.

There was no movement in her, only continual pain. A continual opening and closing, a clamping down hard in her head. It made her head, her eyes, everything in that featured region of her feel like tiny darts stuck into her. The rest of her body was numb, as if it had abandoned her, as if it had vanished. She knew she couldn't walk if she tried—not that she wanted to.

It was Susan's mind that retained reality. It was her mind that kept repeating what it'd heard from the man who called because Connie couldn't.

"Your husband, Mrs. Mack. Your husband—you can imagine. You can imagine …"

How alone she felt in this bed she was in, unable to know anything, only that Billy had hung himself. She knew she'd been medicated. Someone must have called someone, and they came for her. How she got here to Echo Lane Hospital, onto the bed she was lying in, she did not know. But she had been medicated, her body forced into a calm state.

It was supposed to turn her into an empty shell, a zombie—but she felt everything Billy had done to himself in his room. He'd hung himself, and the horror of it was she knew why.

Susan's body jerked. It's when she felt the first signs of life, not like it would die if she just let it.

CHAPTER 19

It was weeks later.

Jimmy had just slipped his jacket on. He zipped it.

"Dad, I just have to go."

"Jimmy, would you wait."

Jimmy had reached the house's front door.

Jimmy turned.

"We've talked so much, Dad. But ..."

Jim grabbed Jimmy and hugged him.

"Three weeks and ..."

"It feels like forever, Jimmy."

"I don't know what to say anymore. What to think ..." Jimmy was sniffling. "We were supposed to start choosing colleges, Dad. Narrow them down."

Jimmy leaned back against the door frame. "Yesterday at football practice, we—how can Coach Bosco expect us to play football?"

Jim's head lowered, and his hands shot into his pants pockets.

"We've dedicated our season to Billy, but ... oh, Dad. Dad!"

Jimmy was grabbing Jim, holding him.

"I'm going, Dad. By myself. That's all there is to it. I'm tired. Tired of talking about it—trying to make sense out of it. I just want to be to myself today. On my own."

Jim said nothing.

"Dad, see you."

"Sure, sure, Jimmy."

Jimmy opened the door and stepped out onto the porch.

It was maybe twenty-five minutes later when Marion entered the house. Jim, who was in the living room, got up and helped Marion with her coat.

"Marion, don't ask for Jimmy. He went out."

Today was Saturday.

"He had to be alone. To himself. Who can blame him."

"When will it end, Jim? For all of us?"

Jim simply shrugged his shoulders.

"Did he say where?"

"Hell, Marion," Jim said with frustration, "you know where: Cunningham Park. Where Jimmy and Judy go."

"Their secret spot." Now Marion was frustrated. "I wish they'd tell us. Why won't they? It really angers me sometimes." Pause.

"Not even Billy knew. Can you believe it?" Jim said, as if to further certify its importance.

Marion sat down on the couch.

"Jim, have you heard anything regarding Connie lately?"

"Uh, yes. I hear Connie's holding up okay."

"The bar?"

"Uh … uh, no. No one's seen him in the bar. Mitch's Sports Bar."

"I mean, Jim … what must it feel like to lose your son, your child?" Marion asked, laying her head on Jim's shoulders.

"Like hell, Marion. Hell. A living hell."

Tears edged Marion's brown eyes. "You know, I didn't know what to say to Susan at Billy's funeral. I felt empty, lifeless. Without an anchor, Jim. Does that sound nutty? Does it?"

Marion gazed up at him from his shoulder. "Will I ever have the right words?"

"Tell me, Marion, please, what are Connie and Susan left with? I wish that someone could tell me that."

"And to second-guess yourself …"

"It'll kill you, Marion. Take all the life from you. It's lousy. Plain lousy."

"And it's what they're doing, Jim. Going over each step of their lives. Susan and Connie. Carefully, critically. In no way actually, really, really trusting themselves."

Pause.

"Do you think there's any communication between them? Has, I wonder if there's been any since Billy's suicide."

Marion barely swallowed. "It's going to be hard, knowing them. They expect that. But their grieving. Blaming themselves. This has to be the worst time of it for them." Marion sighed. "Their past is their biggest burden."

"If I'd just done this or that—then, then the despondency. Deep and real, Marion." Jim's eyes shut.

"And insufferable. It's what Jimmy's going through," Marion said.

"The ifs, what-ifs. Yes, I know, Marion. Gosh, he wishes the football season was over already. That it hadn't, well, begun."

"It's horrible what Billy did. What he's left us with!"

"If Billy only knew. But how could he?" Jim said.

Jimmy was in Cunningham Park. He was there alone.

His head turned when he heard her feet travel through the grass.

"Judy."

"I called the house."

"I had to come out here by myself. Be by myself."

Judy didn't go to him. She stood as if a ring of fire was around him.

"I couldn't stay there in the house. I felt like I was in a cage. My tapes—forget about them. I couldn't play them. Nothing. I couldn't do anything. I had to come out here. Be alone."

"Our spot," Judy said, looking around at Cunningham Park's beauty. The trees in the distance were tall and well spaced, as if preparing themselves for fall and for leaves to drop and dress the ground in bright, sensory colors. Clusters of scented flowers touching the air with mixed fragrances to incite like a gypsy's dance.

"Jimmy," Judy said, looking at the rock Jimmy sat on, "will we ever put our names on the rock, what we said one day we'd do?"

Jimmy looked down at the rock. "What, this?" he said, as if he didn't know what it was he was sitting on.

"I'm not helping, am I?"

"It's not you, Judy. It's just that I won't let you. It's me. Me, not you."

Judy was wearing jeans and a short jacket. She unbuttoned the jacket's top button.

"Alexis, I spoke to her today. She's not coming back to the cheerleading squad this year. She can't do it."

"Judy ... do you blame her?"

Pause.

"They canceled school for a day, one day, but should've canceled the football season. All the games. Cancel everything. Coach Bosco should refuse to coach the Purple Eagles this year. It's not good enough that the team's dedicating the season to Billy. It's not good enough. They should cancel the season.

"How can I play? What do they want from me? What do they expect from me, Judy!"

"Jimmy!"

Judy got to him. She was in his space, grabbing his shoulders.

"But ... but life, it, it—"

"If you say that, what I think you're going to say," Jimmy threatened, "I'll hate you, Judy. Hate you. I mean it!" He ran off, then stopped.

He looked back at her, his eyes glaring at her. "How could you think to say what you were about to say? How ... Life going on. Football, it was always me and Billy. Nothing else. Nothing else mattered. Me and Billy, Judy. Us."

Judy headed toward him.

"Stay away. Don't come any farther," Jimmy said, pushing his hands out in front of him, disgusted by her. "It's why I came out here in the first place—to be alone."

"With Billy."

"Yes, with Billy!"

It was much later in Cunningham Park.

"Jimmy, are you ready to leave? I'll walk back with you to the house, if you'd like."

Up until now, they'd not conversed.

"How do you feel, Judy? I mean, you?" Jimmy asked, as his eyes cut through her.

"I cry a lot. When I think about it. Not every night. But I do cry a lot. And you know, I've tried to help Alexis through this."

Pause.

"You've been a good friend to her throughout this."

"So many times, I'm at a loss for words. She cries so much. So often. Spontaneously. You can't get inside something like that, I don't think."

"No. It's something no one can explain. It has to happen to you. I've found out that it has to happen to you. I see Billy everywhere. Everywhere I go. Wherever I am."

Judy's hand reached for Jimmy's.

"I see Billy now." Jimmy half-laughed. "Steam ... Steamroller. You know he, Billy, really didn't like the name, not at all—even though it didn't catch on with anyone else. Never got as far as me, really."

"But I think he did like it, Jimmy, when you called him that."

Jimmy half-laughed again. "I think he did too, Judy." Pause. "I know Billy did."

"It was in Billy's eyes, Jimmy. Billy's beautiful brown eyes. I'll always remember Billy's beautiful brown eyes."

Jimmy ran his hands through his hair. "It's just that we talked about things. His final, I mean, his last day. I mean we talked about things, Judy, Billy and I. Our futures. And yours, Judy, yours and Alexis's. How we were all going to be together in college. Going over our football offers and then matching them up with yours and Alexis's majors.

"Make ... making sure the schools were strong in your majors. Were right. Suited. You know what I'm saying, Judy?"

"Yes."

"Up to the end, it was like that. And now he's gone."

"Jimmy ..."

Jimmy could feel Judy beckoning him.

"Judy, I want to stay out here by myself." Pause. "A little longer."

Judy's hand was held out to him, hoping there'd be a connection.

"Let me, okay? Okay? Let me. This one time, I just want to be alone. Let me, Judy, this one time, be out here alone with Billy."

"Billy didn't know this spot, did he?" Judy asked, as if she'd come out a dream and had forgotten reality.

"No," Jimmy said, reaffirming the fact.

"Now Billy does, doesn't he, Jimmy?" Judy said innocently.

"Yes, now. Now Steamroller does."

Judy reached Jimmy, and when she did, she kissed him.

She began walking away from him without looking back, knowing Jimmy was sitting on their rock, looking away from her and feeling things she could never feel for Billy. It was that way with Alexis too whenever they spoke.

Jimmy hadn't changed his football locker. It was the same one from his freshman year. Billy's locker was not in use. Jimmy was crouched over on the wooden bench, sweating—his hair mop-wet with sweat, his blue eyes closed for now. The locker room had emptied.

"Coach wants to see me in his office, doesn't he? Is waiting on me."

Jimmy started pulling himself together.

"I can't keep him waiting."

Jimmy looked around at the empty locker room.

"I've been keeping him waiting long enough." Jimmy hurried.

"Sorry, Coach."

Jimmy was in Frank's office.

Frank looked up from his desk, amused.

"For keeping you, Coach. Making you wait."

Frank laughed. "Then you don't know anything about a football coach's life. You mean you haven't been observing me for the past three years? I'm surprised, Jimmy."

Jimmy took a seat.

"We never run out of things to do. Things to deal with during the day. What a great life!"

Jimmy made a halfhearted attempt to smile, but there was this joylessness in him.

"Jimmy, thank you for today's game."

The remark animated Jimmy. "You don't have to do that, Coach. No need, not at all, Coach. None."

"Jimmy, why didn't you come out of the game when I asked?"

Jimmy sat in the chair as if he hadn't heard Frank's question.

"Do you have any idea why?"

"I wanted to play the whole game. Be involved in every play, every down. It … it was our opener, Coach. Our first game of the season. So I wanted to play the whole game."

"But why, Jimmy?" Frank persisted.

"Why Coach, why!" Jimmy said, responding in kind to Frank's persistent tone. "Coach, we sat down. The team. We sat down and talked about Billy. We …"

"But you never said anything during the entire meeting. Not a word. Nothing. Why?"

"Come on, Coach Bosco, I respect you too much. I don't want to in any way be disrespectful toward you, sir."

"Your feelings, Jimmy. We have to get to the bottom of your feelings. We … it looked as if we were running up the score out on the field today. With you still in the game and throwing the way you were, Cardinal High and Coach Phillips thought we were running up the score on them, Jimmy. I can't have that. I can't allow that. That … that's not sport."

"Then, Coach, I'm sorry," Jimmy said with open sincerity. "I know how it looked, but …"

Jimmy's eyes shut as if he were going back into his shell.

"Tell me. Let me in on this."

Jimmy's eyes opened. "Coach, I was playing for Billy too. I was scoring touchdowns for Billy out on the field against Cardinal High today. It was Billy and me out there."

Frank was in tears. "Yeah, it's what I thought, Jimmy. What I came away with."

"It … it wasn't good enough, just me, Coach. I had to play for Billy today. Score touchdowns for him too."

"Billy would have—"

"Run over Cardinal, their guys, defensive line. Steam-steamrolled right over them. Scored a hundred, a zillion touchdowns, Coach."

Frank unloosed himself by rolling the pencil off the lined yellow pad on the desk. "You threw the ball well today."

"Had to, Coach."

"Well … you did."

Frank pushed back his chair, then clasped his hands in back of his head. "You know what amazes me about you, besides your arm, intelligence, poise under fire, and downright natural ability, of course"—Frank winked—"is how you hear everything that's out on the field. It still amazes me when I witness it." Pause.

"When Cardinal did a full-out blitz, I honestly thought you were a goner. But you seemed to hear them before you actually saw them. You pick up on them, their footsteps, as keenly as radar."

Pause.

"Mom, my mom, Coach. I get it from her."

Frank smiled. "So your mom was a football player, huh? Jimmy, that's news to me. So she wore a helmet and shoulder pads and barked out signals too, huh?"

"Yes, Coach. Mom played quarterback for Quarterback U, sir. Number twelve."

Both had a good laugh.

"Mom hears everything in the house, and I mean everything. My dad and I, we're always teasing her. It's who I got my excellent pair of ears from."

Jimmy glanced at his watch.

"Jimmy, thanks for dropping by."

"It's the last time I'll ever do what I did against Cardinal High, Coach."

"I didn't have to hear you say that, but it's good to hear anyway."

"Today, I had to. It is unsportsmanlike. It's not sport."

"Judy's waiting outside?" Frank grinned.

"Yes, sir."

"She doesn't mind?"

"She's like you, Coach."

"Except she's not a football coach."

"She's someone, though, who always finds something to do."

"She's a great young lady, Jimmy."

"Thanks, Coach."

"It's how Mrs. Bosco and I started. We were high school sweethearts." Frank's hand slapped his knees. "You know what? It doesn't seem that long ago either, when I'm reminded of it." Frank crossed his leg. "Jimmy, we're going to do it this time."

"The baby, sir?"

"God's going to shine down on us, let's say. Uh, let's leave it at that."

"How many months, Coach?"

"Three, Jimmy. Mrs. Bosco's in her third month and counting."

"One day, maybe Judy and I, Coach."

"I always thought about it. Family, a bunch of kids. Uh, two or three, but not like my brother-in-law, the mayor. Mrs. Bosco and I are getting started late, granted, but it's an unbelievable feeling, I assure you."

"Yes, one day, Judy and I—"

"Hey, you'd better get out of here. I don't want to be blamed for … Tell her I said hello, Jimmy, even though I heard her loud and clear today."

"Judy does cheer loud."

The car honked outside of Pittsfield High School.

Frank waved. The car with the gorgeous dish inside stopped.

"Get in, will you, you handsome hunk!"

"Am I being kidnapped or what?"

"If you are"—Maria grinned saucily—"do you think I'd tell you?"

Maria leaned over and kissed Frank high on the chin.

"Been waiting long?" Frank spied his watch.

"I'd say long enough."

"So this is how it's going to go for the rest of the evening?"

"You've got it, sugar!"

The drive home in the blue Ford began.

"You know, you've had one hectic day, Maria. The game, then running over to Mrs. Chesterfield's with your latest creation, and then back to the school. I guess one day I'll be a football coach with two cars: one for me and my wife."

Maria ran her eyes over to Frank. "Get off it, Frank. With both our incomes, you know we can afford two cars."

"Yes, you're right." Frank chuckled. "But now it's the baby. All our savings are geared toward the baby. The baby and nothing but the baby. Our baby comes first."

"It's going to happen, Frank."

"I know. It's what I told Jimmy."

"Jimmy?"

"I called him into the office after the game. It's what took me longer than usual. It was important for me to see him. For me to sit down with him. There were things I thought we had to go over."

"He played great today," Maria said enthusiastically. "To be honest with you, I was surprised. I thought without Billy out there, he might—"

"Not play well?" Frank said softly. "But he was there, Maria. Jimmy played for Billy today."

Frank saw surprise on Maria's face.

"It's why Jimmy didn't come out of the game when I tried substituting him."

"It's what he told you?"

"And it did—I think it did him some good. Us, the two of us sitting down, did him a lot of good."

"The last time you talked"—Maria frowned—"you said you didn't get much out of him. It was with the team, right, Frank?"

"Nothing, Maria. Not one word from him. Not one. Everyone on the team said something, bared their souls, except him. Jimmy. But me force him … uh-uh, Maria. Embarrass him? Others at the meeting shared their feelings regarding Billy's suicide. His death. But not Jimmy. Emotionally, Jimmy couldn't. He was shut down. Totally …"

"There's a love, I suppose. And then I suppose there's something that goes way above and beyond that, Frank," Maria said, turning right at the corner of Denver Avenue.

"No one's invented that word yet. It's beyond understanding, any human comprehension, Maria."

"But he's glad, isn't he, that he's got the first game under his belt?"

"You bet. But he played angry, Maria, just like Billy punished tacklers last year when he ran the football. When he was going through his emotional problems at home. Jimmy did that today. Out and out punished people. There was no joy in him. No feeling for the fun of the game. If it wasn't for his anger, a perverse passion in him, he would've been empty on the field, Maria. Like he's been in practice. Not until today. Bringing Billy back to life, back alive."

"When I lost, when—I mean when we lost our baby, Frank ..." Maria released her left hand from the steering wheel. "I—"

"I don't think it's the same. No, it's not. Not that. No, we never got to know the ... our baby, Maria. It was a different kind of loss, emptiness in us. It's not the same," Frank said dismissively. "Simply not the same set of emotions."

"So maybe it's better that we not talk about it, Frank," Maria said, her eyes putting sterner attention on the road.

"As friends, you know, they had it all, Maria. As friends," Frank said achingly.

"Frank, how did you feel today? Billy not being out there, how did it affect you, sweetheart?"

Pause.

"It was miserable. I mean, I got into the game. I'm the coach, for God's sake. I wrapped my head into it, Maria. But my heart ... I'll just leave it at that."

"It felt different for me too."

"Billy left a vacuum. A huge hole in all of us. Every one of our lives."

"Frank, do you think Jimmy's play will be joyless, the way he was today, for the rest of the year?"

Frank held back from answering the question.

"Frank ..."

"I heard you."

"There's no clear answer, is there?" Maria said, to help Frank out of the jam she'd put him in.

"I have to pray there is. Hope and pray, like I prayed we'd have another baby. I'm going to pray as hard as I prayed for the baby you're carrying, Maria."

Pause.

"I saw Jimmy look for Billy on the first play of the game. The first series of downs, Frank."

"Me too. And then it was me, Maria. My turn to. It was sad, I know."

Frank wasn't in his room at the house doing his football business. He'd just walked a tiny bit into Cunningham Park, following a trail he knew. Maria had let him go off like this. He'd taken his jacket out of the closet and told her he was taking a walk over to the park. Maria was cognizant of his habits, of him walking along the trail he was on.

"I wonder where their hideaway is out here."

Frank was aware of Judy Collins and Jimmy Boston having a secret hideaway in the park. It was common knowledge by now to their friends. He heard them get teased because of it—Jimmy by the football team, and Judy by the cheerleading squad. He just laughed at it but passed no opinion to either one.

He knew Cunningham Park pretty well, even though it was huge, and there were places in it he was unfamiliar with (it was deep and wide, mirroring a labyrinth). But how far would they walk into the park until they found their secret spot? Frank thought. A half mile? Not more than a mile. Anything longer would be a hike, knocking the romance out of the experience.

In some ways, he wished he and Maria had such a spot they could have called their own when they were childhood sweethearts. Indeed, this was something Jimmy and Judy would look back on fondly as another chapter in their lives. He and Maria had resonant memories, a truckload of them. Sometimes it was difficult to keep pace with them. Frank chuckled.

Frank hoped Judy and Jimmy would have kids, a whole basketful of beautiful, bouncing bambinos. Judy had to work a miracle for Jimmy. Football wasn't going to do it. Football was Billy's and Jimmy's. It had belonged to them. Football was only a reminder of this. It wouldn't make things better—no way in the world.

Frank looked up the broad dirt trail.

"Boy, how I missed Billy today. It really did hit me hard. Hell."

He remembered back to how he got the news of Billy's death. It was as if he'd been shot, as if his insides had been ripped open by a bullet. The news, too, put Maria in shock.

When did he tell her Billy had committed suicide? When did he tell Maria that Connie Mack had found his son hanging by a belt from the ceiling in his room? How long had it taken him to process it, to tell her once he was able to even say it without feeling like it was his death he'd come upon?

Judy and Jimmy had their private spot in the park. They had a place to meet, something exclusively theirs. Somewhere where Jimmy could cry if he wanted, whenever his depression overtook him. They were teenagers facing up to things even adults found emotionally impossible to handle.

Frank wasn't going to walk far on the trail. He wasn't looking for Judy and Jimmy's hideaway in Cunningham Park. And if he ever found it, he wouldn't tell anyone. Judy and Jimmy could trust him with that.

Frank stopped walking when he looked up at the lazy, cloudy sky.

CHAPTER 20

It was several months later.

"Jim! Did you hear that, Jim!"

Jim Boston had his head under the covers as if he didn't want to hear his own breath.

"Marion …"

"It's down in the basement."

"It is?" Then Jim came to his senses. "What's down in the basement?"

"That."

"What!"

Jim was supported by his elbows and looked about as alert as an Eagle Scout at dawn.

"I don't hear anything."

"I do."

"You would," Jim said, agitated. "Of course you would. No one else I know of. Marion, you could hear a spider when it lands."

"Aren't you going to check on it—do something about it?" Marion asked after feeling Jim's body wind comfortably back to its past state.

"Check on something I can't hear. Do something? Gosh, woman!"

"There … there it goes again."

"Darn it, Marion."

"I'm going down—"

"No, you're not," Jim said, stopping her. "You're not going anywhere. Not on your life. If it's a break-in, which I seriously doubt, I'll risk my life.

I'll be the one to sacrifice my life first. Uh, my life insurance policy's paid up—isn't it, Marion?"

Jim was out the bed. He fetched his robe.

"It's probably a stray squirrel or something," Marion said.

"Oh, so you mean I don't need to carry my baseball bat? I can leave it in the closet?"

"Not for something as innocuous as a squirrel."

"I can't believe it's in the middle of the night—"

"Three sixteen to be accurate." Marion chuckled.

"And I'm being asked to go down into the basement to chase a squirrel. Protect hearth and home. Gosh, Marion!"

"Me either, Jim," Marion said, rubbing it in.

"What's my life coming to? Tell me."

Jim was out of the bedroom and into the hallway.

It was ten minutes later, and Jim was climbing the staircase. Then he was up on the landing.

"Dad …"

Jim opened Jimmy's door.

"Yes, Jimmy?"

"You're not going to turn on the lights, are you?"

"Of course not. I know how you look."

"Thanks."

"And the layout of the room."

"I was thinking."

"About tomorrow's game."

Jim could feel Jimmy's heart as it beat.

"The whole season's been dedicated to Billy, and now it's the payoff. I just want to perform well, Dad. Up to my capabilities."

"Jimmy, you will. You always do. Especially in big games. They're tailor-made for you."

"Tomorrow's going to be the biggest game of my life." Pause. "By the way, what are you doing up, walking the floor, anyway?"

"Oh, who? Me? Oh, gosh, just chasing a scrawny squirrel out of the basement at three sixteen in the morning."

"Don't tell me …"

"Right, your mother again." Jim laughed.

"She heard something moving in the basement, all the way from the bedroom?"

"Ain't the first time that's happened. Heck, you know that, Jimmy."

"Mom and her ears."

"So I escorted the little bugger out the back door once we got on better terms—that is, realized it was far too early in the morning to be running around a dark basement.

"We called it a truce, in other words."

"I wonder how it got in the house in the first place."

"Beats me," Jim said, showing his disinterest.

"I told Coach Bosco at the beginning of the season about Mom. That I'm like her. At least on the football field. I can hear everything out there."

"You are, Jimmy. A replica."

"I hear everything on the field, but under ordinary circumstances, I'm just ordinary."

"I know. Strange, isn't it, how our senses work and adjust?"

Pause.

"So are you all right with tomorrow's game?" Jim asked, yawning.

"Yes, fine."

"Billy's going to be proud, Jimmy. Damn proud of you."

"He, Billy, will."

"Good night—not that there's much left."

"Uh, by the way, Dad, was the squirrel's insurance paid up, or did you bother to ask?"

"Why, you know," Jim said, enticed, "I didn't. But maybe I can catch up with the little fella. Who knows? I'm sure he hasn't gotten too far from the house."

Jim closed Jimmy's door.

"Mr. Squirrel sent his regards, Marion," Jim said, entering the dark bedroom.

"Was his insurance paid up, Jim?"

"Gosh, not you too, Marion. Why, Jimmy said the same thing. Am I that bad?"

Marion held her breath.

"Uh no, I forgot. And we got on such friendly terms down in the basement, Mr. Squirrel and I."

"Jimmy …"

"Pregame, jitters. The usual," Jim said, falling back into bed.

"Now where was I before I was so rudely—"

"He'll do fine, Jim."

"I told him that."

"It's Billy, isn't it?" Marion frowned.

"Oh, how I hope the Purple Eagles win it for Billy too."

"At first, I didn't know how Jimmy would make it through the season, never mind to the championship game."

"Never doubted it in my mind, Marion. Our son's an exceptional young man."

Jim was under the covers. Jim could tell Marion hadn't entered into the same resting position.

"I don't care what you hear for the rest of the night, Marion," Jim grumbled. "Even if Mr. Squirrel comes back, I'm not leaving my warm nest."

"Don't worry, Jim. I've tucked my antennae in for the night."

"Who are you kidding? You hear everything that moves in this damn house," Jim groused.

"I do, don't I?"

Jim remained silent. He wasn't going to pursue this, not with her. What, and lose more sleep?

Judy bounded out of her chair more than once, it had seemed. It's how she and the rest of the Purple Eagle cheerleaders bounded into the air when the team won the state championship today, defying gravity.

Marion enjoyed Judy's exuberance. "All of that, Judy, because I said, 'I'd like to have a glass of punch'? I could have gotten it, honey."

"I know, Mrs. Boston, but I guess I'm still on edge."

"It was some win, wasn't it?"

"Fantastic, Mrs. Boston. Simply amazing!"

Jim, Jimmy, Marion, and Judy had come back to the Boston home to celebrate today's victory. It was the way Jimmy wanted it.

"How do you keep those girls so energized, Judy? Full of pep?"

Judy was still team captain of the Purple Eagles cheerleading squad. "Easy. Tradition, Mrs. Boston. We're used to the Purple Eagles winning."

"It can make all the difference in the world, can't it? Thank you, dear," Marion said, receiving her second glass of punch.

Jimmy came back into the house with an armful of grocery bags; Jim followed him empty-handed.

"You're tilting a bit to the left with the bags, Jimmy."

"Am I, Dad?"

Jim laughed heartily. "Getting heavy, huh? Quarterbacks," Jim said, shaking his head. "Now if you were Billy, a full …" Jim caught himself.

"Billy," Jimmy said. He turned from them and then back to them as if the storm had passed. "It's all right. The Purple Eagles played this season for Billy, didn't we? It's his victory, Billy's victory too."

Jimmy took the grocery bags into the kitchen. Tears had reached his cheeks. The tears were there today when the team beat Randolph High. Jimmy's flowed like champagne. They were mostly for Billy—maybe all of them, since he'd never cried after a football win. But he wasn't the only one who cried. Coach Bosco had too, and those tears had something to do with Billy since he'd never done that. *I wasn't alone,* Jimmy thought.

"Yes, Marion, we bought Italian," Jim said with a sparkle in his eye, taking the glass of punch from Judy. "Thanks, Judy." He sat down in the living room with Marion and Judy.

The Boscos had been invited for dinner. It was unplanned, arranged at the last minute.

"Well, let me get up from here and into the kitchen to prepare some Italian cuisine."

"May I help, Mrs. Boston?"

"Checking in," Marion said to Jimmy, who had just left the kitchen.

"Me too," Judy said. Jimmy hugged her and kissed her.

"Well, here goes," Marion said as Judy stood by her side at the kitchen counter.

"Men," Judy said in a mild huff.

"Get used to it. Men don't want to be anywhere near a kitchen, not unless there's food on the table."

Jimmy, once he got into the living room, sat next to Jim on the couch.

"Dad, there's a heaven, isn't there?"

"Yes, I believe there is. Never mind our religious beliefs, what we're taught to believe. Look, we came from somewhere, Jimmy."

"And Billy's there, isn't he?"

Jim looked at Jimmy, offering no reply.

"One day, Billy and I will reunite. It's what heaven's for too. Right, Dad?"

Suddenly Jim didn't want to take on this kind of talk, let it get too far. This was something new Jimmy was asking, what seemed on the borderline of a new source of pain, or whatever his emotions were now putting him through.

"It was a great win today, Jimmy. The team can feel proud of itself."

"Dad ..." Jimmy felt as if Jim was being evasive.

"Don't, Jimmy. It does no one any good. Those are questions only God can answer, not me, son. No ... not me."

Jimmy got up and walked over to the living room's back window. "Yeah, yeah, Dad."

The phone rang.

"I'll get it, Jim."

"What? I thought you were busy cooking, Marion!" Jim shouted.

"Hello," Marion said, speaking into the phone.

"Susan!"

Judy perked up, along with Jim and Jimmy.

Marion and Susan spoke no more than a minute.

"Jimmy," Marion said.

Jimmy ran into the kitchen.

"It's—"

"I know, Mom. I heard you."

He took the phone out of Marion's hand.

"Hello, Mrs. Mack."

Jimmy was trying his best to control himself, but it was difficult.

They talked for a few minutes.

"Yes, Mrs. Mack. Thank you. Soon, yes, Mrs. Mack, very soon."

Jimmy looked at the phone after hanging it up in total disbelief, as if what had just happened hadn't.

"It, it was Mrs. Mack," Jimmy said, turning to Judy, who was all smiles. "Congratulating me."

Marion held him.

Jim came into the kitchen. "How did she sound, Marion?"

"Like Susan. Wonderful."

"She knew about the game today, Dad. All about it."

"She would," Jim said wistfully.

"Mrs. Mack's calling Coach Bosco to congratulate him."

"She's such a doll," Marion said.

"A real classy lady," Jim added.

Pause.

"Do ... do you think Mr. Mack knows, Dad?"

"Don't worry about Connie. He knows all right."

"I ... we'll never know what was in Billy's suicide note, will we, Mom?" Jimmy said, looking at Marion. "Dad?" Pause.

"I'd never leave a suicide note. Never. I wouldn't know what to say."

Judy, Marion, and Jim trembled at the thought.

The wind whipping the air was merciless, yet he stood there letting it whipsaw his skin.

"You aren't gone, Billy. Not you. You didn't leave me, man!"

He broke his silence. Jimmy finally broke it. He'd been standing out in it, in his silence, out on the grounds of Amity Cemetery where Billy was buried. Billy's gray-slated headstone told the tale: the date of his birth, May 23, 1975, and the date of his death, September 19, 1991. His beginning and end.

"Billy. Man, Billy ..."

Jimmy broke down and cried. He fell to his knees as if they'd been broken off at their kneecaps—some gruesome, violent act.

"Every day, Billy, I try. I try. How, how I try. You know I do."

Jimmy's face pressed against the ground, his cheekbone, the ground cold without a sun to heat it in early December.

"Nothing's enough anymore without you. Nothing, Billy. It's all I can say about my life. Nothing."

The way Jimmy hugged his face to the ground, it was as if it were keeping the ground warm, keeping it from turning colder, protecting it from the blasting wind.

Jimmy's tears seeped into the ground, and he felt alone. His soul no longer felt youthful but old and betrayed. The days had passed. The football season and all its glory had passed. Next year, the new football campaign, the Purple Eagles would not dedicate its season to Billy. The idea, the thought of that happening was repulsive to him even if it was also unrealistic. Billy would all but be forgotten in some respect.

"Don't worry, Billy. Don't you worry," Jimmy said over and over.

When Jimmy got to his feet, he felt no comfort, no relief. His soul felt old, betrayed—no longer young, no longer fresh, no longer tender.

"Billy, see you."

Jimmy was standing and looking down at his Beetle Volkswagen. It was a hot red. It wasn't new but secondhand.

"Dad bought it for me. And he paid for the insurance. Who else but good old Dad, Billy."

It was the first time Jimmy had driven the car to the cemetery, since it was only three days old. It was parked in Amity Cemetery's gravel parking lot, about ninety yards from Billy's plot.

Jimmy kicked the tires. "And the tires are pretty good. Pretty decent."

Jimmy was tired of crying.

"What were you thinking, Billy, when you took your life?"

Then the biggest question loomed. "How did you get, have the courage to do it? To hang yourself. To get, step up on the ladder, and hang yourself, Billy?"

It was what frightened Jimmy, to think Billy could think to kill himself the way he had. He just stood up on the ladder and did the things so he could do the final thing to end his life. Was it courage that did that or anger?

"School finals. Summer vacation. Then a brand-new football season, Billy. It just keeps going on. Life just keeps going on, repeating itself. Revolving round and round and round."

It was the same day.

Judy and Jimmy had left the movie early. Jimmy complained of a headache. They were in the Volkswagen Beetle.

"Are you okay?" Judy asked. "Can you drive?"

"I can drive," Jimmy said.

"Fine then," Judy said, buckling herself in.

"They say, before seat belts in cars, teenagers like us would sit side by side, Jud. Snuggle up real close."

"I know, but it's safety first and foremost."

"Safety first and foremost," Jimmy said, echoing her. "Judy, I'm sorry about the movie."

"That's all right. We can wait for the video. It'll be out in the stores before we know it," Judy said cheerily.

"My head, I don't know."

"It's not something—"

"Uh, no, not … Just tonight for some odd reason. It decided to be a pain in the butt tonight of all nights. Our night out."

"Unless you would've told me right, Jimmy? If, you know, you've been having headaches. Right?" Judy said, hoping she'd get a straight answer.

"Judy, without question." Jimmy smiled.

Pause.

"You went to see Billy today, didn't you? Out to Amity Cemetery?"

"Yes."

"Do you like going without me? Not having me around?" Judy asked, hurt. "Is that it?"

"Judy, it's not that. Has nothing to do with that. Any of that."

"Sorry if I'm overreacting. I don't mean to. I don't, Jimmy. But it just came out that way anyway, I suppose." Judy tucked her chin. "He can't be replaced, can he? Billy, in your life."

"It's really hard. Darn if I don't try. Sometimes, Judy, in my room, I, man … the things I remember we used to do. Billy and me. It all comes back. Every last detail. It's horrible. Ruthless at times. It just won't stop. Let up for me."

"Look what it did to Alexis. What lovely parents she has," Judy said, with admiration. "Understanding. They're great."

"They could've said no, I know. But didn't. They moved from Pittsfield for Alexis's sake. They didn't have to leave," Jimmy said.

"But she couldn't live here anymore inside a memory. She couldn't take it."

"Billy's gone, Judy."

"I miss Alexis." Pause. "A lot."

"She had to go, don't you see? You can see that, can't you?"

Pause.

"At times, I wish ..." Jimmy ended there, went no further.

"One more year of high school. Then we're off to college."

"I know, right," Jimmy said, edgily. "Not until next year." Pause.

"Judy, I didn't mean to say it like that. What's wrong with me? What's going on tonight? You and I saying wrong things. Apologizing like this. Not even being able to talk normally. I ... I don't know," Jimmy said, shaking his head.

Judy's hand held on to the edge of the car's armrest as she watched the night lights on Saddle Road (a beautiful section of Pittsfield) slip on and off the windshield.

Jimmy parked the car outside Judy's house. The car hadn't been running long.

"Not worried about gas?"

"No, uh-uh. Just my toes, Jud." Jimmy laughed.

No longer were they strapped to seat belts.

"I thought cuddling like this kept our toes warm," Judy said, like a seductress.

"Judy, hey ..."

She lifted her head. "Do you feel better?"

"Much."

"I'm glad."

"I'm looking forward to seeing that movie on video when it comes out any day now," Jimmy said, with sarcasm dripping from his tongue.

"Not that soon." Judy laughed. "And I bet I can tell you how it ends. You know there was a predictability about it, wasn't there? A certain—"

"Judy," Jimmy said, "you're too smart for me. I don't have the foggiest idea of how it ends. So ..."

"Well, you see—"

"And don't tell me!"

Playfully, Judy's fist tapped Jimmy's chest. "What a spoilsport. I never knew—"

Jimmy kissed her.

"That … now, that was nice," Judy said, snuggling up to him.

Jimmy hadn't kissed her all night. Not even when he picked her up. But Judy told herself she'd use restraint, that it would happen naturally, as it had. Because she knew Jimmy had gone to Amity Cemetery to visit Billy the second she saw him. It's something she concluded right off, as soon as she saw Jimmy when he came to pick her up.

"Tomorrow, Judy," Jimmy said, as if already bragging, "I'm going to sleep all day. Become a beach bum."

"Not you. Now that I can't believe." Pause. "Why?"

"I don't know. So don't call me before twelve o'clock. Okay?"

"As you know, I'll be up well before then."

"Yes, I'm going to behave like a teenager tomorrow—irresponsibly lazy. How's that?"

"Well, I can find something to do to wile the time away until after twelve without talking to Mr. Wonderful on the phone, I guess," Judy swooned.

"Who me?"

"Yes, you," Judy said, pinching Jimmy's nose.

Jimmy pulled down on her ponytail.

"Ouch!"

"Can't take it, huh? Can dish it out but can't take it!"

"We're, we're," Judy said between laughs, "no better than five … five-year-olds, Jimmy."

"I wish I knew you when you were five."

"And what, spoil all of the mystery and allure of meeting me at—"

"Seriously though, Jud."

"Who knows, Jimmy? At that age, we might've hated each other. Despised each other."

"Boys, huh? That was it, huh?"

"Ugh! They weren't my cup of tea. Not in the least," Judy said snottily.

"Uh-uh, it's how Billy and I, I mean how I felt about girls then, when I was five. Identical. Man, Judy, you could have them. Keep them, as far as I was concerned!"

Jimmy kissed the tip of Judy's nose.

"It's just that I would've known you longer. For a longer period of time, that's all."

"Oh, don't worry," Judy said sexily, "you're going to know me for a long time. A long, long time, baby!"

"Yes, of course. Of course, Jud."

Judy felt comfortable in Jimmy's arms. She always felt comfortable in his arms. It was the sweetest kind of comfort for her.

"My gas!"

"You're not—you're worried about your gas?"

"Have to go, Judy. Gotta go."

"I was thinking," Judy said.

"About—"

"How—oh, never mind."

"Come on. Out with it. Don't do that to me. You know how I hate it when you try—"

"How I could stay like this with you in ... in your arms like this forever. And eternity."

Judy's lips touched Jimmy's hand.

"I love you, Jimmy. Haven't told you all night, have I?"

Jimmy's heart swelled as big as a balloon with far too much air as he took her and kissed her.

"Man, Judy, I love you too. Do I!" Jimmy said, as if his heart had burst.

"I want to marry you, Jimmy, one day. Be your wife. Have your children."

"I do too. So do I. It's what I want too, children with you. All of those beautiful things. They will come, Jud. They will come—don't worry," Jimmy said, with rigid patience in his voice.

"It's what I'm impatient about. It, right now, it seems so far off. So distant. It does ... it really does."

"Maybe it's not good to want things too soon. Too quickly, Judy. Maybe it's not good. Takes the fun out of it. You know—looking too far ahead."

"You could be right. Rushing things."

"College first."

"And then the rest. What follows," Judy said, less eager, timidly, more relaxed. "It's just that I love you so much. It's what's making me feel like this, say these crazy things. As if I'm rushing things along too quickly."

Jimmy shut his eyes, and those same words lived inside him.

They were saying good night.

Judy stood outside the Volkswagen, on the passenger side. Jimmy leaned over and touched her hand when it came through the rolled-down window.

"Call you tomorrow, after twelve. See? I remember. I won't be any trouble."

"You did, Jud. After twelve. I'll be up and about. And you're no trouble. You're never any trouble for me."

"What about your parents? Have they found out about your Saturday-morning plans yet?"

"They'll be the first to know. As soon as I set foot in the house, they'll be perfectly apprised of my situation," Jimmy said officiously.

Their lips met in the middle.

"I had to kiss you, Jimmy. I couldn't resist."

Jimmy smiled. "I'm glad."

"Good night."

"Good night."

Jimmy rolled up the window. Then he leaned over and rolled up the passenger-side window. He watched Judy, waiting until she got onto the house's front porch. Judy waved a second time to him, saying good night.

Honk!

It was ten twenty-five when Jimmy entered the house. Immediately, he sought Marion and Jim out. They could be only one place.

"Come in, Jimmy," Marion said, responding to the knock on the bedroom door.

Marion rested her book, Jim his newspaper.

"Suppose I was a burglar knocking on the door?"

"Burglars don't knock, Jimmy. They're not that polite," Jim said, "before robbing you!"

"How was the movie?" Marion asked.

"Oh, great, Mom."

"Did you and Judy share a super-duper box of popcorn?"

"No, Dad. A box for her and one for me."

"Judy doesn't have to worry about her waistline. I remember once upon a time being that petite. A waistline as small and narrow as an hourglass."

"Hey, you're still not doing so bad, Marion, after all these years," Jim said approvingly.

Jimmy walked over to the queen-sized bed and sat on it (he was on Marion's side).

"Your wedding pictures don't lie, Mom."

"It's like a before-and-after ad, huh, Jimmy?" Marion sighed ponderously.

"No, it's like Dad said. You're doing fine, Mom. Fine for yourself."

"Have to work at it though. Can't be lazy. Can't let a day slip by or … or else …"

"Well, you and Dad taught me that nothing comes easy without hard work."

"Oh … you've been paying attention, have you?"

"Jim," Marion admonished.

"Marion, just because our son's on the honor roll and a football All-American—okay, okay. I need to be quiet. Shut up. Slink away as meekly as a mouse. I know what the two of you are thinking."

Pause.

"Jimmy, are you making any progress with the colleges you're entertaining?"

"I am. I'm on a roll. Clipping them off pretty fast. With Judy's help, of course."

"Of course," Jim said mockingly.

"It's wonderful Judy wants to be a pediatrician."

"A perfect field for her. Kids. That's her thing."

Jim coughed into his hand. "She's just a caring young lady, period. A sweetheart of a girl."

"It's the first time your father's said something we agree on. Right, Jimmy?"

"There're a gang of colleges with great football programs and premed."

"They're dotted across the map." Then Jim turned serious. "As long as they're not too far from Pittsfield, Jimmy. Us."

"Dad, don't tell me—"

"No, don't get things wrong, Jimmy. This is strictly for your mother I'm speaking. Her, not me."

"I love you guys. I really do."

Marion and Jim looked at each other with mutual admiration.

"We're proud of you, Jimmy," Jim said as he watched Jimmy gradually let go of Marion.

"Thanks, Dad." Pause. "By the way, I'm going to sleep in tomorrow."

"Sleep—"

"Oh, act lazy. Get up at no earlier than, say, twelve o'clock. How about that? It's Saturday. I'm going to be an irresponsible teenager for a change."

"A typical teenager you mean, huh?"

"That's it, Dad. A typical teenager."

"You deserve it, honey," Marion said.

"So please hold my calls."

"What about Judy, Jimmy, or the president?"

"Jim …"

"Already told her, Dad. I've got that covered. Not to call before twelve."

"Heck. Should've guessed."

"And as for the president, you can tell him, Dad, what you always tell him when he calls and I'm unavailable."

"Got you, Jimmy." Jim winked. "Wonder if his insurance is paid up?"

"Good night," Jimmy said.

"Good night," Jim said.

"Good night," Marion said.

"My bed's going to feel good tonight," Jimmy said, looking back at his parents. "My head on my pillow, it's going to feel real, real good."

Jimmy shut the door.

Marion and Jim didn't strike up conversation until minutes after Jimmy left.

Jim removed his reading glasses.

"I'm glad he enjoyed the movie tonight," Marion said.

"Me too."

"You know, Jim, I think Jimmy's life's getting back to normal."

"Do you?"

"Don't you?"

"Yes, there are signs. Positive ones. That Jimmy's clearing the waters. Slowly pulling himself out ..."

"But?" Marion asked, sensing reservation in Jim's voice.

"It is an awful thing, Marion, our son's been living with. It just doesn't go away."

"Jim, but it does seem like he's beginning to find some peace, some resolution. Don't you think?"

"Marion, it's like you're trying to force me to say things, the things I can't say yet. Not honestly, at least."

"No, it's the last thing I'm trying to do. No, not at all."

"So why does it feel like you are?"

"Then I'm sorry, Jim, if it does. Not this kind of tragedy. What Jimmy's been through."

"You're looking for things and that's positive, healthy." Jim's hand smoothed out the wrinkled newspaper. "But let's face it. Jimmy's struggling. Billy is still a powerful presence. Billy's there; he hasn't left, been in any way displaced. In any way uprooted." Pause. "We've talked. They've been long, hard talks between us."

Marion agreed.

"But you can only penetrate a person so ... but so deeply. But he is doing better. I'll grant you that much. Much better, I'll grant you."

"Yes, it's all I was saying, commenting on, Jim," Marion said nervously. "Nothing more."

Jim made himself more comfortable. "And he's sleeping in tomorrow."

"Treating himself, you might say, Jim." Marion laughed. "To teenagerdom, if there's such a word—"

"Which I doubt." Pause. "But just make sure you tiptoe around the house, will you?" Jim laughed.

"Look who's talking, Jim. You're the noisemaker. Why, don't you have the nerve. The nerve of a burglar!" Marion faked a yawn. "So maybe I'll sleep in a little late too."

"What, this is rubbing off? What Jimmy said?"

"Could be. Maybe."

"Well, you deserve it. You're another one who deserves a lazy day. Take part of it off."

"Jim Boston, don't tell me you're trying to butter me up?"

"Marion … the way Jimmy said it …" Jim's face glowed. "You know …"

"I know, Jim. What Jimmy said in the living room. His admiration for us. He really does love us."

"I suppose I'm a sentimental old fool." Jim laughed.

"Me too. No better than you. But I'll accept only the sentimental part, not the old fool."

Jim fussed with the newspaper. "Marion, we are getting older. Can't deny it. We've seen our share of sunrises and sunsets."

Marion's hands slid down along her waist. "Yes, Jim, I lost my hourglass figure what seems years ago."

"Not in my eyes," Jim said cunningly, inching himself closer to her.

Jimmy's clothes were halfway off. It's when it struck him, this headache of his. It tore into him. It practically tore his head off.

Jimmy grabbed his head. The hanger he held fell to the floor.

"My head!"

Jimmy reeled. His body kept reeling. And then he sank hard to the floor. He was pleading for his headache to go away, to end then and now.

"Tell me what's wrong with me!"

He'd been thinking too much. *It's what it is. I have to relax*, Jimmy thought.

The headache continued. The headache intensified.

Jimmy was viewing his life. With the intense pain in his brain, Jimmy was on the floor, sunk in it, looking at his life, trying to understand it as best he could.

He had Judy. And she had med school. They'd talked about Stanford University and Duke University as choices. They were great schools for them. They were schools that were spinning through their conversations more and more. He would be far from home if he chose Stanford, on the other side of the world practically.

He had his mom and dad. They were the best, tops. The best parents anyone could have. They didn't want him to travel far from home. They'd miss him. He was important to them.

But these headaches. How much longer would they continue? How much longer would they go on? Would they ever stop?

He could get off the floor now. This he felt. That he could get off the floor.

"All-American quarterback. All … All-American quarterback. Big deal. Big deal."

Jimmy was on his bed damning his headache, knowing why it was still with him, why it wouldn't leave him. End.

"Billy. How did you do it, Billy? How, man!"

Jimmy looked up at the top of the bed, and his hand reached out to the top of the bedspread tucked under the pillow and yanked back the bedspread to cover him, as a certain chill had stabbed him.

There was no defense for what he felt. He was beginning to think, in his mind, that there was no defense for how he felt—the headaches.

"All-American. All-American quarterback. Big deal. Big deal."

Billy was gone. Billy would always be gone. He'd left him. His tomorrows he did not consider. Their tomorrows he did not consider. His life had been distorted, skewed. Billy had reached a desperate state.

Jimmy's hands went back up to his head; it was hurting him so. Relentlessly. Paining him.

"Billy, you didn't feel they were … your parents. You just didn't know about them, Billy. The marriage. What would happen with them. Stood. Where everything stood between them. Reconciliation or …"

Every morning, he was frightened by the thought. Terrified by the thought. *Put yourself in his shoes. Put yourself in Billy's shoes.*

"You were scared, Billy. Terrified. All-American. All-American, big deal. Big deal. What's it mean, Billy? What does it mean?"

Jimmy jumped to his feet. He felt stronger, better. His hands reached down to the bedspread, and neatly, very precisely, he began making his bed. And once it was made, he looked at it, how neat it was, and then put himself back on the bed softly, as if not to put a wrinkle in its look, not one hint of one.

As he lay on the bed, Jimmy's thoughts became tender, fond. He was thinking about all the good times he'd had in Pittsfield: Judy, Coach Bosco, his mom and dad, Billy. Pittsfield was a splendid environment. His dad made a good living selling insurance in Pittsfield. A middle-class living. They lived a great life in Pittsfield.

Jimmy's eyes shut.

He saw Billy's hands in the casket, big and powerful, fleshy—a fullback's hands. His hands were large and his fingers long, a quarterback's hands. He placed his hands on his stomach as they had placed Billy's hands on his stomach. There were so many things he wanted to say to Billy the day of his funeral. But all he did was look at Billy's hands, the ones he handed the football off to so many times, thousands, for so many years of his life.

Jimmy's eyes popped opened.

"And now I'm alone, Billy. All alone without you. It's you who's not coming back. You had that fear. It's what you were afraid of. But maybe your parents … maybe Mr. and Mrs. Mack would've worked things out. Maybe … maybe they would have, Billy. It would have gotten better between your parents, for them, Billy."

Jimmy felt an awful pain strike his head. But he didn't put his hands up to his head like he'd done before, since he knew they were flat to his stomach, holding the stiff position Billy's hands held in the casket at his funeral.

"But you, Billy. But you, you're not coming back. No, man. And now I'm scared. Scared, Steamroller, scared. Can't you see I'm scared!"

Jimmy, for that instant, knew Billy had heard him. For that instant, he knew Billy knew what his insides felt like, how devastating and desperate all of this had become for him. Billy understood everything about him, every part there was of the life living inside him. It was Billy who understood these things, all of this. Billy.

"I know you do, Billy. You do, Steamroller."

Billy had known what loneliness was. Billy Steamroller Mack had lived with it until he took his life in his room, had consciously and deliberately hanged himself.

It was the next morning.

"Marion, don't forget to tiptoe."

Marion's robe lay across her shoulders. She slipped her arms through its sleeves.

"I haven't forgotten."

"I know. Was just checking." Pause. "Gosh." Jim yawned. "I feel like sleeping in today."

Marion grinned.

"When's the last time I did that?"

Marion's robe was fastened to her. "Not anytime I can recall."

"Go-go Boston. I suppose that's my motto!"

"And you live up to it too, Jim. You've been an excellent provider for us."

"Marion, why, thank you."

Marion headed for the bathroom.

When she came back into the bedroom, Jim had dozed off. She was going to do the family's food shopping. While dressing, she was going to make sure she didn't bump into anything to disturb Jim.

"Jim," she whispered, looking at him curled comfortably under the covers, "I'll behave responsibly. As delicate as a ballerina."

When she was dressed, Marion kissed him on his cheek, and he mumbled something inaudible back.

"At least he's alive," Marion whispered again. "Barely, uh, that is."

When Jim awakened, Marion was out of the house.

In bed, Jim's hand felt for her for a second, but then he remembered it was Saturday, that she'd gone food shopping at Bernie's Farms Foods.

"So what time is it anyway? Ten ... ten fifty-two!"

Jim scurried. This was late for him. He was an insurance man. There were things to do. Mountains of them. Always!

His feet had begun making a racket on the floor as if the heels of his feet were actually stomping about.

"Jimmy," Jim said. "Darn it. I … ah … what the heck. If I woke him, if he heard me, that is—he's probably just rolled back over onto his other side."

Jim didn't know what had overcome him, for him to sleep so late.

Jim was down in the kitchen. He'd showered, shaved, and taken his morning coffee (even though it was nearer lunch).

He heard Marion's car. He was out the back door like a shot out of hell.

"Hi, Jim," Marion said, rolling down the car window.

"You kissed me goodbye this morning when you left, didn't you? I know—"

"Who else leaves traces of her lipstick on your cheek as evidence, honey?" Pause.

"You know, I didn't feel a thing."

"Yes, I know. You mumbled as much. Ha, ha."

Jim was helping Marion with the bags, taking them out of the trunk.

"This is usually Jimmy's job."

"I know. But—"

"He's still sleeping, Jim?"

"Uh, I guess. Yeah, I guess so. Is out like a light," Jim said, carrying the shopping bags into the house. "He seduced me too," Jim said over his shoulder as Marion followed close behind.

"Power of suggestion, Jim."

"Probably. I've been up for a little over forty, forty-five minutes."

"Why, that's not like you."

"Half the morning's gone, wasted, shot. Hell, I sell insurance, for God's sake, Marion. What happened to my automatic alarm clock?"

"Beats me. I guess it decided to take the morning off too, along with you. It needed a break," Marion teased.

Marion removed her car coat. She was in jeans. A jean top and loafers.

"Well, I'm going to help you put away the groceries, and then I'm out of here."

"You don't have to. You go ahead. Off to the office. I can manage this."

"Uh-uh. I'm going to do the full nine yards. Do what your son does. Uh, but I'm not competing, mind you."

"But—"

"Nope. I'm yours for the next few minutes."

Jim finished the small chore.

"Marion, I'm at the office. The usual routine. Pitter-patter."

"Go ahead, shoo."

Jim kissed her.

"It should be an early day, even if I lost half the morning," Jim said, leaving the kitchen.

"Hope they don't fire you!"

"Oh yeah. Me too!"

For some odd reason, Marion thought of Susan Mack, but it was fleeting.

"Oh well …"

Marion's many chores were mapped out. She glanced at the wall's round-faced, shiny silver clock. It was 12:10. *Yes*, Marion thought, *I have plenty of things to do.*

Ring.

Marion sensed it was Judy calling. Jimmy had said she'd call after twelve, and it was that. Judy had given him about ten minutes extra.

"Hello.

"Oh, hello, Judy."

"How'd I know it was you?"

"Yes, Jimmy let us know, Mr. Boston and I, before he turned in last night. He said you had permission to call the house after twelve but not before."

"No, not before. I dare say not. Not at all, dear."

"Okay, honey, I'll get him. He hasn't moved from his room, to my knowledge. Of course, I was shopping at Bernie's Farm Foods, so who knows what goes on in this house when I'm not here, when the men are in the house. Be right back."

Marion strode to the front of the staircase.

"Jimmy, it's Judy. Jimmy, it's Judy on the phone!" Marion shouted up the stairs.

Marion stood at the bottom of the stairs, giving Jimmy time, even though he was always quick on his feet when getting out of bed.

"Jimmy, Jimmy …"

Marion was making her way up the staircase because she noticed there was a distinct absence of sound, something her ears must have somehow overlooked earlier.

"Jimmy, honey," Marion said more questioningly.

"Judy, you said she could call after twelve."

There was greater panic in Marion's voice.

She was at Jimmy's door. "Jimmy …"

Instinctively, Marion knew Jimmy wasn't in his room, behind the closed door.

Marion was in the room.

Jimmy wasn't there.

Marion looked at Jimmy's bed. It was made but with wrinkles still in it and a faint imprint of his body.

"Jimmy!"

Judy, Marion thought. *Judy. Judy's on the phone. I left Judy on the phone.*

Marion ran out Jimmy's room.

"Judy. Judy. Uh … honey—I made a mistake. I just found a note. A note from Jimmy on, on the kitchen table. He, uh, Jimmy—I didn't see it before. When I came in from shopping. I must have been distracted. I … overlooked it. Jimmy said he'd be back in a few minutes. And, and it says," Marion said, as if she were actually reading a handwritten note left by Jimmy, "that if Judy calls, tell her I'll call her at her house later.… No, honey. Jimmy didn't say how, uh, when later.… O-okay. Yes, Judy. Yes, dear, I'll tell him. Between one and four, you'll … you'll be out the house. But, yes, but after that, any time after that, it's okay. It's all right to call … Yes, honey. Got it. W-will do."

Marion hung up the phone.

"Jimmy, where are you?"

And automatically, Marion said. "Why didn't I hear you? Why didn't I hear you when you left the house?"

She thought of Jim. She looked at the kitchen clock. He wasn't at the office yet. He'd been gone ten minutes, no more. It was a fifteen-minute drive to his office.

"I must wait."

There was no one in the house. Marion's ears heard no one else in the house.

"But … but I'll have to wait. Wait for Jim. For him to get to the office," Marion said, sitting on the edge of the chair.

"Jim. What could it be, Jim?"

Marion leaped to her feet. It was time.

"Hel … Jim!"

"Marion. What is it?"

"He's not in his room. Jimmy's not in his room!"

"But he said he'd be sleeping late, Marion. Jimmy said—"

"But he's not in his room. Jimmy's not in his room."

"Calm down, Marion. Don't get yourself worked up over this."

"How can I!"

"Maybe Jimmy's—"

"Come home, Jim. Come home. Now!"

"Why, of course. Of course, Marion. I'm on my way."

When Marion got into Jimmy's room, she walked over to Jimmy's bed and looked down at it and saw what she saw before, the marginal wrinkles on the bedspread and his body's imprint.

Marion looked away. She walked over to Jimmy's desk and the chair facing the bed. She pulled out the chair and then turned it. Marion sat and stared at the bed.

"Marion!"

Jim was moving toward the kitchen.

"I'm up here, Jim. In Jimmy's room!"

"Marion!"

Jim grabbed her.

Marion sobbed into Jim's shoulder.

"I don't know where he is, Jim. Where Jimmy is."

He continued to hold her.

"Jimmy didn't sleep in his bed last night, Jim. On … on top of it. But not in it. He didn't sleep in it, Jim."

Jim let Marion stand. "See … see," she said, taking Jim's hand and leading him over to the made bed.

287

He was about to put his hand down on the bed.

"Don't touch it, Jim. Don't touch it," Marion said, as if she were using the bed, its condition, as some kind of evidence, proof.

"No ... I won't, Marion. Forgive me."

"Where is he, Jim? Where's Jimmy? Where'd he go?"

"I ... I thought about it. Thought it through. On the way over, Marion. In the car on the way over, Marion. Cunningham Park. Where else, Marion? Cunningham Park. To think, Marion. Jimmy went there to think—to be alone."

"But why wouldn't he tell us? We'd let him go. It'd be no problem for us. It's been no problem before. Up until now."

Jim was walking Marion back over to Jimmy's desk, Jimmy's chair.

"Sit, Marion. Please. Down here."

"Why so secretive?" Marion asked, looking up at Jim from the chair.

"Oh ... I don't know, Marion. Teenagers ..."

"Not Jimmy, Jim. Jimmy's not like that with us. You know that. We're not treated like, in, in that way."

Jim knew as much.

"He's open with us. Totally. There're no secrets."

"Did ... did Judy call?"

"It's how I found out. Yes. It's how I found out Jimmy wasn't home. She, Judy called."

"What did you tell her?"

"I lied."

"That's okay. All right. Absolutely. Under the circumstances, Marion, it's okay. I would've done the same."

"Jim, do you think I should call her? After all ..."

"I know what you're thinking. You're getting at."

"It's their spot, Jim. It's where Jimmy and Judy go off to together."

"Private. It's private, Marion."

"But ... but I could tell Judy it's where I think he is. Where he might've gone."

"Marion, let's wait. Let's say we wait a little longer, okay? Wait it out some more."

"And then what, Jim? What then?"

"We'll call Judy. Do that, Marion. Call Judy."

Marion had been placated.

Neither had moved from Jimmy's room. Both had been in Jimmy's room for well over two hours. Jimmy hadn't come home.

Marion's face had a distressed look on it.

"We'll … we should call Judy, Marion. I think we call her now."

"Thank you, Jim," Marion said, as if there was to be some final resolution to the situation.

Jim and Marion were in the kitchen (they never used Jimmy's phone, not under any circumstance).

Marion had lost sight of the time. But then she looked at the kitchen clock and remembered Judy's message she was to deliver to Jimmy.

"Jim, I can't call," Marion said, her body sagging more.

Jim was imploring her to say more.

"Judy won't be home until four, Jim. Not before four o'clock. It's the message I was to give Jimmy. Not before four. It … it's 2:39, Jim. It's only 2:39."

Jim looked at the kitchen clock and saw the time. What was happening to them, him and Marion, for now, seemed so damned cruel and heartless, Jim thought.

"Maybe by then …"

"Yes, Jim, maybe by then," Marion said, cutting Jim off, "Jimmy will be home."

They'd been looking at the kitchen clock until it got to 4:05. Jim understood why Marion had not called the minute the clock's hand struck four o'clock.

Marion was back on her feet.

Jim could hear the pressing of Marion's finger on the phone's buttons.

"Judy.… Yes, Judy, it's me. I'm calling you at four o'clock. Uh, not Jimmy, honey.… Oh, everything's okay.… Yes. Yes." Pause. "No. Jimmy hasn't gotten home as of yet.... No, there's no need to worry. None, honey.... But Mr. Boston and I ..." Pause. "Yes, he had a short day today. At the office. Business, he said, was slow.... Jimmy, Judy. Jimmy, we, Mr. Boston and I think he's gone to Cunningham Park, honey.... Yes, honey.... To think, Judy.... Yes, to be alone—that too."

Jim knew that Judy knew why Jimmy went to Cunningham Park: Billy. It was always why he'd go there alone, to be with Billy.

"You'll go, Judy? Go then?... Yes. Yes. I'm sure. I'm sure Jimmy would. He wouldn't mind. No, I'm more than sure."

Marion was about to hang up when she said, "Thank you. Thank you, dear."

"She, she's going, Marion. Judy's going."

"Yes, it's where he is, Jim. Jimmy's in Cunningham Park. I'm positive. Certain of it."

"He won't mind her being there. Being with him. Her company. Not at all. He's had the morning to think, Marion. To clear things out the way in ... in his head."

"Think. I ... we keep saying that, Jim. But maybe there are no more thoughts for him to think. I ... I don't know, Jim. I just don't know anymore," Marion said in an emotional stream of unconscious thought.

"Maybe Jimmy's beyond that now, Jim. Maybe all he can do is feel, not think. Maybe it's all Jimmy can do, Jim—is feel not think. Maybe he's gone back to that again."

"When ... when's it going to end?" Jim responded feebly.

It was a question Jim had asked Marion a dozen or more times.

Judy was apprehensive. How was she to handle this?

Judy was at the edge of the park. Her feelings were darting through her sharply, diagonally. Nothing felt clear or orderly or settled.

Jimmy's in there with Billy. They're inseparable, she thought. *Jimmy and Billy are inseparable.*

Judy exuded her usual brightness when she entered into their space. But Jimmy was not on the rock he normally sat on.

Judy clearly felt pained, out of it.

"Jimmy, why aren't you here?"

She looked over to places she knew Jimmy wouldn't be.

"Why am I doing this?" Judy asked herself.

She thought back to Mrs. Boston, and while her voice on the surface sounded calm, she'd felt all along that there was something pressuring her and that what was happening was beginning to take on a mystery, as if some suspense were controlling it.

"There's something happening that I don't know. Something's wrong."

Jim and Marion hadn't left the kitchen.

Ring.

"Let me get it, Marion."

Jim got to the door and opened it.

"Judy."

"Hello, Mr. Boston."

"Judy," Marion said, now in the hallway.

"He wasn't there, Mrs. Boston. Jimmy's not in Cunningham Park."

"At the spot?" Marion said.

"Come ... come in, Judy," Jim said.

Judy, when she got in the house, wasted no time in asking the question. "Respectfully, can one of you tell me what's going on that I don't know of?"

Jim and Marion looked at each other.

"I lied to you, Judy, before" Marion said, coming to her and walking her into the living room. "I lied to you over the phone. Jimmy didn't leave a note for you on the kitchen table. There was no note."

Jim shook his head.

"There ... there wasn't?"

"No, Judy. I lied to you." Marion did everything she could to harness her emotions. "When you called, honey, you see, Jimmy's been gone, Judy. Missing since ..." Marion couldn't go on.

Jim looked at Judy intently from about ten feet away. "Since, we suspect, this morning, Judy," Jim said, grabbing his wrist and twisting it. "Jimmy, you see, didn't sleep in his bed last night. That much we do know."

"But on top of it, honey, but not in it. On the sheet," Marion said.

Judy was mystified. "May ... may I see for myself? Jimmy's bed? Please?"

"Go ahead, honey. Yes, go ahead," Marion said.

Marion and Jim wouldn't go back upstairs into Jimmy's room—not for now.

Judy stood at the foot of Jimmy's bed. She'd been in his room before. She knew Mr. and Mrs. Boston had not touched the bed. She could tell.

"God, I hate this, Jimmy. Already I hate this."

She saw how the bed looked, how Jimmy left it.

Judy was back downstairs with Jim and Marion.

"What do we do now?"

"We wait, Judy. We wait," Jim said.

Marion held her.

"It's scary, Mrs. Boston. It ... it's just scary."

"Jim ..." Marion looked at him. "The police, Jim?"

"It's still too early to report Jimmy as a ... a missing person."

Pause.

"It's always twenty-four hours. It's what we have to work with, Marion, Judy. Twenty-four hours."

"But we don't know what time Jimmy left the house, Jim."

"We'll have to guess, Marion," Jim said. "I suppose."

"May ... may I stay with you tonight? Here tonight?" Judy asked softly. "I'll call my parents. They'll understand. There'll be no problem with me staying here tonight."

Jim and Marion smiled.

Jim hadn't slept. Neither had Marion. Nothing had changed since yesterday, Saturday. Jimmy hadn't called or come home.

"I ... I think we can call now."

"I'll get Judy."

Jim and Marion were fully dressed. They hadn't changed out of yesterday's attire.

"Judy." Marion was at the guest room door. "We're going to call now."

The door opened. Judy was fully dressed too. Her hair was neatly combed like Marion's and Jim's.

Marion took Judy's hand. Jim joined them.

They went into the kitchen. There was no mention of breakfast.

Jim held the phone in his hand. "Hello, my name is Jim Boston. I'd like to report a missing person. My son, Jimmy Boston." Pause. "Yes, it is twenty-four hours since we last saw him."

It was eight o'clock.

"More than twenty-four hours."

The police were at the house, two of them. They both knew Jim and of course Jimmy Boston (All-American quarterback who played for Pittsfield High, the Purple Eagles).

"This is top priority, Jim. So don't worry."

Jim patted Officer Pat Elkins's back. "Thank you, Pat."

"His clothes are upstairs."

"All of them," Marion said.

"So at least he's coming back, Marion. Jimmy's not going anywhere," Elkins said. "That's a good sign. Always a good sign in situations like this."

This news did nothing to change Jim, Marion, or Judy's mood.

The other officer, Rudy Castro, was at the door, seemingly itching to get started.

"Rudy, be right there. Give me a second."

Elkins was back in the living room. "Again, we're going to work as hard as hell on this case, Jim. Rudy and I."

It was after six. Jim and Marion and Judy had eaten. Jimmy was still missing. Jim and Marion and Judy could do nothing but turn to one another.

Officer Elkins called in periodically to report that nothing up to that specific point had changed. There'd been no progress. The waiting was unnerving them.

"Excuse me," Judy said to Jim and Marion. Judy stepped out the room.

Jim and Marion waited until the bathroom door on the second floor shut.

"This is hell, Jim. Hell."

"I don't want to believe it. That something like this is happening to us, Marion. Not, not this."

"By now, where could he be, Jim? Jimmy. Where, Jim?"

"Damn if I know!" Jim said, furious, finally losing his patience.

"I'm disappointed in him, Jim. In Jimmy."

"I'm downright mad, Marion. Mad as hell at him. About to go out of my mind I'm so mad at him."

"I don't want to say that. I don't want to regret what I say, even now."

"You can stay calm all you want to, but Jimmy … Jimmy …" Jim slapped the kitchen table. "What's gone wrong, Marion? Tell me. What's gone wrong!"

The bathroom door reopened.

"Judy, Jim."

Jim shut his eyes while his body visibly breathed hard.

"Mr. and Mrs. Boston, I've decided I'm going to go home." Pause. "It's … it's time for me to go home. You understand, don't you? I hope you do."

Marion rose to her feet.

Marion put her arms around Judy's waist. Jim came over and kissed her cheek.

Gently, Judy smiled, thanking Jim.

"As … as soon as we get word. As soon as we hear anything, Judy."

"Yes, Mrs. Boston. As soon as you and Mr. Boston hear anything from Officer Elkins and Officer Castro."

"You'll be the first to know."

"Thank you, Mrs. Boston, Mr. Boston."

Judy hugged Marion.

"Get home safely."

"Maybe I should drive you back—"

"No, Mr. Boston. Thank you … but I'll walk. I want to walk home."

Judy was out of the house and on the porch and then on the walkway, and she looked frail and pale and lost, no longer a teenager.

She walked over to the driveway, then up the driveway where Jimmy's red Beetle Volkswagen was parked. This had been discussed between Jim and Marion, then Judy, and then relayed to the police, that Jimmy, wherever he went yesterday morning, had not traveled by car.

"What sadness this day has brought with it."

"There's still hope, Marion. There's always hope. It's how we must think. Approach this."

Ring.

Ring.

Jim dashed to the phone.

"Yes, Pat?... Yes. Yes." Pause. "Thank you, Pat."

Marion's head dropped down and rested on Jim's shoulder.

"Nothing, Jim?"

"Pat's going to call back soon though. It's what he told me, Marion."

This marked the third day Jimmy was officially missing. The whole town of Pittsfield was aware of his disappearance. An enormous search party had been organized. It was searching Pittsfield for Jimmy.

Marion was up in the attic. She was sitting down in beige slacks on the attic's floorboards, which were lightly dusted. Marion was looking through Jimmy's things. They were old photos, toys, a lot of things Jimmy had ultimately outgrown.

The Bostons' attic was where most family items were stored. Marion, at the moment, was looking at a picture Jimmy had taken of her. She was holding it at eye level. In the picture, Marion's blonde hair looked lovely in the sun, and there was a splashy smile covering her face, something looking like a sunny-side-up egg staring up off a plate.

I didn't have my finest jeans on, Marion thought, *because the picture was taken of me in the house's backyard on a Saturday afternoon when I was doing the week's housework so, my, you can imagine.*

It was a candid shot of her. Jimmy, with that camera of his, enjoyed taking candid shots of his subjects. He'd catch them off guard, at random if possible.

It's where she and Jimmy differed. Marion always prepared her subjects before she shot their picture. She'd give them fair warning of what she was about to do to them with her camera. Jimmy was the opposite.

Jim was with the search party looking for Jimmy. She couldn't do that, tolerate that. Jim understood as much. He didn't expect her to react any differently to the search party than what she had. That was not something she could do with Jim and a search party, search for Jimmy.

While sitting on the attic's floor, Marion was looking at other old photos Jimmy had taken of her. She was mindful of why she had those photos spread across her lap. The midday sun shining through the attic's two windows gave enough light for her to adequately study the photos.

Marion still hadn't straightened out Jimmy's bed since he left the house without warning. It still had its look. Jimmy's hands were still the last ones to touch it—no one else's.

"I hear everything, don't I, Jimmy. In the house. Everything, Jimmy."

Marion wiped her eyes.

"If only I heard you, Jimmy. If only I had three mornings ago."

Marion's arms just held rigidly to her body, and she rocked herself in the sun as gently as its warm glow.

Jim was with the search party but physically detached from it. He had been with it at one point but broke away from it like a distant runner away from the pack. He was maybe a hundred and fifty yards ahead of it. It was wonderful that everyone was taking part in trying to find Jimmy, but this was still private, something Jim did not want to share.

He was deep in the woods. Deep in Cunningham Park. The search party was conducting a thorough search inside Cunningham Park for Jimmy. Judy had pretty much been a search party of one when she went off to her and Jimmy's special spot for the Boston family to find him.

There was something about the park, its vastness, largeness, something that haunted Jim at times and at other times appealed to him.

Mentally, he was exhausted. Spiritually, he was trying to hold on with all the faith in God he had inside him. Marion was walking this strange road they were on like him, mentally and physically exhausted, both trying to use their faith as an anchor to hold on. Their son was somewhere, and he'd be found.

Jim stopped for a second just to catch his breath. He'd been walking through the park too fast. He had to keep the distance between him and the search party consistent. That way, there still could be quick communication. He knew communication was the key in something like this, no matter how unfamiliar this was.

He started back up. This area of the park was thick with pines, cedars, and oaks. He'd never been so deep in the woods. *Would Jimmy travel this far?* Jim thought. *And if he did—to do what?*

Jim's knees buckled, practically giving way.

"Jimmy, I'm not mad at you, son. I'm not angry with you now. I was before, son. But not now. It was the first day, that's all. It's why I was angry, Jimmy. It was the first day."

There was so much fear in him, and he knew it. Marion had shut her eyes last night with the same fear in her. They had to sleep, but it wasn't much.

But when they woke, the fear was still there, frozen to them like ice. It was still all they could feel.

Jim was standing before a wall of trees. It was odd the way this section of Cunningham Park was configured, Jim thought. He'd not seen anything in the park quite like this. Jim indulged in a moment of silence and sheer awe, totally awestruck by nature and her exceptional accomplishment.

And then Jim could hear the search party drawing nearer to him. He could hear the men and women and young people's voices and their feet advancing farther.

Jim snapped out of it. The search party had shortened its distance between them, had gotten much closer than what he liked.

Jim moved into that clear setting of trees, of nature at her best. And it was as if he had entered a pristine space where there were no voices, as if this section of Cunningham Park had been sealed off from sound, from the living.

Jim walked into a lovely glade.

The sun poured out of the sky.

There was a tall tree.

Jim looked up.

Jimmy's body hung from the solid branch of the tree.

"Jimmy! Jimmy!"

The search party had arrived and had witnessed the same.

"Cut Jimmy down! Please, please cut my son down!"

Marion was in the attic. The sun was as bright as before. The first sound she heard was the car's door from the outside close slowly. Then the voices. There was news this time. Marion knew there was definite news this time.

Jim's shoes were in the house. Marion was back to hearing everything in the house again. Marion couldn't physically move off the floorboards. Jim wasn't bringing her good news, not something she could store away in the attic for the Boston family to reminisce about through good times and bad. This wasn't to be good news.

"I must meet Jim halfway. I must meet him halfway. He shouldn't have to come up to the attic for me. No, no, no," Marion cried.

Marion got to her feet.

"It would be so unfair. Unfair to him."

She would meet him on the second floor of the house. He would tell her about Jimmy there.

"Won't you, Jim. You will, Jim. Yes, you will."

CHAPTER 21

It was months later.

Jim thought it would be useful; it was why he'd gotten in touch with Judy and Frank Bosco.

"Is ... is everything ready, Marion?" Jim asked with trepidation.

"Yes, Jim."

Jim had come into the kitchen. He'd peeked at his watch.

"They should be here any minute now."

Marion untied her polka-dot apron. She held Jim.

"Relax, honey. Everything's going to turn out well today."

"Yes, I have every confidence it will."

It was Saturday, midafternoon.

Jim was in casual garb: khakis, shirt, and loafers. Marion was outfitted casually too, and their colors practically matched.

Ring.

Jim headed for the front door.

"Who do you think it is, Jim?"

"My money's on Frank Bosco," Jim said pluckily.

"Then I'll have to say Judy. Just to keep the game honest."

"Hi, Judy," Jim said, hugging her.

"Hi, Mr. Boston, Mrs. Boston," Judy said, looking over Jim's shoulder.

Marion was the next to hug Judy.

Jim was just about to shut the door when he spotted the familiar dark blue Ford pull up outside the house.

"Coach Bosco, Jim?"

"Gosh, you called it, Marion," Jim said sarcastically.

"Frank."

"Hi, Jim."

Frank acknowledged Marion and Judy.

"Something cool to drink?" Marion asked. "And I have finger food too, so don't be shy."

"Well, come in and sit down in the living room," Jim said.

Frank hugged Judy.

"Judy, how have you been, by the way?"

"Fine, Coach Bosco. Just fine."

They were all seated in the living room.

In an instant, Marion was in the living room with the punch she'd made and finger foods.

"Let me help you, Mrs. Boston."

"Sit," Jim said demandingly. "Don't you know this is the nineties, Judy? Men know how to do these thing now, you know."

Frank, Marion, and Jim laughed.

"Thank you, Mr. Boston," Judy said, taking her glass of punch from him.

"I really am good at this, you know." Jim chuckled.

They began eating. And before long, silence sat in the room.

"Don't tell me we've all suddenly forgotten how to talk. Our tongues have gone dead on us?" It'd made Jim feel ill at ease.

"No, Jim," Marion replied. "I ... I just think we're all hungry, honey." Marion's eyes took in Judy's and Frank's.

Jim put down his glass. "Frank, is your insurance paid up?" Jim said with the usual twinkle in his eye.

They laughed.

Then Jim targeted the three again as his fingers slid up and down the side of the glass, increasingly eager.

"You know why I called for this ... what you might call a gathering, don't you?"

Frank placed his glass down on the plastic coaster.

"The new football season will begin with, without Jimmy. Last year was hard enough without Billy," Frank said, looking at Jim. "But losing a player through graduation is much different than losing him through ..."

"None of us have had time to talk. Family, Judy," Jim said, looking at Judy, then at Frank. "Friend, Frank." Jim had chosen to categorize them in this way. "It's why Marion and I wanted you here today." Pause. "We both agreed it'd be good for us. Healthy. That this is the time for the healing of, to try to help heal ourselves."

Pause.

"How did I get them? Not one but two. Two great football players," Frank said. "Two All-Americans. Two great young men. How did I get to be so darn lucky? So often I'd pinch myself. Sometimes Maria thought I was crazy, but did I care? She could think what she wanted. Nah ..."

"Football," Jim said. "At one time, I thought it might be able to replace—"

"Jimmy didn't have Billy to hand the ball off to, Jim," Frank said, cutting Jim off. "Billy wasn't there. It wasn't the same. Could never be the same, not being able to hand the football off to Billy."

Silence struck the room again as they all contemplated Frank's remarks.

"Billy left a note," Judy said.

"Yes, Judy, he did," Marion said.

"But ... but not Jimmy."

"No, Judy, not Jimmy."

"Why, Mrs. Boston?"

"I don't know why. I can't answer that for you, honey."

"I'm, I'm sorry," Judy said, almost breaking down. "There are just so many things we don't know, Mrs. Boston. Remain unanswered. Are unaccounted for."

"As for me," Jim said, "I try not to think too much. What Jimmy did was a reaction to Billy's death."

"But Billy ... Billy was angry at ... at ..."

"Say it, Marion. It's why we're here, to be open and honest. We're after the truth."

Marion composed herself. "Billy was mad at Connie, at his father. The Macks had separated. His family split apart—and Billy blamed it on Connie. Mr. Mack, Judy."

"It's why Billy hung himself at home, in his room. Isn't it, Mrs. Boston?" Judy said.

"He was angry with Connie," Jim said.

"Jimmy couldn't do that. Hang ... hang himself in his room. Not to us. Not to his parents," Marion said.

"Jimmy wasn't angry with us, Marion. He just wasn't."

For the four, it seemed like such a small consolation.

"Jimmy didn't want us to see him," Jim continued. "But I did. I found him like Connie found Billy. His son."

Pause.

"I thought the counseling," Frank said. "I mean, I was dumb enough to think—Jimmy and I talked, Judy, Jim, Mrs. Boston. I mean, we talked a lot in my office. I was dumb enough to think ..."

"Who knows what's going on inside of us, Frank," Jim said. "This, this mind of ours." Jim pointed to his head.

"What we're hiding," Marion said.

"We had plans," Judy said. "But ..."

"Jimmy wasn't pretending. Whatever he did up to the end, I'm sure he believed he could accomplish. In his heart, he wanted to. But it was just his mind, like Jim said," Marion said. "It's what overtook him, honey. He thought too much about things. Too deeply."

"Playing football and the college thing. Billy made it fun, worthwhile," Frank said. "They were never in it for themselves, just for each other. Now I realize that. I see that. God, have I thought it through, over and over. Racked my brain. But now it's clear. It's the way it worked for them, between them. Always. It's a lesson, a valuable one I'll keep."

They all sat back in their seats, physically and emotionally drained.

Time had passed, and there was some general cheer among them.

The four stood in the living room. The gathering was gradually drawing to a close. The four had paired off.

"The football season, how does it stack up for the Purple Eagles this year, Frank?"

Frank took a long, winding breath. "Uh, good, Jim. The prospects are good. The team knows how to win. It's learned how." Frank smiled.

"We'll be there. Marion and I will be at the opener, Frank. It hasn't lost its number one fans."

"Thanks, Jim. I appreciate that a lot," Frank said, shaking Jim's hand.

"And Maria? The baby, Frank?"

"Fine, Jim. Maria and Francesca Elizabeth are doing okay, all right." Jim winked.

"Mrs. Boston, guess what? Alexis called me two nights ago."

"She did." Pause. "Judy, how is she?"

"Better, I guess," Judy replied glumly, but then she perked up. "She's looking forward to school though. University of Pennsylvania."

"Good for her."

"Of course, at one time we thought we'd …"

"Of course."

"But Columbia, I'm looking forward to that just as much as Alexis is to her new situation."

Marion smiled.

"I, we, Alexis and I canceled the idea of matriculating at the same school some time ago, Mrs. Boston. It just would've been too much for us emotionally." Pause. "Neither of us wanted that," Judy said, looking down, away from Marion. "It would have been unhealthy." Pause. "Alexis was the one who, at the time, brought it up."

Marion smiled again, more than pleased with Alexis and Judy.

"Good night, Coach Bosco."

"Good night, Judy," Frank said, breaking away from Jim and embracing Judy.

"Good night, Mr. Boston."

Judy embraced Jim.

"You … you first, Judy," Frank said to Judy as both entered the porch.

"Chivalry is not dead." Frank laughed.

Judy and Frank walked down the walk together. Jim and Marion were focused on Judy as she made a left turn, opposite of the direction that would take her home.

Then Sally Ann Schumacher popped out of the house and onto her front porch.

"Hi, Judy," Sally said, waving at her.

"Hi, Sally Ann," Judy said, waving back.

Frank got into his Ford.

Jim and Marion continued to watch Judy, knowing where she was going. It had sometimes annoyed and angered them when Jimmy and Judy did this, practiced this, but not now, not today.

Soon Frank was gone, and Judy was gone, and Jim and Marion stood at the house's front door, his arm linked to her waist and her arm linked to his waist, Marion standing much taller than Jim.

Jim looked up at Marion. "Did it help any, Marion? What just happened today?"

"No, Jim. I can honestly say no it didn't."

The Bostons front door shut.

His car was out of view of the Bostons' house. But he moved it along the street, at times just missing the curb, scraping the tires. He felt good and bad. It was a combination of something he had yet to control, emotions so strong they could only be uneven, patchy, not yet entirely managed. This was very difficult for him, yet he already felt relieved in some kind, charitable way. And now, by trying not to cry, he felt everything in him do just that: cry.

"Jim, before I put things away, do you want anything? There's plenty of finger food left."

"No, nothing for me, Marion. My waistline can't take it."

"By the way, I heard you ask Frank about the baby."

"Who, Francesca Elizabeth?"

"What a gorgeous name. A name from heaven."

"When I first heard it, it's how I reacted. It produces that kind of reaction I think." Pause. "Frank didn't get his boy, but Frank and Francesca are close enough."

"I'm just glad, Jim, that Frank and Maria didn't give up. It's what makes me happy, most satisfied about it."

Marion's head was in the refrigerator. She was putting things on the refrigerator's top back shelf.

Ring.

"Marion ..."

"I heard it, Jim."

"Why, somebody must've left something behind. Won't be the first time it's happened."

Marion's head popped out of the refrigerator. "But we're not expecting anyone, are we, Jim? Not this evening."

Ring.

"But I guess we are now, ready or not. And I better get to the door before whoever it is goes bell crazy."

Ring.

"Coming!"

Jim got to the front door.

"Connie!" Jim said in disbelief.

"Jim."

"Marion. Hi, Marion."

Jim grabbed Connie, holding him.

"Come in, Connie. Come in."

Marion got to Connie and hugged him. She kissed his cheek.

"Oh ... it's so good to see you, Connie. I can't tell you!"

"Yes ... it sure is, Marion."

Marion, Connie, and Jim walked into the living room.

Jim was behind Connie. He looked at this big, powerful man as if he were looking for signs of something, as if Connie's back could reveal all.

"You remember the house, don't you, Connie? It hasn't changed—not that I can tell, at least," Jim joked, taking to his seat.

"No ... no, uh, it hasn't, Jim."

"It is so good to see you," Marion said again, practically hypnotically.

Jim continued to look at Connie as if he were studying him. *What has happened to him over the past year?* Jim thought. *What kind of mental and spiritual state is he in? Physically, yes, he looks fine.*

"Connie, your weight looks good."

"I, uh, think so too, Jim. I hang in there. Stay with the program." He shrugged his shoulders politely. "You guys certainly look the same. Uh, look terrific, that is."

"It's not easy battling the bulge, the old waistline, at our advanced ages, Connie," Jim said, his eyes darting over to Marion. "But I can't very well sell life insurance to my clients and not look 100 percent healthy myself. A perfect picture of health." Jim laughed.

Pause.

"I'm aware of what just occurred here today, Jim, Marion." Connie couldn't take any more of this small talk. He got right down to the point about the nature of his surprise visit with the Bostons.

"I called Frank Bosco's home to wish him and the Purple Eagles well for the upcoming season. For what's ahead," Connie said, looking at Marion and Jim.

"I called for it, the meeting. Of … of course, Marion was all for it."

Marion nodded.

"But I was the one who called for it. It seemed a necessity, Connie. It really did. I … I don't know." Tears welled in Jim's eyes.

"I wasn't at Jimmy's funeral."

"I was disappointed, Connie. Marion and I. Very."

"Susan was there," Connie said.

"Yes, Susan was there," Marion said.

"Jim, Marion, I'm not going to sit here and make an excuse, any excuses. I'm tired, sick and tired of making excuses for myself. For my actions."

"We've forgiven you, Connie," Marion said quickly.

"Thank you, Marion, Jim, but I'm the one responsible for this tragedy."

And in some way, Connie could see Marion and Jim both saw this.

"It all started with me," Connie said grimly. "My guilt is thick. As thick as hell. As thick as hell!"

"Nobody wished this, Connie. God, nobody wished this. You wished this?" Jim said rhetorically.

"You and Susan had problems, Connie," Marion said. "Marital problems. No one knew they would lead to this." Pause.

"But it was my problem, Marion. Mine alone. Mine, not Susan's. I felt trapped. You might as well know. I felt trapped in a white man's world."

Shock was on Jim's and Marion's faces.

"I never knew you felt ... I never knew you felt that way, Connie. Not like—"

"I didn't either, Marion."

"And that ... that the problem between you and Susan had something to do with race. Color, Connie."

"Well, it did, Marion."

Jim remembered back to Mitch's Sports Bar, when he went in there to see Connie. He got a slice of what Connie was saying to them now. But he'd kept it to himself. He never shared that information with Marion. He didn't know then or now why not.

"These feeling were in me somewhere. Buried away. And they came out, surfaced again."

"Again?"

"Yes, Marion, again. When Billy began dating Alexis, a white girl."

"Oh, Connie," Marion anguished.

"Susan was aware of my feelings. I told her, ex-pressed them to her. I felt she didn't want to try ..." Connie was struggling. "What the hell, I was trying to force her to understand. That, that Billy was being swallowed by this false world, this artificial world we'd created for him. Put him in here in Pittsfield."

"Us, me ... me, you mean Jim and I are included, Connie?"

"Yes, you and Jim, Marion. You and Jim."

Marion and Jim felt terrible (Jim for a second time).

"A white world that ... that can reject us, a black person, turn its back on us at any given time. A moment's notice. Whimsically. Nonchalantly. Uncaringly. Without any justification. Cause." Pause.

"It happened to me at Blast Aircrafts. It happens to black folk every day. Every day of their lives. Don't you see?"

"But, Connie, you said this feeling surfaced again. When did you first have it? When, Connie?"

"With Jimmy."

"Connie," Marion said, suffering further shock.

"With Jimmy," Connie said, not intimidated by feelings or sensitivities—sparing absolutely nothing or no one. "I didn't like it."

"Billy's best friend being white, Connie?" Marion asked, still hurting.

"I wanted him to be black, Marion. Black. But how could I," Connie said, looking at both of them, "when Susan and I lived in Pittsfield? This white town?"

"We didn't care, Connie. Jim and I—"

"This isn't about you and me and Jim, Marion. This about identity and culture and passing it onto your child. It was my perception. It's what made up my background. Black friends, girlfriends—a father who, when I went off to a predominantly white school, reminded me I was there for education, to better myself, not to integrate.

"Not ... not to champion some cause but to get a good, solid education so I could make a good, solid living for my family, put food on the table. Be a good provider. And to always know who I was and where I'd come from. I ... I was never to embarrass myself or my race. And that part, the part of always being black, I must not ever forget. Not ever lose or compromise."

Jim and Marion listened intently.

"And you thought you had with Billy, Connie?"

"Yes, Jim. At a point, I thought I had."

"But Susan?"

"Marion, let's leave Susan out of this. Susan wasn't a part of my thinking. The equation. She thought the opposite, just the opposite of me. Antithesis. There's no deception in Susan's thinking, only mine."

Connie rubbed his forehead. "How could he be black in Pittsfield, Marion and Jim? What defined him as black in Pittsfield, a small town like this? White friends? Girlfriends? Teenage things? This was his life, Jim. But Pittsfield isn't every town, city, Marion. Pittsfield was an unreal reality. A mirage." Pause.

"It didn't work for me. You see, it didn't work for me. Not for me."

Marion and Jim felt overwhelmed by Connie's words, this undeniable force of his confession.

"And finally, I told Billy. I told Billy of my feelings. I told him. You see, I taught him all the good things and then taught him how to kill himself. How to kill himself. You see, you see," Connie said, trying to fight back tears, "I-I couldn't go to Jimmy's funeral. I couldn't. I killed him too. I killed Jimmy too. I loved him. Loved him like Billy, no less than Billy."

Jim and Marion gripped themselves, afraid to go back into those dark, emotional waters, those dark places where they'd barely survived.

"But Billy's note. His note to us, to Susan and me. It wasn't angry. Not any of it. Mean or angry. It was loving like Billy. Billy loved us. He loved Susan and me to the end of his life."

"Jimmy too. Jimmy too. But there was no indication," Marion said, "no sign or warning of what was to come."

Jim went over to Marion.

"Cunningham Park. Jimmy chose Cunningham Park, Connie," Marion said as Jim comforted her.

By now, the day had ground Marion down. It had been a long day for her. Connie was leaving the house. The three were back at the front door.

"I'm not drinking."

"I know you aren't, Connie," Jim said, placing his hand on Connie's back.

"You and Marion have been good friends."

Pause.

"Connie, are ... are you—what about your career? What's ahead for you?"

"It's not going to be here, Jim. It's not going to be restarted in Pittsfield."

Pause.

"I'm not a bum, Jim. I've been one, lived like one, and I don't like it. I don't like the feel of it. It doesn't suit me. The seediness of it. There're some very big people who are interested in me, in my talents," Connie said, in no way bragging. "It's just a matter of where I want to live, settle down next. But I'll be leaving Pittsfield. Leaving here for good soon. That I can inform you."

Marion wanted to ask, "What about Susan, Connie?" but knew it would be inappropriate.

"This isn't goodbye, is it, Connie?"

"No, not at all, Jim. Not on your life. You and Marion will see me well before then. Before any decision is made to leave Pittsfield."

Connie reached for Jim and Marion, bringing them into him, and Marion kissed Connie's cheek.

"I ... I needed to talk to someone. I'm glad it was you two. You two were around for me."

"And we'll try to understand, Connie," Marion said. "We'll really try."

"It's a lot to swallow, digest, Marion. I know that. But what you're made of, the stuff you're made from, it's not easy to get rid of, cut away. I have to go through it in, in order to maybe come out of the other end different. Whatever it takes, Marion, Jim. Whatever it takes for me to get to that place."

Connie was about to leave.

"By the way, Connie, Marion and I plan to go to the Purple Eagles' opener."

"Can't wait, in fact," Marion said.

And without any forethought or hesitation, Connie said. "So am I. So am I, Jim, Marion. I'll see you and Marion at the game!"

"You bet, Connie," Marion said. "You bet."

Jim and Marion watched Connie walk down the walk and then get into his car.

Their hands were joined. Jim and Marion shut the front door behind them.

Connie was back on the road. He looked in his rearview mirror. "I'm not a new man by any stretch of the imagination, but I'm getting there, learning more things about myself," he said to himself.

So far, her Saturday was like any other Saturday. The chores were finished, and she was slipping comfortably into the remainder of the evening. The routine, by now, she was accustomed to. What now separated her from the mundane was sitting down at her living room desk, opening her law books, and learning all she could from them while listening to a cool blend of jazz in the background. This was what Mrs. Susan Mack called an exciting Saturday night at home.

Susan reached for her reading glasses. Two months back, her eyes had been diagnosed, and reading glasses were hastily prescribed by her optometrist. She loved them. Susan was having trouble focusing on fine print, and during extensive reading periods, the print suddenly blurred, becoming fuzzy. Now the world had opened back up to her. She loved her glasses; they'd become Susan's right arm.

Susan, if she bragged, would tell you she was the top student in her law class. That was how well she was performing at Tyler College. Her secret ambition to be a lawyer one day was at full throttle. Susan was content with that aspect of her life.

She held the book upright, her fingertips edging the side of it as her feet shifted about beneath the desk as if fishing. Maybe this had something (her feet, that is) to do with the cool jazz floating suavely into her ears, or maybe not. There was a yellow pad on the desk, and Susan was making copious notes. Susan picked up the pen to transfer those notes onto another yellow legal pad when the doorbell rang.

Sharply, this put a surprise in her. Susan's face looked puzzled. Her head turned toward the door. *I'm not expecting anyone*, she thought.

This was atypical, someone ringing her doorbell on a Saturday night (really, any night for that matter).

Susan stood up from her desk. She just stood there. It was as if she was waiting for the doorbell to ring again, to make sure the person ringing the bell had the right apartment number, that there'd been no mistake.

The doorbell did ring again. But whoever rang it knew she was home. *The living room lights are on, after all*, Susan thought.

Susan's heart sped up.

Ring.

Answer it, Susan. Answer it. What are you waiting on? Why don't you answer it!

Susan stepped to the door and opened it. She was so startled she couldn't use his name.

"Susan," Connie said.

Susan's hands covered her mouth as her eyes bubbled, showing total, vivid surprise. Susan stepped back from the door, almost as if frightened.

"Sorry. Sorry to surprise you like this. Shock you."

The disbelief of the moment was still alive.

"I-I expected no less. I expected this kind of reaction from you," Connie said tentatively. "Susan, I did expect this," he said.

Susan was regaining her balance, her emotional level.

"Con-Connie …"

And then the most honest and obvious question came to her. "What are you doing here, Connie?"

"To see you," Connie said, again in perfect control.

Susan walked away from the door.

Connie entered the apartment and closed the door.

Susan's back was to him.

"You've never been here, have you?"

"No … no."

"Then you might as well look around. Go ahead, Connie. Look around," Susan said.

"Susan, I didn't come here to—it … it's a beautiful apartment. It's a beautiful apartment you have here."

"Thank you," Susan replied coldly.

Connie put his hands in his jacket's pockets.

"Sit down, Connie. You might as well."

"Susan, do you want me here?"

"Sit down, Connie. Sit down. You came here for a reason, haven't you?"

Connie knew he wasn't there to fight; he had come to see Susan. When he left Marion and Jim, it's what was on his mind—seeing her.

"You weren't at the funeral, Connie. Jimmy's funeral."

Connie was sitting in an armchair.

Susan continued to stand.

"I wasn't, Susan. No."

"I … I just said that. Didn't I just say that?"

A long pause.

"Why?"

"I-I just came from the Bostons'. Marion and Jim's place."

"What? You did?" True surprise was in her voice.

"Finally, I was able to tell someone why I was not at Jimmy's funeral. Finally, I was able to tell myself."

Pause.

"Jimmy hung himself for Billy. For our son, Connie. To be with him," Susan said, turning around just for that short period just to see Connie's reaction.

"It began with me."

"It most certainly did," Susan said.

"I live with the guilt."

Susan did not care to look at him now (this broken-looking man), turning from him a second time.

"But ... but after today, I'm going to move on."

Susan's arms crossed in front of her. "Now doesn't that sound romantic, poetic, perfectly put," Susan said. "Responsible."

"It doesn't matter how it sounds. It's me. It's what I think of me. What I want to do with my life."

"Well, up to now, you've made a mess of it, haven't you? Don't you think!"

"And I'm not drinking. I've stopped."

"Hurrah, hurrah, and what—I'm supposed to do what, Connie? Jump for joy through imaginary hoops? Is that what you want people to do? Or applaud. Applaud you!"

"No, I—"

"Billy's dead. Jimmy's dead."

"Yes, they are. And now I'm tired from it. Of grieving. Not that I won't, will continue to grieve for the rest of my life."

Her head whirled around to him.

"In ... in a different way, on a different level! I'm going to live again, Susan." Pause. "I've decided to live again. What I did is done, finished, in the past. I'm ... I'm not going to beat myself, continue to beat myself down. Billy didn't hang himself to punish me. He hung himself ... Billy hung himself ..."

"Yes, please tell me why our son hung himself," Susan said, her eyes burning. "Please ... do tell me why, since it seems you're the expert now. You've made yourself one!"

"All right. All right. I killed him! I killed him! All right! All right!"

"Damn right you did. You did!" Susan said, slamming her fist onto the desk, jolting it.

"And I can never make up for it. Not anything I do or say is going to make up for it. But I'm going to live again. I'm not going to give up on myself. I'm a good person. I'm a decent person. Life, I was looking at it differently. It, it was causing me to look at it differently, and, and the results were unspeakable. Reprehensible."

All talk stopped.

Susan sat back down at the desk's chair and put her head in her hands and shut her eyes.

The music in the background played.

Connie sat back in the armchair and shut his eyes.

"Miles ..." Connie said.

"What did you say?"

"Miles Davis."

Susan nodded.

She opened her eyes. She was looking at Connie. Oh how she missed him. Oh how she loved him. In a way, already, she could tell he was back to who he was: warm, thoughtful, and loving.

"How are Jim and Marion?"

Connie's eyes opened. "Fine. They're doing just fine, Susan."

"I ... I call Marion."

"Often?"

"Enough. We girls talk enough."

"It's ..."

"No. It's not like that. It's not dreary, depressing. We talk about our lives." Pause. "What are you doing about your life?"

"Susan, I've actually sent out more résumés and have gotten more responses than imaginable."

"I'm happy for you," Susan said. "To hear that."

"Government, Susan. It looks like I'll be working for the government, not private enterprise. The government is doing some exciting things in terms of its aeronautical projects and concepts."

"But Billy, Connie. Billy. You'll be leaving Billy behind. You have thought of it, haven't you? You have. I know that."

"Yes," Connie said, with strain. "But I have to live, Susan, no matter what has come out of this entire tragedy. I must live. Go on living."

Susan saw Connie's determination. Susan turned to what was on her desk.

"It's what I've been trying to do, live." Susan stretched her arms out. "This is what I call a typical Saturday night in Susan Mack's apartment. For Susan Mack."

Connie crossed the floor. "Schoolwork?" He laughed.

"Yep, schoolwork," Susan said depressingly. "But don't get me wrong, Connie. Don't take the wrong spin on things. I love it. Honestly do."

"You were always an amazing student. Studied like a beaver. Used to get on my last nerve—you and your work habits."

"Yep."

"Glasses?" Connie had spotted the glasses.

"Reading glasses."

"Join the club. Nice to have you on board."

Susan smiled.

"Well … Susan …"

"You're … you're not leaving already, are, are you, Connie?"

"I, I don't want to, but …"

Susan reached for Connie's hand. She stood.

When she did, Connie pulled her to him. "Oh, how I miss you, Susan. If you only knew."

Susan was holding on to Connie with her eyes shut.

"We've been through so much, Connie."

"So much."

"There's so much we had to find out about ourselves. To get to today."

"My thinking, was it—was it warped, Susan?"

Susan paused. "I … I don't know, Connie. There … there're things in this society that make black people think about where they stand. They're always there. Just where we fit in. Present for us to consider."

Pause.

"But not to the point of destroying ourselves, Susan."

Susan was nonresponsive.

Connie let go of her. He walked toward the front door. She put her hand on top of his shoulders as she trailed from behind.

"Susan …" Connie had stopped. "Susan, I want you to consider something."

Susan's arm was around Connie's waist.

"Susan, I need you. In order to start this new life, I want—I need you. To make it complete, I need you. Need you back with me."

Susan's arms remained around Connie's waist, tenderly holding him.

"I need time, Connie. I need time to think. I … I don't know if I can leave Billy here to start this new life you want. A new life with you, without Billy."

"Of course … of course."

Pause.

"Can … can I call you?" Connie asked.

"You still have my number?"

Connie laughed. "It's—"

Susan put her finger to Connie's lips, sexily. "I'm sure you remember. Anything with numbers. Anything that has numbers in it—"

"I remember … Susan, I love you."

"I love you, Connie."

"Oh, Susan, the Purple Eagles' opening game's in a few weeks."

"I know."

"I won't make any commitment regarding my job situation before then. Want to go? Jim and Marion are going to be there. It should be fun for everyone."

"Yes, great. Great!"

Pause.

"Good night."

"Good night, Connie," Susan said softly.

Susan watched as Connie walked down her apartment's short walkway. Connie turned as if it were his last goodbye.

"Good night, Connie," Susan said again.

Susan turned and walked back into the apartment.

The words Connie just used, the passion and respect in them, sat deeply in her.

"Yes, we need each other, Connie," Susan said, not returning to her desk where the books were but sitting down on the couch. "More than ever."

Maybe there is hope, Susan thought.

And the Purple Eagles had their home opener in a few weeks. She and Connie had already made a date to root for them. She and Connie would always root for the Purple Eagles and Frank Bosco, their amazing Coach. Their hearts would always remain there with them.

And Jim and Marion would be there at the game.

Jim and Marion, Susan thought.

Printed in the United States
By Bookmasters